Persuade Me

Persuade Me

Juliet Archer

First published 2011 by Choc Lit Limited
Penrose House, Crawley Drive, Camberley, Surrey GU15 2AB, UK
www.choclitpublishing.com

A CIP catalogue record for this book is available
from the British Library

ISBN 978-1-906931-21-6

Printed and bound by CPI Group (UK) Ltd, Croydon, CR0 4YY

For the best of mothers
Jean and Edith

Acknowledgements

A big thank you to:

All my readers, who have given such encouraging feedback.

The Choc Lit team, for their patience and support.

My panel of experts, for generously sharing
their knowledge – Susan and Rhi (the academic world –
arts and sciences respectively), the Kent family (sailing),
Eve (farming), Linda (journalism),
Michael (hereditary titles).

My wonderful 'locals' for their tours, actual and virtual
– Gill and Paul (Bath, especially the Theatre Royal),
Gerry (The Royal Crescent Hotel), Rosemarie (BRLSI),
the Jane Austen Centre in Bath (the world of Austen
– real and imaginary), Tess and team (Dorset County
Hospital A&E), Barbara (Lyme Regis Library), Steven
(Melbourne – Australia, not Derbyshire!).

The three Sarahs, two Jeans, two Doreens, Alison, Maggie,
Janet, Carol and Edaena, for keeping me going with their
interest and enthusiasm.

Central Newcastle High School and all at
the University of Nottingham's Slavonic Studies Department,
for my love of Russian language and literature.

My fellow Chocliteers and Austen Authors, especially
Jane Odiwe, for their camaraderie – sometimes face to face,
often across thousands of miles, always with goodwill and
good humour.

The Romantic Novelists' Association, for their constant
encouragement and support.

My family, for never telling me to stop writing –
or not loud enough for me to hear.

Jane Austen, for inspiration.

Foreword

A magazine headline, circled in black ink: 'Never forgive, never forget'. You can tell a lot from what's on a person's desk ...

Some years ago, just before I met Elizabeth, I took my sister Georgie to Australia for a much-needed holiday. She was going through a particularly difficult time; so, when she showed a spark of her previous passion for saving the planet, I encouraged it in every possible way.

During a brief visit to Melbourne I discovered that there was an expert in marine conservation based at one of the local universities, a Dr Rick Wentworth. I sent him an email, using the pretext of possible interest from the Pemberley Foundation in his Save the Sea Dragons campaign – although I usually avoid the 'grand benefactor' act at all costs. When I received a terse and somewhat begrudging invitation to meet in his office, I immediately pictured an old, cross, bespectacled nerd.

I couldn't have been more wrong. He turned out to be young, charming and, judging from Georgie's sharp intake of breath, very easy on the female eye. And he was English, with a northern accent that had apparently resisted all attempts at Australianisation.

He even apologised for the tone of his invitation. He told us that, with his work attracting more and more media attention, he'd become wary of requests like mine. This led to a brief discussion about the drawbacks of being a modern celebrity, especially a reluctant one.

As we talked, I realised that he was meticulous about his research – and not just on sea dragons. I'd given him no indication of my sister's troubles and had taken the necessary steps to gag the press, although inevitably some details had leaked out. Yet I sensed he knew – and understood – what she'd been through …

So I watched in genuine admiration as he drew Georgie out of her dark shell into the wider world, if only for an hour. He held us both spellbound with stirring tales of battles against natural elements and man-made disasters, often in the form of short-sighted bureaucracy, and showed us stunning footage of the fragile creatures he was fighting to protect. Of the man himself I learned very little – until we got up to leave.

At this point he scrawled his personal email address on a piece of paper and handed it to a blushing Georgie, urging her to get in touch with any questions. That in itself made me warm to him and decide on a generous donation from the Foundation for his campaign – an unusual instance of my heart ruling my head.

But the piece of paper had been hiding something on his desk, a magazine article with a big bold headline. A headline that obviously had a greater significance because he'd drawn a brutal black ring round it: 'Never forgive, never forget.'

They were words I could relate to completely. Except that I was thinking of the man who'd broken my sister's heart, whereas he – as I discovered much later into our friendship – was thinking of the girl who'd broken his.

Although neither of us knew it then, their paths would cross when he wrote a book and, despite some misgivings, visited England to promote it.

This is their story …

Prologue

Her voice gatecrashed his thoughts. 'Rick, who's that woman you've been dreaming about?'

He frowned. Typical Shelley, scratching at the scab of their relationship just when he was about to leave for the airport. He picked up the last pair of new shirts, still in their cellophane wrapping, and forced them into the suitcase.

Then he looked across at her and said quietly, 'What do you mean?'

Her eyes brimmed with accusation and she took a long gulp of air before she spoke again. 'You've been calling out to her in your sleep. I didn't think that much about it at first, but now it's been three nights in a row.'

He must have had that dream, the one where …

It hurt to breathe, yet his hands were steady as he closed the suitcase; and he held her gaze as though he had nothing to fear. 'What did I say?'

'You said "Annie", over and over again. And you sounded so different, so gentle, as if – as if –' She broke off, but the damage was done. His eyes flinched shut. In a heartbeat he was ten years younger, far away, with someone else.

'Rick, who's Annie?'

Never forgive, never forget.

His eyes snapped open and he swung the case off the bed on to the floor. 'I don't know anyone called Annie,' he said. And he couldn't have made his voice less gentle if he'd tried.

Shelley stepped forward and grabbed his arm. 'Is she in England? Is that why you're going back there all of a sudden?'

He stared down at her, struggling to conceal his

impatience. 'It's not sudden, as you very well know. It takes months to organise a book tour on the other side of the world. And Sophie's been on at me to visit for ages. She and Ed can't afford any more trips over here.'

'But *seven weeks*? You've never been away for that long before. And it's not as if you can study your precious sea dragons over there, is it? Especially in the depths of Somerset or wherever your sister's bought her crummy little garden centre!'

These were basic observations, and she could have made them at any time in the last few months; but she'd waited until he was ready to walk out of the door. He sighed. She sounded so shrill and resentful, as though she really did care.

He smiled as he framed her face in his hands and tilted it up towards him. 'I know. So I'll be coming back. To the sea dragons – to my life in Australia.'

Hardly a profession of love, but it was better than nothing. And maybe, when he did come back, they could make a fresh start. Because, after ten years, it was time to forget the past.

Forgiveness was an entirely different matter.

Chapter One

He made the headlines, naturally.

On Saturday morning, in the neat privacy of her little flat, Anna read them all; from *The Sun*'s 'Sex-in-the-Sea Doc Comes Home' to the more sedate 'Celebrity Scientist on UK Book Tour' in *The Times*.

To her shame, it was the article in *The Sun* that she lingered over. It had the most detail, real or imagined, about Dr Rick Wentworth: a description of his girlfriend, the Australian supermodel Shelley McCourt, in tears as he left for the airport; an interview with a woman on the same flight, featuring some banter about asking him to join the Mile High Club – an invitation he'd apparently refused; his little altercation at Heathrow with a TV reporter who'd had the temerity to question something in his research.

And *The Sun* had the best photo of him – sitting on the deck of a boat, studying some small creature cradled in the palm of his hand, his expression intent yet relaxed, as though he didn't want to be anywhere else in the whole wide world. It was a look she'd known well, once upon a time.

She let out a long breath. If she wanted to, she could meet him again; she had a ticket for his Bath book signing in four weeks' time. She could see herself now: waiting in line, counting the minutes that brought them closer and closer, full of dread yet unable to tear herself away. At last, it would be her turn and she'd stand awkwardly in front of the table as he opened another copy of *Sex in the Sea*. Head down, pen poised, he'd ask 'Name?' and she'd whisper 'Anna Elliot'. Then that sleek blond head would snap up and …

But at this point the picture became blurred. Would he force a smile and write 'To Anna from Rick' as if she were just another of his fans? Or would he jump up, send table and books flying, and carry on where they'd left off all those years ago?

If that happened, it would be an ugly scene. Anger and recriminations on his part, no doubt – tears and resentment on hers; which would probably do his book sales no good at all. And book sales were the main reason he was here; that much was obvious from all the newspapers she'd read this morning. He'd be off to Australia again as soon as the book tour was over and the only people he'd be visiting in England were his sister and her husband. No mention of looking up the girl he'd once begged to sail with him to the other side of the world.

A knock at the door made her start. What if …? She gave a rueful smile. Silly to think, even for a split second, that it could be him; he neither knew nor cared where she was. She got to her feet, scooped up all the newspapers except *The Times* and stuffed them behind the sofa.

It was Jenny, her landlady and work colleague; more than that now – her best friend. She and her husband Tom, wheelchair-bound since a car accident, occupied the ground floor of this large, end-of-terrace house in central Bath, having converted the rest into self-contained flats. That income, together with Jenny's part-time job, could never compensate for Tom's previous salary as a sales director, but they managed. And Jenny always claimed that her frequent visits to Anna on the top floor did her far more good, both physically and mentally, than the gym memberships and theatre trips she could no longer afford.

Now, with no indication that she'd just run up several flights of stairs, she breezed past Anna into the living room. 'Just seeing if you want me to get you anything at the shops.

You're off to Kellynch soon, aren't you? And I thought we could eat together when you get back tomorrow night – unless you've got something else planned?'

They both knew she hadn't, but Jenny's voice was still full of hope.

'Yes, I'd love to eat with you,' Anna said, 'and no, I don't need anything from the shops. I've already been out, to get a paper.'

Jenny went over to the table where *The Times* was spread out next to a solitary mug and an empty cereal bowl. 'Isn't that Rick Wentworth? Good job I got our tickets for his book signing as soon as they went on sale – I was in Molland's last night and there were none left. I bet it's mainly women who've bought them – women with absolutely no interest in marine biology, like me!'

Anna managed a laugh. 'Yes, his marketing's spot on, isn't it? Good-looking bloke writes a book called *Sex in the Sea* and appears half-naked on the cover – I'm sure quite a few people will be disappointed to find they've bought a detailed study on the mating habits of sea slugs and the like.'

'Nice cover photo, though.' Jenny picked up the paper. 'What my Aunt Jane would call a fine specimen of manhood. D'you think he'll sign our books dressed like that? We can but dream.'

Anna glanced at the photo. Jenny would see a man sitting on a beach, in swimming trunks and a baseball cap, his back to the camera, long legs outstretched towards the sea, those tanned, broad, muscular shoulders proclaiming him as a fit outdoor type.

Whereas she ... she saw the restlessness that she'd found so attractive in him; head turned to the side, his attention caught by the slightest of movements; arms and legs tensed, ready to launch him up off the sand; back – ah, his back ... how many times had she traced those muscles, with her fingers, with her lips? Too many times, yet never enough ...

Yes, this photo could easily have been her favourite, but it didn't show his face. How she'd loved watching him at work, waiting for his expression to change: one moment, still with concentration; the next – as she made some provocative remark – alive with laughter and, although she hadn't realised it at first, desire.

That's why she preferred the photo in *The Sun*. You could see his face, and imagine ...

'This is the man,' Jenny was saying, 'who almost made me get satellite TV, remember? That was the only way to see his documentary series, but you talked me out of it. Very sensible too, we need to economise and Tom watches enough TV as it is. Just as well he has his voluntary work at Open Door, since no one wants to employ him.' She gave a little sigh, her eyes still fixed on the newspaper. 'I'm sure they'll bring out a DVD soon, in the meantime the book will do nicely.' Then she chuckled. 'It says here that he's a world expert on sea dragons. Sounds dangerous, doesn't it? They must be huge, although at least they can't breathe fire if they're under water!'

'They're tiny actually, I read somewhere that they're related to the sea horse.' To Anna's relief she sounded more brisk and business-like than she felt. 'Look, I've finished with the paper for now – why don't you take it? Tell Tom I expect him to get all the Sudoku done, even the Killer, before I see him tomorrow.' She checked her watch. 'I'd better get going, or I'll be late for our special family meeting and Walter will say all the important stuff while I'm not there.'

Jenny pulled a face as she folded up the newspaper. 'I'll never understand why your father insists on you girls calling him by his Christian name, it's not natural.'

'But then,' Anna said, with a little shrug, '*nothing* about my father is natural.'

'Except his preference for your obnoxious older sister. She's a chip off the old block, if ever there was one.' Newspaper in hand, Jenny turned towards the door and stopped short. 'Ah, there's the other thing I came for.'

Anna followed her gaze to the DVD case lying on top of the TV. '*Anna Karenina*?'

'Yes, the very thought of Sean Bean as Vronsky ... Tom likes watching him in *Sharpe*, as you know, but I want something more romantic.' Jenny picked up the DVD and hesitated. 'Are you in the middle of watching it?'

'No, take it. I'll just need it back a week on Monday, when term starts.'

Jenny grinned. 'For your opening lecture to the first years? They're always full of it when they come into my office afterwards – you're so good at getting them to relate to nineteenth-century Russian literature. How does it go again? "Would you give up everything for your lover ..."'

'"Would you give up everything in your life – family, friends, your place at this university – for your lover?"' Anna said softly. '"Anna Karenina did. She ignored the advice of those closest to her and left everything she had – husband, child and social position – for Vronsky. When it all went wrong, she threw herself under a train."' A pause. '"Tragic heroine – or selfish fool?"'

'Brilliant opening to a brilliant lecture!' A wry chuckle. 'Of course, the students who *have* given up their place at Bath & Western University for their lover aren't there to hear it, but you certainly make an impression on the students who are. I've always meant to ask you – which one do *you* think Anna Karenina was?'

'A selfish fool.' The response was automatic, a consequence of subtle indoctrination since childhood. Besides, if Jenny knew what had happened all those years ago, she'd realise it was the obvious response from a woman like Anna Elliot.

A woman who'd followed the advice of those closest to her: to keep her family, friends and place at university – and give up her lover instead.

Chapter Two

Sir Walter Elliot ran an elegantly manicured fingertip over the faded gold lettering on the cover of his most treasured possession: *Burke's Peerage & Baronetage*, 106th edition, Volume One. Published shortly after his wife's death, it had become a trusty anchor in the storm-tossed sea of his life, a symbol of hope in a darkening world; a world where, increasingly, people worshipped the false god of celebrity in preference to the true and solid worth of an hereditary title.

He turned to the page where the red satin bookmark had taken up permanent residence and read the words he knew by heart: 'SIR WALTER WILLIAM ELLIOT, 8TH BT, of Kellynch, Somerset; *b* 5th April 1953 ... *m* 1975 Princess Irina Grigoryevna Petrova (*d* 1998), dau of Prince Grigori Ivanovich Petrov, of Paris, and has: Elisabeth Irina, *b* 1978; Anna Elena, *b* 1982; Mona Katerina, *b* 1984 ...'

He let out a little sigh. The absence of a son to inherit his title had always been a severe blow, but at least he could be proud of two of his daughters: Lisa, made in his own image, tall, golden-haired and utterly beautiful, the only one who understood him; and Mona, incomprehensibly freckled, something of a disappointment until she made a respectable marriage to Charles Musgrove and produced two fine boys. The Musgrove family might not possess a title, but they had a nine-hundred-acre farm, a decent-sized manor house and generally clear complexions.

Which left Anna: small and dark and studious like her mother; but, unlike her mother, unable – or unwilling – to find a suitable man. And, since she'd started living with that Smith woman and her layabout of a husband, showing a rebellious streak that would no doubt manifest itself at the meeting today. He shook his head sadly. It had all started so well! The degree at Oxford and trips to Russia that he'd magnanimously funded – out of the trust fund that Irina had purposely set up, but even so ... (He'd never understood why Irina sold the Petrov diamonds and invested the proceeds for the girls' education – unless it was to favour Anna, who was always going to need more than her fair share.) The PhD that he'd tolerated, so long as Anna earned enough to support herself ... But then, instead of doing something useful with her life and finding a desirable husband, as Irina had, she'd become a lecturer at the Bath & Western University! Oxford itself would have been preferable, and further away ... 'My middle daughter's an Oxford professor, you know. Always was a bit eccentric.' Thank God Irina couldn't see her favourite daughter now, mixing with the working class and – on the rare occasions that she visited Kellynch – dressing as scruffily as one of her students ...

A car sweeping past the library window roused him from his reverie. His nearest neighbour Minty – or Lady Russell, to use her formal name – in her vintage Rolls; like him, she was a stickler for appearances. In fact, they had so much in common that he found himself wondering why they'd never married. He could see several advantages in such an alliance. As the widow of a mere knight, she'd always been more than willing to look up to a baronet; she dressed with a certain style and, as she often reminded him, on a much smaller budget than Lisa; and, from the far side of a dimly lit room, she could easily pass for forty-five.

Then he remembered the downside. As his wife's closest friend and confidante, she had an unfortunate habit of imagining what 'dear Irina' would have thought about everything; her hair was as grey as dust and she refused to contemplate any sort of flattering rinse; what he called the necessities of life, she termed pure extravagance; and, last but by no means least, she was too old to bear him a son, a scenario that had suddenly become a distinct possibility, thanks to–

'Walter, *darling*!'

Minty, somewhere behind him. He hadn't heard her come in, but he could smell her perfume – Je Reviens, or 'I'll be back'. Wasn't that a famous line from a film? He could vaguely recall the actor, a splendid figure of a man with an unfortunate guttural accent ... Yes, he reflected, dear Minty had been as good as her word, or rather her perfume's word; over the years she'd been back time and again to Kellynch, worldly wisdom and well-meant advice always at the ready.

He placed *Burke's* carefully on a nearby secretaire, got languidly to his feet and proffered a silk-smooth cheek for her kiss. 'Still wearing that old Jaeger jacket, Minty? It looks almost as good as new, you must tell me how you do it. I'm afraid I feel rather wretched this morning, my masseuse phoned to say–'

'Masseuse?' Minty's eyes widened in horror, then narrowed; she had a deplorable lack of concern for crow's feet. 'Walter, we discussed this last time I was here and I'm sure you said you'd dispense with her services *immediately*. Imagine what dear Irina–'

He interrupted her with a sharp, 'She wouldn't have minded in the least.' Sometimes, just sometimes, Minty overstepped the mark and assumed that the widow of old Sir Reginald 'Rusty' Russell knew better than the 8th Baronet of Kellynch. He went on, 'As I was saying, my masseuse phoned to say she's delayed, so I'm not at my best. Which is a great pity, in view of the stressful nature of this meeting–' He broke off. 'That reminds me, Mona's not coming. The usual.'

Minty gave a little snort of derision. 'That girl needs a

decent doctor or a firm husband, and she doesn't seem to have either. Heaven knows I've tried to tell her often enough, but I've lost all patience with her since she told me to keep my opinions to myself.' She went over to the window and peered out. 'Any sign of Anna?'

'No. She'd better not be late.' He glanced across at Minty defiantly. 'I'll be going for my massage as soon as Cleopatra arrives.'

'Cleopatra?' She made a little moue of distaste. 'Oh, the masseuse.'

'A real find,' he said, flexing his wrists. 'I feel ten years younger already. Lisa's started having her too, I'm sure you'll see a difference.'

As if on cue, the library door swung open and a slim, bronzed goddess in black leggings and a long cream cashmere sweater made her entrance. Lisa, his loveliest and most loving daughter. He gazed at her fondly as she glided over to Minty, kissed her lightly on the cheek and came to stand next to him.

'Coffee's on its way,' she said in a high, breathless, Marilyn Monroe voice that had shattered countless male hearts, 'and I've had a text from Cleo. She'll be here by half-past, thank God.'

'Excellent, darling, let's make a start.'

Minty frowned. 'But it's only ten to, and Anna's not–'

'You can tell her what she's missed,' he said coolly.

Then, like a pair of synchronised swimmers, he and Lisa crossed to the sofa facing the window and sank gracefully into it, while Minty perched on a high-backed chair opposite.

Walter adopted a slightly troubled look and began, 'As you both know–'

Immediately, there was a half-hearted tap at the door and the latest in a long line of unsatisfactory housekeepers tottered into the library with the coffee tray. He'd stopped trying to remember their names; Minty handled the whole boring business for him, recruiting them from the surrounding villages, recording their hours, dispensing their wages and dealing with the ghastly tax people. They always started off suitably grateful to work at Kellynch – then, after a month or two, the rot would set in. The excuses ranged from advanced decrepitude – dodgy hips and dicky hearts were the favourites – to family revolt – 'my son says I'm working for a pittance and he'll report you to the national minimum wage helpline' – or transport problems, with heavy-handed hints that Walter should meet the cost of a taxi. It was a sign of the times; people judged the privilege of serving a baronet and a job at the local Tesco by the same lamentable criteria.

When the creature had slopped coffee into the cups, handed round a plate of limp-looking ginger snaps and sloped off again, Walter resumed his troubled look. 'As you both know, I take my responsibilities very seriously, very seriously indeed. *Noblesse oblige* is my way of life. And so, in the midst of another recession, with the estate farm yields well down on last year, I feel I must set an example and be even more of a shining light in these dark times. I've accepted–'

He broke off in irritation as the door opened again and his middle daughter came into the room – looking so like Irina that it hurt, ever so briefly.

And that husky voice, so like Irina's. 'Am I late? I thought–'

'You're not late, Anna dear, Walter started early.' Minty patted the chair next to hers.

His other daughters would have come straight over and kissed him, but not Anna. He watched her sit down beside Minty and rub her temples, as if the very sight of him produced a headache.

He cleared his throat. 'As I was saying, I've accepted an

offer that will bring in a substantial amount of income over the next year and allow me to finance the necessities of life.' He paused long enough to hear Minty's sharp intake of breath, then continued in a louder tone, as if to quell any thoughts of insubordination, 'I've been approached by the couple who've bought Graham Farley's garden centre. To make a proper go of it, they need to rent more greenhouse space and they'd also prefer to live off the premises, but not too far away. I'm sure you'll agree that Kellynch meets their requirements admirably.'

Lisa's hand flew to her mouth. 'You're not suggesting they live *here*, with us?'

He smiled his reassurance. 'Of course not, darling, I'm thinking of The Lodge.'

'The Lodge?' Minty's jaw dropped, rather unattractively. 'But Walter, it needs a lot of work, and you may not recover the cost of that in the rental, especially if the business fails and they only stay a few months. Who are these people anyway? What if they bring ...' her eyebrows straggled upwards, 'an undesirable element to Kellynch?'

Walter spread his hands in an eloquent gesture of despair. 'I've thought long and hard about this, Minty, and talked it over with my professional advisors.' He put a tiny but audible emphasis on the word 'professional'. 'Shepherd feels that we can get away with the minimum of refurbishment and still charge the maximum rent. And the couple themselves, Sophie and Edward Croft, come with very solid references.'

Minty pursed her lips. 'Croft ... Croft ... I wonder if they're related to the Ashford Crofts?'

'I'll look it up in *Burke's*.' He reached towards the secretaire.

'They can't be,' she said hurriedly. 'I'd have heard about it from Tuppy if any of them were planning to run a garden centre.' She gave a little shudder.

Walter reluctantly withdrew his hand. 'I've made my own enquiries, of course,' he went on. 'In Uppercross, where they're renting one of those poky cottages on the main street. Roger Musgrove thinks they're rather dull, but very pleasant and hard-working. And, as he's Mona's father-in-law, I'm perfectly happy to take his opinions into account – in spite of the fact that he never trims that revolting beard of his. Anyway, he says things should liven up soon, Sophie's expecting her brother from Australia. Somebody quite famous apparently, a scientist who writes books, which sounds respectable enough. Except he's called Woolworth … Woolworth … Wasn't that the name of that young upstart we had to sort out in France, Minty?'

'Wentworth,' came a low voice.

Walter looked across at his middle daughter. 'What?'

'Rick Wentworth.'

He had to strain to catch her words. 'Speak up, anyone would think you couldn't bear to say his name.'

'That's hardly surprising, Walter, when you remember the circumstances,' Minty said crisply.

Walter allowed his lip to curl. He remembered the circumstances extremely well: the collar of his favourite Eton shirt twisted completely out of shape as the young upstart hissed some very unsavoury words in his ear. 'Well, if it's the same man, which I doubt, we'll have to hope he's mended his arrogant ways. But in any case I'm not renting anything to *him*, just his sister. Everything's signed and the builders are starting work on The Lodge next week, which is why I wanted you all to know.'

He gave Anna an accusing look. 'Are you sure it wasn't Woolworth?'

Anna made no answer; it was taking all her self-control not to run out of the room. She stared down at her lap, outwardly composed but secretly chasing wild thoughts around in her head.

A famous scientist who wrote books ... from Australia ... a sister called Sophie. It must be him. He'd talked about Sophie, all those years ago ... To think that his sister would be living in The Lodge and running the garden centre on the main road between here and Uppercross ... She decided she would make an effort to meet her. It would be – interesting. And it might help her to prepare for meeting *him*.

Her father was saying, 'At Cleopatra's recommendation, of course. An excellent place for the more advanced treatments, a sort of revival of its former glory days as a spa town. And I won't be too far away if there's anything to sort out at Kellynch, which there usually is.' He paused and gave a little sigh.

Anna closed her eyes; she knew perfectly well what was coming next.

'*Noblesse oblige*,' he murmured, savouring the words like nectar. '*Noblesse oblige*.'

Then Minty said, 'At least you'll see a lot more of Anna.'

Anna looked up, blinking in confusion. Was her father moving to Bath? She could feel the blood draining from her face.

Minty went on, warming to her task, 'You could even see if the flat below hers is still vacant. Bennett Street's so handy for everything and Jenny Smith charges a very reasonable rent.'

Anna's confusion turned to undisguised horror; but, as usual, Walter didn't appear to notice. He glanced impatiently at his watch, stood up and crossed the room to the large ormolu mirror over the fireplace. 'Definitely ...' he paused to study his reflection from several angles, while Anna held her breath for his next words, 'not. We have our standards and I guarantee that they're a far cry from anything that

16

Smith woman might aspire to.' He turned to Lisa with a brilliant smile. 'Don't worry, darling, I've booked us into The Royal Crescent Hotel.'

'I should bloody well hope so,' Lisa muttered. 'If we have to go to Bath and not London, then I'm certainly not slumming it.'

Anna went over in her mind what she'd just heard – blocking out the unkind reference to Jenny, knowing from experience that retaliation was pointless. The Royal Crescent was only a short walk from Bennett Street, but her work would take her several miles in the opposite direction, and her social life even further away, metaphorically speaking ... She felt her shoulders relax; in reality there'd be little chance of their paths crossing and, with any luck, Walter and Lisa would be too busy enjoying their five-star surroundings to parade themselves around Bath like C-list celebrities.

Minty leaned forward and glared at Walter. 'The rent from The Lodge and a few greenhouses won't go very far at The Royal Crescent. Quite frankly, I'm astonished that you're even considering living in Bath when you'll still be paying for the upkeep of this enormous house.'

Walter ignored her and fixed his cold blue eyes on Anna. 'We will, of course, expect to see you occasionally. Although I find it incomprehensible that a daughter of mine wishes to waste her life being a university lecturer, I'm not above offering her a helping hand with her career. I imagine the head of your department will be honoured to receive an invitation to dinner from Sir Walter Elliot, 8th Baronet.'

Anna smiled sweetly at him. 'As she's a committed socialist, I imagine she'll be anything but.' She had no intention of letting her father disrupt the measured pace of her life in Bath. It had been years since she'd let his bullying – there was no other word for it – affect her. Still, might as well show some interest; and, after all, forewarned was

17

forearmed. She said, 'When do you–'

Lisa cut in with, 'Here's Cleo now, coming up the drive. She'll have to do me first, I've an appointment with my stylist at one. Party at Pen's tonight, and my hair's a complete and utter mess.' She gave her perfectly groomed mane a petulant flick; then added, in Anna's direction, 'They won't mind if you tag along. You can do the driving, I'll be having a few drinks.'

Just as Anna opened her mouth to object, Walter intervened. 'I'm afraid she's wanted at Uppercross, darling. Mona's not well and it's Harvest Festival tomorrow morning at St Stephen's, someone has to take the boys and Charles is off fishing as usual.' He half-turned to Anna. 'And you really need to go there this afternoon and make their harvest baskets. The boys want a dinosaur theme, nothing too taxing.'

Anna weighed up her options. Stay at Kellynch and have Lisa throw a tantrum if she refused to act as her chauffeur, or go to Uppercross and witness Mona's wall-to-wall misery? But Mona had two redeeming features: her children – Oliver, seven, and Harry, almost three. And there'd be no chance of Rick Wentworth visiting his sister; according to his website, he was starting his book tour in London and had two solid days of signings arranged.

She looked straight at her father. 'I'll go where I'm wanted, then. And I might as well go now.'

No one voiced the slightest objection, so she got abruptly to her feet and left the room. On her way to the front door, she paused to stare mutinously at the two full-length portraits that dominated the hall: her parents, in the second year of their marriage. On the left, Walter preened in front of a banner carrying the Elliot coat of arms, one hand resting reverently on *Burke's Peerage*; the 106th edition, of course – an anachronism added many years later. On the right stood

Irina, stunning in a coral-pink evening dress, a diamond tiara in her dark hair and more diamonds at her throat. The expression in those grey eyes was enigmatic; Anna suspected a mixture of disenchantment with Walter and relief at being apart, if only in an oil painting.

'I'll never – *ever* – understand why you ended up with him. Except – well, sometimes I wonder if you were an even bigger snob than he is.'

She must have said the words out loud, because here was Minty beside her, resting a heavy hand on her shoulder and saying quietly, 'As I told you after she died, your mother made a mistake that she regretted all her days. She was very young when she met Walter, and she couldn't wait to marry him and settle down at Kellynch.' A heartfelt sigh. 'She wouldn't contemplate divorce, so she lived for her children – especially you. But that youthful haste cost her dear. That's why–' She stopped.

Anna stiffened. 'That's why you talked me out of ...' it had been a taboo subject for so long that she stumbled over the words, 'out of going to Australia, with Rick Wentworth.'

Minty pursed her lips. 'Your mother wouldn't have wanted you to make the same mistake and put your life, your many talents, on hold for a man who didn't deserve you.'

'Were you and Walter the best people to judge?'

The bitterness in Anna's voice suggested this was a purely rhetorical question, but Minty chose to answer it.

'Absolutely. You were completely under his spell, remember? And your cousin Natasha backed us up–'

'I don't want to talk about it.'

'But Anna, if he's back in England he may come looking for you!'

'Fat chance, when there's been no communication between us for ten years.'

A slight pause; then Minty said, 'Exactly. If you'd really been the one he wanted to spend the rest of his life with, wouldn't he have been in touch?'

Anna stifled a small stirring of sadness. 'Yes. Yes, he would.'

Chapter Three

In the back seat of the black Jaguar, Rick slumped against the cool leather upholstery and enjoyed his first scowl of the day. What a prospect – another twenty or so events like this, up and down the country. He felt drained; was it the long flight, or the effort of signing books for three hours at a stretch?

He became vaguely aware of his publicist's irritatingly chirpy voice. '... Great boost to sales having you over here. I mean, look at today – hundreds of women in some sort of frenzy. If that's going to happen each time, you'll need bodyguards.'

'Dream on, Guy. I'm hardly an A-list celebrity.'

'At this rate, you soon will be.'

'When that happens, mate, you'll be paying for this chauffeur-driven Jag.'

Guy gave the lazy, lopsided grin that masked a will of iron, as Rick was already learning. 'Forgive me for saying this, but you're going to great lengths to behave like an A-list celebrity, even if you're not. Why the flash car? Why the driver? Don't get me wrong, I'm glad I don't have to ferry you round the country in my old BMW – but it's an expensive way of doing a book tour.'

'That's my business.' Rick tilted his head back and closed his eyes.

If Guy recognised the hint to leave him in peace, he certainly didn't take it. 'It's a pity we can't get Shelley over, the tabloids would wet themselves to get an interview with the two of you together.'

Rick opened his eyes and kept his face expressionless;

no need for Guy to know that his last phone call with Shelley had ended with her hanging up on him. 'I'd hoped to be more than just tabloid fodder – although it's hardly surprising since the publishers decided on that idiotic book title. *Sex in the Sea* gives people completely the wrong idea.'

'But it's a lot snappier than the original *Risk and Reproduction: modern challenges for marine life*. And it's all about appealing to a whole new market.'

'Yeah, the chattering classes. They'll never get past that ridiculous front cover.'

'More to the point, they'll fork out the money for your impressive physique to adorn their coffee tables.'

Rick couldn't help laughing. 'Only in photo form, thank God. I'd charge a hell of a lot more to be there in person.'

'So, now that I've got you in a good mood again, what shall we do tonight? Dinner at your hotel, then that party I told you about?'

Rick sighed. This was networking, pure and simple, dressed up as socialising; but it had to be done, for the sake of book sales. He was saved from answering, however, by the annoyingly cheerful trill of a mobile.

'Excuse me a moment,' Guy said, glancing at the number. His voice dropped an octave as he talked to the unknown caller in fluent French. A love interest, Rick thought, although it was too early for him to tell whether male or female; his first impression of Guy was that he was an ex-public school type, which meant that his sexual preferences were anyone's guess.

Embarrassingly, he could understand almost every word, because he had once spoken the language on a daily basis. It was the summer he'd worked at a sailing club in Brittany, and met the girl he'd denied knowing when Shelley challenged him about the dreams.

Which was technically correct, since her name was Anna;

he'd only called her Annie when they were–

But now he was determined to forget her. He'd even bought some self-help books at Melbourne airport and practised the techniques on the plane. By the time he'd landed at Heathrow, he'd cracked it. Easy. Shelley had actually done him a favour, exposing that secret corner of his past …

'Sorry,' Guy said, when he'd finished the call. 'New girlfriend, Marie-Claude, very keen. So, dinner first – then the party?'

All of a sudden, the last thing Rick felt like was being sociable; he pretended to consult his mobile. 'Afraid not, my sister's sent me a message. She needs to see me urgently, so I'll pick up a few things from the hotel and get on my way.'

For the first time since they'd met, Rick saw Guy frown. 'But you've got to be at Charing Cross Road for three o'clock tomorrow, quite a trek from Suffolk.'

'That's Dave the driver's problem, not mine. And it's Somerset, not Suffolk.' Rick closed his eyes again to discourage further conversation. As soon as he'd got rid of Guy, he'd ring Sophie; he hoped she'd be staying in for the evening, but it didn't matter if she wasn't. All he wanted was to unwind for a few hours, in a place where no one was watching his every move. Not much to ask, was it?

It all worked out perfectly. Sophie was ecstatic at the prospect of seeing him a few days ahead of schedule. She and Ed had planned a quiet dinner at home, but the meal could easily stretch to three. Or four – what about his driver? Rick said no, Dave would sort himself out food-wise, but if she could book him a bed at some local pub … As for him, the prodigal brother, he'd rather keep a low profile – so could she put him up at her cottage for the night? The sofa would be fine, even the floor.

She could offer something better than that, although not

much. It turned out that she had a small second bedroom with a single bed and a lumpy mattress, a far cry from his plush hotel in London.

But he drank too much to notice and had too good a time to care.

Just before eleven the next morning, after a slap-up breakfast and more laughter, he set off for London. He felt relaxed, almost happy; when Dave arrived with the car, he got into the front seat beside him – ready to chat, even cracking a joke.

The Jag cruised along the main street. It was empty – except for a woman with two little boys half-running towards the church, obviously late for the service. She was holding the smaller one's hand and clutching something to her, while the other boy skipped along in front carrying a most peculiar object, a little makeshift cardboard dragon. The next minute, predictably, he dropped it. It split open – or was that thing with brown spines sticking up some sort of lid? – and disgorged its contents far and wide. Three bright green apples tumbled into the gutter, plums scattered and squashed under the boy's dancing feet, a banana landed awkwardly in a pile of damp leaves.

The car drew near. Rick heard the inevitable wail as the boy realised what had happened and looked to his mother for a miracle. The woman ignored the spilled, spoiled fruit and bent to offer comfort. Rick's mouth twisted into an unpleasant smile. How touching. His own mother would have boxed his ears and walked on …

Then, as the woman straightened up, came a stab of recognition. The hair was longer than before, the face paler and thinner, but the resemblance was uncanny. What he was looking at now, and what he'd filed away to forget, matched. Perfectly.

So much for the self-help. All the memories came flooding back; not erased, as he'd thought – or wanted to think – but safely stored, and expertly retouched.

Dave slowed the car, as if debating whether to stop and help.

Rick found his voice. 'Drive on. Drive *on*.'

Chapter Four

Jenny ignored Anna's protests and poured her a generous glass of red wine. 'From the sound of your weekend, you *need* this. And I'll need the rest of the bottle to calm myself down. Who did you say your father's shagging?'

Sunday evening and, as promised, Anna was having dinner with Jenny and Tom. They were in the kitchen – shabbier and more cluttered than the dining room, but far warmer. And it allowed Jenny to direct the cooking and the conversation at the same time. She was the better cook but, since his accident, she encouraged Tom to do as much as possible round the house. Anna felt a surge of admiration for them both. She knew Jenny's relentless optimism and Tom's quiet acceptance were masks, but she'd rarely seen them slip.

She pretended to be affronted by Jenny's question. 'I never said he was shagging her, I just couldn't understand why they went into his bedroom and locked the door. I mean, it's only a massage.'

Tom stopped mashing the potatoes and grinned. 'There are massages – and there are *massages*, if you know what I mean.'

'No, we don't – are you going to enlighten us?' Jenny gave Anna a sly wink.

'Certainly not, use your imagination.' He turned his wheelchair expertly towards Anna. 'But give me this woman's contact details when *she's* not looking.'

'Quick, take them now, you know she's blind as a bat without her specs,' Anna said in a stage whisper. She rummaged in her bag and handed Tom a brightly coloured leaflet, which Jenny – as expected – snatched away with a crow of triumph.

'Ha, looks like Barbie on the front cover, let me just put my specs on ...' Jenny perched her spectacles on her nose and did a double take. 'Good grief, it *is* Barbie! Wearing her Mad Scientist outfit, except the white coat's so tight that most of her buttons have popped off, and it's so short that she's obviously forgotten the matching trousers. "Cléopatra Clé, the Science of Healing, the Hands of Love, the Key to a Better Life." Bloody Nora!'

'I need a Better Life,' Tom said. 'And Barbie's a vast improvement on my usual masseuse, Frumpie, with her Hands of Torture.'

Jenny's throaty laugh filled the kitchen. 'How dare you! Just don't expect Frumpie to help you into bed later on, you can spend the night in your chair.' She threw the leaflet down on the table in mock disgust. 'So, your father's taking *noblesse oblige* to a new level, is he? Actually, a rather old level, that sort of thing's gone on for centuries. You know, lord of the manor tumbling the servant girls.'

'No, it can't be that, he's never been very interested in sex.' Anna frowned as she recalled a low-voiced conversation between her mother and Minty years ago, all about Walter's Little Problem in That Department. She and Mona had giggled about it afterwards and Lisa had told them they were pathetically immature.

Jenny sniffed. 'Don't you believe it, sunshine – if you're looking for the ladle, Tom, it's on the draining board.' She gave Anna a shrewd look. 'And did you meet this surgically enhanced miracle worker?'

'I did. She arrived just as I was leaving Kellynch for Uppercross. Walter rushed out to see her, with Minty hot on his trail – you know she can't bear the thought of him throwing his money away on what she calls frivolities. So there we all were, watching Cleopatra squeeze herself out of this tiny sports car. A delightful little welcome party – Walter almost slobbering, Minty scowling, Lisa pushing to the front of the queue as usual–'

'And you in the background, not missing a thing,' Tom put in, smiling. 'What did you make of her?'

'She's a fake.'

Jenny almost choked on her wine. 'That's very direct, for you. What makes you think–'

'It's not just her fake tan and her fake boobs. She's got a fake French accent as well. I spoke French to her and she didn't seem to understand a word. I could even accept *that*, she probably just wants to sound glamorous as well as look it. But there's something else I can't quite put my finger on ... And how can he even look at a creature like that after Mummy, it makes me want to–' She broke off in frustration.

'So, after you'd recovered from Walter's shock announcement about coming to Bath next weekend, you went to Uppercross to mop Mona's brow,' Jenny said, swiftly changing the subject. 'What had the poor thing done? Broken a nail?'

Anna gave a wan smile. 'The usual.'

'Oh. How bad this time?'

She shrugged, stared at her untouched wine and pushed the glass away.

For a while, the only sounds were the ticking of the clock and the scrape of metal against china as Tom served lamb stew, mashed potato and broccoli on to the plates.

Jenny said, 'And the boys?'

'Great.' Anna smiled, in spite of herself. 'Ollie loves his new teacher and Harry's settled well at nursery. We had a lovely time on Saturday afternoon making harvest baskets out of shoeboxes. They're both mad about dinosaurs and I had to make the boxes look like a stegosaurus or something, can you imagine? It took me ages! Then would you believe it, on the way to the Harvest Festival Ollie dropped his and all the fruit fell out. But I salvaged some, and Harry offered him an apple from his basket, it was so sweet.'

'What about Charles?'

'I hardly saw him. He went over to the Great House as soon as I arrived and didn't come back until late. Then today he was up at the lake until lunch time. I took the boys there after church, but of course he couldn't say much in front of them.' She bit her lip. 'He's asked me to go back next weekend, it's Roger's birthday on Saturday and there's a party at night. They've got a babysitter but he wants another pair of eyes at the party, in case Mona–'

'Don't make a rod for your own back,' Tom said, setting a plate in front of her.

'I hardly do a thing for them, it's the Musgroves who help out most of the time. I wish Walter and Lisa would do more, but until Mona's last birthday they didn't seem to realise there was a problem–'

'Your father never seems to realise *anything*,' Jenny put in. 'He certainly doesn't seem to realise that Charles and Mona only got married because she was pregnant and Charles felt he had to do the decent thing. But Walter prances about pretending the Musgroves are embarrassingly grateful to be part of the Elliot dynasty and refusing to accept that it's a marriage made in hell.'

'I just feel sorry for the children,' Anna said quietly. Then, with forced cheerfulness, 'Mmmm, this looks delicious.' She picked up her fork and ploughed her way through a meal that may as well have been sawdust.

Chapter Five

After a heavy session at the hotel gym, Rick sat in his room nursing a whisky and reliving that brush with the past in Uppercross.

If it *was* her … No, there was no mistake, it was her all right. And the betrayal had been even greater than he'd thought. From the look of it, she hadn't finished her precious degree – probably hadn't gone to university at all. She'd fallen in love with someone else, had a couple of kids and was now festering in Sleepy Hollow. God knows, she could have had all that – and an awful lot more – with *him*, out in Australia. But she'd preferred to listen to her pompous old fart of a father and her evil godmother. If he let himself, he could remember – as if it were yesterday – the moment when she'd told him she would do what her mother had always planned for her, a degree in Russian at Oxford …

Except she obviously hadn't. Instead here she was, a dowdy mother of two, living close enough to her beloved Kellynch to make a daily bloody pilgrimage if she wanted.

Women. You couldn't trust them as far as you could throw them.

He phoned Shelley, but there was no answer. Maybe she was away on an assignment and had left her mobile behind; she was always forgetting something.

He phoned Sophie.

'Hi,' she said brightly. 'How did Charing Cross Road go?'

'Fine. Just wanted to check it's still OK for me to come on Friday.'

'Of course. Although I should warn you – one of our neighbours, Roger Musgrove, is having a party on Saturday and Ed let slip that you were here for the weekend, so we're all invited. I couldn't really refuse, Roger's been very kind.'

'Who else is going?'

'Oh, it'll be mainly family. Barbara, his wife, we'll have to hope she's not doing the catering.' She giggled, but didn't share the joke. 'His two daughters, Louisa and Henrietta, they run the stables at the far end of the village. His son, Charles, and his dreadful wife. A few other neighbours, I think, and us.'

'Do you know someone in Uppercross with two little boys?' He paused, calculating their ages. 'One's six or seven and the other's a lot younger.'

'There aren't many families with young children round here. Could be Charles Musgrove, his boys are that sort of age.'

'The one with the dreadful wife?' He held his breath for her answer.

'Well, I've only met her once and that was enough. Can't remember her name but she's actually the daughter of Sir Walter Elliot.'

Bingo. 'Sir Walter Elliot?' He hoped he sounded appropriately curious. He'd never discussed Anna with Sophie. By the time he'd seen his sister again after France, he was working his way through a succession of women at the University of Melbourne. So why mention yet another meaningless fling?

'Yes, the man who's renting us the greenhouses and Kellynch Lodge,' Sophie went on. 'He's dreadful too, drones on and on about being a baronet and looks down his nose at me as if I should be tugging my forelock–' She stopped, and Rick could imagine her impish grin. Then she said, 'How do you know the boys?'

'I don't, I just saw them as we left this morning. With the mother.'

'Who'd be shouting her head off, she's hopeless with them.'

He hesitated. 'Something like that. Anyway, it was great to see you and I'll phone during the week. Give my best to Ed, will you?'

She said goodbye and rang off, leaving him alone with his thoughts.

Anna ... Musgrove.

In six days he'd meet her again. And he'd prove he was over her, if it was the last thing he did.

Chapter Six

The last Monday in September saw the start of Freshers'
Week at university. For Anna, it was the run-up to another
academic year when she would focus on giving her students
a grounding in – and, if possible, a passion for – her chosen
subject. Strange, though; while the tide of nineteenth-century
Russian literature swept inexorably from Romanticism to
Realism, she often felt she was swimming against it. Her
mother's death may have turned her into more of a realist
than most teenagers, but, as she grew older, she found herself
drawn to romance – or at least the memory of it.

This year, however, she felt different. It was as if the
knowledge that Rick Wentworth was nearby – or, at least, in
the same part of the world – gave her an energy that moved
everything up a gear. Because, as she was only now realising,
she'd spent the last ten years in neutral. Oh, she'd got her
degree, a First, as Mummy would have wanted. She'd won
a measure of independence – financial and emotional – from
the Ancient Principality of Kellynch. She enjoyed her job,
overall. And she had plenty of opportunities to socialise,
mainly with Jenny and Tom and their friends in the more
bohemian parts of Bath.

But these were all superficial signs of life and, if she
died today, they'd make a painfully short obituary. 'At her
untimely death aged twenty-eight, Dr Anna Elliot was a
lecturer in Russian Studies at Bath & Western University.
Long fascinated by the great figures of nineteenth-century
Russian literature, Elliot was continuing her research into
their impact on western culture, the subject of her earlier
PhD (the actual title was far too long and boring). She leaves

a grieving father (Walter always reckoned he looked good in black), two sisters and a few close friends. The owner of her favourite bookshop said he knew her name but couldn't quite put a face to it.'

And that was the sum total of Anna Elliot. Except …

Somewhere deep down was another Anna, the one she'd been at eighteen during that summer in France. The one Rick Wentworth had coaxed into being, then left to shrivel and die. And she hadn't really looked at another man since. Oh, she'd tried; at Oxford, there'd been a few boyfriends, but they simply couldn't compare. It was like warming yourself on a radiator when you were used to basking in the sun.

She'd grown accustomed to it now, this quiet longing for another life.

By the time she drove into Uppercross on the following Saturday morning, she was obsessed by the thought of meeting him. Each car she passed, each man walking along the pavement, could be *him*. He was bound to be visiting his sister this weekend; according to his website, never a source of anything but purely factual information, he had no events scheduled until Tuesday evening.

Of course, she knew nothing could come of it. Too much water had gone under the bridge; and anyway, he had a girlfriend, Shelley someone, absolutely stunning. But meeting him again would close the chapter, put the other Anna out of her misery. It had to. She didn't allow herself to dwell on the alternative.

Mona lived on the fringes of the Musgrove estate, at Uppercross Cottage; the name rankled as a reminder of its unsavoury origins – two little farm labourers' cottages knocked together. The resulting four-bedroomed house was big enough to satisfy her ambitions – for now – and small enough to limit her spending, theoretically at least. Anna remembered how, even before she'd moved in, Mona had rebranded it as 'Uppercross Manor' with new signage and a range of personalised stationery. Apparently it impressed her London friends but had little effect closer to home; much to her annoyance the locals, especially her in-laws, still referred to it as 'the Cottage'.

Anna parked her Mini next to Charles's old Range Rover and sat for a few minutes, summoning all her reserves of patience. Although she'd always been closer to Mona than to Lisa – which wasn't saying much – their relationship had cooled when Mona married and became a mother. Anna wouldn't have minded if it was because Mona was too absorbed in her husband and children. But she wasn't; the reasons were altogether more complex.

And one of them was coming out of the house and walking this way; a thin dark-haired man two years older than herself, whose tense face lit up at the sight of her. She fixed her smile in place and got out of the car.

'Charles! I thought you were going out this morning?'

He held her, didn't kiss her, but looked deep into her eyes. 'Good to see you, as always.'

'And you.' She moved away to get her bags from the back seat. Then, with an anxious glance, 'Is everything all right?'

'Not too bad, actually. Mum and Dad had the boys overnight.' He gave a sheepish grin and Anna guessed that he and Mona had stopped arguing long enough to have sex. He went on, 'I'm just going to fetch them now and take them to feed the horses. Mona's had a lie-in, but she seems to be stirring.'

'I'll go and see her, it'll be good to have a chat while the boys aren't around.' A pause. 'How's she been?'

'A lot better. I think your visit last weekend did her good.' His face clouded. 'But she's all worked up about tonight, that's why I thought if there were two of us …'

'Yes, of course.' She gave him a reassuring smile.

He smiled back, then frowned. 'Have you heard of Rick Wentworth, some Australian celebrity who's over here on a book tour? Turns out he's not really Australian, he's Sophie Croft's brother and he's staying with her this weekend. Came down last night apparently, although nobody's seen him. Anyway, Dad's invited him to the party. Sounds harmless enough, doesn't it, except it's got Mona all hyper and Lou and Henrietta almost in hysterics.'

'Mmmm.'

'Lou went up to London specially for one of his book signings, she thinks he's even more gorgeous in the flesh. Can't understand his appeal myself. I mean, he's good-looking, I'll grant you that, but I bet there's not much between the ears, someone probably has to write his books for him. But then Lou's always been impressed by a nice set of pecs, whereas you're more interested in a man's mind, aren't you?' He touched her arm. 'Anna?'

She started. 'Oh! ... Yes ...'

His hand was still on her arm. 'You and I can form our own club, the Rick Wentworth Non-Appreciation Society, inaugural meeting tonight. You never know, by the end of the evening we might get more members, although at this stage it looks very doubtful. Even Mum's besotted, and of course Dad thinks that anyone who can fight off a shark with his bare hands must be – Do you think it really was a shark? Probably just a dolphin, same sort of fins, easy mistake to make.'

'Mmmm.'

'Well, good to chat but I'd better get going. Come up to the Great House for Dad's birthday lunch, they're expecting you. Should be safe to eat, Henrietta's on kitchen duty. Here, I'll take those.'

He let go of her arm at last, grabbed her bags and herded

her into the house; then shambled off, taking a well-trodden path across the fields opposite – the short cut to his parents'.

Just inside the front door, Anna leaned against the wall and closed her eyes. She'd meet Rick tonight, for sure. No surprises there, she'd expected to see him this weekend. But now she had a time, and a place, and the clock was ticking. Should she spend time tarting herself up in some pathetic little act of defiance – or go as she normally did, wearing the first thing to hand and sporting an invisible 'I'm Allergic to Male Pheromones So Don't Even Think About It' badge?

In the end, the decision was made for her.

'Anna, is that you?' Mona's sulky voice from upstairs. 'Come here. I feel like shit, it's going to take all day to get me ready for the party.'

Chapter Seven

The evening before, Rick had returned to Sophie and Ed's and heard their progress report on the garden centre refurbishment. He'd responded with a brief – and sanitised – account of the week's book signing events. In reality, it had been an unnerving experience. Some of the women he'd met made the deep sea angler fish – famous for biting on to its mate and never letting go – look sexually inhibited. And, for God's sake, if he wanted a girl's phone number he certainly wouldn't ask her to write it on her knickers, recently worn or not. With a grim smile, he'd passed the offending article to Guy and left him to deal with the disappointed owner.

And when Sophie had asked about Shelley, he'd fobbed her off. Shelley was neither answering her phone nor returning his calls, but he didn't want Sophie to make a big deal out of it. There'd be a simple explanation, he was sure.

Now, on Saturday morning, he was preparing himself to see Anna Musgrove later in the day. He started with his usual routine of a hundred sit-ups and fifty press-ups, had a protein-packed breakfast of smoked haddock and scrambled eggs, read the paper, then announced to Sophie that he was going for a run. When she asked how long he'd be, he told her not to expect him for lunch.

He went over his route on Ed's Ordnance Survey map, but refused to take it with him; the pockets of his shorts weren't big enough and he had his mobile if he got lost. Then he headed for Kellynch, telling himself he wanted to check out the greenhouses and The Lodge and take in the garden centre on the way. It was certainly not for sentimental reasons; although, if he chose to, he could recall the warmth in Anna's voice as she described her home and its happy associations with her mother. No, if there was an ulterior motive, it was purely to remind himself of the gulf between his background and hers. How had her father put it, the one and only time they'd met? Something along the lines of 'You're not fit for my daughter to wipe her feet on.' He'd found some satisfaction in retorting, 'But I made sure she enjoyed every single minute of it.'

The main road out of Uppercross was narrow and winding, its high hedgerows jewelled with late blackberries. For safety he ran against the traffic – and once or twice had to swerve into the grassy ditch to avoid an oncoming car. He didn't like running on tarmac, too unyielding, but there was no obvious alternative route. It was very warm for an English October and he was glad he'd remembered his water bottle.

He stopped after four miles when he reached the garden centre. The place was easily accessible from the road, had ample car parking and seemed well maintained. The refurbishment was limited to the main part of the shop, where Sophie and Ed had changed the layout; they were reluctant to spend time and money making the first-floor living accommodation habitable and, anyway, Sophie wanted a place to unwind away from the business. As far as Rick could tell, everything was on target for the grand opening in early November, shortly before he returned to Australia. Not the best time of year to open a garden centre, but Sophie wanted to try out some Christmas decorations and gifts, and Ed planned to test the local market for pet products and animal feed.

After a swig of water he set off for Kellynch, which he reckoned was only another couple of miles further on. And indeed, the hedgerow beside him soon gave way to a crumbling stone wall and a weathered sign where he could just make out the words 'Kellynch Estate, Private Property – Keep Out'. Although he could have easily scaled the wall, he kept to the road, noting the lie of the land he passed: open fields with a few sheep grazing, then more formal gardens as the house came briefly into sight.

At the wrought iron gates he paused. They were tall and ornate, but riddled with rust and half-askew, as though they'd forgotten why they were there. As he jogged along the weed-ravaged drive, an elegant Palladian mansion came into view, glowing in the sunshine like a large pearl on a green velvet cushion. But when he reached it, he saw that the elegance was a mirage; the walls of the house were damp-stained and peeling, the lawns patchy with neglect.

He wondered what he was doing this side of the gates; he'd probably get accused of trespassing. That in itself didn't bother him, it was more the thought of having to explain his presence to someone when he didn't understand it himself. Sure enough, at that moment two women appeared at the front door; both tall and blonde and wearing immaculate designer gym outfits, one pale pink, the other lilac. They saw him – and their conversation came to an abrupt halt.

'Yes?' Pink said imperiously. Her eyes fixed on his damp, clinging T-shirt, as if seeking enlightenment from the words 'Beauty is in the eye of the beer holder' emblazoned across his chest.

Lilac ran her tongue over her already glistening lips. 'I nuh oo yuh aargh,' she said. 'Yuh aargh Reek Wantwart.'

Rick looked at her, totally baffled.

Pink, however, seemed to have no difficulty in understanding this gibberish. 'Well, well, Rick Wentworth,' she breathed, in a much more encouraging tone. 'Are there any photographers with you?'

'There might have been, but they couldn't keep up,' he

said brusquely, then forced a smile. No point in antagonising the woman; at least, not yet.

'Welcome to Kellynch.' She fluttered her eyelashes at him. 'Were you after anything – or anyone – in particular?'

'I'm here on behalf of Sophie and Ed Croft.' That was partly true, wasn't it? 'They want me to report back on the state of The Lodge.'

'Checking up on us, are they? Come along, I'll give you a personal tour.' She slipped her bare arm through his – skin as smooth and cold as marble – then turned to her companion and said, 'Bring the car round to The Lodge, we'll go to the gym from there.'

He let her guide him away from the house, down a wide, overgrown path at right angles to the gates he'd just walked through. He wondered if she was related to Anna; at first glance, it didn't seem possible. But he didn't have to speculate for long, because she talked without any prompting. And her favourite subject seemed to be … herself.

She had a silly, little-girl voice which was profoundly irritating and completely at odds with her sophisticated image. He made himself listen, however, and soon learned that she was Elisabeth-with-an-s, Lisa for short, eldest daughter of Sir Walter Elliot, 8th Baronet. She'd apparently given up a successful career in the City – she didn't say what – to devote her time to various worthy causes connected with Kellynch. First impressions led Rick to suspect that there was no worthier cause than the beautification of Elisabeth Elliot.

The Lodge nestled beside a pair of gates that were even more impressive – and, on closer inspection, even more run down – than the previous ones. Rick guessed that they'd once been the main entrance and the path he was walking along had originally been a proper drive. There were signs that workmen had been: the grass outside The Lodge was flattened and muddied, and most of the windows were ajar, their frames freshly painted. Lisa bent down to retrieve a key from under an empty terracotta plant pot – giving him ample opportunity to observe her taste in underwear, a black thong – and unlocked the front door.

There wasn't much to see. It was basically small, with two bedrooms, and in need of a good clean and a lick of paint; the kitchen and bathroom had been cleared, presumably in preparation for new fittings. Lisa stayed close, which wasn't difficult in such a confined space.

'So, when's it due to be finished?' he said, as they went out again into the sultry air.

She shrugged. 'No idea. When do you *want* it finished? Are you coming to stay? Just give me a date and I'll have them working day and night to deliver.'

He gave her an appraising look – she'd probably enjoy cracking the whip, metaphorically at least – but merely said, 'I'll be visiting Sophie and Ed whenever I can. It doesn't matter to me whether they're here or in Uppercross.' He added, in the hope of learning something useful about Anna before tonight, 'Sophie tells me you've got a sister there. Do you see much of her?'

Just then a horn blared and a silver, open-topped sports car swung into the lay-by on the other side of the gates, with Lilac behind the wheel. She leaned across the passenger seat and called, 'Urree, or we'll meess ze class.'

Lisa smirked and gave her slim, pink-clad thigh a light tap. 'Mustn't be late, have to keep the cellulite at bay.' She treated him to a full-on smile, an advertisement for a Harley Street orthodontist no doubt. 'But don't worry – I'll pop over to see my sister more often, now that I know *you* might be just round the corner.' Before he could think up a non-committal reply, she sauntered through a little side gate and slipped into the car next to Lilac. As they drove off Lisa tilted the wing mirror towards her, checked her make-up and flicked her fingers in a careless wave.

He stood for several minutes staring after her. Not in admiration, however; he was casting his mind back to Anna's comments about her older sister. They'd been few and uncharacteristically dismissive.

And now he could understand why.

Chapter Eight

At Uppercross, despite all Anna's coaxing, Mona was still in bed.

'I'm not going there for lunch,' she said flatly. 'Even if it is Roger's birthday. Tell them I'm resting before the party.'

'But you've only just woken up.'

'They don't know that.' Mona examined her fingernails. 'You can give me one of your special manicures when I've had a bath.'

'I really think you should go,' Anna said, with a frown. 'We needn't stay long.'

'They never normally bother with *me*, it's only because *you're* here.'

'"Never" seems a bit harsh, weren't you there for lunch the other weekend?'

'Don't be so bloody pedantic.' Mona paused. 'Maybe I'll see how I feel after my bath. Henrietta said I could borrow her red dress for tonight, which means I'll have to go there to fetch it. She never calls here if she can help it.'

This time Anna refrained from questioning the 'never' word. 'I'll run your bath,' she said, knowing that this would get Mona out of bed – if only to spend the next half-hour in the warm, fragrant water reading a celebrity magazine, envying other people's lives. 'And I'll do a bit of tidying up while the boys aren't here.'

'Every room in the house looks like it's been hit by a bomb. I keep telling Charles I need the cleaners here more often, but oh no, he won't even talk about it. You're so lucky to live by yourself, you don't have any of the stresses I've got to put up with. Let me know when my bath's ready.'

Anna watched in silence as her sister yawned and reached for a magazine from the pile on the bedside table. At times, especially in the dark maze of a sleepless night, she would have given a lot for Mona's stresses: a husband who was basically kind and loving, when given the chance; two adorable children; no real financial worries; and the happy-go-lucky Musgrove family on her doorstep. But the grass was always greener on the other side of the street, wasn't it?

An hour later, after much complaining, Mona accompanied Anna to lunch at the Great House. They didn't take the short cut across the fields because of Mona's new shoes, which meant a guided tour of some current bones of contention: the money her parents-in-law had spent on the new boundary fence, the cost of the recently resurfaced drive, and so on. As they neared the house, a jolly hand-painted sign propped against the porch informed them that 'We're in the garden' and they walked round to a plain wooden door set in a high stone wall. Anna opened it and went in, while Mona hung back in a fit of pique at the lack of attention.

Anna closed her eyes for a moment and let the waves of sound wash over her. Children whooping, men shouting affably at each other, women shrieking with laughter. The Land of Musgrove, where everyone was welcome – whatever Mona might say – and life was lived at a glorious, noisy gallop.

Then she heard Ollie call her name and Harry squeal with delight; she opened her eyes just as they hurled themselves at her legs like boisterous puppies.

She laughed, picked Harry up and ruffled Ollie's dark curls. 'My favourite nephews.'

Ollie thought for a minute. 'We're your *only* nephews, Aunty Anna. You'll have to do better than that.'

She laughed even more. 'What are they teaching you at

that school – philosophy?'

Mona joined them, giving Harry a sharp glance. 'What's that round your mouth? Has Grandma been stuffing you with chocolate again? God knows, I'll be the one they blame when all your teeth fall out!'

Silence, then a heartfelt whimper from Harry as he took in the full horror of his mother's words.

Anna rummaged in her bag. 'Let's see what I've got here – ah yes, red package for Ollie, blue for Harry.'

The distraction worked; Harry stopped crying and clambered down. In a few seconds the boys had opened their presents, yelled their thanks and rushed off to show Charles their toy dinosaurs.

'Is Harry's suitable for a two-year-old?' Mona said, in a deceptively sugary tone. 'The childless never think about things like that.'

Anna was saved from replying by Barbara Musgrove, a large, red-faced woman with cropped brown hair and, as Mona put it, the dress sense of one of her horses. Today she was resplendent in a tight orange skirt and a sparkly yellow vest top, revealing an alarming amount of flabby cleavage. She cornered the newcomers in a stable-scented embrace, then swept Anna off to the far end of the garden.

With Barbara's disconcerting tendency to talk about two subjects at once, Anna had to focus all her attention on disentangling the daughter-in-law from the dahlias. 'How did you manage it?' Barbara gave her an admiring glance. 'Charles was convinced Mona wouldn't come, he thinks she's keeping a tally of the number of times we invite her here … Here's one you won't have seen before – Charlie Dimmock, grown from a cutting my sister gave me … Ridiculous, isn't it? As if she needs to wait for an invitation … and neither do you, we see far too little of you, Harry's always asking where "Tee-Anna" is … That big pink one's Sir Alf Ramsey … He can be a right little imp though, much worse than his brother, needs a firm hand. But, as I tell Charles, it's not my place to discipline them, grandchildren are for spoiling. Maybe if Mona *did* more with them, they'd be less of a handful – don't suppose you could drop a few hints? … Barbara's Pastelle, a medium semi-cactus variety, Roger's favourite because of the name. Not the Barbara bit, he says, more the suggestion of fruit pastilles. Cheeky old thing … And I often have to bribe them with biscuits, but at least they're home made, none of that shop-bought rubbish Mona gives them. That reminds me, come into the kitchen and try one of my cheese straws, there's something wrong with them but I can't decide what.'

Roger came striding towards them. 'An-na!' A hug and a kiss – more of a brush with his beard – then a frown as she handed him a card and a present. 'What's this, what's this? I gave strict orders, no presents.' His face brightened as he undid the wrapping paper. 'Marvellous! Where on earth did you find it? I've been looking for one of these.' He turned the little horse brass over in his hands. 'Two bells, not just one, you see?' Another kiss, a furtive look round and a lowering of the voice. 'By the way, will you have a word with Mona? They're overdrawn again and Charles can't seem to get through to her. Poor chap hates coming to us to bail them out, doesn't he, Barb?'

But Barbara wasn't listening; she was looking anxiously at Anna. 'You need fattening up, my dear. Let's go and see what Henrietta's doing with the lunch.'

She hustled Anna back up the garden and into the kitchen, where both her daughters were giggling uncontrollably.

'I – dare – you,' Henrietta gasped, the tears rolling down her cheeks. 'He might think – oh, Anna, great to see you. Lou's just been practising her chat-up line for Rick Wentworth, it's hysterical, she's going to–'

'I'll be hysterical in a minute,' Barbara put in. 'For one thing, Rick Wentworth's practically engaged and the only person who's allowed to chat him up is a respectable married woman, like me. For another thing, where's the lunch? If we want to eat all frisky, we'd better get a move on. Your father says it's going to rain.'

This set Lou and Henrietta off again. 'All – frisky!' they spluttered.

Barbara turned to Anna and tried to sound cross. 'They're horrible, aren't they? What's wrong with all frisky? That'll be Roger after a few drinks, I can tell you.'

Anna laughed, for the third time in little more than ten minutes; the Land of Musgrove was already working its magic. With her offers of help refused, and Barbara's offer of a cheese straw reluctantly accepted, she leaned back against the dresser to survey the scene. It was utter chaos, but she saw only three women whose mutual bond of affection made everything else irrelevant. Lou – *'never* call me Louisa, it takes far too long to say' – was big-boned like her mother but dark-haired and dark-eyed like her father, with an attractive vitality that Anna almost envied. Henrietta – *'always* call me Henrietta, I hate anything shorter' – was small, brown-haired and, on the face of it, far quieter; but she was never content to be in her elder sister's shadow. And Barbara was like an indulgent mother hen; she may have given up on Charles's happiness, but she was still full of hope for her girls.

Barbara's words had the desired effect and lunch was soon ready. In anticipation of rain, the food was set out indoors on the large kitchen table. Everyone came and helped themselves, then drifted outside again to eat 'all frisky' and enjoy the sunshine while it lasted. Everyone, that is, except Mona.

Anna noticed her slip out of the kitchen into the hall,

glass in one hand, bottle in the other. She hastily piled some food on to an extra plate and followed her into the large square sitting room. In the soft light that filtered through its small mullioned windows, the horse brasses lining its walls winked at each other surreptitiously.

'I brought you some lunch,' Anna said, sitting down on the sofa next to her sister.

'I'm not hungry.'

'Come on, at least it's not Barbara's handiwork, I've spared you her cheese straws. And you're better not drinking on an empty stomach.'

Mona gave a bitter little laugh. 'Don't you mean I'm better not drinking at all?'

'Don't you ever ask yourself that?' Anna said quietly.

'It's all right for you, you don't have a husband who hates you, or children who never do as they're told, or in-laws who are spending your inheritance as if there's no tomorrow.' Mona's large baby-blue eyes filled with tears. 'And tonight with Rick Wentworth will be the ultimate humiliation!'

Anna looked at her in alarm. 'Wh-what do you mean?'

But Mona could see no further than her own concerns. 'The Musgroves will treat him as if he's one of them – a huntin', shootin', fishin' country yokel – and they'll play those awful party games. What if the press turn up? Think of the embarrassment, it'll be "Rick Wentworth caught in a compromising position with Mrs Barbara Musgrove and an orange" splashed all over the national papers, complete with photos. I've told Charles a million times, we should have had the party at Kellynch, done things with style and good taste.'

Anna looked down. There'd been precious little style or good taste the one time Walter and Rick had met. She'd seen her father in a temper before, of course; no surprises there.

Rick, however, was a different matter. She'd thought she

knew him so well – but this man, with his reckless, almost uncontrollable anger, had been a complete stranger. The Rick she knew was persuasive, yes, and passionate; but gentle with it. And surprisingly romantic. The first time they'd made love, he'd–

Oh God, it was still so real, she could even smell the rose petals.

In the heavy silence Mona drank undisturbed, while Anna stared unseeingly at her lap and wondered if she could bear to meet the man she'd once loved.

Chapter Nine

Earlier that day, Sir Walter Elliot's mind had been occupied by far more important reflections, as he reassured himself that – for a man in his position – mirrors were a necessity of life, whatever Minty might say.

He had just had an extra one installed in his dressing room, the free-standing cheval type, properly bevelled and oak-framed. He felt a huge sense of achievement now that he could view his appearance from 360 degrees. Lisa was enchanted and wanted the same arrangement in one of her dressing rooms; they'd decided it would be better in the second, more spacious one. Her original dressing room had proved too small when she returned after those traumatic few months in London, and moving her surplus clothes into the room next door had been the obvious solution. He vaguely remembered it being Anna's bedroom – but she'd never live here again, so that was no longer a consideration.

His morning ritual completed, Walter adjusted the cuffs of his peach silk shirt and slipped on his taupe linen jacket, turning this way and that to admire the full effect. The expression 'Clothes maketh the man' was as true today as it had always been. How many men of fifty – he always rounded down, not up – looked this good?

He gave a little sigh. Inevitably, heads would turn at Luigi's later, when he went to lunch with Lisa and Cleopatra after their gym class. 'Isn't that Sir Walter Elliot, 8th Baronet?' 'Can't be, looks far too young.' 'The one on the right is his daughter, beautiful girl, still single, but of course there's no man round here good enough for her.' 'Wasn't there someone in London?' 'Yes, but she's well rid of him. William Elliot-Dunne, a distant relative actually, even more distant since he ran off to America with a rich divorcee.' 'The other girl's a stunner too, and French from the sound of it. Hangs on Sir Walter's every word, can't take her eyes off him. Not that I blame her.'

Yes, he'd been blessed with far more than his fair share of good looks and it was his duty to preserve them. Most men went to seed as soon as they turned thirty. Take Edward Croft; dressed like an old tramp, with soil and goodness knows what else under his fingernails, and had the skin of an alligator. As Lisa said, 'What do you expect from a gardener? And remember, that's the only way some people get a tan.' He'd responded with 'Thank God for tinted moisturiser!' and they'd both laughed.

His thoughts returned to Cleopatra. How overwhelmed she'd been when he'd invited her to Bath as his guest – almost speechless, in fact. She managed to babble something about 'an 'eart zrobbing wiz gratitude'; then, with typical Gallic exuberance, she placed his hand where he could feel the 'zrobbing' for himself ... And Minty, too, when she heard that Cleo was going to Bath with him and Lisa tomorrow, was almost speechless – for quite a different reason. She couldn't decide which was more outrageous: the expense of yet another person staying at The Royal Crescent Hotel, or the implied insult to her darling Anna. When Walter asked her what she could possibly mean, Minty replied that, if he wanted to splash his money around, Anna was a far more deserving cause. He'd taken great pleasure in pointing out that, by boosting Bath's tourist economy, he was effectively subsidising its permanent residents – as someone with Minty's knowledge of economics should have realised. That had taken the wind out of her sails, he recalled contentedly.

Still smiling, he went into his bedroom and paused beside the window to enjoy the view. His eyesight was less than perfect these days; but he had no intention of wearing those hideous spectacles Minty had ordered for him, terribly ageing, and he'd never got the hang of contact lenses. Anyway, being ever so slightly short-sighted was an advantage; he saw Kellynch as it used to be, before the last recession or whenever it was that his income had ceased to keep pace with his expenditure. The well-kept Kellynch that he remembered from his childhood, his youth and the halcyon years of his marriage – when rare and noble breeds of sheep had gambolled in its rolling fields, alongside the equally rare and noble breed who held court over garden parties and balls galore. Times of plenty; ah well, perhaps one day those times would return.

Then he noticed a figure in shorts and a T-shirt running towards the house from The Lodge – a young man, tanned and blond and pounding along the path like a god of vengeance. Walter thought the blurred face looked vaguely familiar; perhaps a model from the Sport section of the latest Ermenegildo Zegna catalogue? He couldn't help admiring the broad shoulders and strong legs, and quite forgot to wonder what the man was doing on his property. He wondered instead if he should take another look at the catalogue, a deliciously expensive-looking hardback that had occupied many a happy interlude already. Dressed in some Zegna sportswear, he might even accompany Lisa and Cleopatra to the gym. Not actually *do* anything in the way of exercise, of course, but that was hardly the point.

As the man drew level with the house, he seemed to glance up at the window where Walter was standing and give a jaunty salute. Walter waved grandly back at him, one magnificent physical specimen acknowledging another, then watched him head down the drive, out of the gates and on to the Uppercross road.

Walter would not have been quite so complacent if he'd been wearing those hideous spectacles. Then he might have recognised the man as that young upstart from France and responded far less charitably to his V-sign.

Chapter Ten

'Mona!'

Anna jerked her head up, Rick Wentworth temporarily forgotten. Charles was at the sitting-room door, his face ashen, his breath coming in great gulps.

Mona quickly drained her glass and glared at him. 'Can't I have a quiet drink without–'

'It's Ollie ... he's had ... an accident,' he said, between gasps.

As Mona burst into noisy sobs, Anna asked, 'Is it serious?'

At the sound of her voice, his breathing seemed to steady. 'I don't think so, but – but I want to take him to hospital, have him checked out.'

'Of course,' she said. 'Do you need to call for an ambulance?'

He shook his head. 'It's just his ankle, he twisted it when he fell out of the tree–'

'*Tree?*' Mona cut in, angrily. 'What the hell was he doing up a tree? Weren't any of you watching him, for God's sake?'

His thin face flushed. 'You can't watch them every single minute.'

'Evidently not.' Mona got to her feet, knocking over the empty wine bottle. 'Shit, who left that there?'

Charles's lips tightened. 'Anna, will you walk her home? I'm going there now for my car, but I'm in a hurry, got to bring it up here for Ollie. Shall I call for you on my way to Yeovil? I could do with some moral support, in case–'

'He's *my* son, I'll go to the effing hospital with you!' Mona kicked the bottle aside and slammed her glass down on a nearby table.

For a minute or so, nobody spoke; yet it seemed to Anna that bitter words hung in the air, too exhausted to find a voice. At last she stood up, collected the two plates – the food barely touched – and gave Charles a reassuring smile.

'You get the car, I'll take Mona to see Ollie so she can put her mind at rest. Where is he?'

'In the garden,' he said, and went.

They found Ollie lying on a sunlounger, pale and silent, with his left leg raised on a pile of cushions. Barbara was kneeling at his side and holding a bag of frozen peas on his ankle.

She glanced up and said cheerfully, 'Charles fell from the same tree when he was seven too, or was it eight? Such a fright at the time, but boys will be boys.'

Mona sat gingerly on the edge of the sunlounger. 'My poor baby, Mummy's here now.'

Ollie's hand crept into hers. 'Hurts.'

'No wonder.' She scowled at Barbara. 'I'll sit with him until Charles arrives. You'd better phone round and cancel the party.'

Barbara looked puzzled. 'Not sure I follow you, dear.'

'You can't possibly be going ahead after this!'

'But everything's arranged and Roger's so looking forward to it. And you weren't coming anyway, were you, my pet?' Barbara patted Ollie's arm kindly, then smiled at Mona. 'I'll give Gemma a ring for you, though, and tell her not to come and babysit. This young man'll want his mother with him tonight.'

Mona's scowl deepened. 'You can cancel the babysitter, but I'll decide what my own son wants, thank you very much. And it's Charles who'll be staying at home with Ollie – it's all his fault anyway, letting the poor kid fall from a *tree*.'

Anna eyed her sister's flushed face and quickly intervened.

'Why don't you leave me your house key? Then I'll make sure Harry has his tea and goes to bed at the usual time, if you're still at the hospital.'

'Be my guest.' Mona turned abruptly towards the door out of the garden, which Charles had left ajar. 'That sounds like our car. Here's to a fun afternoon in Accident and Emergency.'

Harry was running wildly about with the dogs, Belle and Bracken. Anna let him play; as soon as he started to flag, however, she put him in the stroller and set off for the village shop to get something for Ollie. They dawdled down the lane, stopping every so often to examine butterflies or teasels or whatever else Harry found intriguing. The rain held off, but the air was heavy and still.

The shop was set back a little way from the main road and its owners, Penny and Iain, made full use of the extra pavement space. Trays of winter pansies glowed between bags of freshly dug potatoes and baskets of logs, while wellington boots of all sizes and colours guarded neat stacks of plastic storage boxes. Inside, Anna steered Harry away from the sweets to the small selection of colouring books. As they debated which one Ollie would like, the shop door pinged and a couple came in, chatting amicably.

Anna glanced up. The man was stocky and sandy-haired with a friendly, weather-beaten face; the woman, tall and blonde and athletic-looking. Anna didn't know either of them and was on the verge of looking away, when something about the woman – her dark, deep-set eyes perhaps – stopped her in her tracks.

'So he helped you move all those paving slabs?' The woman sounded surprised.

'Yes, quite handy having him turn up like that,' the man said. 'I showed him round the garden centre, of course, and he seemed very impressed.'

'But he'd just been on a long run, hadn't he?' Her voice was anxious now. 'I hope he's not overdoing it, he's got such an intensive schedule over the next few weeks.'

'Don't fuss, Sophie, he's fighting fit. He'd have run all the way back home if I'd let him. I know you feel protective about your little brother, but I think at thirty-two years old he's quite capable of looking after himself.' His bantering tone grew more business-like. 'Aren't the cards along here?'

As the couple walked past, Anna turned blindly away. So these were the Crofts; she felt instinctively that she would like them, especially Sophie. In a daze, she let Harry choose something totally unsuitable for Ollie, but didn't notice her mistake until they were at the counter. By then it was too late. The Crofts were right behind her; she could hear them discussing what time they'd go to Roger's party. She couldn't bear to turn round and see the family likeness all over again, so she handed Iain the money and hustled Harry out of the shop.

All the way to the Cottage, she scolded herself. What if Rick had been there? She *must* pull herself together before they met, or else she'd look like a complete fool.

Just as they reached home, the rain started; it seemed somehow to match her mood.

Towards six-thirty, the others returned.

'Not broken, but a nasty sprain,' Charles announced as he laid Ollie carefully on the sofa. 'We've got to make him rest for the next few days, that'll be a trick and a half.' He gave Anna a weary smile. 'Thanks for looking after Harry – shall I put him to bed while you get ready for the party?' A glance across the room, where Harry was playing happily with his Lego. 'I'll just have a shower first, won't take long.'

Mona shot him a look of pure poison. 'Excuse me? Who's looking after these two while you're at the party?'

He frowned. 'I thought you–'

'Me?' She gave a mirthless laugh. 'We've been through this already, remember? Several times! You expect me to stay and babysit while you and Anna–'

'For God's sake,' he said testily, 'I didn't think you were serious about me babysitting. Ollie's had a hell of a time, he just wants his mother.'

'While his father goes off enjoying himself–'

'There's no point both of us staying at home, is there, you stupid–' He stopped and glared at Mona. 'You didn't really want to go to Dad's party, so why kick up such a fuss?'

'That's hardly the point. Why should you go and not me?' Her voice rose to a crescendo. 'It's always the same, you have all the fun while I'm stuck here–'

'I'll babysit,' Anna put in, sitting down next to Ollie and ruffling his curls.

Mona brightened instantly. 'Of course, that's the ideal solution! If I stay, I'll worry myself sick and have to ring the doctor every five minutes, whereas you don't understand what a mother goes through, so–'

Charles cut in with an exasperated, 'Absolutely not, Anna. Let me see if Gemma's still available.'

'No, I've made up my mind, please explain to everyone how sorry I am,' Anna said firmly. 'And, in the circumstances, isn't it best if the boys are with someone they know well?'

He shook his head. 'You're probably right, but it's still not fair.'

Mona checked her watch. 'Charles, there's no time to argue, we must get ready *now*. We'll have to be up at the Great House in good time so that I can try on Henrietta's dress, needless to say she couldn't be bothered to drop it off here. And Anna –' a dazzling smile – 'if you want anything, just ring us on the mobile.'

But they all knew she wouldn't.

Chapter Eleven

The Crofts and their celebrity guest were the last to arrive at the party.

Rick had spent so long in his bedroom that Sophie asked if he'd fallen asleep after all his exertions. He shrugged off her concerns, however, and said that he'd been catching up with emails and missed calls on his BlackBerry. This was not quite true; he'd spent most of the time rehearsing a range of facial expressions – from bland indifference to studied surprise – in anticipation of meeting Anna Musgrove. When he did get round to checking his missed calls, he discovered that Shelley had rung at last. She hadn't left a message and it was now the middle of the night in Australia, so he made a mental note to try her in the morning.

As a courtesy, they rang the doorbell; when no one answered, however, they tracked everyone down in the walled garden round the side of the house. There were probably only about twenty people on the well-lit terrace, but it sounded like a lot more. Rick's arrival didn't cause a noticeable stir, thank God, although a couple of girls squealed when they saw him. Roger Musgrove, a jovial, loudly dressed man, introduced them as his daughters, Lou and Henrietta.

Next came his wife, Barbara. 'Now Rick, don't hold back on the food front, we've got enough to feed an army. Village caterers, all local produce, trout from our very own lake. Which reminds me, I need your opinion on our koi carp. Too dark to see them now, maybe you'll come over in the morning?'

It was something he encountered time and again – the

idiotic assumption that he was an authority on anything that lived in water. But somehow he warmed to this woman; so he smiled and said he'd be delighted and left it at that.

He handed Roger his gift, a signed copy of *Sex in the Sea* with a personal birthday message. Roger went into such raptures that Rick winced with embarrassment, especially when Lou let slip that this was the fourth copy in the family. She'd apparently bought books for herself, Henrietta and Barbara at one of his signings. He did the decent thing and pretended he remembered which seemed to make her ludicrously happy.

Infected with the others' enthusiasm, he almost relaxed, almost let down his guard. But all the time his eyes searched for *her* face ...

As it turned out, he met the husband first; dark-haired and weedy-looking, with watchful eyes.

'Let me introduce my son, Charles,' Roger said heartily. 'We run the estate together – would you believe he actually *likes* dealing with all that EU Single Payment Scheme paperwork?'

The two younger men shook hands and, feeling a sudden need to test the other man's strength, Rick made it one of his bone-crunching specials. No contest; now it was just a matter of establishing that he was superior in mind as well as body.

Charles's mouth tightened in what may have been a smile or, more likely, a grimace of pain. 'Ah, the shark wrestler. We're all itching to hear about your incredible exploits.'

This sort of remark irritated Rick. It always came from men and was usually accompanied by some limp-wristed posturing, as if he'd challenged their manhood.

And so, when Roger went off to refill their glasses, he heard himself say, 'I knew your wife, a long time ago. Rather well.' He cursed himself under his breath. Why tell this man anything?

Charles gave a sardonic laugh. 'Lucky you. Maybe you'd like to get reacquainted?' He glanced round. 'Ah, there she is, I'll just bring her over.'

A sudden pounding in his ears, blotting everything else out. Rick closed his eyes and let his lungs fill with air. Hold – two, three, four, five. And out again, slowly, slowly.

Charles's voice, quite sharp. 'Darling, you didn't tell me you'd met Rick Wentworth. Says he knew you rather well, once upon a time.'

Rick forced his eyes open and stared down at a face he'd never seen before. Broad, heavily made-up, pretty enough but with none of *her* delicate features, and framed by long, wavy, dark red – almost maroon – hair.

'*Have* we met?' The woman hiccupped and tried to cover it up with a suggestive giggle. 'I'm sure I'd have remembered.'

He pulled himself together, switched on the charm. 'I'm sure I would too, obviously got you mixed up with someone else.' He turned to Charles and attempted a smile. 'Sorry, my mistake, wrong Musgrove. Unless you've got another wife tucked away somewhere?'

'I wish. Anyway, why don't I leave you two to get acquainted, as opposed to reacquainted. I'm just popping home to check on Ollie – or have you been already, Mona?'

She didn't answer; so, after a moment, Charles shrugged and sloped off.

As soon as he'd gone, she put her hand on Rick's arm and simpered, 'Let me introduce myself properly. I'm Mona Musgrove, formerly an Elliot of Kellynch, my father's the 8th Baronet. And where do you think we've met?'

Was she thick, deaf or merely drunk? 'I've just said we haven't. But I have met an Elliot of Kellynch before, Annette or something. Perhaps your younger sister?' He couldn't resist that last little jibe.

'You must mean Anna.' Her tone was distinctly cooler. 'She's my older sister, actually. And it's funny that she's never mentioned you.'

He felt the blood rush to his face; had he been that insignificant in her life? 'It was in France, years ago, and we only saw each other a few times,' he said stiffly. 'She was an au pair and I was teaching kids how to sail, a bit of responsibility after four years at university.' It sounded more like an entry on his bloody CV, but that way there was no chance of anyone guessing the truth.

And Mona seemed less curious than most. 'Oh, that explains it,' she said airily. 'She was miserable in France, I remember my father having to fetch her home. I wasn't around that summer – Lady Helen Carnegie, a good friend from boarding school, invited me up to Scotland. Her family seat is Sanders Castle, you must have heard of it, in the–'

He was barely listening. 'Is she married now?'

'Lady Helen? Not yet, but she's engaged to–'

'I meant your sister.'

'Anna? God, no.' He waited for her to elaborate, but instead she went on, 'She's just next door actually, babysitting for us. At Uppercross Manor – that's our house, rather small, we're looking for something much bigger. I don't know how she and Charles persuaded me to come out this evening, I can't bear to be away from my boys for long. In fact, why don't we take a little walk over there? Best to go now, before Barbara gets her oranges out, so degrading.'

Rick declined as politely as he could. Why on earth would he find Barbara and her oranges degrading? If it was a quaint euphemism for Barbara going topless – well, he lived in Australia, for God's sake; bare breasts were part of the bloody landscape.

And he was in no hurry to meet Anna Elliot again, married or not.

By the time Charles arrived at the Cottage, Anna had put both children to bed; Harry was asleep and she was in Ollie's room, reading him his favourite Roald Dahl story.

He greeted his father with an enormous yawn and said, 'Where's Mummy?'

'Talking to a shark wrestler,' Charles replied.

'*Really*?' Ollie's eyes were wide with wonder.

'Well, so everyone says. Anyway, how are you feeling?'

'Good. Except Harry gave me the silliest colouring book, all fairies and stuff. Aunty Anna says they're special fairies and they're going to make my ankle as good as new.' He pulled the duvet over his head in disgust.

Charles looked across at Anna and smiled. 'If Aunty Anna says so, it must be true.' He sighed. 'I suppose I'd better be going back, Mum wants me to help with the party games. Rick Wentworth doesn't know what he's letting himself in for. Do you know, I think the man's unhinged? Tried to tell me he'd – slept with Mona!' He mouthed the last three words so that Ollie didn't hear, then went on, 'Of course he didn't put it quite like that, just said he knew my wife a long time ago "rather well", but I could read between the lines. Then, when they met, it was obvious he'd never seen her before in his life, and he actually admitted he'd made a mistake. Weird.'

Anna stared down at the jumble of words on the page in front of her. 'Maybe he was confusing her with someone else.'

'God knows who, there's only one Mona.' A short laugh. 'Well, goodnight, Ollie boy. And you, Anna.'

She was dimly aware of Charles leaving the room ... of reading to the end of the chapter as if on autopilot ... of

Ollie demanding that she read it all over again, but this time with her usual funny voices. Somehow she remembered to reassure him that, if he woke up and needed anything, he only had to shout and she'd come. Then she sat and listened to the tick of the clock, until his breathing settled into the gentle rhythm of sleep.

And still she sat, turning Charles's words over and over in her mind. It sounded as if Rick had expected her to be at the party – as Charles's wife! She wondered how he'd react when they did meet, and he found out that she was no one's wife ... But he had a girlfriend, so what was the point of wondering anything at all?

Anyway, although she'd avoided a meeting tonight, one thing was certain: she wouldn't have to wait until his book signing in Bath to see him. Now that he'd met the Musgroves, he could walk back into her life at any moment.

Waiting in line while an orange was passed from one person to the next – an excuse for much giggling, bawdy remarks and occasional shrieks of 'No hands allowed!' from Barbara – Rick almost regretted turning down Mona Musgrove's suggestion. A stroll to call on Anna Elliot, with Mona name-dropping every few seconds, would definitely have been the lesser of two evils.

He wondered when he could escape back to Sophie and Ed's. At least they seemed to be enjoying themselves; he watched them pass the orange rather deftly from one to the other, using the chest technique. He decided that this was a game best played by married couples, or people trying to get each other into bed; anything else was downright embarrassing.

But, before he could slip away, the girl in front – Lou? – turned to him with the orange wedged under her chin. Knees slightly bent, head at an awkward angle, hands clenched behind his back, he attempted to take it from her using only his neck muscles.

Shit! Out of the corner of his eye, he watched it roll down inside her shirt and nestle in her not inconsiderable cleavage. She burst out laughing, making the fruit wobble rather endearingly.

And he recalled other fruit, spilling out of a dragon box; and a little boy in distress; and a pale, haunting face ...

He stared at the face next to him, bright with amusement and admiration. Yes, admiration. This girl fancied the pants off him and all he had to do was give her a word of encouragement. Oh, he was tempted; he could do with someone warm and willing in his bed tonight. But he'd never cheat on Shelley.

So he calmly put out one hand and retrieved the orange as quickly as possible, much to the girl's disappointment. In an effort to console her, he tucked it back under her chin, grabbed her by the shoulders and expertly transferred it – without using his hands – to her sister, who was waiting on his other side.

Later, after he'd left the party, he stood at the back door of Sophie's cottage, staring into the whispering darkness of the garden. For the first time since he'd arrived in England, he allowed himself to think long and hard about Shelley. On his part, the relationship was pretty sterile: hardly a word of affection, let alone commitment. He knew she wanted – and deserved – more.

When he returned to Australia, it would be different. He'd open up, tell her about the past, make plans for a long, leisurely holiday together. It would make her happy. As for himself ...

But why wait another few weeks? He'd start tomorrow, with the phone call.

Chapter Twelve

Rick woke with a start. It took him a few seconds to realise that the insistent buzz from the bedside table was his mobile. He fumbled for the light switch. Six-thirty; and it was Shelley's number showing on the display.

'Hi,' he said, smiling into the phone.

'Hi, I hoped you'd pick up.' She sounded nervous.

'Where've you been? I've missed you.' His smile broadened. 'Especially last night.'

A pause. 'Why last night?'

'Because that was when I knew just how much you mean to me.'

Silence.

'Shell?'

'Yes?'

'I just wanted to say–'

'Whatever you wanted to say, it's too late.'

He must be doing this all wrong; her voice was like ice cracking.

'Too late for what?'

'Us.' Before he could speak, she went on, rushing the words out as if she couldn't wait to be rid of them, 'I wanted to tell you before it – well, it's probably in all the papers already. I've met someone else and I'm going to move in with him. You and me – that's over, so don't even think about trying to change my mind. And you know what? Maybe it was over as soon as you went back to England.'

Then she hung up.

The call had lasted barely a minute, but he lay in bed for a long time afterwards. It was as if he'd been floored by a single punch, all the more lethal because he'd never seen it coming.

He wondered who she was with, and when, and where – but not why. That was the easy bit. It wasn't just about his failings and her needs and the demands of both their careers. They were the context, not the cause.

The cause was only a few hundred yards away, visiting her spoilt brat of a sister at Uppercross Manor.

Harry crept into Anna's bed shortly after eight o'clock. He lay still for precisely five seconds, then whispered in her ear 'Tee-Anna up' and started his wriggling routine. This had been perfected over many mornings and was carefully designed to wear down the strongest resolve. Anna lasted less than half a minute.

She got up, struggled into a faded pink dressing gown – one of Mona's cast-offs that she used whenever she was here – and wondered why her head felt like cotton wool. Ah yes, Ollie had called for her several times in the night. She looked for her slippers but couldn't find them, checked on Ollie – who was sleeping peacefully – and went down to the kitchen with Harry.

Charles was already up and dressed. He took one look at the dark circles under her eyes and apologised profusely for her broken night. Then he made a fresh pot of tea and insisted on getting Harry's breakfast ready before he went up to the lake.

He paused at the back door, rod and tackle in his hand. 'Need anything from the shop?' He'd be calling for the paper on his way, as usual.

Anna took a sip of tea. 'Don't think so, unless – what about lunch?'

'We're all invited up to the Great House.'

'All?'

'Just the family – which includes you, of course. See you later.' And off he went.

So Rick hadn't been invited; she didn't know whether to be relieved or disappointed. She'd make herself presentable, though, in case their paths crossed in the village. Wash her hair – it felt as lifeless as the rest of her. Find that newish jumper she'd left here last weekend. Put on a brave face with the help of Mona's make-up bag.

Which meant that, when Harry smeared the remains of his soft-boiled egg in her hair, it didn't really matter. And when she spilt tea down the front of her dressing gown, she simply made a mental note to pop it in the washing machine later; there was probably enough in the laundry basket to make up a full load. And when Harry sat astride her outstretched leg and counted her bare toes in a language known only to himself, she couldn't resist chanting 'One, two, buckle my shoe' in its entirety.

Which meant she hardly noticed the back door opening; and Charles rushing through into the utility room; and a tall figure coming in behind him, then stopping abruptly.

'Nineteen, twenty, my plate's empty!' She finished with a triumphant wiggle of her toes and glanced across at the newcomer.

Their eyes locked. It was Rick.

As she looked away in shock and confusion, she had the strange, random thought that his stony gaze fitted the last three words of the nursery rhyme to a T.

Chapter Thirteen

Rick hadn't felt like telling Sophie and Ed about Shelley. Not yet.

He'd refused breakfast, claiming a bad head and saying he was going for a long walk to clear it. Then he'd made straight for the village shop and its piles of Sunday newspapers.

He found what he was looking for in the first tabloid he opened, *The Sunday Reporter*. 'Sex-in-the-Sea Rick's Shell Shock!' screamed the headline on page two; if he'd been in a better frame of mind, he might have appreciated the wit. There were two photos – one of Shelley and a dark-haired man, both wearing sunglasses and guilty expressions, and one of him at a recent book signing, looking sullen. He discovered who – someone called Andy Stuart; he didn't recognise the name. And when – they'd 'grown close' over the last ten days; that was how long he'd been away from Melbourne. And where – she'd been seen leaving his 'millionaire's mansion' in Toorak; some distance – geographically and socially – from Rick's house by one of the more remote beaches. And why – according to the *Reporter*, at any rate. Apparently Andy Stuart had not just the money but also the time for Shelley McCourt. They were inseparable and there was already talk of marriage, and children, and Shelley giving up her career to devote herself to domesticity. Or whatever passed for domesticity in a millionaire's household.

And Rick learned that he himself was 'devastated' by the break-up. Apparently this was fantastic news for the female population of Britain, because he'd be looking to them for consolation. The *Reporter* wanted feedback on their progress.

There were only two copies of this particular newspaper left in the shop; out of spite or panic – he wasn't sure which – he bought them both, along with a *Sunday Times* and a *Sunday Telegraph*. He'd need plenty of reading material for the next couple of days; he had no plans to go out and throw himself into the arms of a passing *Reporter* reader.

The guy at the counter gave him a plastic carrier bag and a look of pity; but whether the pity was for the amount of newsprint or the state of his love life, Rick couldn't tell. Just as he was pocketing his change, he heard a man behind him say cheerfully, "Morning, Iain. *Sunday Times*, as usual. 'Morning, Rick.' It was Charles.

Rick turned round and forced a smile. 'You're out and about early.'

'Always am on a Sunday, I go fishing.' Charles hesitated, then went on, 'Why don't you come up and check out the lake? Rainbow and brown trout mainly, I'd really appreciate your opinion on what improvements we could make.'

For crying out loud, did marine biology make him an expert on trout fishing? Rick almost cut him dead, then thought better of it. Why not while away an hour or so in the sunshine? It might prolong this feeling of numbness, delay the black mood that he suspected was inevitable.

He made a huge effort to sound enthusiastic. 'Thanks, I'd really like that.'

As they left the shop together, Charles said, 'There's a spare rod at home that you could use, we'll call for it on the way. And I've got a paper, so you could park all those –' he indicated Rick's carrier bag – 'and pick them up later.' He chuckled. 'Anna – that's my sister-in-law – finds it rather amusing that I take my *Sunday Times* with me to the lake. She says the fishing's obviously just a cover for reading the paper in peace and quiet, especially as I hardly ever catch anything.'

So, Anna Elliot still had a sense of humour; that was more than could be said for him at this precise moment. He heard himself mutter, 'Typical woman, never satisfied.'

'Believe me, Anna's not your typical woman.'

Something in his voice made Rick look at him sharply, but Charles's face gave nothing away. They walked on in silence and Rick felt his state of mind slip from its current limbo into an older, bigger emptiness. No, Anna was not 'your typical woman' ...

But Charles couldn't possibly know her as Rick had once known her; otherwise how could he have ended up with someone like Mona?

And then his thoughts took a different turn. Last night hadn't it been Charles, not Mona, who popped home – supposedly to check on the kids? And didn't Mona say that it was Anna and Charles who'd persuaded her to go out for the evening? What if they were having an affair behind her back?

He knew he was jumping to conclusions, but ... 'Believe me, Anna's not your typical woman.' He'd detected a quiet conviction in this remark, the sort of conviction that grew from a special knowledge of someone, from intimacy, and love ...

Charles took a little turning off the lane, beside a large sign saying 'Uppercross Manor', and Rick followed him blindly. Down a side path, into a sudden fragrance of lavender, across a wide sunny terrace strewn with kids' toys. Then through a door and–

Two worlds collided. The one he inhabited now, with its ship-like order and restraint; and the one he'd glimpsed ten years ago. With a girl who'd once wiggled her toes at him until he'd caught hold of her small, perfect foot and covered it in kisses.

This girl. Those toes. That foot.

He dragged his gaze to her face. She was too busy with the little boy to notice him, so he had several long seconds to study her haggard, unkempt appearance. He felt oddly pleased that she'd lost her looks; especially since she wouldn't see much change in his.

At last, she glanced up and their eyes met. He watched her smile fade and her face go rigid with disbelief; then she flushed and looked away.

The boy broke the strained silence. 'Who dat man?'

Charles breezed in – Rick hadn't even realised that he'd gone out of the room – and said, 'That's Rick, he's coming up to see our lake. Sorry, Rick, haven't introduced you. This is Anna, Mona's sister, and my son, Harry. By the way, Anna, have you seen my spare rod?'

She gave him a stunned look, but said nothing.

Charles's voice softened noticeably. 'Don't worry, you're obviously on another planet, I'll check the shed.' He turned to Rick and added, 'She's whacked – my other son sprained his ankle yesterday and he's had a bit of a restless night. Poor Anna bore the brunt, she's wonderful with the children, always happy to come and help us out.'

Quite the little *ménage à trois*, Rick thought sourly. He cleared his throat, muttered 'Hi' and followed Charles outside.

It was over. He'd met her again and he'd felt nothing. Nothing at all.

It was over. And it was just beginning, all over again.

Anna remembered the first time she'd seen him. The sailing club in La Baule had been running courses throughout the school holidays and Natasha had wanted to enrol her children, then aged ten and eight. On the day the beginners' lessons had started, Natasha had taken the reluctant pair along, satisfied herself that everything was done properly and signed them up for a full month.

That evening, all Katya and Alyosha could talk about was their sailing instructor. They called him 'Rique' and Anna imagined a swarthy Frenchman, or even a Spaniard. He was apparently the bravest, strongest, funniest man they'd ever met.

So, when Anna took them to the club the next day as part of her au pair duties, she wouldn't have been surprised to see 'Rique' walking towards them on the water. Instead, however, he came on dry land, a mere human, and welcomed the children by name. And, although his skin was tanned to a healthy copper-bronze, he didn't have the dark colouring she'd expected. Not surprising, since he was actually 'Rick', from England.

At first glance, his hair was as blond as the sand; yet, on closer inspection, it was far more intriguing – sun-bleached at the front and tawny-gold round the sides and back. He fixed his deep-set, deep-brown eyes on her, while replying to the children's questions in monosyllabic French. But it was his smile that she fell in love with first: warm and caressing, like the summer breeze.

It took them a week of eyeing each other up before he asked her out. One day, Alyosha stayed at home with an upset stomach; which meant that Katya hung back instead of competing with her brother for attention.

Rick seized his chance in the most surprising way. '*Ty ochen krasiva*,' he said, looking straight at Anna.

She blushed at his words; then, to cover her embarrassment, she said, 'I didn't know you spoke Russian.' So far, they'd all been talking to each other in French, as she was doing now. Alyosha and Katya went to school in Paris and were fluent, although they usually lapsed into Russian at home. It was after all their heritage, a source of family pride. As Natasha never ceased to remind them, they were descended from the

St Petersburg Petrovs; and so was Anna, whose mother had been Natasha's aunt.

Katya grinned at Rick. 'Not bad, considering you only started practising yesterday. At first it felt weird me teaching you stuff, but I got used to it.'

He laughed, then looked again at Anna. 'Did you understand what I said?'

'Yes.' Another blush. Shit, he'd think no one had ever told her she was beautiful. Which they hadn't.

'I take it you don't believe me?'

And he smiled that incredible smile. When he did that, he could say there were fairies at the bottom of the garden and she'd believe him, from here to eternity.

But all she said was, 'It makes me think you want something.'

'Oh, I do.' His eyes danced. 'I want you to come out with me tonight.'

Katya giggled, but Anna's heart began to pound; he couldn't possibly mean it, this was some sort of trick.

'Sorry, no,' she said shyly.

'Why ever not? You can't be staying in to wash your hair, or whatever the usual excuse is.' He reached out and brushed one or two tendrils back from her face. 'As I thought, like silk.'

At his touch she flinched, though not with distaste; far from it.

'It's nothing to do with her hair,' Katya put in, helpfully. 'She's taking Alyosha and me to Le Moulin à Vent for crêpes because Mum and Dad won't be home for dinner.' She cocked her head on one side and looked at Rick, all wide-eyed innocence. 'So if she comes out with you tonight, she'll have to bring us as well.'

Rick raised one eyebrow. 'Crêpes? That should be interesting, with Alyosha's upset stomach.'

'Oh, he'll be fine, you wait and see,' Katya said. 'He never stops eating for long.'

So they'd gone to the Le Moulin à Vent together and, over the meal, Anna and Rick exchanged some basic information. She discovered that he came from northern mining stock, a far cry from the sort of lineage that would impress her father. He was twenty-two, four years older than her, and had just done his MSc in marine biology at Bangor University, reckoning that the extra year of student debt would be worth it in the long term. After the summer, he planned to start his PhD and, although he didn't say where, she got the impression that he was staying on at Bangor. She told him she'd be going up to Lady Margaret Hall to study Russian, and that led to a discussion about her mother, a loss still raw after only eighteen months. He said he wished he was as close to his mother, and then made her laugh with tales of a childhood that seemed to have been devoted to disappointing every parental hope.

He was easy to be with, even easier to fall in love with. She found herself secretly wondering how many miles Bangor was from Oxford; but that was looking too far ahead, wasn't it?

When he kissed her, it was the perfect end to a perfect evening. He'd walked them home – even though it was still light, and not far, and the streets were perfectly safe. Katya and Alyosha rushed indoors to watch something on TV, but she and Rick lingered outside. And there, under the pine trees, he took her in his arms, bent his head and teased her lips apart. He was so obviously experienced, and she wasn't. But, after a while, that didn't matter at all …

'Aunty An-na!'

Ollie, from upstairs. She looked wildly round for Harry; she hadn't noticed him wander off. To her relief, he was under the table playing with his toy dinosaur.

Stupid, *stupid* to let herself be so – so distracted at seeing Rick again. But she hadn't wanted it to be quite so soon, and certainly not when she looked – and felt – a total wreck! Lucky for her, though, that Charles had put her state of confusion down to lack of sleep. Because, with none of the Musgroves – including Mona – aware of their history, maybe it was best to keep it that way. And, after that *faux pas* with Charles about knowing his wife, she hoped that Rick too was in no hurry to tell anyone about the past.

But Anna had reckoned without her sister's point-scoring skills. When she and Harry went to find out what Ollie wanted, they found Mona sitting on his bed. As soon as she saw Anna, she narrowed her eyes and said, 'You didn't tell me you'd met Rick Wentworth.'

Anna kept her gaze steady and her tone casual. 'It was ages ago, in France, before he was famous. And we didn't see that much of each other.'

Only every day, and one wonderful weekend, filled with loving …

'Actually, I got the distinct impression he couldn't stand you,' Mona said, with a delighted little laugh. 'Whereas he and I got on extremely well, much to Charles's annoyance. Nice to think I can still make my husband jealous, it isn't as if he–'

'Mummy,' Ollie put in, 'my leg's hurting.'

'Aunty Anna'll sort it, I need to get dressed.' With a dazzling smile, Mona leapt to her feet and almost ran out of the room.

When she came downstairs over an hour later in full regalia – new designer jeans and shirt, hair and make-up immaculate – Anna was still in her dressing gown. There hadn't been time for a shower, what with getting the boys ready and coaxing Ollie to eat some breakfast. At least, Anna reflected miserably, meeting Rick seemed to have given Mona a new lease of life. Up before nine on a Sunday, dressed by half-past ten, whatever next?

Voices at the back door interrupted her thoughts and made her heart race. What if this was Rick again? Not that it mattered. Nothing mattered any more, it was over, utterly and completely. She wished she could go home and–

The door burst open and Lou and Henrietta almost fell into the kitchen.

'Oh-God-oh-God-oh-God, you'll never guess what's happened!' they said, clutching at each other and giggling hysterically.

The children stared at them open-mouthed, while Mona said, 'It must be very important if you've bothered to come all the way to our humble little abode.'

Henrietta simply stood there, speechless with excitement, but Lou gabbled, 'It's Rick, he's split with Shelley. We googled him this morning, just for the hell of it, and found it all on *The Sunday Reporter*'s website. She's dumped him for this other bloke, nothing much to look at – she must be mental, mustn't she?'

Anna's cotton-wool brain could hardly take it in. Rick's girlfriend, with someone else?

As Lou paused for breath, Henrietta managed to gasp, 'So now we're off to the lake.'

'The lake?' Mona made it sound like the ends of the earth. 'Whatever for?'

'*He's* there.' Lou flapped her hand in front of her face to calm herself. 'You know. Rick.'

Mona rolled her eyes. 'You're such a drama queen, he's hardly the type to throw himself in the lake just because some bimbo's dumped him.'

'Don't be ridiculous, he's there to fish, with Charles,' Lou said. 'We saw them from my bedroom window.'

Mona whirled round and gave Anna an accusing look.

'You never told me – I *thought* I heard Charles come back and clatter about. Was Rick with him?'

'Yes, Charles wanted him to have his spare rod,' Anna said quietly.

'Right, I'm going to the lake, just need my boots.' And Mona rushed out into the hall.

Lou frowned. 'Why don't you come too, Anna? We don't mind waiting while you go and get ready, and I'm sure between us we could carry Ollie. That reminds me, Master Musgrove, how are you feeling this morning?'

While Lou and Henrietta inspected Ollie's ankle, Mona came back into the kitchen. As she bent down to adjust one of her boots, Anna saw that they were last year's and remembered that the path round the lake was notoriously muddy, even after the driest summer. That showed Rick's true place in Mona's affections – he wasn't worth sacrificing her new ones for … Oh God, it was only two hours since he'd come back into her life and here she was, seeing everything in terms of him all over again …

And now when they met he'd be unattached – like her. Stupid to think that would make any difference … *stupid*.

Mona straightened up. 'We'd better be quick, Rick must be desperate for someone to talk to, I had *such* a nice chat with him last night.' She marched to the back door and turned to Lou and Henrietta. 'Come on.'

Harry clung to her legs. 'Me go too.'

'No, no, darling. Stay here with Aunty Anna.' She picked him up and sat him firmly in Anna's lap.

'Anna?' Lou gave her an enquiring look.

She hugged Harry's sturdy little body and shook her head. 'I'll stay here with the children, but we'll see you at the Great House for lunch. We might go there early and play with Belle and Bracken. You'd like that, Harry, wouldn't you?'

When they'd gone, she sat the boys in front of a DVD and

dashed upstairs for a quick shower. The hot water soothed her enough to allow a mental replay of that awful silent scene in the kitchen. The look on Rick's face – blank, and at the same time tortured, as if grieving for someone. At the time, the thought had flashed through her mind that maybe ...

But now she knew the reason for it, and it was nothing to do with her.

Chapter Fourteen

Up at the lake, Rick found himself relaxing more than he'd anticipated. He went through the motions of fly-tying and casting, but for once he couldn't be bothered to compete. It was the peace, the closeness to nature and the undemanding companionship that he needed most. He stretched out his legs, leaned back and rested his head on the bag of newspapers. In his hurry to be out of that kitchen, he'd ended up carrying it here after all.

'Going to sleep already, are you?' Charles said, with a chuckle.

'No, just sky gazing.'

'Thinking about your girlfriend?'

'My ex-girlfriend, you mean.'

A pause; then, in a much more serious tone, 'What's happened?'

'You obviously haven't read *The Sunday Reporter* this morning.'

'I'm a *Times* man, as you can see.'

'It's probably in there, too – I haven't looked yet. Anyway, the *Reporter* tells you all you need to know, and makes up the rest. Page two.'

He rolled over, selected the right paper from the bag under his head and handed it to Charles. Then he lay on his back again and stared up at a bank of cloud drifting in from the west. To his left he heard the rustle of pages and a sharp intake of breath, followed by a heavy sigh.

At last, Charles spoke. 'I had no idea. Must be terrible for you, dealing with all this media crap on top of the break-up.'

'Doesn't help.'

'You put on a brave face last night.'

Rick debated whether to admit that he hadn't known then, but decided to keep quiet. He was still feeling numb about the whole Shelley thing. And his phone was strangely silent, when he was half-expecting a call from Guy. Or maybe Guy was too busy talking to the tabloids ...

Charles went on, 'I can completely relate to what you're going through. Ten years ago, near enough, I was madly in love and she dumped me. In the nicest possible way, of course, but it hurt like hell.'

Rick thought he detected a catch in his voice. Obviously still not over her, whoever she was.

A chorus of shrieks in the distance. He turned his head and saw three women bearing down on them. Charles's sisters, with Mona. No one else.

He let out a long breath. 'Didn't realise your womenfolk were interested in fishing.'

Charles gave a rueful laugh. 'It'll be you they're interested in, not the fishing.'

'Just what a badly bruised ego needs,' Rick said lightly.

And he spent the next hour proving it. Flirting with Lou and Henrietta. Dodging Mona's 'sympathetic ear' overtures with unusual tact. And keeping thoughts of Anna Elliot at bay.

No fish caught. No papers read. But a sense of self restored.

Anna and the boys went the long way round to the Great House, so that she could call at the village shop. It seemed a better option than checking *The Sunday Reporter*'s website on Mona's computer, which would mean phoning her for login details and facing an inquisition.

Ollie had to sit in the stroller, leaving Harry to walk, and progress was painfully slow. When at last they reached the shop, Anna was relieved to find it empty – apart from old Mrs Stokes who'd apparently come to buy her weekly ticket for the National Lottery. Iain was explaining at the top of his voice that it had taken place last night, she must have got her days mixed up, and did she want to buy next week's instead?

Anna stopped the stroller in front of the colouring books and told the boys to choose one, then turned her attention to the Sunday papers. Not many left, and no sign of the one she was after.

As soon as Mrs Stokes shuffled off, Anna approached the counter. 'Don't suppose you've got any spare copies of *The Sunday Reporter*? A friend's asked me to get hold of one for her.'

'Sorry, no. I never order many in, not much call for it round here most of the time,' Iain said, brusquely. Maybe he'd had a queue of women already this morning, all wanting that particular paper 'for a friend', all refusing to spend their money on anything else. He went on, 'Rick Wentworth bought the last two early this morning, you could always track him down and ask him if one's a spare.'

Yeah, right.

But she smiled her thanks and handed over the money for the colouring book Ollie had found. Much nicer than yesterday's, thank you, he informed her gleefully when they'd left the shop; not one single fairy from cover to cover.

When they reached the lane leading to the Great House, she paused. There was more activity than usual on the high street. Cars parked nose to tail, men chatting to each other – some with those cumbersome cameras that looked like weapons. Just then, the Crofts came out of their cottage and the men clustered round them like flies, shouted questions, fired their gun-cameras.

The media had arrived in Uppercross. Poor Rick. Poor Sophie and Ed.

She continued up the lane, chilled – despite the unseasonable warmth – by a sudden thought. Rick might have to take refuge somewhere until the fuss died down. Somewhere that stood in extensive grounds, to prevent prying eyes – and cameras – from tracking his every move. Somewhere like the Great House, where she was taking the boys.

She wasn't sure she could face another meeting; at least, not yet. But how could she get out of lunch? Impossible without letting people down, or having them wonder ... Like a rabbit trapped in car headlights, she couldn't think which way to run; then Harry tugged on her hand and pointed. On a nearby nettle was a Red Admiral, experimentally flexing its wings as if surprised by this resurgence of summer, and instantly her mood brightened. She had to meet Rick again some time, she reasoned. And at least now she'd made an effort with her appearance. Washed and blow-dried her hair; used make-up to disguise the dark circles under her eyes and add a little colour to her face; found that jumper, and decided she looked OK in it.

Footsteps behind her, where one of the paths from the lake joined the lane. But it was only Charles.

'Hi there – great idea to come in the stroller, Ollie, I thought Aunty Anna would have to drive you. What's that, Harry? Yes, I'll take you to see Belle and Bracken, I just need to speak to Grandma first.' An appraising look at Anna. 'Feeling better?'

'Fine, thanks.' She gave him a reassuring smile. 'Catch anything?'

'No, too much going on. Half the bloody family turned up – Lou, Henrietta, even Mona.' A pause. 'You've heard about Rick and his girlfriend splitting up?'

'Yes.' She forced herself to imagine Rick as a passing acquaintance, to put on a convincing act, to ask after him with just the right amount of concern. 'Such a shame. How is he?'

'Seems to be taking it all in his stride, actually, and it doesn't seem to have put him off female company. Which is amazing when you think he's got Lou and Henrietta giggling at everything he says, funny or not, and Mona badgering him to pour out his troubles.'

They were nearing the house; she could hear the dogs barking. 'So ... what about the Non-Appreciation Society?'

'The what?' He looked at her blankly.

She didn't want to elaborate too much in front of the children. 'We talked about it yesterday, remember? The inaugural meeting was going to be last night, but you didn't think there'd be much support.' And even less now, by the sound of it.

'Oh, *that*. Maybe we should give it a miss, I feel rather sorry for him. Seems like a nice bloke, underneath.'

Male solidarity. You couldn't beat it, so you may as well give in gracefully.

'By the way,' Charles went on, 'the press are here in force. Sophie Croft phoned Rick and warned him to stay away from her place. So he'll be joining us for lunch – and probably longer. My sisters are in ecstasies. As far as Henrietta's concerned it's nothing serious, you know, she just can't resist a bit of sibling rivalry. I mean, she's almost engaged, for God's sake. In fact, I may see if Kyle wants to have lunch with us. Nip anything between Henrietta and Rick in the bud.'

Kyle McIntyre ran the Musgrove farm and had been going out with Henrietta for two years. With good farm managers thin on the ground, Roger and Barbara thought the world of him; whether Henrietta did was harder to tell.

Charles added, 'Lou, on the other hand ...' He raised his eyebrows and grinned expressively.

Anna knew exactly what he was thinking. Lou was unattached and much more single-minded than her sister. Whatever Lou wanted, Lou usually got.

Chapter Fifteen

Rick found himself unexpectedly back at Uppercross Manor shortly before lunch, but in a much happier frame of mind. They'd packed up fishing half-an-hour earlier, when Barbara phoned Charles to ask if he'd seen her spectacles. He hadn't, but went off to the Great House anyway to 'do a proper briefing'.

Handling the press invasion seemed to have brought out hidden depths in Charles. He was now behaving as though he had the lead role in a third-rate war movie, planning 'Operation Dunkirk' in enthusiastic detail and firing off a barrage of instructions at the slightest opportunity. He told Rick to 'lie low' at the Great House and call his driver to fetch him – not on Tuesday morning, as 'the enemy' would expect, but at dead of night on Monday. He also ordered Sophie and Ed to take a leisurely stroll with rucksacks on their backs. Ideal cover, he explained, for bringing Rick his belongings – but they must take a particularly circuitous route to the Great House and throw those 'paparazzi johnnies' well and truly off the scent. Rick suggested that he went to see Barbara too; but Charles insisted on going alone – he could 'check that the coast was clear' at the same time – leaving the others to follow at a more leisurely pace.

The path round the lake was only wide enough for two, and Rick was relieved when Lou – as opposed to Mona – manoeuvred herself alongside him. She was the tactile sort, grabbing his arm at every opportunity to steady herself, or alert him to sightings of monster trout – largely imaginary, he suspected. Eventually her arm simply stayed locked in his, and he felt it would be rude to ask her to remove it. Anyway, what was the harm in exchanging mindless banter with a young adoring female? Although it didn't seem to go down well with Mona; as soon as the path widened, she took his other arm and demanded a detour via Uppercross Manor so that she could change her boots.

On this visit, Rick took a lot more notice of his surroundings. Uppercross Manor was little more than a couple of cottages knocked into one; clearly the name reflected Mona's pretensions rather than reality. Thinking that Anna might be inside, he chose to wait out on the terrace – and Lou and Henrietta immediately did the same. But Anna wasn't there; and the whole boot-changing exercise took far longer because Mona kept popping outside to see what she was missing.

Once, when Mona was safely indoors, Henrietta observed that Anna's car was still here – a five-year-old Mini, Rick noted – and hoped that she hadn't attempted to carry Ollie to the Great House. Lou retorted that Anna gave those children too much attention for their own good – and was it all that surprising when she seemed to be on a permanent guilt trip where Mona and Charles were concerned? Rick listened and wondered, but said nothing – yet.

At last Mona was ready and they set off for the Great House. Charles came to meet them, anxious because Rick had been back to the Cottage – 'too near the enemy lines for comfort'. When he realised that the Cottage was Charles's name for Uppercross Manor, Rick smiled to himself. He'd known Charles and Mona less than twenty-four hours, but already he'd have been amazed if they could even agree which day of the week it was.

And so, when he found himself in the same room as Anna once again, it was quite different from last time. More people, more noise … He sensed her, rather than saw her …

For a moment, he was distracted by Lou putting an ice-cold beer in his hand – and a red-hot, as yet unspoken, invitation in his mind; but she was called away, and he was alone, and preparing himself ...

Then something cannoned into his legs and he almost spilt his drink.

'Careful, Harry.'

Her voice – and the years crumbled away ... He was jumping over the rocks to be with her and she was saying, 'Careful, Rick.' She never shouted, never had to; he always heard her, as if his brain was tuned to a special frequency ... Other memories intruded. On the boat, just the two of them. His voice, strangely hesitant: 'My grandmother used to say – if you can't be good, be careful.' And her laugh, soft and seductive, like her skin against his: 'Well then, we'd better be careful, hadn't we?'

He screwed his eyes shut. To hell with the past, and to hell with her–

'Are you all right?'

Her voice again, all husky with concern as if he was a bloody basket case. His eyes flicked open. Her face, too near, and white as a ghost.

She had a child in her arms, the same little boy as before. He stared at Rick, eyes round and bright with concern, lower lip trembling. 'Man hurt?'

Spot on, Harry, but it wasn't anything *you* did. I can tell you about it, if you're interested. Trouble is, it's not the sort of hurt you can see or touch. And you probably haven't covered metaphysics yet on the nursery school curriculum, although I'm sure it's just a matter of time ...

Aloud he said tersely, 'No, I'm fine,' and made for the nearest door.

Sophie Croft was puzzled.

She and Rick were very close, even though they'd lived on different continents for most of their adult lives. And her marriage to Ed hadn't made the slightest difference. If anything, both relationships seemed the better for it, with the men either competing for her approval or ganging up on her. All very good-natured, of course.

But she'd seen a change in Rick since his unexpected visit the previous weekend. More withdrawn, more edgy. And what puzzled her was that she didn't believe it had much to do with Shelley, although she knew that they'd quarrelled before he'd left.

She'd been furious with him earlier in the day. Partly because she'd only found out about Shelley from an obliging journalist; partly because she didn't know where he'd gone and he wasn't answering his phone. When he finally condescended to pick up and she heard the peals of girlish laughter in the background, she saw red.

'You really piss me off sometimes! How do you imagine I felt when I opened the front door this morning and found a load of journalists outside? It put the fear of God into me, and Ed too. For one awful moment, we thought–'

He cut her short with, 'Don't worry, I'm not suicidal.' She could barely make out the words above another burst of laughter at the other end of the phone.

'No, doesn't sound like it,' she said, more sharply than she'd intended. 'Where the hell are you?'

'I'm fishing.'

'What for? Loud women?'

'Definitely.' She could hear the grin in his voice.

'I must say,' she went on, 'it was *so* kind of you to arrange for the media to enlighten us about your private life. And we're *so* pleased that you're enjoying your fishing, let's hope you don't catch something too soon. You might be better analysing what went wrong with your last relationship before rushing on to the next one.'

A pause; then he said, in a more serious tone, 'I'm not discussing that now.'

'When are you going to discuss it, then?'

He muttered something about ringing her back and hung up. But it was Charles who phoned a few minutes later, with some gibberish about Operation Dunkirk and a stream of ridiculous instructions. She'd wanted to tell him where to go, but Ed said they should just do it.

Bad sign, Rick not talking to her.

And now she was back at the Great House for the second time in two days. Staying for lunch, when all she wanted to do was go home and chill out after lugging that bloody rucksack half-way across Somerset. She suspected Ed felt the same. To cap it all, she couldn't find Rick, even though Roger had assured her that he'd just seen him here, in the sitting room. She gave one last look round and let out a great sigh of exasperation.

'If you're after Rick, he's outside.'

She turned and looked down into a pale heart-shaped face with large grey eyes. A tired face, but with a fragile beauty that she imagined most men would find irresistible, once they noticed it.

The woman spoke again; an attractive voice, low and soothing. 'Would you like me to show you?'

'That would be great. Thanks.'

Sophie followed the woman out of the room and along a hallway, where they stopped at a half-glazed door. Beyond it was the walled garden that she'd seen once or twice before; large and square, with a stunning profusion of colours and textures even in early autumn. Mind, she'd have done it a bit differently – made the paths curve a bit more and moved those hostas to the other side for more shade.

'I imagine he's at the far end by now,' her guide said, with a shy smile.

'Excuse me, you are–?'

'Anna Elliot, Mona Musgrove's sister.'

Sophie waited for the catchphrase 'and daughter of Sir Walter Elliot, 8th Baronet', but it didn't materialise.

She smiled back. 'I'm Rick's sister, Sophie Croft. How did you guess it was him I wanted?'

Anna blushed. 'You look very similar.' She added, rather disjointedly, 'Based on his newspaper photos, I mean. I've only met him briefly today.' She hesitated, then said, 'See you,' and hurried off.

Sophie found Rick at the far end of the garden, where Anna had predicted, sitting on a bench and staring at the ground in front of him. As she approached, he looked up and frowned.

'Look, Soph, I'm sorry I didn't tell you about Shelley this morning. Believe it or not, I wanted to get away and think, rather than talk. And when Charles invited me fishing, I didn't expect his sisters to turn up.'

She shrugged. 'That's OK. And I'm in a better mood than I was earlier. I've just met an Elliot of Kellynch who I feel I could actually like.'

'Really.' He focused his gaze on something in the distance.

'Her name's Anna, she reminds me of a violet. Yes, a shrinking violet. You know – a lovely little thing, but easily overlooked.'

'Especially by men who don't want anything to shrink.'

She couldn't help laughing. 'Trust you. And I forgot, you're fishing for loud women, aren't you? Like those big showy dahlias over there.'

'Exactly. Give me a big showy dahlia rather than a shrinking violet, every time. By the way, what plant am I?'

'Giant knotweed, I suspect, after this latest assault on

your ego.' She pulled him to his feet. 'Ready to run rampant and sow its seed here, there and everywhere.'

'Ouch. You always did know how to cut me down to size.'

They smiled at each other, linked arms and walked back to the house.

Chapter Sixteen

Lunch proved to be quite an ordeal for Anna. Not only because she was opposite Rick and hearing his voice at length, its familiar northern lilt intact despite all those years in Australia; but also for other reasons ... The boys played up and everyone seemed to expect her to control them. Kyle couldn't make it, which meant that Henrietta competed with Lou for Rick's attention. Mona was even more abrasive than usual, mainly because Charles – well, Anna would be having a little chat with Charles. Sophie sat next to her and was so nice that it hurt. And, last but by no means least, Barbara had one of her culinary disasters.

The prawn cocktail starter looked harmless enough, appetisingly served on a bed of crisp lettuce with lemon wedges and the local bakery's renowned wholemeal bread. Anna stared at it, fighting off unpleasant memories. The Marie Rose sauce reminded her of that silk emulsion she'd once used on her bedroom walls at Kellynch. Walter hadn't noticed this little act of defiance until weeks later, when the door was open and he happened to be passing. He'd turned a similar colour to the walls, only much, much deeper–

'What exactly are these, Barb?'

Anna glanced up. Roger was chewing warily and examining his fork, which had a couple of glistening sauce-smeared lumps on the end. She sneaked a look round the table and found that everyone seemed to be waiting with bated breath for Barbara's reply. Or perhaps they were glad of the excuse to stop eating.

'Prawns, dear.' Unperturbed, Barbara speared a lump from her own plate and popped it into her mouth.

Silence. Then Lou said, stifling a giggle, 'No, Mum, they're more like lychees.'

'Oh, shit.' Barbara dropped her fork, jumped up and ran out of the dining room.

'That means it's prawn trifle for dessert,' Roger explained, with a sigh. 'And she's gone to see if she can rustle up something else. We need to find her specs, and soon.'

'For God's sake, this is ridiculous.' Mona yanked Harry's plate away and he gave a loud wail.

'Let him have it, Mona, it won't do him any harm,' Roger said. 'Everyone else can leave theirs, though. It's an acquired taste.'

But Mona ignored him and Harry's wails continued – until Anna made him a lettuce sandwich from her own starter, which she no longer felt like tackling. Not after Lou whispered something to Rick and, for the first time in ten years, Anna felt the warmth of his smile. No longer directed at her, of course ...

Ed cleared his plate with apparent relish. 'When Sophie and I did a few trips round Europe in our camper van, we took a supply of tinned food and ate all sorts of weird combinations. Tuna with peaches in syrup was a particular favourite, wasn't it, Soph?'

Sophie laughed. 'I remember. Actually, this is pretty good – although I'm not sure I could cope with prawn trifle. More water, Anna?'

And Anna smiled and nodded and went through the motions of enjoying herself.

Until during the main course, when – out of nowhere – Ollie said in his clear piping voice, 'Daddy, I saw you kiss Aunty Anna in the middle of the night.'

Rick thought that they covered it up rather well. Anna looked startled, rather than guilty. But then she would, wouldn't she? Just to brazen it out. Charles, on the other hand, tried to laugh it off.

'I thought you were asleep, Oliver Musgrove! Aunty Anna certainly was, in that chair by your bed. Looked so peaceful, I couldn't resist. And I kissed you too, didn't I? Silly old Daddy.'

Ollie opened his mouth to say more, but his father promptly changed the subject. 'This beef's delicious, Mum, more than makes up for the starter. Nothing like a traditional English roast dinner, is there, Rick?'

For Barbara's sake, Rick agreed – with an enthusiasm he certainly didn't feel. What he did feel was his throat constricting each time he forced his food down. How could Anna and Charles do this – to Mona, to the kids, to the whole family? The Musgroves seemed to believe Charles's pathetic story without any problem, although he detected a faint air of embarrassment. Not so Mona, however. Judging by the way she carved up the meat on Harry's plate, a radical solution to family planning was in store for Charles.

Now Henrietta was murmuring in his ear and he had to lean closer to catch her words.

'What do you mean, am I a bit of a barnacle?' he said, his thoughts elsewhere.

On his other side, Lou let out a little shriek. 'Oh Henrietta, how could you? That was *my* line!'

Henrietta shrugged. 'You had your chance to use it and you didn't.'

'I was going to, you had no right–'

'Calm down, girls!' Barbara put in, with mock severity. 'And please explain yourselves. No one knows what you're talking about, especially Rick.'

'It's in his book,' Henrietta began, then giggled. 'Which I've read three times so far.'

'Page fifty-six, to be exact,' Lou went on. 'Rick's

comparing different fish in terms of their sex organs–'

'The males, that is.'

'Well, obviously.'

'It's not obvious at all, is it, Rick? Some of the females–'

'Hey, leave me out of this.' By now Rick had a fair idea of where the conversation was heading. The barnacle had the longest penis in the world – in relation to its body size. There must be worse things to discuss over a dinner table with the present company, but none came to mind immediately. For one mad moment, he imagined asking Anna – in front of everyone – if she'd like to reply to Henrietta's question from first-hand experience. He might even suggest that she justified her answer with some intimate details about her current relationship. He was confident that he'd outperform Charles on all counts.

Huh, that'd wipe the butter-wouldn't-melt look off her face.

He turned to Henrietta and said, as patiently as he could, 'The whole point of my book is that, for sea creatures, sex isn't driven by the same considerations as modern-day humans. It's about adapting to a hostile environment and maximising the chances of reproduction. That's why – with the barnacle, for example – size matters. All very straightforward, none of that love and commitment crap.'

Across the table, Sophie grinned. 'Actually, that sounds like one or two men I know.'

He frowned at her. 'They probably have their reasons. If women were more like the females of most other species – well, the world would be a happier place.'

Ed gave a great guffaw. 'I bet none of you realised that Rick is a leading expert on misogyny, as well as sea dragons.'

'And Mum, before you ask, you won't find misogyny swimming about off the coast of Australia,' Charles added.

Barbara pretended to take offence. 'I know perfectly well

what misogyny is, I've been married to your father for thirty odd years.' She gave Rick a sympathetic look. 'You just haven't met the right person yet, it makes all the difference.'

'Or maybe he has and she's hurt him, very very badly.' Sophie again, on a little fishing expedition of her own.

He looked straight at his sister, shutting out the woman next to her, who he sensed was waiting – more than anyone – for his reply, and selected his words with care.

'I've been let down, if that's what you mean. But I wasn't hurt, except for my pride. And she did me a big favour, actually, because she wasn't the right person for me. She wasn't the right person at all.'

Chapter Seventeen

Anna hoped she left the table without arousing any suspicions. In the downstairs cloakroom she took long gulps of air and willed the tears to stop.

Everyone would assume that Rick was referring to Shelley, but she suspected that his remarks were meant for her. He was sending a message, loud and clear: in the end, it didn't matter that she'd let him down because 'she wasn't the right person at all'.

How could he say such a thing? How *could* he, after all the times he'd told her that she was the one he wanted to spend the rest of his life with?

Of course, maybe he still needed closure – maybe they both did. Because, after that horrible confrontation with Walter and Minty, the lines of communication had been swiftly severed: Natasha stopped sending the children to the sailing club, Anna's mobile and laptop were removed 'for repair', and Anna herself was soon spirited back to England.

Katya told her later that Rick had called at the house and asked to see her, very politely; but Natasha sent him away, and he never came back …

A thump on the door.

Sod it, was there no privacy – not even in the bloody loo? 'Need a wee.'

Harry. If she didn't let him in, there'd be an accident – and she'd be the one clearing it up, no doubt. As for privacy, she'd have that soon enough, on the drive back to Bath and during the long days – and nights – ahead.

By the time she and Harry returned to the dining room, all the plates had been cleared away – even her meal, only half-eaten. She felt a surge of resentment. The Musgroves took it for granted that she wasn't interested in food, just as they took *her* for granted as someone who could wave a magic wand and turn Mona into a reasonable human being.

She took her seat, aware of Rick looking in her direction; but she refused to meet his gaze. Why give him the satisfaction of knowing that his words had hit their target?

Then Barbara announced that there'd be a ten-minute wait for dessert; the rhubarb crumble she'd unearthed from the freezer needed a little longer in the oven to heat through.

Henrietta grinned at her mother. 'Are you sure it's just rhubarb?'

'Absolutely,' Barbara replied calmly. 'We'd be able to smell it otherwise, wouldn't we?'

Lou nudged Rick and leaned in close. 'They're talking about Mum's legendary rhubarb and garlic crumble. Can you pour me some more wine?'

Rick was just about to do so when Lou's hand pounced on his, almost making him drop the bottle. 'Let me help,' she said, looking up at him from under her lashes. 'You seem a little out of practice.'

He responded with the ghost of a smile, as if acknowledging the subtext. And that was all the encouragement Lou needed; her strong brown fingers clamped his to the bottle and lingered long after they'd poured the wine together. Anna forced her gaze away from their coupled hands to her own, clenched together on her lap.

'Rhubarb and garlic?' Sophie put in. 'How did that come about?' There was a definite hint of distaste in her voice; hardly surprising, but Anna wondered if it had more to do with Lou and Rick.

Lou didn't answer, so Barbara took up the story. 'Oh, as usual I was trying to do too many things at once – making a stew at the same time as a crumble – and the phone rang, and while I was talking I stirred the chopped garlic into the rhubarb by mistake.' She added, with a rueful smile, 'I couldn't smell anything because I had a cold, so I simply carried on and served up the crumble, beautifully cooked but stinking to high heaven. The family have never let me forget it.'

Roger chuckled. 'You see what we have to put up with? Surprised I'm still alive, all things considered.'

Barbara got to her feet. 'Let me see if it's ready.' As she passed behind Roger, she ruffled his hair affectionately. 'And don't worry, dear. If I really wanted to kill you I'd have done it long ago and quite differently. A lot can happen on a farm.'

The crumble was voted garlic free and utterly delicious. Anna managed a few mouthfuls, while everyone else had seconds and then complained of feeling stuffed.

'Let's all go for a walk round the estate,' Charles said. 'Don't worry, Rick, I'll choose a route where there's no chance of you being seen.'

Ed glanced at Sophie. 'We'll give it a miss, if you don't mind. We've done enough walking for today.'

'I'm not going either,' Anna said, as she helped Barbara to clear the table. 'I'll stay behind with the boys.'

'Nonsense, dear.' Barbara's tone was kind but firm. 'You could do with the fresh air, you're looking peaky. I can lend you a coat if you like, but you should be fine in that jumper. Roger and I will look after the boys – he can take Harry out with the dogs and I'll play cards with Ollie.' And she almost bundled Anna into the hall.

With a sigh of resignation, Anna knelt down to retie her shoelace. Maybe this would be a good opportunity to take Charles to one side and tell him to get his act together – for the children's sake, at least. How *dare* he kiss her when she was asleep, and in front of Ollie?

As the others waited outside, the clean country air carried

their voices to her – Lou and Henrietta's giggles, Charles and Mona's bickering. And Rick? He'd be shifting from foot to foot, anxious to get moving and work off that huge lunch. In France he'd wanted to walk everywhere; and that's what they'd done, holding hands, talking, kissing …

A sudden crowing laugh behind her, a child's weight pressing down on her back, hot little hands round her neck in a boisterous stranglehold.

'Me go with Tee-Anna!'

Hard to speak, need to loosen Harry's grip–

And then, cool fingers on her neck – the slightest, lightest touch – and Harry's hands were prised away.

'No, Harry.' Rick's voice, stern, uncompromising. 'Let's go and find your grandma.'

A grateful glance upwards – and there was Rick towering over her, Harry penned in his arms, a smile softening his words as he looked at the little boy. Harry offered no resistance, for once stunned into wide-eyed silence.

They'd gone before she could croak a thank you.

Hard to speak, still; and now hard to breathe. Hard to forget a lover's touch. Not the brief, business-like contact of a minute ago, but those tender caresses from the past.

Chapter Eighteen

Rick held Harry close while he headed towards the kitchen. Although he told himself it was to keep the child safe, he was vaguely aware of another reason.

Something to do with Anna.

A moment ago, this little boy's hands had been clasped around her neck – a part of her anatomy that, long ago, Rick had found irresistible. Now the same small stubby fingers were splayed like stars on his chest. Next to his heart, ironically enough. A heart that had once been hers ...

The child stirred in his arms, brought him back to the present. 'It all happened long before you were born,' he said; and Harry stared solemnly up at him, as if he understood this was no laughing matter.

By now they'd arrived at a kitchen full of dirty dishes, but empty of people.

'Bet Grandma's in the garden,' Rick went on. He bloody well hoped she was; then he could rejoin the others without going back through the house and having another close encounter in the hall.

Because, actually, it wasn't meant to be like this; it wasn't meant to be like this at all.

He'd bought a whole set of expensive clothes, invested in the Jag and a driver, so that he'd look the part of a man who'd made it, big time. And as long as that information reached a certain corner of Somerset, via *The Times*, or the TV, or even *Snobs & Knobs* – if such a magazine existed, her father was bound to read it – he would be satisfied. And yes, he'd prepared himself for the possibility of Anna herself turning up at one of his book signings; but he was sure he'd be able to cope with a ten-second meeting in a public place.

Instead, he'd been suffocating in the same room as her for over an hour, picking his way through a conversational minefield that was obvious to no one except her, stomaching the realisation that she was sleeping with her brother-in-law ...

'Tee-Anna hurt?' Ah, another of Harry's penetrating questions; the sort that could be answered in three words or three thousand, depending on how you were feeling.

Rick paused by the half-glazed door into the walled garden. Hallelujah, there was Barbara settling Ollie on a sunlounger; he'd leave Harry with her and simply follow the gravel path out of the garden and round to the front of the house.

'Aunty Anna's fine,' he said briskly. He opened the door, then hesitated. How the hell did he know? He forced his brain to rewind. OK, during the meal she'd been subdued, but that was understandable around the over-exuberant Musgroves. And at one point she'd been upset, he could tell; although it gave him no pleasure to see how hard his remarks had hit her.

On the whole, though, she seemed fine – in spite of Charles's pathetic attempt to cover up their sordid little affair. She just wasn't the girl he remembered – the girl with golden skin, and ideals to match.

Difficult to tell which was uppermost, relief or disappointment. Masking both with a nonchalant smile, he stepped into the Musgroves' garden and delivered Harry safely to his grandma.

Anna straightened up and leaned against the old oak bureau to collect herself. When Rick returned, she would try to behave naturally with him. Maybe touch his arm to attract his attention; laugh, as she thanked him for rescuing her from Harry's clutches.

But the minutes passed and he didn't return.

She felt strangely bereft, and began to hope that the others had set off without her so that she didn't have to put on an act. No such luck; just as she was retreating to the kitchen, Henrietta flung open the front door, announced cheerfully, 'She's here!' and shepherded her outside.

Anna immediately looked round for Charles; but he was already walking off with Rick, who'd obviously taken the alternative route through the garden to avoid her. Lou and Henrietta followed, heads close together, a 'Do not disturb' sign all but visible. This left Mona on her own; as soon as she took Anna's arm and gave a gloating little laugh, Anna knew that trouble was brewing. If only Ollie had kept quiet ...

'If you think you've got a chance with Rick, you can forget it,' Mona said. 'I just asked him if you'd changed much and he said "Yes, and not for the better".' She paused, to let the words sink in. 'So it looks like he's all Henrietta's.'

Anna swallowed. Was Mona telling the truth, or was she getting revenge for what she would see as her public humiliation earlier? And if she *was* telling the truth – then OK, Anna was not the same person, and never could be after ten years ... So maybe Rick had a point; but it still hurt to hear it.

Aloud she said slowly, 'Henrietta? He seems more interested in Lou.'

'I don't think there's much to choose between them, as far as he's concerned. But Henrietta needs to set her sights a lot higher than Kyle McIntyre. I've been telling Charles for months, there's no way she should be sleeping with one of her father's farmhands.'

'He's hardly that.'

Mona ignored this and went on, 'I'm going to give her a piece of my mind, right now–'

'I don't think they want to be disturbed–'

'Tough, you watch me.'

She marched up to the two sisters and wedged herself between them. Immediately, Lou ran forward and slipped her arm through Rick's; a few moments later, Charles walked purposefully on ahead, leaving Lou and Rick on their own. Anna noticed that he was leading them to the estate farm, where Kyle McIntyre was no doubt hard at work; and, in an instant, she understood the hidden agendas. Charles and Lou wanted Henrietta with Kyle, so that Kyle would stay on as farm manager and Lou could pair off with Rick. Mona wanted Henrietta with Rick, so that she wouldn't be with Kyle.

And Rick? What – who – did he want? He certainly didn't want Anna Elliot. And yet there was a time when he didn't want anyone – anything – else. Or so he'd said.

She shivered. The sky had clouded over and the once bright fields and hedgerows were a dull patchwork of greens and browns. As she trudged along the tree-lined road to the farm, leaves drifted past to carpet the ground in swirls of copper and gold. She'd always loved autumn, associating its blaze of colour with the hopes and challenges of a new academic year. But today she saw only the onset of winter.

In front of her, the drama was playing out, a farce and a tragedy at the same time. Mona had realised where they were heading and was holding on to Henrietta for dear life. Charles came back and tried to pull Henrietta away, his face flushed and angry. Their voices blurred with the breeze, but Anna could fill in the words and detect the fast-burning fuse of emotions behind them. Henrietta slumped between them like a rag doll until, at last, Charles managed to wrench her from Mona's grasp.

Anna looked round for Lou and Rick. They were standing a little distance from the road, either side of an old wooden stile set into a high, winding hedge. As if on cue, Lou stepped on to the crossbar at the top of the stile and jumped into his arms. He held her to him, turned his head very slightly and stared straight at Anna. She was too far away to read his expression, but she knew it wouldn't be friendly. And then – did he make the first move, or was it Lou?

There was something horribly fascinating about seeing them kiss – as if Anna was watching her own past, brought vividly and unexpectedly back to life. But closing her eyes was not an option; darkness would merely intensify the memories ...

Eventually, she tore her gaze away and stumbled on towards the farm, dimly aware of Charles hurrying Henrietta into the barn some hundred yards ahead. Next thing she knew, Mona had barred her path and grabbed her by the wrist.

'Did you *see* that? He nearly pulled her arm out of its bloody socket to get her away from me! I've had it with him, I really have. I'm going to leave him, I'm going to leave the whole effing family and go back to Kellynch with the boys.' She dug her nails into Anna's flesh. 'You can move into the Manor and make him happy after all these years. I'll go and tell him, shall I?' And before Anna could stop her, she stormed off.

The last thing Anna wanted to do was follow her. Instead, she huddled by the hedge; out of the breeze, but not too close to the entwined hawthorn, bramble and hazel in case she snagged her new jumper. She would stay here until the others returned, then take Charles to one side for a private word; or maybe she'd wait for him at the Cottage. Whatever she did, no one would care. In fact, if she hadn't needed to speak to Charles, she'd have walked back to the Great House to say her goodbyes and driven straight home to Bath.

Then, on the other side of the hedge, she heard voices: Lou and Rick. They paused almost directly behind her.

'Looks like they've all gone to the farm,' Rick said.

'Thank God for that. You know,' Lou's tone hardened, 'Henrietta's been going out with Kyle for two years now, but she still won't commit. If I were her, I'd have moved into that farmhouse with him and made it work – or at least found out that it didn't. You only live once, don't you?'

'That's always been my philosophy.'

'Right, but it's certainly not Henrietta's. If I hadn't gone on and on at her today, she'd never have called on Kyle. She's too used to waiting for him to come running, even though I've told her he won't do that forever.'

'Good job she's got you to keep her on track.' His voice was warm with approval.

'I suppose I'm a typical older sister. Isn't yours like that?'

'When I let her.'

Lou giggled, then gave a little sigh of resignation. 'I'm not sure she likes me.'

'She's just over-protective,' he said, curtly. 'I wouldn't be surprised if she and Ed were parked at the top of that field, watching us through their binoculars.'

Another giggle. 'They're always out together. Dad says they take a thermos of tea everywhere, like a couple of pensioners.'

'I think it's good that they enjoy each other's company.' He was on the defensive now. 'They were quite adventurous when they were younger, it's hardly surprising that they prefer the quiet life. Although you wouldn't think so, the way Ed drives that old Land Rover – one day they'll end up in a ditch, or worse.'

'I'd rather end up in a ditch with the man I love than

be without him.' A pause; then, 'Cheer up – it might never happen.'

'What might never happen?'

'Whatever it is you're thinking about. And look – we're in a ditch right now!' Lou's voice dropped to a slow, seductive murmur. 'See if this cheers you up.'

Silence, interrupted by Lou again. 'Mmm, that was … What if your sister's looking at us through her binoculars?'

His voice, low and ragged. 'Let's give her something really worth watching, then.'

Another silence, much longer.

Anna tensed; just because she couldn't actually see them kissing didn't make it any easier. He wasn't wasting any time, was he? Shelley one day, Lou the next; unless, of course, the Shelley relationship had been over before he came to England. She chewed her lip, desperate to escape but terrified to move, in case she made a noise. The humiliation of being caught would be worse – if only slightly – than the agony of listening, and imagining, and remembering …

A sharp intake of breath; then Rick said, 'No, Lou, the others might come back.' But his rebuke was gentle, almost apologetic, and he went on in a bantering tone, 'Here, have a blackberry, or a nut. Isn't this a hazelnut? You know, most people are like blackberries, they turn to pulp at the slightest pressure. You're not, though. You're like this nut, not easily crushed – that's a compliment, by the way. Go on, take it as a souvenir.'

'The only nuts I'm interested in are yours, Rick Wentworth.'

And, for the first time in ten years, Anna heard his laugh; deep and rich and unhurried, as if he'd just heard the funniest thing in the world. She used to call it his bedroom laugh, and once he'd asked if that was a threat or a promise, and she'd told him it was anything he wanted it to be. In response, he'd kissed her over and over again; until she was breathless, and he wasn't laughing any more ...

Now he said, 'We'd better go and find the others before they come and find us.'

'Actually, I'd quite like them to find us,' Lou replied. 'I can just imagine Mona's face.'

'Why do you say that?'

'She's a stupid, stuck-up cow. She doesn't think Kyle's good enough for a Musgrove and she's hoping you'll be Henrietta's reason to drop him. So you and me getting together isn't part of her little plan at all.'

'Hmm, maybe I should tell her I'm quite happy to have both of you.'

A half-hearted giggle. 'Don't even think about it, Henrietta and I aren't very good at sharing.'

'Is Mona?'

'What do you mean?' Lou sounded puzzled.

'Doesn't she have to share Charles?' His voice was dark with condemnation. 'With her sister?'

Anna's eyes widened. What the hell–?

'In a way, you're right,' Lou said thoughtfully. 'Charles hasn't completely moved on from Anna, although he's a lot better than he was.'

'Moved on?' A pause. 'Were they – did she go out with Charles?'

'Yes, they met at Oxford. Before that, we didn't know the Elliot girls very well, even though Kellynch is so near. They were either away at boarding school or moving in far grander circles than gymkhana events and the Young Farmers' Club. Anyway, Charles was in his last year at Oxford and Anna had just started. When she dumped him, he was devastated. He went out with Mona on the rebound and kept breaking up with her. But, in the end, she got pregnant and he married her.' Lou added dryly, 'He's been regretting it ever since, as you must have noticed. They're like chalk and cheese, he'd have been much better off with Anna.'

Anna thought that Lou made it sound so simple: a short sequence of cause and effect, with all the heartache erased – hers, Charles's, even Mona's, when she first knew she was pregnant.

'Why did she dump him?' Rick said abruptly.

'Well, Mum and Dad think it was Lady Russell – or Minty, as the chosen few call her. Anna's her favourite goddaughter, the child she never had, and Minty's an awful snob. So, although Charles was just about good enough to make an honest woman of Mona, Minty never considered him worthy of Anna.'

'And now?'

'Now – what?'

'It seems to me – from everything I've seen and heard – that Anna and Charles are having an affair behind Mona's back.'

Anna flinched. His voice was soft, but she recognised its latent anger; primed and ready to explode, like that terrible scene in France …

'I can see how you might think that, but Anna would *never* …' Lou gave a deep sigh. 'What really gets me is how she puts up with absolute crap from Mona – I know she feels responsible for her unhappy marriage, but still … As for Charles, remember his little confession at lunch? He obviously kissed Anna when she was unconscious with exhaustion – from looking after *his* kids! But, believe me, it's nothing to worry about. She'll give him a pep talk and he'll be fine again – or as fine as he can be with Mona. And Anna will return home to Bath–'

'Bath? Not Kellynch?'

'She hasn't lived at Kellynch since she went to university.'

A sardonic laugh. 'And who can blame her? If Sir Walter Elliot was *my* father, I'd have run away long ago.'

'But how do you know that she and Charles aren't just putting on an act, to fool everyone?'

Anna held her breath for Lou's reply.

'Because I trust her. I don't trust my brother in this particular situation, although he's basically a decent man. But I'd trust Anna with my life.'

Silence; and this time Anna knew that they weren't kissing.

Then Rick said, so quietly that she could barely hear, 'What a mess.'

Chapter Nineteen

'What a mess.' Rick wasn't sure whose love life he was describing – Charles's, Anna's, or his own. 'Let's go and find the others,' he added, forcing a smile.

After a moment Lou unglued herself from him, but kept tight hold of his hand and murmured, 'Watch Mona's face when she sees us.'

He had a sudden thought: was it Mona's reaction that he was interested in, or someone else's?

As they entered the barn, he had a good look round. Henrietta was in the far corner, talking animatedly to a tall, lean man with wiry red hair – presumably Kyle. In the opposite corner, Charles and Mona weren't talking at all. Mona was using a stick to scrape something nasty off the sole of her expensive-looking boot, while Charles stood scowling at her, hands in pockets.

Anna wasn't there.

Rick had last seen her when he and Lou were fooling around at the stile. In fact, he'd been thinking about her and Charles; and, on the spur of the moment, he'd wanted to show that, unlike her, he could be open and upfront about kissing someone.

Then Lou had knocked his little theory for six and everything had changed. Now he was fighting new feelings alongside old memories. Shame at jumping so readily to the wrong conclusion. Hesitation about his behaviour with Lou. And a growing fear of 'what if': what if, like Charles, he wasn't over Anna Elliot at all?

Anna let a good five minutes pass before she too set off for the barn. Just as she arrived, Mona and Charles came out with Lou and Rick. Tired from the fresh air and her broken night, Anna stumbled and almost fell; but no one seemed to notice.

Charles greeted her warmly. 'Anna, at last! I wondered where you were, thought you must be having a nice little rest somewhere.' He gave a triumphant grin. 'Henrietta's staying here with Kyle, but we're going back to the Great House now. Taking the long route – still got an awful lot of crumble to walk off. Is that OK with you?'

It wasn't; but she merely said, 'Yes, it's fine,' then crouched down to retie her shoelace. The others didn't wait and she kept her eyes lowered until they'd filed past. She'd already seen that Lou had draped herself around Rick and she didn't think she could handle any more displays of affection, not yet. As for Charles and Mona, she'd hoped to walk with them to avoid being alone with her thoughts for a while longer. But she could tell that they were in the middle of one of their arguments, and she of all people should keep her distance. So she waited until they were all a good fifty yards in front before setting off again.

With nobody to distract her, she found herself brooding. Stupid idea to come on this walk, she should have stood up to Barbara. And, if she was this tired, the drive home would be more of a pain than usual. But all that was nothing compared to the realisation that Rick wanted to be with Lou. How would she get through the next few weeks? She could put off meeting them – claim pressure of work and stay in Bath – but that wouldn't stop Mona from giving her spiteful little updates.

She forced herself to look up and saw Rick stop to answer his mobile; obviously not a simple call, because he waved Lou on ahead. Anna decided to overtake him while he was on the phone; that way there'd be less chance of another agonising non-conversation.

As soon as she'd quickened her pace and walked past, she heard him say, 'My sister's offering you a lift back to the Great House. Or the Cottage, if you prefer.'

She kept going; he couldn't possibly be talking to *her*.

'Anna.'

It was the first time he'd used her name to her face, or at least to the back of her head. She spun round and stared at him.

He avoided her gaze. 'I said, Sophie and Ed can give you a lift.'

She ignored her aching legs, and squared her shoulders. 'I don't need one.'

He looked straight at her for a moment, his eyes flashing. 'Don't be so bloody-minded, you can hardly put one foot in front of the other!' Then he gestured at the road, just visible through a hedge to his left, and said in a calmer tone, 'They'll be coming along there any minute now.'

Sure enough, a Land Rover came lurching into view and screeched to a halt next to a gap in the hedge. Anna bit her lip. To refuse again would probably earn her another accusation of being bloody-minded; and, anyway, he was right – she was struggling.

She headed towards the gap, then stopped dead. It was guarded by a stile; not so much a physical barrier as a psychological one, given what she'd witnessed earlier. As she hesitated, Rick jumped on to the lower plank, stepped over the crossbar to the other side – and held out his hand.

His eyes wouldn't meet hers and he seemed tense and impatient; but she placed her hand in his as though the last ten years had never been.

When she relived it all later, it was like a slow-motion dance where they touched in mocking memory of more intimate encounters. Her fingers embraced in his as he helped her on to the stile ... His hands on her waist, lifting her over and down ... His arm guiding her gently to the Land Rover ... Both hands again at her waist, lifting her up ...

'Budge up, Soph,' his voice behind her, so close that she felt his breath ruffle her hair, 'make some room for your passenger. Any tea left in that thermos – or is it gin today? Either'll do, she needs looking after.'

While Sophie laughed and shuffled further along the front seat, he set Anna carefully down beside her, holding on for a split second longer than necessary – or was she imagining it? Then he simply turned away, vaulted the stile and walked off without a backward glance.

Whereas she ...

Sophie's voice roused her. 'Quite the gentleman, our Rick. When he wants to be.' She gave Anna an appraising look. 'No wonder he was concerned, you seem rather ... out of breath.'

Anna felt her cheeks flush, and made sure her face was hidden as she fastened her seat belt. 'Yes, I'm whacked, lucky for me that you were passing.'

Ed chuckled as he drove off. 'Not really passing. Rick phoned us ten minutes ago – didn't you fall over or something? He checked where we could meet you with the Land Rover and told us to get up here quick.'

She frowned. 'But didn't you ring him, just now?'

'Yes, to say we were only a couple of minutes away,' Sophie put in; after a slight pause, she went on, 'He seemed quite anxious – you've obviously made an impression.'

Anna closed her eyes briefly. If only Sophie knew how wrong she was to speculate about a Rick-Anna romance. She obviously didn't know a thing about their previous relationship.

'I think it was because I was holding everyone up,' she said, adding, 'and I should tell you that – well, it looks like Rick's getting together with Lou.'

'God, what an *idiot*!' Sophie's lips tightened. 'Although, given the way she's been throwing herself at him, who can blame him? Of course, it'll all end in tears – and they won't be his.'

Anna said nothing. She was a little surprised at the speed of events herself; Rick had taken things far more slowly with her. But they'd both been so much younger, overflowing with hopes and dreams ...

She stared silently out of the window while Sophie and Ed negotiated a particularly tricky set of road junctions. If she'd been in a happier mood, she'd have found it amusing: a few wrong turns by Ed despite Sophie's calm directions, all accompanied by occasional swearing and much good-natured banter. Anna suspected it was a fair indication of how they got through life generally.

As the Great House came into sight, Ed let out a low whistle. 'Can't believe we're here already – Sophie, you're a genius. Now, Anna, where shall we drop you – Great House or Cottage?'

'Unless you fancy a cup of tea at our place first? Or gin, as Rick suggested?' Sophie added, eyes crinkling at the corners. So like her brother's, Anna thought; huh, as if she needed any more reminders of *him* today.

Aloud she said, 'Sounds wonderful, but I'd better go straight to the Cottage and get my stuff together. I need to be back in Bath tonight.'

'Lucky you.' Sophie gave an envious sigh. 'I'd love to live in Bath.'

Ed grinned, and the Land Rover swerved slightly. 'No way, you're moving into Kellynch Lodge, remember?'

'Of course I do. That reminds me, Anna, we're very grateful to your father for all the improvements he's making.'

'Don't mention it.' She went on, with a smile, 'At least,

not to me. Feel free to tell him, though – I know exactly what he'll say.'

Sophie groaned loudly. '*Noblesse oblige*. We've heard that quite a few times already.'

The main guest room was at the far end of the Great House; here, the blare of the TV was reduced to a soothing drone and the only other sounds were the hoot of an owl or the bark of a fox. Rick stripped down to his boxers and got into bed. After such a stressful day and a huge supper, he was ready for sleep.

He was just dozing off when his mobile rang; it was Sophie's number.

'What is it? I'm in bed.'

'On your own?' Her voice was edgy.

'I believe so.' He flapped the duvet against the phone, as if he was checking. 'Yep, there's only me, the giant knotweed, alone and unloved.'

She didn't laugh, but said sternly, 'I left a message for you a couple of hours ago, on your mobile. The press went earlier this afternoon, and they don't seem to have returned. So I thought you should move back here.'

He frowned. 'It's too late to move back tonight. And if I'm staying tonight I might as well stay tomorrow night, as planned.'

'Suit yourself. I'm sure you'll be in touch if you want us to rescue any more damsels in distress.'

'Oh yes, thanks again for helping out with Anna.' A pause. 'She doesn't know, does she, that I asked you to come and get her?'

'Why should that bother you? Haven't you got other fish to fry?' And Sophie hung up.

He slammed the phone down on the bedside table and stretched out under the duvet, burying his face in the cool, fragrant pillow. What was Sophie's problem? Did she honestly think he was gagging for a cramped night's sleep at her place and a big-sister-knows-best chat over breakfast? Whereas here … here the bed was large and comfortable, and the company more … appreciative.

Except that he'd had to tell Lou to slow down. Out in the open air, kissing her had seemed like a good idea; whereas back at the house, in a confined space, he'd felt cornered. He hadn't said that, of course. Instead, he'd apologised for getting carried away, asked for a bit of space to adjust to the Shelley situation and suggested they spent some time getting to know each other.

Lou had nodded understandingly, then pinned him to the sofa and–

He'd been saved by a call on his mobile: Guy, confirming the next week's events. Three days of talks in North Wales, followed by book signings in Dorset. As requested, Guy had booked him into a hotel in Lyme Regis for the weekend.

'I *love* Lyme Regis!' Lou said, when the call was over. 'I'll come down and we can spend some time *getting to know each other*.' She giggled and rubbed her foot up and down his leg.

He stood up and moved out of range. 'Difficult. One of my best mates lives there, so I'll be spending any spare time with him.'

'Not *all* your spare time, though? Not every single minute?' Her dark eyes fixed on his, bright with expectation.

He hesitated. What did he have to lose? She was a very attractive girl, and he was single again. So he said slowly, 'OK, I'll book you a room in the same hotel.'

From the look on her face, that wasn't quite what she'd had in mind; but he was determined to pace things. Especially as he was only around for another few weeks.

What had Sophie said earlier? 'Analyse what went wrong

with your last relationship before you rush into the next one.' Well, here he was following her advice, although he wouldn't give her the satisfaction of knowing it.

That night, it took him ages to get to sleep; and even then he had the most disturbing dreams – about a dark-haired girl, looking deep into his eyes as he lifted her down from a stile.

Not a future lover, but one from his past.

Chapter Twenty

The following week, despite the usual sense of relief that the new academic year had finally started, Anna found it impossible to settle into her term-time routine. Lectures went well, especially the one on *Anna Karenina*, but there were too few of them to provide the focus she needed. And, even though the many attractions of Bath were now enhanced by the presence of Sir Walter Elliot, 8th Baronet, she couldn't blame the disruption on her father.

It was the fallout from seeing Rick again.

She read Monday's *Times* with some trepidation, expecting to find him still in the news; but there was nothing. In her lunch hour she went out to buy *The Sun*, and found only a short article about the break-up: according to Rick, speaking from his 'secret' Somerset hideout, it was amicable and he wished Shelley well. A quick glance at the front pages suggested that the tabloids had moved on; several new stories had broken, including a far more salacious one involving Premier League footballers.

So, reading the papers wouldn't add to the fallout; she wished she could say the same for sisterly telepathy. Because, on the few occasions she succeeded in switching her thoughts away from Rick, Mona sent her thoughtful little text messages. Such as 'Lou + Rick went on v early run – sharing same alarm already? ☺' and 'OMG! Lou planning dirty weekend!' She seemed to have completely forgotten her little campaign to get him off with Henrietta.

And then Anna had the phone call. It came on Tuesday night, when she and Jenny were going to their yoga class at the local school. She debated whether to answer; she didn't recognise the number and Jenny had just found a parking space with only two minutes to spare.

In the end, however, curiosity got the better of her. 'Hi – who is this?'

'Rick Wentworth.'

She nearly dropped her mobile. 'Wh-what do you want?' Her heart was pounding and, in spite of the chilly evening air, she felt herself breaking into a sweat.

'I'll make it quick.' His tone was cold and clipped. 'If you're wondering how I got your number, I asked Lou for it, said I wanted to check something about Bath. But I really wanted to check something else.' A pause. 'Did you get pregnant when we – after that weekend on the boat?'

'*What*?'

Jenny gave her a swift, searching look as she turned off the engine, but said nothing.

'Just tell me,' he said, impatiently. 'Please.'

Anna got out of the car, slammed the door and hissed into the phone, 'How dare you ask me *that*, after–'

He cut in with, 'Look, I know we took the necessary precautions, but it's not an impossibility.'

'You're a biologist – and it's taken you ten years to work that out?' She let out a long steadying breath. 'Why do you want to know all of a sudden?'

Silence, as if she'd wrong-footed him with the vehemence of her response; then, 'Just something I heard – not about you, about someone else – and it made me wonder ... I should have been in touch again when I got to Australia.'

'Oh, that's a good one. Because I emailed you in the October and you never bothered to reply.' In the stark lighting of the car park, she saw Jenny gesturing to her that she was going into the school hall. Anna gave her a relieved thumbs-up; she didn't want anyone – even Jenny – overhearing this conversation. She wasn't sure that she wanted to hear it herself.

'You emailed me? ... I don't remember anything. Which address did you use – Uni or Hotmail?'

'The one on the University of Melbourne website. You never gave me your Hotmail one.'

'No need, was there? We were with each other every day, and I was expecting that to continue.' He sounded defensive, even though she'd tried not to turn it into an accusation. Then he cleared his throat. 'Anyway, wherever you sent it, I never saw it.'

'You didn't?' Something – disbelief? hope? – fluttered in her chest. 'When I heard nothing back, I thought you mustn't want any more contact.' She added quietly, 'I wasn't that surprised after – well, you know, the way it all ended.'

Another silence. When at last he spoke, his voice was gentler, more hesitant. 'I had a lot of diving trips that first semester. Had to be doing something, you know? Physical stuff helped, tired me out. And I was pretty ruthless with my emails to keep on top of it. If yours was buried in my spam folder, I'd have deleted it without even noticing.' A pause. 'Were you replying to my letter?'

'Your *letter*?'

He went on, 'I knew I was taking a risk sending it to Kellynch, but it was the only way to reach you after you changed your mobile number.'

Her stomach felt as if it had been kicked, and then some. Her mind seemed to empty of all coherent thought – before the familiar ache of self-recrimination seeped back, altered and sharpened by this new information.

She forced herself to confront that part of the past and remember ... Minty taking away her mobile and laptop 'for repair', presumably enlisting Natasha's help with the technicalities of new contracts and contact details – 'a fresh start for Oxford,' Minty called it ... The journey home, with Minty or Walter always by her side, as if she might make a bid for freedom and stow away on a plane bound for Australia … Lisa taking an unnatural interest, arranging cosy little expeditions to Harrods for 'student basics' … And she'd let it all happen, convinced that it was for the best – that Minty had saved her from making a mess of her life, as her mother had.

But she'd never seen a letter.

Rick said, his tone distant again, 'So, you emailed me … Were you replying to my letter – or getting in touch because you were pregnant?'

'Neither.' She'd actually been going to tell him that she'd made a mistake, the biggest mistake of her life.

A sort of sigh, barely audible. 'Thanks, that's all I wanted to know. And don't worry, I won't bother you again.' With that, he hung up.

Anna almost rang him straight back, but stopped herself. What was the point? He hadn't even pressed her to explain why she'd emailed him; he'd been focused on one thing: finding out if he'd got her pregnant. And she knew what had triggered it – when Lou had told him about Charles and Mona, he'd started examining his own conscience.

But, just as he was putting the record straight with her, she had a score to settle with someone else.

Minty answered the phone with her usual brisk cheerfulness. 'Anna, *darling*! I was just going to ring you – they're doing Chekhov at the Theatre Royal later this month. Shall I get us tickets?'

'What did you do with Rick Wentworth's letter?'

A slight pause. 'What letter?'

'The one he sent to Kellynch shortly after – after I came back from France,' Anna said, through clenched teeth. 'And don't pretend you can't remember!'

'If you mean the letter that Walter opened by accident–'

'Oh, come on – surely you can do better than that? It must have been a classic case of *noblesse oblige* – he saw it was addressed to me and opened it anyway, to protect the family name!'

'Calm down, remember who you are–'

'Have you or Walter ever let me forget?'

'Imagine what your dear mother–'

'My mother's no longer here, Minty.' Anna was surprised at how steady her voice sounded. 'And I'm not my mother, however much you may want me to be.' She took a deep breath. 'Now, what did the letter say?'

'Nothing that you didn't already know,' Minty said, frostily. 'He wasn't much of a writer then, and I don't suppose he's any good now – and I certainly won't be buying his book to find out.'

But Anna wasn't going to be put off that easily. 'If you won't tell me, I'll just have to ask him myself the next time I see him.'

Silence. Then Minty said, 'You've met him, then?'

'On Sunday, at Uppercross.'

'And?'

Anna swallowed. 'He made it very clear that he wasn't interested any more, if that's what you mean.'

A pause. 'So why do you want to know what the letter said?'

'Because I've got nothing to remind me of the happiest time of my life – except a few memories and a lot of regrets!'

'I'm sorry you feel that way, darling.' Minty's voice was muffled now, as if she was choking back tears. 'I was simply doing what I thought was best – and what your dear mother would have wanted.'

Anna closed her eyes. This was Minty's defence for most of her actions and, as neither point could be disproved, arguing with her was hopeless. At the first opportunity, Anna ended the call.

By now, there was a tight knot in her chest that even an hour of yoga couldn't unravel. On the way home, she went through the motions of conversation, on tenterhooks in case Jenny asked who'd phoned her. But if she was dying to know, she didn't show it. One of the things Anna loved about her friend was that, despite having an opinion on everything and everyone, she didn't pry; she was content to wait to be told.

The week dragged by. Anna made a determined effort to get to know her new students and inject enthusiasm into her lectures, cursing Rick Wentworth for disrupting her life all over again. Time after time she looked at his number in the list of calls on her mobile, but couldn't bring herself to ring him. It was over; it really was.

Thursday brought more texts from Mona: 'L + R in Lyme Regis Sat.', then 'Me + C too!' and, finally, a cryptic 'Asked H'. Even these brief headlines were too much information; they nagged like a dull ache at the back of Anna's mind.

Then, that evening, another phone call. She was slumped in front of the TV watching a repeat of *Friends*; normally her comfort food, but tonight it may as well have been a documentary on spread betting. When she saw that the phone number was withheld, her mouth went dry and her heart started to thud. It must be *him*. In a fever of justification, she reminded herself that her mobile had run out of battery and she hadn't yet put it on charge, which meant he'd had to get her landline number. He was ringing to ask why she'd emailed him that October, and he was withholding his number so that she wouldn't ignore the call.

She picked up the receiver, ready to tell him everything.

'Anna?' A man's voice, but not his ... 'Are you there?' the voice prompted, anxiously.

Charles. Her shoulders sagged. No wonder he'd withheld his number; she'd told him last Sunday not to contact her for a while. Their little chat had been a rushed, awkward exchange beside her car – while he was checking her tyre pressure, with Mona watching them the whole time from Harry's bedroom window. Still, Anna felt that she'd got her point across. Ollie's embarrassing revelation at lunch had been a wake-up call, made her more assertive and less guilt-ridden. She'd told Charles that he had to decide before it was too late: was he going to waste the rest of his life on regrets – or make the most of what he'd got?

How she'd cringed at her own hypocrisy.

Now she said quietly, 'Why are you ringing me?'

'Because I've got a big favour to ask.'

She closed her eyes and counted to ten.

'Anna?'

'I told you not to contact me, you and Mona need some space.'

'I know, and I took on board what you said – well, most of it – and things have been a bit better.' A pause; then, in that familiar wheedling tone, 'But Lou and Rick are meeting in Lyme Regis this weekend, and Rick told me that he's looking up a mate of his who lives there, and it just happens to be Ben Harville, the guru on fishing management. So I said I'd pop down for the day, but Mona thought it would be a good idea for us – her and me, that is – to have a weekend away.'

'And you want me to look after the boys.' At least that would leave her little time – or energy – for thinking.

He gave a rueful laugh. 'No, they're going to Mum and Dad's, it's Mona I need you to look after. And not just to keep her off the booze. You see, she says she'll be bored while I'm talking to Ben, and of course Lou will just want to be with Rick, so she's asked Henrietta along.' Another pause. 'I have this horrible feeling she's going to try and split Lou and Rick up, then wheel in Henrietta as Lou's replacement.'

'That's absurd.' Anna couldn't help a flicker of hope that the first part of Mona's supposed plan would succeed, but not the second.

'Not to Mona, anything's possible as far as she's concerned. So I need you to keep an eye on her, you can manage her better than anyone.'

'That's not saying much. And she certainly won't want me there.' A deep breath. 'The answer's no.'

'But Anna–'

'I said no.' It wasn't so much Mona; more the thought of having to watch Rick with Lou …

'You don't understand how important this weekend is.' Charles hesitated, then went on, 'It's make or break with me and Mona. Looking at it positively, it's a chance to get to know each other again. And being negative, if she messes things up for Henrietta or Lou, then God help me I'll–'

'That's emotional blackmail!'

'It's not, it's asking my sister-in-law – and very close friend – for a big favour. The last one for a long time, I promise you.'

'Get lost, Charles.' And she put down the receiver.

Chapter Twenty-One

Eight o'clock on Friday morning, and the first of Rick's daily phone calls from Lou. He'd tried ignoring them earlier in the week, but she kept on ringing until he answered. He supposed he should be flattered by her persistence.

He let her voice wash over him, his thoughts elsewhere.

'... And I wish I could get out of this Pony Club thing tonight, but I can't. It's their anniversary year and Mum's giving a speech.'

'Mmm?' The word 'anniversary' caught his attention. In a couple of weeks it would be Sophie and Ed's fifth wedding anniversary; maybe he'd get back into Sophie's good books with a special present ...

'I just want to be with you – *now*. And the thought of waiting until tomorrow is driving me crazy.'

'Deferred gratification's good for the soul,' he said, forcing a laugh.

'And how come a quiet little weekend, just the two of us, has turned into a bloody group outing?' Her mood had changed abruptly; she sounded sulky and cross. 'I knew it was a mistake when you invited Charles. Now we've got Mona, Henrietta and Anna as well–'

'What the–?'

'Didn't you know? Mona's asked Henrietta along and Charles has retaliated with Anna. I'm bringing Henrietta tomorrow, but the others will get there this evening. Lucky you.'

So, this evening they'd meet for the first time since that phone call. How would she react? Would she even speak to him? He cursed his own stupidity; he was building her up into some sort of threat, when she was just someone he used to know …

Lou went on, 'Although for once Anna played hard to get.'

'What do you mean?' Something made him add, 'Did her boyfriend object?'

'Boyfriend? Hasn't got one as far as we know, seems to prefer her men to stay between the covers of a book, especially if it's a nineteenth-century Russian novel. I'm not sure she's had anyone serious since Charles – hang on, won't be a minute, I just need a word with Mum before she goes out.'

While he waited, he mulled over this new information. Anna had gone out with Charles in her first year at Oxford – but was it before she'd tried to email him, or after? And what did the email say? 'I've got someone else, and I'm over you'? Or 'I'm not interested in anyone else, because I still love you'?

And did 'serious' mean 'sleeping with'? How many men had she slept with? He knew he'd been her first, that weekend on the boat …

Something stinging at the back of his eyes; he shut them, tight.

'Which is half the problem, if you ask me,' Lou was saying in his ear. 'Makes Charles think Anna's at his beck and call – Rick, are you still there?'

'Yes.' He opened his eyes again. Better now. Back to normal, in fact.

'But this time, when he asked her to come along and look after Mona – who's on the way to becoming an alcoholic, in case you hadn't noticed – Anna refused. She changed her mind in the end, though, when Mum put her oar in. Anna's far too soft-hearted for her own good.' She giggled. 'Don't worry, you won't have to entertain them on your own, by the time they arrive at Lyme you'll be in the pub with Ben. Anna's got a hair appointment in Bath – or is it the dentist? Anyway, Charles and Mona aren't picking her up from wherever it is until six o'clock and he reckons it's a two-hour drive at that time on a Friday.'

When at last she rang off, he let out a long, ragged breath. If only Charles hadn't invited Anna. What should have been a straightforward weekend had become more ... complicated.

The journey from Bangor to Lyme Regis took even longer than expected, as a result of road works on the M5. He passed the time chatting to Dave; or rather, punctuating a seven-hour monologue on model railways with appropriate questions. Strange that he'd uncovered the man's secret passion with a random comment about his misadventures as a student on the North Wales Coast trains. And strange that he couldn't recall the last time he'd talked about anything with as much enthusiasm as Dave.

Inevitably his thoughts returned to that summer in France, when he'd had several passions on the go and none of them secret. He'd worn his heart on his sleeve – about teaching kids how to sail dinghies, about conserving marine life and about wanting Anna Elliot. Especially about wanting Anna Elliot. He'd known from the start that she was different from the others, but he'd thought it was simply because she was younger and more innocent. So, until that weekend on the boat, it had been a slow burn of a summer ... Especially as they had no privacy; he shared a dormitory with three others and, although she had her own room, her cousin's kids were always around.

In the end, he was so focused on physical self-restraint that he completely underestimated the other effects Anna had on him. Like the way the sun only seemed to start shining when she came to the sailing club; or the urge he had in the middle of the night to phone her, just to hear her voice. And he only realised all this when it was too late, when he was in too deep ...

They reached Lyme Regis just before five and checked into the hotel. It was situated up a hill on the outskirts of the town and called – optimistically, given the blanket of mist – the Cobb View Hotel. Rick took an instant dislike to the proprietor, Evan Pargeter, a long-faced stork of a man with black greasy hair and an oily smile.

He confirmed arrangements with Dave for the next day – there was an event at eleven-thirty in nearby Dorchester – then inspected his room. The second best in the hotel, Pargeter assured him; only an earlier booking by another 'celebwity' had deprived him of the best, known as the 'pwesidential suite'. Rick's room was certainly a good size, although the decor was a bit too flowery for his taste. A quick shower and a change of clothes, and then it was time to meet Ben.

Dave had the night off and anyway, after the long journey, Rick needed a walk. He set off at a brisk pace, following the directions Ben had given him, and by six o'clock was ringing the doorbell of a neat little terraced house. The smart, bottle-green door opened tentatively and a curly-haired, snotty-nosed child – three or four years old, he guessed, and of indeterminate sex – stared up at him as if he'd just landed from outer space.

'Hi there,' Rick said, slightly disconcerted by the blood-curdling yells from upstairs. 'Is your dad in? Or your mum?'

The child just gawped.

And then someone else came to the door; a face he knew, although not one he was expecting.

'James!' Rick groped for the few details passed on by Ben over the years about James Benwick, a contemporary of theirs at Bangor. Teaching at some poncy boys' school in Sussex; presumably English, his degree subject. Engaged to Julie, the girl he'd immortalised in excruciatingly bad verse all those years ago in the student magazine; it only got printed because James was the editor. And he recalled that James was still writing poetry and now publishing stuff on the Internet; Rick hadn't yet steeled himself to look at the website.

'Good to see you.' James's response was muted, but that could have been due to the deafening noise from above. 'Ben won't be long – the twins had simultaneous bowel movements, so he's changing one nappy and Megan's doing the other. Cassie, let Uncle Rick in.'

The child – Cassie – shuffled aside and Rick stepped into the tiny hall. It was surprisingly free of clutter – thanks, he assumed, to the neat array of cupboards lining one wall. And the same in the sitting room; just a small pile of toys in one corner that Cassie scampered to defend, as though Rick had designs on her dolls.

He grinned at James. 'Good to see you too, Ben didn't say you were coming.'

'Didn't know myself until a few hours ago, just needed a weekend away.'

'How's Julie?'

James's face darkened. 'Ben obviously hasn't kept you up to date – she's run off with the art teacher.'

The bitterness in his voice made Rick wince.

At that moment Ben came in, a matching baby in each arm and an apologetic grin on his face; he'd obviously heard James's last words. 'I was hoping to tell you about that as soon as you got here, but the twins conspired against me. Anyway, how are you, mate? Here, James, take Joshua.' He thrust one of the babies at James and shook Rick's hand for several seconds.

Rick answered automatically, 'Fine, thanks.' But he

wasn't; he was stunned by James's news. In their university days, he'd mocked James and Julie for being too wrapped up in each other. Then, in France, he'd experienced for himself that all-consuming need to share every moment with another person. He'd decided to apologise to James and Julie when he next had the opportunity; now it seemed he never would.

Ben gave him a shrewd look. 'Megan's having a few girlfriends round to watch a film so I thought we'd eat at the pub up the road, since we're going there anyway. Do you want to let your mate know?'

Just as Rick was texting directions to Charles, Megan came downstairs. He'd met her only once before, when she and Ben had visited him in Australia a few years ago. She didn't seem to have changed much; still those frequent, amused looks at Ben and that infectious laugh. He couldn't help comparing this couple – with their well-organised house and relaxed, team-based approach – to Charles and Mona.

Once they got to the pub and downed a few drinks, Rick started to feel better. He and Ben did the talking; James sat hunched over his pint and gave monosyllabic replies to their questions. Towards eight o'clock the pub started to fill up and Ben suggested getting ready to order the food as soon as the others arrived. No menus, just a neatly written list on a blackboard by the bar. Rick went over to take a look and glanced discreetly at his watch. Anna could walk in any minute now; he'd keep his distance, behave as if that strained phone call had never taken place, avoid any further conversation beyond the basic courtesies. What was there to say? That chapter of his life was closed and, now that the potential pregnancy issue was out of the way, he had nothing to reproach himself for.

Because I emailed you in the October and you never bothered to reply.

He closed his eyes briefly, then flicked them open and

gave his full attention to the blackboard. The seared salmon with a lemongrass-honey sauce sounded good, as did the slow-cooked pork and red cabbage–

To his left, the door of the lounge bar swung open and three people entered. Charles, looking harassed and scanning the room anxiously. Mona, turning her discontented face to the mirrored alcove opposite and checking her make-up. And Anna, staring down at the floor. A subtly different Anna, yet startlingly familiar; dark hair now cut short, drawing the eye to the slender neck that, once upon a time, his mouth had traced and tasted on its slow, sweet journey to the base of her throat ...

He twisted blindly away and elbowed a path across the room to the door marked 'Gents'.

Chapter Twenty-Two

'Odd that Rick's not here,' Charles said. 'I'll ring him.'

Anna touched her hair nervously. She usually just had it trimmed, but today – on some mad impulse – she'd asked for something more drastic. Now she was regretting it; Rick might think she was trying to recapture the past.

A mobile trilled behind her and, as if she sensed his approach, she whirled round and saw him. She felt her heart start to race, just like it used to at the sailing club whenever she had that first glimpse of him and couldn't believe her luck that he singled her out for his smile. Caught off guard, she looked straight at him, willing him to do the same.

His gaze slid skilfully past her to Charles and Mona. 'Hi there, was that you calling me? Sorry I wasn't here when you arrived – what would you like to drink?'

'A glass of Shiraz for me,' Mona put in; then, with a smirk, 'Actually, make that a bottle – I'm sure Charles and Anna will help me drink it.'

'I'd rather have a pint of bitter,' Charles said heavily. 'What about you, Anna?'

'I'm fine with the Shiraz,' Anna replied, resigning herself to her role as Mona's minder. She'd have preferred a longer, more refreshing drink too; but that would leave Mona with the whole bottle to herself – the first of several, if she could get away with it.

Rick fidgeted with the cuff of his sweater and still didn't look at her. 'On second thoughts, having seen the queue at the bar I'll take you to meet Ben and James first.'

He led them through the crush to a table in the far corner, where two men were sitting. One – short brown hair, tanned face – glanced up with a welcoming smile; the other – dark, shoulder-length hair and a smattering of stubble – stared fixedly into his pint.

While Rick made the introductions, Anna took off her jacket, sat down and wondered how soon she could get away to the solitude of her hotel room.

Then she heard him say, 'And this is Annie.'

Oh God, he'd only ever called her that in bed ...

He quickly covered up his mistake, his tone almost dismissive. 'Anna, Mona's sister.'

From under lowered lashes she watched him hurry off to the bar. But *she* couldn't escape. She had to sit there, praying that no one noticed the colour flooding her cheeks, and remembering ... Remembering the last time they'd made love – not that they'd realised it was the last time – and how afterwards, after he'd said 'Annie' over and over in that breathless way that she loved, after their bodies had stilled, he'd kissed the damp skin at her throat and told her that he couldn't live without her ...

He'd just called her Annie. Didn't that mean he was remembering, too?

'Are you all right?'

Shit, the miserable-looking man had noticed. She'd thought she'd be fine tucked next to him; it was opposite Mona and well away from the other end of the table, where she reckoned Rick would sit. Charles and Ben were there, already deep in discussion about fishing, and Mona – predictably – wasn't bothering to hide a yawn.

Anna gave the man a bright smile. 'I'm fine, thank you. Sorry, I didn't catch your name?'

'James Benwick. I'm staying with Ben for the weekend, I know him and Rick from university.' A half-hearted shrug. 'Didn't mean to intrude, it's just – well, you looked exactly how I feel.'

Her smile froze. 'Which is?'

'And is this what you wanted, to live in a house that is haunted, by the ghost of you and me?' He spoke the words with a curious lilting reverence that made her think it must be poetry. Too close for comfort, whatever it was.

She stared at him, debating how to respond; in the end, all she could manage was, 'Is that a quote from somewhere?'

'It's a Leonard Cohen song.'

'That explains it. I don't know any of his, apart from "Hallelujah".'

James's eyes gleamed. 'Want to listen to him on my iPod?'

She was about to refuse, when Rick returned with a tray and distributed the drinks; his hands looked so strong and sure, yet she knew just how delicate their touch could be ...

Great, she thought, even listening to Leonard Cohen must be less depressing than this. She nodded at James; instantly he brought out an iPod, took one of the earphones and passed her the other. She wouldn't have minded if he'd let her listen in peace, but he kept up a running commentary above the music. Something about him and Julie and how much he still loved her, how much he still hoped, even though almost five weeks had passed. She felt her fragile spirits spiral further and further down, until at last she couldn't stand it any longer.

'Have you got any other music on here?' she said, more loudly than she'd intended, judging by the way everyone stared at her. It was only now that she noticed Rick sitting beside Mona, opposite her and James. And she saw that there were three glasses next to the bottle of Shiraz – hers full, his and Mona's half-empty. And, amazingly, he was looking at her. She ventured a smile; he immediately looked away.

James was saying, 'Probably, but I prefer listening to stuff that matches my mood.'

Anna waited until the other conversations had started up again – although what Rick was finding to talk to Mona about, she daren't imagine – then took out her earphone. James did the same, with obvious reluctance.

She smiled encouragingly at him, kept her voice low. 'It's so tempting to do that, isn't it? But if you're not careful you never move on.' A pause. 'We can't change what's happened – but we can accept it, and learn from it.' That sounded awful – a cross between clichéd and self-righteous.

He returned her smile, but only briefly; then it was back to his comfort blanket of gloom. 'I've tried, of course I have, but what makes it worse is that I'm a poet, which means I'm always writing about my darkest moments. I've got my own website,' in a burst of animation, he fished out a little card from his pocket, 'so you can have a read and let me know what you think.'

She studied the card: his name, website address and a few words about his latest collection, 'Come Up and See My Retchings'. 'I will,' she said, fighting a sudden urge to giggle, 'although I tend to read novels more than poems.'

He gave her a pitying look. 'If you fill yourself up with bread, there's no room for cake.'

'I hadn't thought of it like that.' She slipped his card into her bag. 'Call it an occupational hazard – I teach nineteenth-century Russian literature. Some poetry, Pushkin for example, and of course there's Chekhov with his plays. But it's mostly novels.'

Another smile; this time it lingered and reached his eyes. 'I teach too, English, in a boys' school. And that's all novels, apart from a few First World War poets and a bit of Shakespeare. I prefer poetry, though, don't you?'

'Not usually. Too much emotion, without any moving on. Whereas a good novel always has a resolution–'

'A happy ending? How many of us believe in those any

more?' His hollow, ringing laugh cut the other conversations short.

'You two OK?' Ben said, casually.

James rolled his eyes. 'Don't nursemaid me, I'm fine. Just beginning to enjoy myself, actually.' He turned back to Anna. 'Sorry, I interrupted you.'

Apparently reassured, Ben continued talking to Charles; Rick and Mona, however, remained silent. Anna wondered if they were each contemplating their own chances of a happy ending.

She took a deep breath and said, 'Resolution doesn't necessarily mean a happy ending – or, at least, not for everyone – but it is about moving on.'

'That's a very practical point of view. I'm more of a romantic, as you can probably tell. I write what I feel, and – believe me – I feel a *lot*.' He moved closer, lowered his voice. 'You see Rick over there? He writes about the sexual activity of little rubbery creatures lying around at the bottom of the sea, whereas I'm helping people understand human suffering. Funny thing is, he's the celebrity, and I'm unknown! How does that happen?'

Anna sipped her wine. Mona was busy texting; but she was pretty sure that Rick was listening. 'Do you want to be a celebrity?' she said quietly.

'Not really, I just think it's ironic – why are celebrities treated like bloody heroes when they can't even cope with everyday life?'

Rick's head jerked up. 'The media haven't exactly treated me like a hero in the last week. And, believe me, I'm quite able to cope with everyday life.' But his tone suggested otherwise – stressed, almost angry.

On impulse, Anna said, 'Heroism comes in different forms, though, doesn't it? Pechorin, for example–' She interrupted herself with an embarrassed laugh. 'Sorry, I almost launched into a lecture on the superfluous man in nineteenth-century Russian literature.'

A broad grin from James. 'I bet your lectures are fascinating. Who's Pechorin?'

She ignored the clumsy compliment and focused on the question. 'Have you heard of *A Hero of Our Time*, by Lermontov? Pechorin's very much in the Byronic tradition–'

'Byron? That's more familiar territory.' He stroked his chin thoughtfully. 'Pechorin's a man of contradiction, then?'

'Understatement of the year.' She frowned slightly. 'He's cynical, but wants to believe in something. Intelligent and talented, yet can't find personal fulfilment. So he becomes Action Man – seeking danger, taking risks, just for the hell of it–'

'Sounds rather like Rick.' A shout of laughter from James. 'Fighting off sharks one minute, women the next – from what I read in the papers.'

Anna glanced across; Rick was fidgeting with a beer mat, his face expressionless. She said softly, 'I find Pechorin rather intriguing–'

'But not good relationship material,' James put in. 'Who, out of all the heroes of Russian literature, would you most want to be with?'

She took another sip of wine to collect her thoughts. If James would let her finish a sentence, she might be able to communicate directly with Rick, establish some sort of truce after Tuesday's phone call. This blank, black mood of his worried her …

'It would have to be a hybrid,' she said at last. 'Action Man Pechorin, because I'd never be bored, combined with the good qualities of Prince Myshkin–'

'Where's Prince What's-his-name from?' James again, when it was Rick she was really talking to.

She forced a smile. '*The Idiot* – Dostoevsky. The Prince is thoughtful and kind, a man of honour and–'

'An honourable Action Man.' James gave a forlorn sigh. 'Maybe I should get down the gym, I used to be–'

'Why's it called *The Idiot*?' Rick said abruptly, his eyes drilling into hers.

She stared back, trying to detect some warmth in his gaze; OK, maybe the truce idea was a non-starter. 'It's more a comment on society,' she began; then noticed that Mona's seat was empty, and so was the wine bottle. It didn't take a genius to work out that she'd gone after more Shiraz; the question was – how much more?

'Excuse me, I have to find my sister.' With something like relief, she stumbled to her feet and made her way to the bar.

Rick knew he'd drunk too much when he heard Anna implying he was her ideal man. Huh, how likely was *that* after all these years?

He must have imagined it. Or, if he hadn't, it was pure coincidence that she'd used the words 'Action Man', and 'thoughtful', and 'kind'. Words she'd once written about him in the hot summer sand, during a game of 'Guess Who?' with Katya and Alyosha. Words she'd later turned into kisses ...

So, when she reappeared with Mona and another bottle of Shiraz, and they ordered the food, it irritated him that she chose salmon, like him. And, as he responded automatically to Mona's chatter and shared out the wine, he was annoyed that it was *her* voice he listened to most. She and James were discussing American literature now, something about Edith Wharton. He had to admit that James was looking the better for it, like a dog who'd glimpsed the possibility of a walk.

When their food was served, it was after nine o'clock;

by the time they'd finished eating, it was nearly ten. Ben suggested calling back at his place for a coffee and, as it was just down the road, Charles left his car at the pub. At the small, tidy, terraced house with the green door, peace reigned; Megan's friends had gone and the kids were in bed.

Rick sipped his good – but extremely hot – black coffee and looked around the sitting room. Ben had managed to give Charles the slip and was talking to Anna; from his gestures, Rick guessed he was describing his next DIY project. Charles was enthusing about fishing to a silent James, while Megan seemed to be making equally slow progress with Mona on the subject of playgroups.

It was only natural, then, that his gaze was drawn back to Ben and Anna; to the dark neatness of her hair, the contrasting pallor of her face and neck and hands, the large expressive eyes, the slightly parted lips. Only natural that he found the breath knocked out of him by an explosion of memories. Only natural that his heart slammed against the tight bands of his chest at the thought, however impossible, of making those memories real again …

Later, in the back of Charles's Range Rover, he was only inches from her – and yet separated by an emotional chasm. Throughout the short journey back to the hotel, he felt weighed down by ifs. If her family hadn't interfered, if they hadn't quarrelled, if he hadn't stormed off, if he'd got her email … they might still be here, in this car. Except that it would be so different; right now they'd be holding hands, and in a few minutes he'd be taking her in his arms and–

They turned into the Cobb View Hotel's floodlit parking area. He got out of the car as soon as it stopped, flinging 'Goodnight!' at the others before they could even hint at a nightcap in the bar, taking the steps to the front entrance two at a time. No Pargeter lurking at Reception, thank God, just a far-too-cheerful young girl. He managed a smile in her direction, then made for the stairs and the sanctuary of his room.

It wasn't until he switched his mobile off 'silent' – and noticed the missed calls – that he realised he hadn't given Lou a thought all evening.

Chapter Twenty-Three

Fingers of sunlight crept into the room through tiny chinks above the heavy chintz curtains. Anna, already awake, watched them steal along the floral border at the top of the wall, then fade as clouds passed over. Rain was forecast for later – why not get up and enjoy the best of the day?

She'd slept soundly; no doubt the wine had helped. And the sight of Charles and Mona heading for their room last night, arm in arm, had reassured her that they were at least making an effort. As the evening wore on, James too had rallied; once he'd weaned himself off Leonard Cohen and allowed her to finish her sentences, he'd proved surprisingly good company.

She shut her mind to Rick's behaviour. Time enough to analyse that when she'd got through this weekend.

A quick shower, then on with jeans, a jade-green, long-sleeved T-shirt and a black jacket, and she was ready to blow the cobwebs away. No one at Reception; but, after all, it was only quarter to eight on a sleepy Saturday in October. Outside, not a soul about; and in the distance the sea, a gunmetal gleam on the horizon. She went down the hill towards it and felt her spirits lift at the sight of the Cobb, shimmering mirage-like in the pastel sun. The breeze ruffled her hair and stung her lips with salt.

She remembered coming here as a child with her mother, usually on day trips; hunting for fossils, visiting the Philpot museum, watching the toings and froings on Victoria Pier. Once they'd stayed for a whole month, holidaying with Stephanie Elliot, the widow of one of Walter's distant cousins, and her silent son, William. And now that Anna was here again, in the chill of an autumn morning, she felt the loss in her life all the more keenly. Her childhood, when fairy-tale endings were a given. Her mother, the woman she'd adored. And Rick …

Through the park, past the row of pretty painted cottages – sugar-almond pink, cream and blue – and the little harbour was in front of her. It was bustling even at this time of year, so she made for the Cobb, curving emptily into the sea under the screaming gulls. Now she had a choice: walk along the top level, exposed to the elements, or take the more sheltered lower path that hugged one side. She chose the top level, daunted at first by its sloping surface; as a child, hadn't she skipped along here without a second thought? Smiling at the memory, she lifted her chin and stretched out her arms like a plane, feeling the full force of the wind.

And then, some yards in front, the lone figure of a man appeared at the top of the steps leading from the lower path. She studied him with mounting resentment as he walked ahead of her. What right had he to be here, spoiling her view and her solitude? Begrudgingly, she lowered her arms, tucked her hands into her pockets and followed him in a more sedate fashion to the furthest point.

When he turned, she was only a few steps away and ready with a brusque, Good morning. But the words died in her throat. This man – it was like looking at her father! Of course, he *wasn't* her father; far too young, and with more interested eyes. She gave an embarrassed half-smile, averted her gaze and dodged past him to avoid speaking; then went as near to the end of the Cobb as she dared, keeping her back to him. When at last she risked a look round, she was relieved to see him walking briskly away.

Silly to let the stranger unsettle her; but she waited a good ten minutes before returning. This time she opted for the lower path, before skirting round the beach with its gaily coloured huts and neatly demarcated areas of gravel and sand. As she climbed the road up through the town, she felt the first spots of rain.

At the hotel, she went straight to the dining room – and immediately stopped in the doorway. The only person there – sitting in the deep bay of the window, reading a newspaper wedged between a portly silver teapot and an arc of pink orchids – was Rick.

She wondered briefly what sort of mood she'd find him in today; then squared her shoulders, and made for the vacant chair at his table for two.

Chapter Twenty-Four

Rick glanced up from his paper, thinking it was the waitress with his cooked breakfast. Saw instead a slim figure in tight-fitting jeans, hair tousled and face glowing from the morning breeze. Felt a jolt in his chest …

She slipped off her jacket and hung it on the back of the chair opposite him.

'It would look odd if I sat somewhere else,' she said, in that low, husky voice. 'Odd to Mona and Charles, I mean – although somehow I don't think they'll be down for a while.' A pause. 'Is anything the matter?'

With an effort, he switched his stare from her to the window beside him; in the distance, sea and sky were one, a soft blur as grey as her eyes …

He made an attempt at normal conversation. 'Didn't you get wet out there?'

'The rain's only just started.' Out of the corner of his eye, he watched the graceful turn of her neck as she followed his gaze. She went on, 'No view now. An hour ago, it was spectacular.'

He cleared his throat. 'They should change the name of this place, then. How about the Occasional Cobb View Hotel?'

She grinned. 'Or the Cobb View If You're Lucky?'

He laughed, and their eyes met. In a sudden slip of time, he was back on the boat with her, off the coast of France. A rush of tenderness, the words on the tip of his tongue – Remember that view, the morning after our first night together? He took a deep breath, readied himself to speak–

But then his full English arrived and, sensing the need

for self-preservation, he launched himself into a flurry of activity. Straightened his cutlery, removed the newspaper, almost sent the orchids flying. The waitress fussed over him, bringing extra marmalade that he didn't want, before taking Anna's order.

By the time they were alone again, the moment for intimate reminiscences had passed.

Instead, he asked another question – one of several that had been playing on his mind for the past six days. 'I heard you went out with Charles at university – when exactly was that?'

She gave him a wary look. 'Why do you want to know?'

He could hardly say, 'I'm trying to piece together the sequence of events ten years ago – Charles, your email, my letter.' Especially if he couldn't face the answer …

Dark feelings tightened their grip. Having breakfast with this woman was never meant to be like this, as stiff and soulless as an early-morning business meeting. It was meant to be as it had been on the boat: food as foreplay, an interlude between the fevered intensity of their nights and the slow burn of their afternoons on the sun-drenched deck …

He twisted his mouth into a smile and answered her question. 'Just look at the poor sod. He must have been your ex for almost as long as I have, but he still can't handle it. Do you think I should give him lessons?'

Silence, taut as a wire between them, while the waitress returned with Anna's tea and toast. When she'd gone, Anna poured her tea and sipped it, eyes cool and reproachful over the rim of her cup. Even without that, he felt a complete bastard; hardly the thoughtful, kind man she'd said she was looking for last night – but why the hell should he care?

Except he did care; he just wasn't sure how much.

'I'm sorry,' he heard himself mutter, 'I don't know what got into me.'

She avoided his gaze and concentrated on cutting her toast into neat halves. 'What's important is – it's been over between Charles and me for years, and he accepts where his responsibilities lie.'

'I believe you,' he said quietly, 'although I have to admit ...'

He was about to apologise for his previous suspicions and tell her how fiercely Lou had defended her, when a man came in and sat at the next table. Rick cursed him under his breath and managed to refrain from pointing out that there were twenty other sodding tables to choose from. But then this man looked as if he always did just as he pleased; well-heeled, judging from his clothes, with a face like an impossibly youthful Sir Walter Elliot, smug and smooth and goading you to wipe the smirk off it. Most of all, Rick didn't care for the way the stranger edged his chair nearer to Anna, at an angle which gave him a better view of her, and stared at her face as if in divine contemplation.

Anna hadn't even noticed him. She clattered her cup down on her saucer and glared across the table – eyes dark now, like a storm at sea. One false move and you'd be swept overboard ...

'You can "have to admit" whatever you like, but it's really none of your business, is it?' Her icy tone made him flinch; but that was nothing compared to what happened next.

The stranger leaned over, laid his hand reverently on her arm and said, 'Is this man bothering you, Anna? Just say the word and I'll have him removed.'

Anna looked across into concerned blue eyes and felt the colour drain from her face. It was the man from the Cobb – and how on earth did he know her name?

Forget breakfast – after that little exchange with Rick, she had to get some time to herself and calm down. With a tight-lipped smile, she jumped to her feet and moved out of touching distance. 'Thanks, it's fine. I've finished here anyway.' She snatched up her jacket and headed for the door.

'Men!' she hissed as she crossed Reception, avoiding the beady gaze of Mr Pargeter at the desk. Idiots, most of them. Especially Rick Wentworth – laughing with her one minute, condemning her the next.

'Anna – wait!'

The stranger again, close behind her.

She whirled round, made her voice cold and imperious. 'Do I know you?' Then groaned inwardly as she realised how like Lisa she sounded.

Undaunted, the man went on, 'Don't you recognise me?'

His face lit up in a boyish grin and she let out a gasp. It was William, Stephanie's son! Not surprisingly, he'd changed – grown tall, filled out – since their holiday here in Lyme Regis. She cast her mind back to the boy she'd got to know as the days dawdled by. At first he'd hardly said a word; later, he'd broken his silence to confide in her – about his mother, his detested soon-to-be-stepfather, Jeremy Dunne, and their plans to send him to boarding school. In this confident, almost brash man, she could see no trace of that vulnerable fourteen-year-old, anxious to please the girl who listened and smiled and shared a little of her boundless optimism.

And she couldn't forget that this was also the man who'd left her sister high and dry a few years ago. They'd met through work – investment banking – and moved in together within a week. Anna, up against her PhD deadline and still smarting from a spectacular falling-out with Lisa, had never visited the happy couple in their ludicrously expensive Kensington apartment. Walter, on the other hand, had gone to London for frequent fawning sessions combined with mysterious appointments at a Harley Street clinic;

while Mona – complaining bitterly about being trapped at Uppercross Manor with an unruly toddler – waited for an invitation that never came.

Around the same time, Cousin Archie dropped dead and Walter's joy knew no bounds. He wasted no time in consulting *Burke's Peerage & Baronetage* and announced triumphantly to anyone who would listen that William was now his nearest living male relative. Barring the inconceivable – Walter having a son and passing the title on through his direct male line – William would become the 9th Baronet; which meant that the future mistress of Kellynch would be none other than his favourite daughter, Lisa.

But William ruined all his plans by running off with a rich Texan divorcee. Lawyers were called in – at great expense – but could find no grounds for any charges. A stony-faced, stony-broke Lisa returned to Kellynch and Walter vowed he would stop William inheriting the title if it killed him. Anna had felt obliged to remind him that dying would simply hand William the baronetcy on a plate.

So it was very strange that William Elliot-Dunne should turn up again, apparently eager to renew a distant summer friendship with another member of the Elliot family. Anna didn't know whether to smile back at him – or slap his face because of how he'd treated Lisa, however much she might have deserved it.

In the end she did neither, just gave him an appraising look. 'What on earth are you doing here? Last I heard, you had a better offer and went to Texas.'

Under his tan she detected a faint flush, but his voice was calm and composed. 'As you can see, I've come back to England – only last week, in fact. Spent a few days up on the Isle of Skye with my mother, until her bastard of a husband returned unexpectedly early from his business trip. Then I drove down here.' He smiled – a smile of such brilliance that she blinked, momentarily dazzled. 'I've been reliving that holiday we had, visiting old haunts, but I certainly didn't expect to find *you* here, looking the very image of your beautiful mother.'

Her face grew warm under his gaze, and warmer still as she registered the compliment. But she wasn't in the mood for flirtatious banter, however gratifying she might find the comparison with her mother.

She was edging away, anxious to get back to her room, when she heard Mr Pargeter call out in his unctuous way, 'Good morning once again, Sir William. Anything else I can do for you?'

Sir William? She turned swiftly to William and raised her eyebrows; but he simply grinned and tucked her arm through his.

'Breakfast for two in my suite, Pargeter,' he drawled. 'Miss Elliot will be joining me.' And he steered Anna firmly up the stairs.

She let her irritation show in her voice. 'No thank you, I've had all the breakfast I want.'

But he just laughed. 'Nonsense, all that sea air earlier must have made you ravenous. And we've got lots of catching up to do.'

'Including how you've suddenly become a Sir.'

He put his finger to his lips. 'Shh, don't blow my cover, it works like a dream on people like Pargeter, every time.'

She couldn't think what to say. She was struggling to make sense of this transformation from stuttering schoolboy to smooth operator. When they reached her landing she stopped, still undecided about breakfast. 'Did you know who I was, when we met on the Cobb?'

He fixed those eyes on her and a shiver ran down her back. It really was as if her father was looking at her, with a degree of warmth that she hadn't seen since her mother died. Then he shook his head. 'I was struck by your likeness to Irina, but I didn't want to say anything until I was sure – I'm not the sort that rushes into things. When I got back just now, I had Pargeter check the guest register. And there you were, the one and only Anna Elliot.' He gave her arm a gentle tug. 'Come on, let's see who remembers the most about that holiday.'

She allowed him to guide her up a further staircase, past a sign saying 'Presidential Suite Only'. To another landing, smaller but more opulent than the previous one; gold leaf in the wallpaper, crystal in the light fittings. Into a sitting room three times the size of her bedroom, with several doors off it, and tall windows looking out over the Jurassic Coast where they'd once hunted for fossils ...

She was only sharing memories over breakfast, wasn't she? And afterwards she'd probably never see him again.

So she shrugged off her doubts along with her jacket. Sank into the squashy embrace of a white leather sofa. And defied Walter's lifetime ban on any further communication with William Elliot-Dunne.

Chapter Twenty-Five

Back in his room Rick fielded a call from Lou, aware that he was only half-listening to her non-stop chatter, his head still full of something else ... How many more of Anna Elliot's male friends would turn up in Lyme Regis, for God's sake? Maybe there was a reunion of her ex-lovers that he was the last to know about?

When he caught the words 'all afternoon' and 'getting to know each other', however, he pulled himself together. 'Sorry, Lou, run that by me again?'

'Henrietta and I are leaving now, we should be with you by eleven. I'd have set off at the crack of dawn, but she wanted to see Kyle – all of a sudden, she can't bear to be away from him!' An exasperated sigh. 'Anyway, you and I are going out for lunch – then spending all afternoon *getting to know each other*.' She giggled. 'Your room or mine?'

He fabricated a sigh of disappointment. 'I can't, I'm in Dorchester, remember? But we could do dinner instead.'

'Just the two of us?' Her voice sharpened.

'Why not? I'll ring you when I'm on my way back to Lyme.'

She made a loud kissing noise down the phone, making him wince at the thought of what she might do to him in person. After the call was over, he slumped in the armchair with his laptop. Was he taking the right approach with Lou? She was unlikely to give him enough space to analyse his last relationship, or however Sophie had put it. Not that he knew where to start with that particular activity; maybe he should stick to analysing sea dragon specimens.

He prodded the keyboard, hunting for information about

Dorchester – something he always did before an event. It focused his mind, gave him a feel for the people he might meet. As he sifted through the search results, he felt even more dispirited. Small market town, scene of the Tolpuddle Martyrs' trial – hadn't they been transported to Australia? Right now he almost envied them, leg irons and all … Population little more than 16,000 – what was that publicist of his thinking, getting him an event in a place that size? On second thoughts, knowing Guy, the local bookshop owner was probably some old public school pal who'd called in a favour … Supposedly the inspiration for Thomas Hardy's Casterbridge – huh, that was the sort of trivia James used to come in handy for, in those Bangor pub quizzes …

Which reminded him, in his pocket from last night was James's card with his website details. May as well give him some feedback – as positive as he could make it. He took out the card and typed in the address.

The first thing he saw on James's gloomy-looking home page was the heading 'Move On You' in large red letters. Underneath was a brief explanation: 'My latest poem, written in Lyme Regis after a sleepless night. Let me know what you think, especially if you're the person who inspired it!' Rick followed the link, wondering idly where James had got his inspiration. And then it hit him, like a runaway train …

Up came a stark white page with a few lines of heavy black Gothic script framed in red roses. How convenient, how clinical – romance at the click of a sodding mouse; flowers you could neither touch nor smell.

In contrast, he'd once made a considerable investment in a grand romantic gesture of his own – with Anna. He'd been a lovesick fool, borrowing the sailing club's forty-four-foot Jeanneau Sun Magic and preparing the skipper's cabin as if it was his bloody wedding night: scented candles, champagne, and the petals of six dozen red roses strewn across the bed. He'd been on tenterhooks in case Stefan, the boat's owner, paid a surprise visit and took the piss. But at the time, he had to admit, it had been worth all the hassle. He could still remember the look on her face when he'd opened the cabin door ...

And now he suspected that James had fallen under her spell, poor sod.

He forced himself to read the almost indecipherable Gothic script – not once but twice, just to make sure of the sentiments behind the words:

Too much emotion,
You said about poetry,
Without any moving on.
I could move on, I thought,
To your dove-grey eyes.
I could move on
To your soft red lips.
Oh yes, I could make a
Move on you.

Rick felt his throat constrict – and it was nothing to do with James's crap poetry. He shut down the laptop and sat staring at the blank screen. At last he roused himself, and checked his watch; Dave would be knocking on the door at any moment.

Time for him to move on, too.

Chapter Twenty-Six

Rick phoned Guy from the car on the way to Dorchester and went straight on the offensive. 'I've got a little bet with myself – the only reason I'm doing this signing is because you owe someone a favour. Am I right?'

'You're not wrong,' came the guarded reply. 'Is there a problem?'

'Not yet. But there will be if hardly anyone turns up.'

'If you recall the events brief you gave me months ago,' Guy said dryly, 'you said you didn't want too many big venues. Something like "I get enough of that on the conference circuit in my day job." That's why I've gone for some small ones, like Dorchester – and Bath, where the bookshop only holds about thirty people. As long as the media are interested, it'll all be worthwhile. So chill out, and be nice to the journalists, won't you?'

It was the reality check Rick needed; he felt some of the tension ease from his neck and shoulders. 'Sorry,' he said. 'I didn't mean to take my bad mood out on you. How about a drink on me when we next meet up?'

And, in the end, his fears about the Dorchester event proved unfounded. Judging by the way they streamed through the doors of Brett's Books, the locals had an avid – and genuine – interest in *Sex in the Sea*. He enjoyed four hours of stimulating conversation and even made a couple of good academic contacts at the University of Southampton.

At quarter-past four, as Dave was driving him back to Lyme Regis, he rang Lou. 'Hi, where are you?'

'Rick!' An ear-splitting squeal. 'We're just leaving the hotel, Ben's organised a walk along the Cobb. Then it's off to the pub, although I've told everyone that you and I are going somewhere else for dinner.' Her voice dropped to a caressing murmur. 'On second thoughts, scrap all that. I'll stay here and wait for you instead – your room or mine?'

It was an echo of their earlier conversation, and he admired her determination. But he also felt slightly insulted – how could he convince her that he wasn't desperate to go to bed on their first date? He said firmly, 'No, I'll meet you at the Cobb – I could do with stretching my legs and I need a word with Ben.' Then, in a gentler tone, 'Let's give the pub a miss, though. We'll get changed back at the hotel and find a nice little restaurant.'

An evening away from the others would do him good. That way he could focus on getting to know Lou without any distractions whatsoever.

In the reception area of the Cobb View Hotel, Lou pocketed her mobile and did a celebratory twirl in front of Anna and Henrietta.

'I'm meeting Rick at the Cobb,' she said breathlessly, 'then we're coming back here. Oh-God-oh-God-oh-God, I can't wait!' She narrowed her eyes at Henrietta. 'There's more than dinner on the agenda, so don't make a fuss if I'm back late – or not at all.'

Anna looked down at the floor. After spending the afternoon with the Musgroves in various cafés and shops, she knew more than she ever wanted to about Lou's plans for the weekend. The fact that Rick had booked a room for the two sisters to share didn't bother Lou in the slightest. She merely assumed that it was a smokescreen, in case the media were tracking his private life. These 'failure is not an option' tactics were typical of Lou, although Anna secretly believed that they'd never work with Rick.

In the last few minutes, however, reality had hit home.

Rick's phone call to Lou, his obvious agreement to her plans, proved that he was up for whatever was on offer. And this was a thousand times worse than dealing with the idea of him and his Australian girlfriend, because ...

Because for years Anna had cherished the fantasy that she and Rick had shared something special on the boat. Not just physical intimacy, but a meeting of hearts and minds. Sex enriched by love of the deepest, truest kind – an experience that she knew she could never recapture with anyone else. Now, right in front of her, Rick would be swinging into action with another woman. She'd had a foretaste on the walk at Uppercross, when he and Lou had kissed, but that was nothing compared with facing them across the breakfast table and *knowing* ...

Tears scratched at the back of her eyes; she felt like a little girl who'd just heard that Santa Claus didn't exist. Why did the past have to lose some of its magic?

A nudge from Henrietta. 'Hey, do you know that man over there? He's been staring at us for the last five minutes. Nice-looking, except he reminds me of your father – creepy, or what?'

Anna knew who it would be before she even turned her head. Yes, lounging at the desk was William Elliot-Dunne, in an expensive-looking raincoat of palest grey. As their eyes met, he winked – and she blushed.

Fortunately no one else noticed, because at that moment Mona and Charles arrived; by the time they set off, William Elliot-Dunne had disappeared. As they passed the desk, however, Mr Pargeter called out, 'Miss Elliot! So sorry to trouble you, I meant to check with Sir William before he went out. Is it to be a table in the dining room tonight, or would you prefer a more private dinner in the presidential suite?'

Anna felt her face flame. 'There's been a misunderstanding,' she said, quickly. 'I'm not having dinner with him tonight or any other night.'

'Oh dear.' Mr Pargeter drooped visibly. 'Sir William *will* be disappointed and–'

'Who the hell is Sir William?' Charles put in, glancing at Anna.

Mr Pargeter drew himself up to his full height and announced grandly, 'Sir William Elliot-Dunne, 9th Baronet of Kellynch.'

The reaction of his audience was probably not what he'd expected. 'Isn't that the jerk who messed with your sister?' Charles said, while Mona yelled 'How *dare* he use our title!' Instantly, through the half-glazed front door they saw a long, sleek, silver-grey car surge out of its parking space and zoom towards the exit. Mona pushed forward, craned her neck to watch it – then turned to the others, a rapt expression on her face.

'Nice-looking, isn't he?' Henrietta began. 'But–'

Mona gave her a withering look. 'I didn't notice, I was too busy looking at his Bentley – he's obviously not done too badly out of his affair with the Texan divorcee. But, since he's the heir to our title, we need to find out why he's back and what he's up to. And it sounds as though *you*,' she rounded on Anna, 'are the one he wants to talk to, for some incomprehensible reason. So be nice to him until he tells you everything we need to know.' She added, with a smirk, '*Noblesse oblige*, darling, *noblesse oblige*.'

Chapter Twenty-Seven

A thin drizzle was falling as Rick strode out towards the Cobb. In the fading light he recognised Lou and Henrietta deep in conversation on the top level, and Ben walking jauntily along the lower path with Cassie bobbing on his shoulders. Rick had already passed Charles and Mona looking for shelter; Mona was holding Charles's coat over her hair and complaining, as usual, while Charles looked thoroughly wet and miserable.

Lou hadn't seen him; so he hurried after Ben and Cassie and caught up with them about fifty yards from the far end of the Cobb. After a brief discussion about the event in Dorchester and the timings for tomorrow's signing in Bournemouth, Rick got to the point.

'I wanted a quick chat about James.' He paused, glanced at Cassie and chose his words carefully. 'Judging by what he's put on his website today, he's starting to get over Julie – but I'm worried that he's jumping from the frying pan into the fire.'

Cassie turned large solemn eyes on him, obviously taking his meaning literally.

Ben grinned. 'In that case, look up ahead and you'll see a raging inferno.'

Rick jerked round. At the end of the Cobb he could make out two people standing next to a bench: Anna, unmistakable even in the misty rain, gazing out to sea; and James, pointing at something on the horizon and casually resting his other arm across her shoulders.

'She seems a lovely girl, so why worry?' Ben went on. 'Or are you after her yourself?'

Rick forced a laugh. 'God no, she's not my type. But I suggest you keep an eye on James tonight – you don't want him to get hurt all over again.'

They turned back towards the harbour. Rick hunched further into his coat and made small talk to distract his mind from the end of the Cobb. At the first set of steps – a safer alternative to the worn stumps of Granny's Teeth – he stopped and let Ben and Cassie continue without him. Waited until Lou, still talking animatedly to Henrietta, came nearer. Called her name and heard her shriek in delight.

She clattered down the steps and, with three to go, skidded to a halt.

'Catch me,' she said, giggling.

No time for a reply – she simply jumped. His arms shot out to take her weight – pure reflex – and the slam of her body almost knocked the breath out of him. But he kept his balance, and his sense of humour. 'Trying to get me hospitalised?'

'You bet,' she said, moulding herself to him. 'At least that way you'd be stuck in a horizontal position for a while. In the meantime, try and imagine we're standing in a ditch at Uppercross.'

A not-so-subtle hint that she wanted a kiss. Her persistence irritated him and – pure reflex again – he stepped back out of range. Made the mistake of looking along the Cobb, to its furthest point. Found himself short of breath, and this time it was nothing to do with Lou ...

Because, as the two figures turned and walked towards him, he saw the smaller one slip on the wet ground. Instinctively, he put out his hand; but he was too far away, and it was James's hand that stopped her from falling–

It should have been his.

A long way off, it seemed, someone shouted, 'Rick, catch me!'

Lou, on the top step now – too high. Even if he got there in time, her weight would knock them both flying. How could she be so stupid – so bloody *stupid*!

A stranger's voice – it might have been his own – roaring 'No, Lou!' just as she launched herself towards him. A two-second eternity, her legs twisting under her and her hands scratching the air.

He made a desperate lunge to reach her.

Too late.

The sickening crack of her head hitting the hard, hard stone.

And deathly silence, save for the mocking cry of the gulls.

Chapter Twenty-Eight

He shut his eyes. That's right, blank it all out – as if it's a dream. No, a nightmare.

Any minute now, he'd wake up. Back home, in his own bed, with the surf rumbling on the beach and the sunlight slicing through the blinds.

But wasn't that *her* voice, so close that he could reach out and touch her? Oh yes, definitely a dream – or a nightmare.

His eyes opened.

It wasn't a dream. Lou was still lying there, sprawled in a heap, facing away from him. No wonder! he thought, as he crouched beside her. No wonder she couldn't bear to look at him – the great useless lump who'd let her fall.

And that *was* Anna's voice. She was kneeling on the other side of Lou and saying, 'Open your eyes, Lou. It's Anna, can you hear me?' Over and over again she said it, and quite loud. But then she had to be loud to make herself heard above that God-awful din on top of the Cobb – a woman, sobbing hysterically. That would be Henrietta; huh, maybe he could make himself useful there, at least, and offer her a shoulder to sodding well cry on.

Then Anna stopped talking to Lou and called out 'James!'; and, for the first time, Rick noticed James standing a little distance away, his face frozen in horror. When he heard his name, however, he twitched into life and shuffled forward. 'Yes?'

Anna looked up at him and said firmly, 'Ring 999 for an ambulance. Tell them she fell from a height of around six feet, landed on stone. Then take Henrietta and catch up with Ben, get him to bring Charles. *Quickly*, James.'

'Yes – yes, of course. 999, then Henrietta, then Ben.'
In a series of surprisingly coordinated movements, James produced a mobile, stabbed at it a few times with his finger and started talking; at the same time, he carefully skirted round Lou and climbed up the steps. His air of authority must have impressed Henrietta, because the sobbing stopped and Rick heard their footsteps hurrying away.

So much for making himself useful. It was James who'd turned into Action Man, while he …

He felt Anna's eyes on him. Instantly, he gazed into their clear grey depths, drawing on her strength even as he questioned his own.

'Come on, Rick,' she said, gently. 'You know what to do.'

But he didn't. His mind was a cotton-wool cloud, blotting out all coherent thought.

She bit her lip; and he realised that she was probably as agitated as he was, but much more in control of herself. 'Your first-aid training – you used it in La Baule, remember? And you must have used it since.' She paused to give him time to respond, but he still couldn't speak. She went on, her voice soft and soothing, 'Talk me through what you're going to do until the ambulance gets here.' Another pause; then, like the flick of a switch, her tone changed. 'Come *on*, Rick. It could make all the difference!' He'd never heard her so – so *commanding*.

And she was right; every action, every second counted.

He took a long, deep breath, looked down at Lou, forced the words out between dry, stiff lips. 'I'm assessing the casualty … Unconscious,' he watched for the rise and fall of her rib cage, 'but breathing.' He placed his fingertips lightly against the clammy skin of her neck. 'Pulse good.' He swallowed. 'I'd normally tilt her head back to keep her airway open, but she may have injured her spine so I daren't move her neck.' He glanced across at Anna and heard his voice falter. 'I-I don't think there's anything else I can do.'

Her eyes held no reproach, only encouragement. 'That's OK, at least you've been through the process. What about covering her with your coat, keeping her warm?'

'Yes, I should have thought of that.'

He got clumsily to his feet, tore off his coat, knelt down again. As Anna took one side of the coat and helped him spread it over Lou's inert body, he watched her hands, with their small, calm movements. And he remembered their butterfly touch on his temples when he'd wanted to unwind after a long day at the sailing club ... For God's sake, this was hardly the place for indulging in happy memories; he had to focus on Lou, not his own badly timed needs.

Anna looked back towards the harbour. 'Not long now, I can hear the siren.' She turned, reached across and rested her small, calm hand briefly on his shoulder. 'You did all you could. Remember that.'

Chapter Twenty-Nine

Only later, in the back of Charles's car as they followed the ambulance, did Anna have time to think over what had happened. The paramedics had made it all look so simple – assessing the situation and strapping Lou to a spinal board in a matter of minutes. She knew, however, that it was anything but simple; the longer Lou was unconscious, the more serious her injuries were likely to be.

Before Lou's fall, Anna had been too distracted by James to pay much attention to anyone else. Once she realised he was making a pass at her, it was a case of wondering how to fend him off without hurting his feelings.

And then she'd heard Lou's first shout of excitement – seen her in Rick's arms – lost her concentration – and slipped. It was as if reality had slapped her in the face again and, in childish retaliation, she'd given James a chance to act the hero.

But she'd heard Lou shout again, then Rick; and, although she couldn't make out his words, she felt his despair.

What had been going on?

Charles had asked Rick that very question as soon as he arrived, just after the paramedics. Rick, his eyes fixed on Lou's face, had whispered, 'I let her down, big time.' Which made no sense to anyone, unless it was a joke in very bad taste.

Now they were following the ambulance to the Accident & Emergency department at Dorchester; Charles, Mona, Henrietta and Anna in one car, Rick and his driver in the other. James and Ben had stayed in Lyme, on the condition that the others would contact them if there was anything they could do.

Mona broke the silence. 'You should ring your parents as soon as we get to the hospital, Charles. I heard the paramedics discussing her and it didn't sound good. Something about giving her oxygen and the A&E trauma team standing by.'

In the back of the car, Henrietta let out a long, shuddering breath; Anna reached across and held her hand.

'Thanks for reminding me,' Charles said heavily, 'but I'll wait until A&E have seen her and we know what's happening.'

'Really? I'd have thought it'll take days, if not weeks, to find out how permanent the brain damage is.' Mona glanced round as Henrietta started to cry. 'Sorry, but we have to be realistic, she could end up a complete vegetable. Better to tell your parents sooner rather than later – don't you agree, Henrietta? You should–'

Charles cut in savagely with, 'I don't think Henrietta's in a fit state to answer that question and *I* want to wait until Lou's been seen in A&E.'

'I'm only trying to be helpful,' Mona said huffily. 'As usual, you're picking a fight over nothing – just when we need to put on a united front.' She took a brush from her handbag and flicked it through her hair. 'The press will turn up, you know, to interview Rick. It'll make quite a story – "Celebrity author's new girlfriend in mysterious fall".' She put the brush away and mused, 'He should get the sympathy vote, unless it turns out he pushed her.'

Anna gasped. 'He didn't push her! How could he – when he was standing below her?'

Charles eyed her in the rear-view mirror. 'So you saw what happened?'

'N-no, not really. But I know he couldn't have pushed her.' She gave Henrietta's hand a little squeeze. She'd been close by, she must have seen or heard something; but she obviously wasn't ready to talk about it.

Mona shrugged. 'Either way, it'll do his book sales no harm. Maybe it was a publicity-seeking stunt that went horribly wrong. You know – Lou staging a fall so that Rick could play the hero and have even more women drooling over him.'

'For God's sake, shut up!' Driving too close, Charles had to brake sharply as the ambulance slowed to turn in at the hospital gates. He swung the car after it and swerved into the first empty parking space he saw.

Mona seemed oblivious to his tension. 'Crap parking, aren't you bothering to straighten up?' she said, as he switched off the engine.

Anna took one look at Charles's clenched fists on the steering wheel and said hurriedly, 'Mona, why don't we take Henrietta to the Ladies? Charles, we'll come and find you later.'

As they got out of the car, she glanced at her watch.

Only six o'clock. It felt like the middle of the night.

Chapter Thirty

Rick found Charles in the A&E waiting area, slumped on one of the dark grey plastic seats. He sat down awkwardly next to him and took a deep breath. 'Any news?'

Charles shook his head. 'Not really. They've taken her for a CT scan and they're monitoring her regularly – the Glasgow Coma Scale or something. Whatever the outcome, they'll have to keep her here until tomorrow. It's too late to transfer her to the specialist unit in Southampton today – apparently the helicopter doesn't fly at night.'

Rick stared at the walls, which were decorated with randomly placed coloured glass panels in vivid cobalt. They reminded him of the sea ... How he wished he could envelop his whole being in its blue warmth right now, go on a long swim to stretch his cramped muscles and numb his restless mind.

And how he wished he could rewind the last couple of hours and change them completely.

'Is there anything you want me to do?' he said quietly, half-expecting Charles to retort, 'Haven't you done enough already?'

But Charles didn't; for the first time since Lou's fall, he looked Rick straight in the eye and said, 'Help me think things through. I don't see much point in us all spending the next God knows how many hours here. I want to stay, and I think one of the others should too. Ideally Henrietta, she's closest to Lou, but I don't think she's up to it. And then at some point someone's got to tell my parents. Mona thinks I should ring them now – but I can't face that. And what would I say? It's likely she's brain damaged, but we don't know how bad it is yet.'

Rick looked down at the floor again. Brain damage covered a whole continuum, from minor behavioural changes to permanent and total disability. And it was all his fault …

A deep breath. 'I'm so sorry this happened, Charles, and I-I must take most – all of the responsibility.' He lifted his head and met Charles's weary gaze. 'For what it's worth, I want to give Lou – give all of you – any support I can. I've got a car, and a driver – why don't I take Henrietta home and tell your parents?'

Charles's eyes seemed to lose a little of their haunted look. 'That would be one weight off my mind. But then – who stays here with me, Mona or Anna?'

A week ago, when he'd believed that Anna was having an affair with Charles, he would have almost choked on the thought of leaving them here together. But now he heard himself say loudly and clearly, as if announcing it to the whole world, 'I think Anna should stay. Lou told me she would trust Anna with her life.'

Light footsteps behind him. He turned to see who it was – and his eyes locked with Anna's.

Anna went over to the drinks machine and selected a bottle of water. In less tragic circumstances, she would have treasured Rick's words. They marked an about-turn from his earlier suspicions, a bridge half-built between them, a bitter-sweet peace offering by an old love.

It was just … well, she felt they were said purely to secure the best possible outcome for Lou. And yet, who could blame him for that?

She turned to the two men. 'I can certainly stay for the next day or so,' she said evenly. 'Then I've got lectures on Monday, from eleven onwards – but I could rearrange some things in the second half of the week.'

Charles gave her a tremulous smile. 'I'll probably have Mum or Dad with me by that time. But it'll be great to have you around tonight and tomorrow, in case Lou wakes up or,' a telling pause, 'in case she doesn't.' He added, with a ragged sigh, 'She's fallen off her fair share of horses over the years, but she was always wearing a hard hat.'

Rick stood up. 'Here are Mona and Henrietta. We might as well tell them the plan, then the three of us can get going.'

Anna glanced round and saw the others approaching. She'd left them in the Ladies, where Mona had obviously been retouching her make-up and restyling her hair; Henrietta, on the other hand, looked a total wreck.

Mona's eyes widened as she saw their serious faces. 'Bad news?'

'No news,' Charles said dully. 'But Rick's offered to take you and Henrietta home and tell Mum and Dad in person. He thinks Anna's the best person to stay here.'

Mona scowled. '*Anna*? How come? She's not even family, and Lou's never thought of her as a particular friend. Anyway, she wouldn't have a clue how to handle the press – whereas, with the sort of circles I move in, it's second nature to me.' She flashed Rick a brilliant smile. 'I agree Henrietta shouldn't stay – she's emotionally unstable – but *I'm* not leaving my husband's side. I supported him through a traumatic time in A&E last Saturday, and I'll do exactly the same this weekend.'

Rick's expression was impossible to read. 'Let's hope it doesn't become a regular weekly event.' He swung round to Charles. 'Is it OK with you if I take Anna home instead?'

Charles covered his face with his hands and mumbled, 'Whatever.'

Rick turned to Anna. 'And is it OK with you?'

She looked down at the floor, her heart still racing from his words 'take Anna home' and all that they'd once conveyed, in the pine-tree scent of a French garden. Everything was different now; but, even so, she found herself filled with a strange anticipation ... Would he drop Henrietta off first? If he did, they'd have over an hour in the car together; not quite alone, although she imagined his driver would have been selected for his discretion. Would they pass the time with a strained question-and-answer session; or would they talk as naturally as they had in the old days? Except – and here anticipation turned to dread – he might want to confide in her about his feelings for Lou ...

Oh shit, what the hell did that matter when Lou was lying there seriously injured?

So she merely said, 'Of course,' kissed Mona on the cheek, gave Charles a reassuring hug and slipped her arm through Henrietta's.

Then she looked over at Rick. 'Ready when you are.'

Chapter Thirty-One

Sir Walter Elliot lay face down on the crisp white linen sheet and abandoned himself once again to old and not entirely forgotten sensations.

Ah, the exquisite pleasure of a woman's touch! Irina had massaged his shoulders whenever he demanded, but she usually took advantage of the situation to ask him awkward questions about their finances; hardly conducive to relaxation. Whereas Cleo's only agenda seemed to be his well-being, in mind as well as body.

Of course, the massages had been going on for some weeks now; almost from the beginning Cleo had used ylang-ylang oil, which she described as a stimulant. And in her strong, warm, capable hands, it certainly was. Naturally, only he was aware of its effects, since he remained face down and partly clothed throughout. Since they'd arrived in Bath, however, Cleo had proposed a change to this routine in the form of a bath massage. At first, after a witty little aside about having baths in Bath, Walter could see nothing but drawbacks in exposing himself – literally – to this new experience. But gradually, as her hands worked their miracles on his back, her words worked with equal skill on his mind. And soon he became obsessed with that higher level of youthfulness which Cleo promised a bath massage would bring – something to do with her working on his sacral chakra, whatever that was.

At this point, perversely, Cleo postponed the longed-for moment. When he asked her why, she simply said in that mysterious way of hers – so utterly *French* – 'Ah, Sir Voltaire, for everyzing zere is ze right time and ze right place.'

Hearing her address him as 'Sir Voltaire' always gave him an agreeable little frisson. He recalled vaguely that there were one or two books in his library by someone called Voltaire; obviously an intellectual heavyweight since Irina used to quote him frequently. What was her favourite saying again? 'Love is a canvas furnished by Nature and embroidered by imagination.' He'd never quite understood that one.

But then Irina had been a highly educated woman. Initially, that had been part of her appeal; as the years passed, however, he'd found it more and more intimidating – he never knew what she was going to come out with next. He was sure it was one of her casual little remarks, another quotation no doubt, that had caused the rift with Dottie Dalrymple. Something about prejudice being opinion without judgement, which he feared dear Dottie had taken personally.

Cleo, on the other hand, had the uncanny gift of articulating his innermost thoughts! What had she said the other day? 'You weel 'ave ze pick of ze ladies, zey weel all be fighting over you. Such an 'andsome man wiz a title and in eez prime – irresistible!'

It was true that he attracted attention wherever he went in Bath. Modesty – and that slightly-less-than-perfect eyesight – prevented him from knowing the details, but he had no doubt that he was on the receiving end of many admiring glances. Hardly surprising when he looked around – for such a fine city, the place had a real shortage of elegant men. Yes, he must appear to the women of Bath like an oasis shimmering in the desert.

And it was especially gratifying to find that he was attracting the attention of one of them in particular – old Dottie Dalrymple herself. It had been a touching reconciliation, even if she'd initially mistaken him for someone else. And it was already bearing fruit: she'd invited them all – including Anna – for drinks one night next week, in her suite. Just a few steps along the garden path, but a giant leap in terms of his rehabilitation with her.

So, all things considered, life here was divine. He felt like a god, worshipped for simply being himself – Sir Walter Elliot, 8th Baronet of Kellynch. And gods could make anything happen, couldn't they? They could even father sons with mere mortals ... although he still preferred to think of such possibilities as more of a concept than a reality. Reality could be horribly disappointing.

As if reading his mind yet again, Cleo paused in the middle of her long rhythmic strokes down his back and said softly, 'Eet weel be soon, ze bath massage, I zink. And of course eet weel be ze bath for me, too.'

Walter's heart gave an alarming little flutter; but whether this was from an understandable interest in seeing Cleo without her white coat or the prospect of coming face to face with reality, he had no idea. 'What do you mean?' he croaked.

'I weel join you in ze bath, *au naturel*. 'Ow else can I attend to ze sacral chakra?'

'But what about Lisa? She might wonder–'

'I will book 'er a full afternoon of treatments – I do not zink she weel spare us a zought.'

'Oh, I see.' Walter stirred uneasily. 'It's just – well, I'm still not sure that a man in my position–'

'*Au contraire, cher* Sir Voltaire,' she purred, resuming that delicious stroking, 'eet eez as you yourself 'ave said – *noblesse oblige.*'

Chapter Thirty-Two

On the journey back to Lyme Regis, conversation in the Jaguar was minimal until they arrived at the Cobb View Hotel. Then there were practicalities to discuss: Rick decided to wait in the car with Dave while Anna and Henrietta went to pack and check out. He took the opportunity to phone Guy and tell him to cancel the next day's event at Bournemouth. When Guy asked why, he gave the reason as 'personal' and refused to elaborate.

Half-an-hour later, Anna and Henrietta returned and they set off again. Henrietta seemed a little better; at any rate, she started talking to Anna in the back of the car and even reminded Dave of the best route to Uppercross, despite the satnav's confident directions.

Then, out of the blue, she said earnestly, 'Rick, please don't blame yourself. I've been going over and over it all in my mind and, believe me, you couldn't have prevented what happened. When Lou's determined to do something, you can't reason with her – she just does it.'

Rick felt the blood drain from his face. Now the chain of cause and effect was crystal clear. He hadn't just let Lou fall, he'd driven her to jump in the first place. On the walk at Uppercross, leaving aside those ill-advised kisses, hadn't he praised her for being resistant to pressure, compared her to a nut? Oh, she was a nut all right. And so was he …

'Rick?' Henrietta prompted, obviously expecting some response. 'Are you OK?'

Such a stupid, *stupid* question that it didn't deserve to be answered.

'Leave it, Henrietta, maybe he can't talk about it just yet.'

This from Anna, slipping easily into the role of peacemaker.

Except she hadn't preserved the peace very well that time between him and her up-his-own-arse father, had she? She'd added just enough fuel to the fire to send it exploding out of control.

Didn't she realise that this whole sodding mess was her fault, too?

Anna wasn't sure exactly what was eating away at Rick: guilt, frustration, genuine feelings for Lou – or a potent combination of all three.

And now they were pulling up outside the Great House. Should she offer to break the news to Barbara and Roger, or give him a chance to recover some of his self-esteem, as she'd done on the Cobb?

Before she could say anything, however, he was out of the car and marching up to the front door. Inside the house the dogs erupted into noisy barking, then subsided to low growls at Roger's reprimand. Lights came on and Barbara appeared; Henrietta burst into tears and rushed from the car into her mother's arms.

By the time Anna followed with Henrietta's case, they were all in the kitchen – even a wide-awake Ollie in his Spiderman pyjamas.

'And I hold myself responsible,' Rick was saying quietly. 'If I'd been paying attention, it wouldn't have happened. As it is–'

'I've told him it's not his fault!' Henrietta wailed, looking up from Barbara's shoulder. 'Mum, you know what she's like–'

'Shhh, that's enough.' Barbara stroked Henrietta's hair and gave Rick a wan smile. 'You're a lovely, lovely man, standing by her like this. She must mean an awful lot to you.'

Rick flushed and said nothing.

Roger said shakily, 'You say you've heard nothing more from Charles? I'll give him a ring, see what's what, then I'll go straight down to Dorchester.' He glanced at Anna. 'Do you want a drink, my dear, or something to eat?'

She hesitated and looked across at Rick, but he was staring at the floor. She suspected that he was anxious to be back at the hospital, so she said, 'No thank you, we'd better get on our way. You'll let me know as soon as you hear anything, won't you?'

Barbara and Roger quietly assured her that they would. She gave them and Henrietta a hug, then knelt in front of Ollie. 'Mummy and Daddy want you to be specially good while they're away. Do you think you can do that?'

He nodded brightly, clasped his arms fiercely round her neck and whispered, 'Isn't that the shark wrestler? Will he tell me about his adventures?'

She whispered back, 'He's not feeling like talking just now, maybe next time.'

A kiss on the little boy's warm downy cheek, then she was out of the kitchen and walking quickly to the car, tears pricking her eyes. She couldn't remember when she'd last seen the Musgroves so subdued. She was vaguely aware of Rick only a few steps behind her, but she didn't turn round. As before, she got into the back of the car and he got into the front.

They'd hardly pulled away from the house when he said bleakly, 'God, that was awful.'

She waited, in case the comment was addressed to Dave, not her; after all, since he'd arrived in England Rick must have spent more time with him than with anyone. But Dave was too busy adjusting something on the dashboard, so it was up to her to give reassurance.

'It could have been worse,' she said slowly. 'At least they

want you to be involved. Some parents would have–' She stopped, realising too late just where her good intentions were leading her.

'Told me to stay away, because I wasn't fit for their daughter to wipe her feet on?' His voice was dangerously soft.

After that, she made no further attempt at conversation, except to give Dave her postcode for the satnav.

Chapter Thirty-Three

Saturday night in Bath, and the road into the city was buzzing. They headed for the centre, a labyrinth of lights and one-way systems. As soon as they turned into a street of tall terraced houses, Anna said, 'There won't be anywhere to park, so you can just drop me here.'

An unfortunate choice of words – maybe in retaliation for his earlier dig at her father? But Rick thought not; she'd never been one for scoring points.

He weighed up his options: do as she suggested and drive straight back to Dorchester? Or see her to her front door, make sure she was all right, then stretch his legs? That way, he could give Dave a decent break – time to find a parking space and get himself something to eat.

As the car came to a halt in the middle of the street, Rick made up his mind. He jumped out, retrieved Anna's small case from the boot and tapped on Dave's window. In an instant, it was all arranged: Dave would take a break – he reckoned half-an-hour would do it – then phone Rick and find out where to pick him up.

Anna looked as though she might object; but after a few seconds she got out of the car, thanked Dave for the lift and set off along the street. Rick followed in silence, debating whether he'd done the right thing. At the far end she stopped and held out her hand for the case. Instead of passing it to her and walking off, he heard himself say, 'I'll bring it inside for you.' She hesitated, then withdrew her hand, rummaged in her bag and produced a key.

While she unlocked the front door, he studied the house where she lived. In the patchy outside lighting, it seemed well cared for; and adapted for wheelchair access, judging by the ramp and grab rail. His next impressions were of a good-sized hall, its plain walls relieved by stained-glass pictures; the tangy aroma of dinner cooking; a snatch of canned laughter from a distant TV. A ten-second trailer for other people's lives.

Anna led him up several flights of stairs to the top floor. On the tiny landing, they stood close together while she unlocked another door. Then, without any discussion – as if by mutual consent – he entered her private space.

As she flicked on the light, shrugged off her coat and moved away, he stopped and looked around. He was in a square living room, all cream and white and saved from being clinical by touches of vibrant colour – sofa and curtains of deep earthy terracotta, beaded cushions of sparkling sea green, a rug in a chaotic but pleasing pattern of burnt orange and turquoise, a big bold painting and a couple of small watercolours. Three – no, four doors opened off it: kitchen, bathroom, bedroom, he guessed, and – where she was hanging her coat – a full-length cupboard.

He put down the case, struggling with the realisation that this flat reflected the woman who lived there: small, and neat, and perfectly self-contained. Yet once, for almost three whole days, they'd revelled in their need for each other – and hers had been just as urgent as his. Need? What a short, understated word for something so amazing, so all-consuming. Never – before or since – had he touched those heights, that beautiful sense of belonging, that place – emotional and spiritual, as well as physical – where he could simply *be* with a woman.

He let out a long, steadying breath. 'Where do you want your case?'

She came out of the first door on the right – the kitchen, judging by the glimpse of rustic tiles – and replied, 'In the bedroom – here, I'll take it.'

Just as she reached down for the handle, he did the same. For one brief, electric moment their fingers touched, and he felt his heart start to pound. No, this was insane. With Lou's future in the balance, the last thing he should be doing was stirring up the past.

He grabbed the case first and pulled it away.

'Where's the bedroom?' Not that he needed to ask – there were just two doors left to choose from – but it seemed only polite. And that was how he had to be with this woman – polite and distant.

She gave him an odd look. 'Door at the end. Do you want a coffee?'

'OK.' That would keep her occupied for a few minutes.

He opened the furthest door as wide as possible to let in the light from the living room and did a quick stock take. Double bed, fitted wardrobes, laundry basket; under the window, a desk with a laptop and a comfortable-looking armchair. He couldn't imagine having a computer in his bedroom – too much a reminder of work when he wanted to focus on sex or sleep; but, from what Lou had said, Anna had one less competing priority. There was certainly no evidence here of a man's presence – occasional or permanent. No clothes or toiletries or magazines – nothing obvious, anyway.

Another steadying breath. Now that this strange urge to see her bedroom was satisfied, what next? Bathroom inspection? Kitchen survey? Or a cosy post-mortem of their previous relationship over coffee?

He put the case down and made to leave, then caught sight of a book lying on the desk. Recalled Lou's comment about Anna preferring her men to stay between the covers of a nineteenth-century Russian novel. Listened for sounds from the kitchen – and, reassured, stole across the floor.

On the book's cover a single word in large Cyrillic letters, presumably the title, jumped out at him: Идиот. He fixed it in his memory for further investigation; it would be interesting to know which hero she was fantasising about at this precise moment.

But right now he'd better get out of this room before she wondered what he was doing.

When Anna came out of the kitchen, Rick was pacing the living-room floor.

She handed him the mug of coffee, on edge in case their fingers touched again; he made sure they didn't. 'Black, no sugar – is that still how you take it?'

'Yes. Thanks.'

'What about something to eat?'

'No thanks.'

He stopped his pacing, but didn't sit down; just stared silently at the floor. She wondered why he'd come in if he had nothing to say. Maybe he wanted her to tell him that everything would be all right? But she couldn't do that; she wasn't one for empty promises, whatever he might think.

So she sank on to the sofa and made conversation, while he drank his coffee. Talked about her work and her students, dwelling on the highs rather than the lows. About her friends and her social life, which sounded more exciting than it actually was. About Bath and its many attractions, as if she was after a job at the bloody Tourist Information Office.

At last he put down his mug. 'Thanks.'

If he said 'thanks' one more time, she'd scream. 'Henrietta's right, you know. You mustn't blame yourself for what happened – Lou's very single-minded.' There – she'd got that off her chest.

'I know. But the fact remains that if ...' he paused, and cleared his throat, 'if I'd behaved differently, she wouldn't be in hospital now.'

He looked so forlorn that she didn't stop to think, just jumped up and slipped her arms around him. Not inside his coat – safely on top, so that she couldn't feel the warmth of his skin through his shirt. And he didn't flinch; he simply sighed, and she felt his body relax against her. It seemed perfectly natural to press her cheek to his chest – where, even through the thickness of his coat, his heart drummed in her ear.

Except, once upon a time, it would also have been perfectly natural for him to put his arms round her. And he didn't.

After a moment she stepped back, turning away so that he wouldn't see her embarrassment. 'Sorry, I thought you needed a hug.'

Behind her, she heard him say, 'You have no idea what I need.'

It wasn't just the words, it was the harshness of his tone that made her gasp. The door clicked open and shut – she spun round, but it was too late. He was nothing but the muffled clatter of steps on the stairs, the distant slam of the front door – then silence, settling like a shroud.

He'd been here barely twenty minutes, but he'd destroyed ten years of self-preservation. She picked up the mug, still warm from his touch, and stumbled into the kitchen.

You have no idea what I need.

It was nothing personal, she told herself. He wasn't getting at her; he was exhausted, and worried sick about Lou.

But all the excuses in the world didn't stop the tears from falling.

He'd walked round the same circular road God knows how many times before Dave rang. And then, of course, he couldn't tell him where he was – he'd been in a blind fury when he left her flat. Because ... because he'd just realised how much he'd screwed everything up.

As soon as he mentioned a circle, Dave said, 'That'll be The Circus.' Very appropriate; he felt exactly like a caged animal.

By the time Dave picked him up, he didn't feel in the mood for small talk. So he avoided the passenger seat and got into the back of the car, at the side where she'd sat. Huh, it was as though he couldn't keep away from her; just why had he gone up to her flat, snooped round her bedroom, drunk her coffee?

But all that was as nothing compared to the moment when she'd held him close. He'd been a breath away from taking her in his arms and pouring it all out – every detail of his irresponsible behaviour towards Lou, the overwhelming sense of guilt and obligation, this bewildering need to be here, with her, in her little flat, away from the real world.

Thank God he hadn't. She'd hugged him because she was a caring person, simple as that. And she'd also made it clear that she was completely content with her life, a constant stream of lectures and tutorials and evenings out with her arty-farty friends – God, he felt like he'd been on a tour of every bookshop, bistro and theatre in Bath.

But, unexpectedly, something in her flat – that stark reflection of a life without him – had disturbed a distant memory. He closed his eyes and concentrated on what he'd seen. The bedroom? No, nothing familiar there. The living room, then? He visualised it – the sofa, the rug, the bookcase in the corner – maybe they shared the same tastes in reading, assuming she ever got beyond her security blanket of Russian literature? Above the bookcase, slightly to the left, there'd been that large abstract painting, oils on canvas. An oblong of cyan, split horizontally by a string of angular shapes in white and orange and brown, with splashes of red and yellow and green; and, across the bottom right-hand corner, a thin curving silver-grey line. As he stood drinking his coffee, listening intently to her words without appearing to, he'd focused on that painting, trying to make sense of it – and of so much else.

Now, in the car, the pieces slotted into place. The cyan was both sea and sky. With a bit of imagination, the string of shapes became a coastline of cliffs and sandy beaches and hotels and houses, ending in a small harbour and a white lighthouse with a distinctive green band. The curving grey line looked very like the handrail of a boat.

He could have left it there, as a nice little exercise in art appreciation.

Except that this was a view he'd actually seen.

And so he found himself sucked under by a riptide of emotions. He recalled the exhilaration of borrowing the Jeanneau and sailing south towards the Côte d'Amour. The first night, he'd dropped anchor opposite a resort called Pornichet. Oh, that first night he hadn't noticed the view at all ... But early the next morning he'd stood on the deck and gazed out at this very place, framed by a cyan sea and a cyan sky, each of its colours burnished by the sun, like the dawn of a new world.

Then he'd turned to the girl beside him, kissed her wonderingly on her soft red lips and said, 'Anna, I think I'm in heaven.'

Chapter Thirty-Four

The following Friday morning, Anna stood by the window in her room at the Department of Russian Studies, staring out at the scene below. Bronze leaves stuck to wet paths like a child's collage. Black umbrellas – lecturers and a few of the more organised students, from the look of it – scuttled beetle-like between buildings. Cars swished along the road, not a single black Jaguar among them. And even if there was, it wouldn't be the one she had in mind. *That* was no doubt parked outside Southampton General Hospital, where Lou had been taken last Sunday with a suspected skull fracture.

A knock at the door made her jump, even though she was expecting it.

'Only me.' Jenny came in, put two mugs of coffee on the desk, slumped on to the nearest chair and smothered a yawn. 'Am I glad this week's almost over! Arranging next year's placements in Russia is stressing me out – I don't want to see another student ever again.' A rueful smile. 'Well, not until Monday, the little darlings.'

'It's certainly been a long week.' Anna sat down at her desk and cradled one of the mugs in her hands. 'Thanks, this'll warm me up before I head off. My afternoon tutorial's cancelled so I thought I'd work from home, especially as Barbara said she might ring and I don't seem to have my mobile with me.'

Jenny gave her a sympathetic look. 'Any more news of Lou?'

'Nothing since Wednesday.'

'So they're still saying that the operation to drain the blood from her brain was a success?'

'Oh yes. It's amazing, she can walk – with help – and talk, although her mouth's droopy and her speech is slurred. They're giving her intensive physio and speech therapy.' A pause. 'Henrietta says she's not her normal self, too quiet, but it could have been so much worse.' Anna forced a brighter note into her voice. 'I told you that Charles and Mona were due to go home yesterday, didn't I? Now that Barbara's at the hospital, there didn't seem much point in them all staying. Anyway, Henrietta and Roger are too busy with the stables and the estate to look after the boys properly.'

'And Rick Wentworth's in Southampton too?'

'He visits whenever he can, apparently.'

'What about his book signings?'

'Henrietta said he nearly fell out with his publisher because he wanted to cancel them all.' When she'd heard this, Anna had wondered what to make of it; did it indicate the depth of his feelings for Lou, or simply his current state of mind? She added briskly, 'In the end, though, he only missed two.'

'So he's still coming to Bath next Friday evening?'

'I expect so.' Was that couldn't-care-less tone convincing?

'All this waiting must have been awful for him as well as the family.' Jenny sipped her coffee thoughtfully. 'And then he's had the press to contend with. One paper even implied he might have pushed Lou – where could they have got that idea?'

'I don't know,' Anna said, making a mental note to find out exactly who Mona had been talking to.

Jenny frowned. 'It's weird to think that her personality may have changed. I've read about that sort of thing, of course, but never actually known anyone affected by it.'

Anna shrugged. 'It's too early to tell if it's permanent. Perhaps being quiet is a natural part of the recovery process.'

'Well, all I can say is – if I had Rick Wentworth waiting

at my bedside, I'd do my damnedest to recover as quickly as possible.' Jenny's voice hardened. 'And how's your delightful father?'

'As delightful as ever.' Anna finished her coffee and started packing her briefcase. 'I've just been summoned to dinner tomorrow night at The Royal Crescent Hotel. He's got someone special coming.'

'You mean other than you?'

'Very funny. Anyway, I've said I'll go. After all, I've managed to avoid actually seeing him since he came to Bath – the phone calls have been bad enough.' A sigh as she recalled the one earlier in the week, when she'd turned down drinks with Lady Dalrymple. She'd explained that she'd already arranged a night out with Jenny and Tom and their crowd; that had made him splutter something about her needing to get her priorities right.

'And you've no idea who the "someone special" is? You could be in for an even worse evening than usual.'

'Probably.' Anna crammed another folder into the already bulging briefcase. Apart from dinner on Saturday night, she planned to spend the entire weekend working; far more productive than wondering what was happening in Southampton. 'It'll be Lady Dalrymple, he's been bleating on and on about her ever since he got here. They fell out years ago, but she's staying at the hotel – practically lives there – so they're back on speaking terms.'

Jenny stared. 'Lady What? Dalrymple? Never heard of her. Am I meant to be impressed?'

'Definitely. She's a viscountess – a dowager viscountess, of course, now that her husband's dead – so Walter's in ecstasies.'

'If you're not careful, he'll be living at that hotel too. Keeping up with the Dalrymples, whatever it costs.'

'Not if Minty can help it,' Anna said. 'I suppose I

should be grateful that she's always poking her nose in our affairs, whether we like it or not.' And, with thoughts of one particular example of her godmother's interference uppermost in her mind, she continued haltingly, 'I never told you about the only time Minty and I really fell out ... I was just eighteen and, until then, I didn't even think to question her – we'd always been so close, especially after Mummy died ... But I'd met this guy when I was staying at my cousin's in France, and things got serious, and he was going off to – somewhere, and he wanted me to go with him. Which meant shelving Oxford and all that Mummy had planned for me ... And, although that's a decision I'd never have made lightly, it was taken out of my hands when Walter and Minty turned up unexpectedly. Walter ranted on and on – which wouldn't have made the slightest difference – but then Minty weighed in ... By the time she'd finished, my whole perspective had changed. I'd been the victim of nothing more than a holiday romance – those were her exact words – and no *reasonable* man would expect me to give up my place at Oxford. And then the killer blow – what would my mother have thought?' She turned away and stared out of the rain-streaked window.

'What do you think now?' Jenny said softly. 'Did you do the right thing?'

Anna shrugged, still unable to speak. After a while, she felt firm hands on her shoulders and heard Jenny say, 'Sorry, I shouldn't have asked. I guess you don't want to talk about it?'

She shook her head miserably.

'But you know where I am if you ever want to.'

The clunk of the mugs as Jenny picked them up, the click of the door as she left the room – and Anna was alone with her thoughts once again.

Chapter Thirty-Five

It had been a long hard week and, Rick suspected, it was about to get worse.

He and Guy were having lunch in Brighton with Duncan Taylor, a freelance journalist. Apparently Guy owed him a favour and the payback involved Rick giving Duncan an exclusive interview. So here they were, going through the charade of a 'frank and revealing conversation'; but Rick had no intention of making it easy.

'What's *Sex in the Sea* about?' was Duncan's first question.

Rick scowled at him. 'Haven't you done your research and read it?'

'Of course, but the readers like it summed up in your own words.'

'Just use the blurb on the back of the book.'

Duncan paused, then changed tack. 'What are you writing next?'

'Nothing. I don't want to write this sort of stuff any more.'

The other man pounced. 'Why is that, do you think?' he said, stroking his unkempt beard. 'Scarred by the experience of becoming a coffee-table celebrity?'

Silence, while Rick carried on eating his lunch.

Guy put down his fork with an exasperated sigh. 'To answer your first question, Duncan, Rick would say that the book's a powerful statement about how far some creatures go in order to procreate, and a timely reminder of what we humans take for granted in that department. Rick's other key message is that life under the sea is precarious enough – but, when you add to this our generally irresponsible attitude to fishing and pollution, you have an ecological disaster waiting to happen. As for what he's writing next, sales of *Sex in the Sea* have been so fantastic that we're already in discussions about a sequel. It's called "Parents of the Deep" and it'll show the extraordinary ways in which some sea creatures rear their young. Put Rick on the cover again, this time holding a child's hand, and it'll sell like the proverbial hot cakes.'

Rick let this bullshit flow uninterrupted. He wasn't contracted for a second book and Guy was exaggerating when he said that they were in discussions. Right now, he wanted nothing more than to return to writing scientific papers and presenting them in the rarefied air of academic conferences – only if and when he felt like it. But he had to admit that 'Parents of the Deep' could be an interesting project.

His mind wandered to Barbara and Roger and the loving concern for their daughter that he'd seen on their faces – God, no, he couldn't bear to revisit the past week. He let himself dwell instead on Ollie and Harry Musgrove, back in the care of a self-absorbed, manipulative mother and a father who wouldn't stand up to her. Huh, they could certainly feature in 'Parents of the Deep'. Mona would be *Vampyroteuthis infernalis*, literally the vampire squid from hell, a blue-blooded cephalopod living in the deepest parts of the ocean; or, in her case, a twilight world of her own making. And Charles? Ah, yes – *Osedax*, the zombie sea worm; enough said.

No! That was grossly unfair. Even when Rick was thinking the worst of him, Charles had been unfailingly pleasant. He deserved sympathy, not sarcasm; especially as he'd lost the woman he'd really loved.

And inevitably, like the pull of the tide, Rick's thoughts turned to Anna. She'd captivated him right from the start –

even though physically she wasn't his usual type. Of course, he hadn't bargained for her other attractions, such as a tender heart, quicksilver mind and quiet sense of humour; and he'd completely underestimated the sexual chemistry ...

He remembered that moment of pure irony, after it was all over between them, when he'd finally understood her physical appeal. Diving at Kangaroo Island, off Australia's south coast, he'd caught his first glimpse of a sea dragon in the wild. Small, delicate, exquisitely beautiful, moving with measured grace, it reminded him of Anna. For some time afterwards, he felt a tightness in his chest every time he studied the creatures, as if she was haunting – or taunting – him.

He dragged his thoughts back to the present. The sea dragon was an obvious candidate for 'Parents of the Deep', since the female delegated all parenting duties, even egg hatching, to the male. In contrast, he was sure that Anna would make a loving mother. He recalled that first unexpected sighting of her in Uppercross, when she stopped to comfort the dark-haired little boy he'd mistakenly thought was her son. For one crazy moment he imagined another boy in Ollie's place: slightly older, tall for his age – blond like his father or dark like his mother? The child they might have had, made from a love that was somehow still so real ...

He scraped his chair back and rose abruptly from the table. 'I need some fresh air.' He shot Guy an angry look. 'Call me when you've finished giving my interview.'

'Hold on a minute.' Obviously still hungry for something frank and revealing, Duncan put a heavy hand on Rick's arm. 'This is a question that only you can answer. What do all these observations of sea creatures tell you about yourself and your fellow man?'

Rick twisted his mouth into a grim smile, shook off

Duncan's hand and threw caution to the winds. 'That I generally prefer hanging out with bottom dwellers than with human beings. That the rules of male-female relationships are much more straightforward under the sea. And that my perfect mate is a sea dragon.'

Chapter Thirty-Six

Anna walked briskly towards the Royal Crescent – partly because she wanted to arrive early and pre-empt any comments from her father about her timekeeping, and partly to keep warm. She'd decided to wear the coral dress that she'd bought for the wedding of an old Oxford friend. But that had been in the summer; now, even under her wool coat, the flimsy fabric was no proof against the chill of an October night.

Then, in spite of the cold, she stopped. In the golden glow of old-fashioned streetlights, the elegant sweep of Georgian houses unfurled before her like the stunning backdrop to an empty stage, waiting for the show to begin. Even the prospect of an evening with Walter and Lisa couldn't subdue a little thrill of excitement. It wasn't every day that she had an invitation to dinner at a world-famous hotel, was it?

Moments later she was inside number sixteen. A welcoming smile from the doorman, a polite enquiry, and she was following a member of staff through the reception area and out into softly lit private gardens. She stared across at a row of renovated outbuildings – 'originally coach houses for Royal Crescent residents, madam – the first two are now our spa, The Bath House, and our restaurant, known as The Dower House'. The man led her towards the building next to the restaurant – 'The Pavilion, madam, where Sir Walter and his guests are staying' – and she stepped into an entrance hall almost the size of her flat.

To her right, on a red leather sofa, sat Lisa – in a dazzling white off-the-shoulder creation that showed her golden limbs to perfection and left Anna feeling pale and uninteresting.

She was on her mobile, deep in conversation – if that wasn't a contradiction in terms. 'Oh God, yes,' she was saying, 'we'll be getting the meal over as soon as possible … Nine-thirty I would think, so let's meet there at ten … No, just the three of us. See you later.'

Anna didn't know whether to be relieved that dinner would be finished in a couple of hours, or worried that she was included in Lisa's plans for the evening.

Lisa snapped her phone shut and greeted Anna with unusual enthusiasm. 'Come and see my suite, it's absolutely divine!' She almost dragged Anna through the nearest door and gave her a guided tour of a beautifully furnished bedroom, bathroom and conservatory-style sitting room. As they stopped to admire every antique bureau and original painting, this took longer than Anna expected.

'Just like being at home,' Lisa said complacently, 'but the service is far better. Nothing's too much trouble.'

Knowing the scale of Lisa's demands, Anna couldn't help but be impressed.

'Cleo's got a room down the hall, very handy if I need her,' Lisa went on. 'And Walter's in the Beau Nash suite, named after the famous Regency fashionista, you know, *so* appropriate. Come on, I'll show you.'

Anna followed her sister, wondering whether to point out that Lisa must be thinking of Beau Brummell, because Beau Nash pre-dated the Regency period by several decades. But she didn't. And she could have added that Walter had better take note since, despite helping to make Bath the most fashionable resort in eighteenth-century England, Beau Nash had died in poverty as a result of his extravagances. But she didn't. Lisa had never had much time for accuracy, historical or otherwise.

They returned to the entrance hall and crossed to the door opposite; when Lisa tried to open it, however, it was locked.

'I've got Anna here, she's dying to see your suite,' she called out imperiously.

Muffled voices from inside. Then Cleo's throaty laugh and Walter's pompous tones, 'It'll have to be another time, I'm getting dressed. Meet you at the restaurant.'

Lisa gave a little shrug and moved away.

'Don't you think that's weird?' Anna said, as she and Lisa left The Pavilion and turned along the path to their right.

'What – that he wants some privacy to get dressed?' Lisa gave a languid wave to someone across the garden.

'No – the fact that Cleo's part of that privacy.'

A laugh of tinkling condescension. 'You really don't get it, do you? She's his masseuse – naturally she sees him with no clothes on, but it doesn't *mean* anything. I suppose I shouldn't be surprised at your ignorance – the nearest you ever got to a massage was being flogged with birch twigs in that Russian bath house.'

They were at The Dower House and Lisa was about to step through the doorway, when Anna caught hold of her arm. 'Listen, does Cleo lock the door when she gives *you* a massage?'

Lisa lowered her voice to a contemptuous hiss. 'No need, I don't care who comes in and sees me naked. But Walter's a different generation, although I know it's sometimes hard to believe.' She shook off Anna's hand, her face contorted with rage. 'And for God's sake don't make a scene – remember where you are!'

A split second later, however, she composed her features in a serene mask and glided swan-like into another spacious entrance hall. She paused expectantly, and the waiters flocked. Anna's coat was whisked away as if by magic, and she found herself swept into the main dining room in Lisa's wake, ushered towards the conservatory area and seated at a table for five, opposite a rather unnerving expanse of mirror.

'Not there!' Lisa said, eyes narrowing. 'She can go on the end, then the four of us will be in our usual places.'

Lisa must be referring to herself, Walter, Cleo and the 'someone special' – who, by the sound of it, was a frequent dining companion; obviously Lady Dalrymple, as she was staying in the same hotel. Anna exchanged a smile with the nearest waiter and moved to the chair at the end of the table.

While Lisa stood fidgeting with her mobile, Anna took the opportunity to look around. Classy furnishings in neutral tones of soft beige and olive green, white damask tablecloths, sparkling silver and crystal – it was a style of restaurant to which she was totally unaccustomed. Walter and Lisa, on the other hand, would feel completely at home – in fact, with its subdued lighting and that huge mirror overlooking the table, this place might have been designed for Walter.

Just then a man's voice interrupted her thoughts – a voice she'd heard only a week ago but never expected to encounter here.

'Lisa darling, you look sensational!' She watched William Elliot-Dunne hold her sister close, saw his lips brush hers, intimate and teasing, for several seconds. Eventually, he seemed to recollect where he was and escorted her to one of the chairs under the mirror. Then, as if he sensed Anna's stare, he turned and looked down at her, eyes wide in disbelief. 'Anna! Nobody told me you'd be here.'

'Same,' she said tersely.

He lifted up her hand and she felt the heat of his lips on her skin. 'You look even more beautiful than your mother,' he murmured, so that only she could hear.

She blushed and shook her head. 'Don't be silly.'

As he pulled out the chair on Anna's left, Lisa said sharply, 'Not there, Bill darling, that's for Cleo. You're over here, beside me.'

Another kiss on the hand, a rueful grin – and he was off to sit next to Lisa, full of apologetic charm. When Walter and Cleo arrived, Anna found herself marooned as Lisa and Cleo monopolised the two men. Not that it mattered; their conversation might as well have been in Japanese, revolving as it did around fashion labels and beauty treatments and people she didn't know.

But she learned a couple of things. First, she needn't have worried that she was part of Lisa's plans for three later as it became obvious that Lisa, Cleo and 'Bill darling' went out together most nights. And second, watching William Elliot-Dunne at work was like watching a puppet show: he was the master puppeteer, pulling everyone's strings.

Except hers, of course.

Chapter Thirty-Seven

Dinner was even more of a triumph than Walter had anticipated – although it hadn't got off to the most promising start.

Really, Anna had no business to change her appearance, however subtly, without telling him! At first, he actually thought it was Irina sitting there ... The short hairstyle showing off the shape of her neck; the softly glowing skin that had never needed any cosmetic retouching; the coral dress – Irina's favourite colour and, he recalled with distaste, the shade Anna had once painted the walls of her room at Kellynch. The table blurred before him and he clutched Cleo's arm more tightly – thank God for Cleo!

And thank God, too, for William. As soon as he saw Walter and Cleo, he jumped up, rushed to embrace them, then stepped back in awe and fixed stunned eyes on Walter.

'We're wearing the same clothes again! It's uncanny – as if I've found an identical twin I didn't know I had.' The dear boy seemed overcome with emotion.

Walter glanced automatically at the large mirror opposite. He saw a misty figure in a taupe suit and ivory shirt, nearly identical to the man facing him – the same crisp blond hair, smooth tanned face, piercing blue gaze. Not identical twins – William's features had one or two little irregularities – but they would certainly pass for brothers.

They sat in their usual places: he faced the mirror, with Cleo next to him, William directly opposite and Lisa next to William. It was an ideal arrangement – Lisa and William made a beautiful couple and, if he tired of watching them, he could always watch himself. Just a pity about William's slightly receding chin – more noticeable tonight because of the number of times he turned to look at the woman at the end of the table. But then, as Cleo reminded him when he'd mentioned it to her previously, there was only one man in Bath blessed with a perfect profile.

The orders were taken, the champagne served, and a toast made by William in a gratifyingly loud voice – 'To the 8th Baronet of Kellynch, Sir Walter Elliot, a name synonymous with everything that's made England what it is today!' Walter responded with a gracious nod of the head; but, out of the corner of his eye, he noticed Anna smile – and wondered what she found so amusing.

So he wasn't surprised when, shortly afterwards, she tried to spoil it all. As soon as William left the room – and his exquisite-looking *foie gras* starter – to answer a call on his mobile, she couldn't resist saying, 'That's odd. When I met William in Lyme Regis only a week ago, he never mentioned he was coming to Bath.'

'Don't be ridiculous, you can't have met him in Lyme Regis,' Lisa said, with understandable irritation. 'He told us himself – he was in London last weekend, going to all our old haunts. On the Sunday evening he drove like a madman to Kellynch, but found we'd gone to Bath. He stayed overnight with Minty and came here first thing Monday morning.'

'I'm not being ridiculous, he was–'

'He can't have been in two places at once, just accept you made a mistake,' Walter put in, magnanimously. At that moment, William returned to his seat and Walter leaned forward to confide, 'My other daughter seems to be under the illusion that she met you in Lyme Regis last weekend. Have you got a double, or shall we call in the psychiatrists?'

Everyone laughed at his little joke, except Anna.

But then William's face clouded and he said quietly, 'I'm afraid she's right. Remember I said I was revisiting old haunts? Well, not just in London, I went to Lyme Regis where I had that wonderful holiday with my mother, and Irina, and of course Anna ... Naturally, I didn't mention it because I didn't want to cause *you* in particular,' a tormented look at Walter, 'any unnecessary pain. I know from my mother what a devoted couple you and Irina were.'

Walter blinked back a tear. So thoughtful – the dear boy had obviously matured a lot during that traumatic time with the Texan divorcee. Not that William himself had breathed a word about it; but Walter had bumped into the friends William was staying with, the Wallises, and they'd reluctantly explained the whole sad story ...

No wonder William had been looking so often in Anna's direction; he'd be trying to signal to her not to let on about Lyme. Little did he know that *she* never bothered to spare her father's feelings.

And now William was asking very kindly after one of the Musgrove girls, something about an accident, and Anna was talking about hospitals and operations – a subject that she very well knew Walter *detested*.

He intervened swiftly. 'My dear friend Lady Dalrymple has hired some boxes at the Theatre Royal next Saturday. We're all invited, of course.' A stern look at Anna. 'It's a Russian play, so she'd particularly like *you* to be there.'

Anna's eyes lit up; she really did look distressingly like Irina tonight. 'Yes, it's Chekhov's *Three Sisters*. I tried to get tickets for Jenny and me, but they only had the most expensive ones left.'

If that was a hint to invite the Smith woman, he was having none of it. Instead, he turned the conversation adroitly to the hotel spa, and which treatments they should sample over the coming week, a discussion he knew Anna would have no interest in. And he would have held court like this all through dinner, if William hadn't left the table again – and this time his *filet mignon* – to answer another call on his mobile.

Taking advantage of a natural lull in the conversation, Anna said in that deceptively gentle voice of hers, 'I don't understand. After all William's done, after all the blustering about never speaking to him again, how are we sitting here having dinner together?' She ignored Lisa's anguished 'You just don't want me to be happy!' and stared fearlessly at Walter.

Walter stared fearlessly back, knowing he had nothing to reproach himself for. 'It's quite simple. When William left Lisa so suddenly, he was not in control of his own mind. Brandi Berette is by all accounts an exceptionally beautiful creature, been on the cover of *Vogue*–'

'It was *Playboy*,' Lisa put in, with a little sob.

'Either way, a force to be reckoned with, and that's without taking her $4 million dollar divorce settlement into account. If you recall, she hired William to give her investment advice – then it all went horribly wrong. She threw herself at his feet, plied him with alcohol and drugs, seduced him and dragged him off to Texas as her live-in adviser.' Walter let out a little shuddering sigh. 'One simply can't imagine what he went through ... he was virtually a prisoner for her pleasure ... but at least it kept him out of the sun, so terribly *ageing*.'

Anna gave a nasty little laugh. 'If you believe all that, you're even more gullible than I thought. What else has he told you – he only escaped when the Marines turned up?'

Walter felt his face purpling with rage – and then Cleo's fingers were soothing his clenched fist and Anna's rudeness didn't seem to matter quite so much.

Thankfully, Lisa stepped in. 'He hasn't told us anything,' she said hotly. 'Walter had to force the truth out of his friends, and they warned us not to discuss it with Bill in case he breaks down.'

Anna merely smiled. 'How convenient – to be too traumatised to explain himself and to have friends lined up to do it for him. I bet they didn't need much forcing, whoever they are.'

'You're wrong, Torquil and Jemima Wallis aren't the sort of people who lower themselves to gossip.' Lisa gave her sister a pitying look. 'I don't expect you know them – they live in one of those huge luxury apartments in The Circus.'

'A very attractive couple, quite a rarity in Bath,' Walter mused. 'Such a shame Torquil's prematurely grey. He must be only in his early thirties, but he looks as old as me!' He gazed expectantly round the table.

Cleo made a little moue of disgust. 'No, Sir Voltaire, I 'ave to disagree wiz you – 'e looks *much* older.'

This led to an enthralling conversation about youth versus the appearance of it. Walter was flattered to learn that he was generally thought to be no more than forty; and his happiness was complete when William returned and let slip that he'd been asked if he and Sir Walter were brothers.

Chapter Thirty-Eight

At the bar of his hotel in Southampton, Rick knocked back another whisky and frowned at Guy.

'So now you're telling me I'm not just a recluse, I'm a rude and abusive recluse?' he said carefully, wondering if Guy was using this bizarre tongue twister as some kind of breathalyser.

'That's right.' Guy leaned his face in close, as though Rick was hard of hearing. 'You're making my job almost impossible and you're not doing yourself any favours. For God's sake, if you're depressed don't take it out on other people – go for a run or something!'

Rick let out a heavy sigh. 'I can't be bothered.'

'It would help if you didn't drink so much. How many's that you've had?'

A shrug. 'Not enough.'

Guy narrowed his eyes. 'Something happen at the hospital this evening?'

'You could say that.'

Silence; then Guy prompted, 'Aren't you going to tell me?'

Rick hesitated; he wasn't sure he wanted to put his misgivings into words ... Oh, what the hell! 'Look, Lou's doing really well – today she even walked along the corridor with me – and they're talking about transferring her to Frenchay Hospital at Bristol, nearer her home. It's all good news.' He gave Guy a despairing look. 'So why don't I feel happy?'

Now it was Guy's turn to shrug. 'Sorry, only you can answer that. Do you want me to fix you up with someone to talk to?'

'No thanks.' The last thing he needed was a psychotherapist; it would be like opening Pandora's bloody box.

'At least she's on the road to recovery.' Guy paused. 'I can't understand why you've let yourself get so involved. You hardly know the girl, you don't seem to be in love with her and it sounds as though the accident was her own fault – why beat yourself up like this?'

Rick bowed his head. 'Things aren't that simple. I promised her family that I'd be there for her–'

'Why the hell did you do that?'

He shrugged. 'Guilt, I suppose. You see, when Shelley dumped me, Lou was great for my ego. Trouble is, I didn't handle it very well – I'd bumped into this woman, and I thought I had something to prove ... So I told Lou we had to slow down, get to know each other, like I did with this woman. But Lou isn't a very good listener. Unlike this woman I know, or used to know ...'

'Stop rambling on about "this woman".' Guy sounded impatient. 'Is it the same one, or are there three of them? No – don't tell me,' he added hurriedly. 'Just remember, guilt is never a good reason for doing something.'

'What about honour?'

'Honour?'

'Knowing and doing what's morally right–'

'I know what it means,' Guy put in, 'but surely you've got no moral obligation towards Lou?'

'It's ... complicated. I want to do the right thing, because ... there's this woman, and her ideal hero is–'

'Not "this woman" again! For God's sake, Rick, go to bed. You're not making any sense.'

Rick studied his glass; hadn't there been some whisky in it, a minute ago? And now he'd lost his train of thought ... 'Anyway, as I was saying, I'm not sure if I'm doing Lou any good by visiting, she doesn't seem to mind if I'm there or not.'

'You weren't saying anything of the sort,' Guy said briskly, 'but it's just as well Lou isn't desperate to see you. Your next events are in South Wales, you can't keep travelling back to Southampton. It's Bristol and Bath towards the end of the week, handy if she's moved to Frenchay, but still ... Did I tell you I was coming to Bath next Saturday, with Marie-Claude? There's a play on at the Theatre Royal that she wants to see, and by sheer coincidence I can impress her with my knowledge, because I studied it for Russian A level–'

Something clicked in Rick's befuddled brain. 'You did Russian? Here, tell me what this says.' He fumbled along the bar for a coaster, dug a pen out of his pocket and scrawled what he could remember of the book title in Anna's bedroom. 'Look, the first and third letters are like 'N' backwards, and the last two are 'OT', but the second letter's weird – a sort of rectangle with little legs.'

Guy glanced at the scrawl and laughed. 'Idiot.'

Rick scowled. 'Yeah, maybe I am, but there wasn't much opportunity to learn the Cyrillic alphabet at my failing secondary school in north-east England.'

Guy laughed even louder. 'That's what the word means – "idiot"!'

'Oh, I see ... Isn't it the name of a novel?'

'By Dostoevsky.'

'About ...?'

'The hero's this well-meaning idealist – think Forrest Gump with brains. He has an overdeveloped sense of duty and tries to help people, in particular a woman who's in a mess.' A pause. 'Eventually he realises that everyone thinks he's an idiot.'

Rick was silent for a few moments; then, ignoring Guy's

protests, he ordered another whisky. For consolation, he told himself; because, rather than the expected insight into Anna's life, this was an uncomfortably accurate picture of his own.

Chapter Thirty-Nine

After a dream of a dessert – mango and jasmine mousse – Anna refused anything else; the coffee would be worth staying for, but not the conversation that went with it. Two hours of her father's Dorian Gray syndrome and her sister's vacuousness were more than enough.

To her surprise, and the others' displeasure, William insisted on walking her home.

'But I'm about to order our taxi,' Lisa said, with a baleful look at Anna.

William flashed her a grin that would have melted half of Greenland. 'No probs, darling, order it to come in half-an-hour. By the time you've all had coffee, I'll be back.'

And, before she knew it, Anna was in her coat – with William's scarf wrapped snugly round her neck – and leaving the restaurant by its other door on Crescent Lane. She told him she lived in Bennett Street; but it turned out that he already knew her address, had got it from Minty – or Araminta, as he called her. He'd wanted to look her up as soon as he arrived in Bath; once he went to build some bridges at The Royal Crescent Hotel, however – another tip-off from Araminta – he found himself without a moment to spare.

He held her arm as they walked along, steered her smoothly across the road and steered the conversation just as smoothly to their breakfast together in Lyme Regis. 'There was so much I wanted to know about you, but I thought I'd see you again that night.' His grip on her arm tightened. 'I was devastated when I heard you'd checked out. That moron Pargeter wouldn't give me your address – went all officious on me and quoted the Data Protection Act. So I decided to head for Kellynch and get the information I wanted there. Another setback when I found Walter and Lisa had decamped to Bath, then – luckily – I remembered where Araminta lived.' He gave a deep chuckle. 'She was a bit frosty to begin with, but she soon thawed.'

They reached the corner of Bennett Street and instantly, even in the dark, he decided he loved everything about it. So central, he told her, yet quiet, and not as intimidating as The Circus. As they neared her front door, he noticed Tom's car with its disabled sticker and started discussing the Smiths' situation. Araminta thought they managed their finances amazingly well, considering Tom was on a pittance of a disability allowance and Jenny didn't earn much more. But then, renting out one's property could be quite a little gold mine, as he and Araminta hoped Walter would come to realise. And although they both admired Anna tremendously for making her own way in life, they felt that she deserved far more than a one-bedroomed rented flat. In fact, they agreed about most things where Anna was concerned ...

Anna let it all wash over her. She wasn't sure if she felt treasured – or trapped. In fact, she wasn't sure about William, full stop.

At the door, she fished the key out of her bag and smiled up at him. 'Thank you for seeing me home, there was really no need. How long are you staying in Bath?'

'My plans are fairly flexible at the moment. One of the advantages of being an investment trader nowadays is that I carry my office with me. Bath has some wonderful little corners where I can hide myself away and still be on the job.' He cleared his throat. 'Actually, Anna, it all depends on what happens in the next week or so.' His face was in shadow, so she couldn't make out his expression; but something in his voice – a suggestion that he was thinking of *her* – rang warning bells.

She said, keeping her tone light and casual, 'Well, if you're still around, maybe we could have a coffee together next weekend?' That sounded perfect – friendly, for old times' sake, without being encouraging.

'I'd love that, although I'm sure we'll see each other before then.'

Not if she could help it. 'Goodnight, William.'

'Goodnight, Anna.' He pulled her close – too close – and murmured, 'I'm so happy I found you again.'

She broke away, stabbed her key into the lock and opened the door wide enough to let herself in but keep him out. Then she shut it firmly behind her, slumped against it and closed her eyes.

The ordeal was over. Except – was she thinking of dinner with her family, or her strange vulnerability to this man?

I'm so happy I found you again.

How she'd longed to hear those words; but from someone else.

Chapter Forty

Anna rang Minty early the next morning. She was determined to catch her before she went off to All Saints – where, needless to say, she was churchwarden, offertory steward and choir stalwart all rolled into one.

It turned out that someone had beaten Anna to it. The first thing Minty said was, 'Anna, *darling*! Have your ears been burning? William's just been on the phone telling me what happened last night.'

Anna was puzzled. 'You mean when he went clubbing with Lisa and Cleo? Why should my ears be burning? I wasn't even there.'

'Silly girl, he hardly mentioned *that* part of the evening.' A knowing laugh. 'It was all about meeting you again and walking you home.'

'As I told him at the time, there was really no need.'

'But he's that sort of man, isn't he? Considerate ... protective ... and *such* good company. Last Sunday we had the most wonderful evening together–'

'That reminds me,' Anna put in, 'why didn't you let me know you'd seen him, or that he was in Bath? I got quite a shock when he turned up at dinner.'

'Don't tease – you mean a lovely surprise, I'm sure. Come to that, why didn't you let me know you'd met him in Lyme Regis? When you rang me last weekend – Sunday afternoon, wasn't it? – you never even mentioned him.'

'I forgot, what with everything else that was going on.'

Minty gave a little sigh. 'Ah yes, poor Louisa Musgrove. Have you been to see her yet?'

'No, I decided to wait until she's been moved to Bristol.'

'Very sensible, it's much nearer.'

That wasn't the only reason, but Anna let it pass; she was in no hurry to bring Rick's name into the conversation.

'And how is she?' Minty went on.

'Quieter than she's ever been in her life, but making a good recovery by the sound of it.' Then she frowned. 'Although Barbara was a bit worried the other day – one of the visitors read some poetry to Lou and afterwards she was even more subdued than usual.'

'How odd, I can imagine a little Keats or Tennyson being quite therapeutic–'

'This guy writes his own stuff – not that I've read any yet, I haven't got round to looking at his website. And he's just split from his long-term girlfriend, so he's not exactly the life and soul of the party.'

Anna recalled how surprised she'd been to hear about James; not so much the depressing effect of his poems – more the fact that he'd turned up at the hospital midweek and visited every day since. Barbara had reminded her that it was his half-term holiday – but that explained only the circumstances, not the motivation. Except that Lou was a captive audience for his poetry; and maybe he mistook her silences for appreciation.

Apparently James kept away from the hospital whenever Rick was around, so Rick knew nothing about these visits. Anna was half-relieved that James seemed to have forgotten she existed – and half-worried that the two men would meet accidentally. She still wasn't sure how Rick felt about Lou …

Minty was saying, '… it wouldn't have happened, would it, my dear?'

'Sorry?'

'If it had been William with Louisa on the Cobb, he would never have let her fall like that. As I said, he's a very considerate and protective man.'

'Rick *didn't* let her fall, he–' Anna broke off, struggling to bring herself under control. No point even trying to convince Minty that William Elliot-Dunne wasn't the only man who could be considerate and protective and good company. Rick had once been all of those and much, much more …

She took a deep breath and changed the subject. 'When are you next coming to Bath?'

'In a couple of weeks or so, although William wants me to come earlier. Says he's missing me already!'

So the phone call ended as it had begun, with Minty singing William's praises and implying that William was singing Anna's. All rather disturbing – like William himself, Anna thought. On the one hand, he was undeniably attractive; and he seemed sincere enough, particularly when he talked about that holiday they'd had in Lyme. On the other hand, he looked too much like Walter for comfort, and what she knew of his past history with Lisa and Brandi Berette suggested he was a rampant opportunist.

Anna looked at the pile of essays that she'd brought home to mark. It would do her good to open that new pack of filter coffee, put on some music and settle down to work. No need for a man in her life at all.

For once Rick didn't give any advance warning of his visit to Lou. He had a Sunday afternoon signing in Exeter and coming back to Southampton afterwards didn't make sense; not when he and Dave should be heading in the opposite direction, to South Wales.

So he called at the hospital in the morning, well before normal visiting hours, on the off chance that they would let him see Lou for a few minutes. And he wanted to thank the nursing staff personally for their superb care; if everything went to plan, Lou would be transferred to Bristol in the next couple of days.

But when he popped his head round the door of Lou's room, he did a double take. There she was, sitting up in bed as he'd expected; but hunched in the chair next to her was none other than James Benwick. Hair flopping over his face, hands gripping hers, he was murmuring something in low urgent tones and, incredibly, she seemed to be hanging on his every word.

Arms folded, Rick leaned against the door frame and said coolly, 'So you've got special visiting rights this morning too, have you?'

James started, glanced nervously across at him and went bright red. 'Yes, well, just dropping by, you know. Been staying with Ben and Megan, going back to Sussex now, got things to do.'

If he was 'just dropping by', Rick thought, why the guilty body language? But he uncrossed his arms, moved towards the bed and said in a gentler voice, 'Hi Lou, how are you today?'

She looked up at him as if she was trying to remember who he was. He frowned; in their different ways, they both made him feel like an intruder. So, after he'd explained why he wouldn't see her until Thursday, he said goodbye and hurried off.

During the two-hour car journey to Exeter, however, he had plenty of time to think. If James and Lou were becoming infatuated with each other, it would solve two problems.

First, it would allow James, not Rick, to play the hero in Lou's life; and second, it would mean that James was no longer infatuated with Anna Elliot.

Anna stretched out on the rug, clasped her hands behind her head and collected her thoughts. She'd finished the marking – now it was time for lunch; she still had the remains of a cooked chicken in the fridge and she'd make some pasta.

This afternoon she'd catch up on her reading and go over the notes for tomorrow's lectures. After a bath, some TV and an early night, she'd feel better prepared for the week ahead and its biggest challenges – a visit to Lou, followed by Rick's book signing at Molland's. She knew she would go through with both, whatever the consequences for her peace of mind.

So when the doorbell rang and threatened to put paid to her plans for the rest of the day, she wasn't best pleased. She got reluctantly to her feet and switched on the intercom. 'Who is it?'

'The owner of a rather nice navy cashmere scarf. Or should that be "the rather nice owner of a navy cashmere scarf"?' William's voice, self-assured with a hint of amusement. She remembered how he'd insisted she wore his scarf last night; in her hurry to leave him on the doorstep, she'd forgotten to give it back.

'May I come up and get it?' he prompted.

Flustered, she pressed the front door release – and immediately regretted it. She should have taken the scarf down to him, chatted for a minute or two, then excused herself with 'too much work'.

The rap at her door seemed to come only seconds later; she took a deep breath and opened it. But just when she expected William to waltz in, he hung back.

'Am I interrupting anything?' he said, with a contrite smile. 'I never thought to ask.'

Caught off guard, she heard herself murmur, 'No, I've just finished my marking and I'm ready for a break. Come in.'

And then she was hanging up his coat and offering him a coffee, and he was following her into the kitchen and marvelling at how neat and compact it was.

Just how did that happen, when she didn't really want him here?

In the living room, over coffee, he seemed transfixed by the picture of Pornichet. So bold and fresh – who was the artist? She explained that it was her cousin's daughter, Katya, who she saw most summers. Based on an old sketch, it had been done four years ago, when Katya was only sixteen and happy to paint whatever people asked for; now she was at the Pont-Aven School of Contemporary Art and far more choosy about her commissions. He wondered aloud why Anna had wanted this particular scene – special memories, perhaps? Anna sidestepped the question by inviting him to lunch.

Which wasn't what she'd meant to do at all.

Back in the kitchen, they made a good team. He cooked the pasta to perfection and created a delicious-smelling sauce from whatever he found in her fridge. She chopped the chicken, mixed everything together, sprinkled cheese on top and put the dish under the grill to brown.

When she brought it into the living room a little while later, he handed her a glass of red wine. 'Can't eat pasta without it, hope you don't mind me opening your last bottle. I'll replace it, I promise.'

She *did* mind – she wanted a clear head for work this afternoon – but she found herself clinking glasses and drinking a toast to 'the future'.

As she served out the food, she couldn't resist saying, 'Congratulations. From what I saw last night, you actually have got a future – with our family, I mean. Amazing, considering what happened.'

He put down his glass, leaned across the table and tilted her chin with his fingertip. 'Please don't judge me – you don't know my side of the story.'

She blushed and looked away from that intent gaze. 'True. But what I do know makes me doubt whether I can *ever* trust you.'

'Anna.' He waited until she looked back at him. 'I've trusted you since I was fourteen, and I'm confident you'll come to trust me over time – otherwise I wouldn't be here. So I'm going to share something that mustn't go any further than these four walls.' He settled back in his chair and sipped his wine, confident of her full attention. 'How much do you know about Cléopatra Clé?'

Anna frowned. 'Hardly anything. She's a masseuse, she and Lisa got friendly at the gym and Walter's become more and more besotted with her, I can't imagine why.'

'Whereas I can, she's another Brandi Berette.' He gave a mirthless laugh. 'How do you think Brandi became a rich divorcee? That woman was Viagra on legs, in the right circumstances she'd get you to sign your life away.' He closed his eyes briefly, as if trying to banish an unpleasant memory. 'Anyway, I'm doing some research on Cleo, finding out who she really is and what she's up to. I can't say much more at this stage, but I can assure you I'm working very hard to protect your interests.'

Anna toyed with her pasta. 'That's very thoughtful of you, William, but there's really no need. Walter's so proud of his heritage that he'd never sign Kellynch away in a moment of passion.' She looked up at him with a wry smile. 'Assuming he even gets that far – he may enjoy the thought but, believe me, he's unlikely to be up to the deed itself. So don't worry – you're not going to lose out.'

Did she imagine it, or were his eyes suddenly hostile? 'What do you mean?' he said, softly.

'Oh, come on – if Walter has a son, bang goes your chance of being Sir William Elliot, 9th Baronet. I realise having the title gives you no direct financial gain – it can't be sold, or at least not legally – but it must come in handy when you want to impress. Whether it's Mr Pargeter at the Cobb View Hotel, or potential investment clients, everyone seems to think that a title makes you more trustworthy. Except me, obviously.'

His eyes creased in a disarming grin. 'Such a shame, because you're the one person I want to impress. Guess I'll just have to come up with a different strategy.' He didn't elaborate, but tucked into his pasta with relish.

As they ate, Anna thought over what William had said. Walter might not have ready cash, but he had two things of value: the title and Kellynch. As things stood, only William could inherit the title – but Kellynch was Walter's to dispose of as he wished. Even in its current run-down state, it would be worth several million pounds to the right buyer.

William interrupted her thoughts. 'Let me put a couple of scenarios to you. One is that Walter simply carries on doing whatever he's doing – or thinking of doing – with Cleo. From what you say, there's no danger of any children coming along or Walter handing Kellynch over to her.' A pause, while Anna nodded in agreement. He went on, 'So, apart from him lavishing money he hasn't got on massages and rooms at The Royal Crescent, there'd be no lasting harm done.' He poured them both some more wine. 'But another scenario is – what if she persuaded him to marry her?'

'Impossible,' Anna said. And it was – wasn't it?

'In what way?'

'He just wouldn't. How could he marry *her* after – after–'

'After Irina?' William raised one eyebrow. 'I might just as well ask myself why a woman like you is still single.'

Anna got abruptly to her feet and took her plate into the kitchen.

His voice followed her. 'The answer in both cases is "Difficult to understand, but it happens." Leaving your love life aside for the moment, I don't see how Cleo can lose by marrying Walter. She'll make sure there's a crippling prenup agreement in the event of a divorce, but otherwise she'll have plenty of opportunity to change his mind about selling Kellynch to the highest bidder. And there's the added bonus that, if she miraculously has a son and the DNA tests prove it's his, the child's well and truly legitimate.'

Anna silently fetched his coat – not forgetting his scarf – and handed it to him.

'You may not like what I'm saying, Anna, but it's not beyond the realms of possibility. Just think – a heritage that's been built up over centuries, poured down the drain in a matter of months.'

'I *will* think about it, but right now I need to prepare for my lectures tomorrow.' She forced a smile. 'Sorry, I know I'm being rude.'

He stood up, put on his coat and scarf and knocked back the last of his wine. Then he reached out and cupped her face in his hands. 'No, you're just being honest, very refreshing. And thank you for lunch – wonderful food and even better company. To show my appreciation, let me take you out to dinner on Friday night.'

She stepped quickly away. 'I'm out with Jenny – a talk and a book signing at Molland's.'

'Which will be finished by quarter to eight, I saw the flyer on your notice board in the kitchen.' He paused, as if considering something; then his face brightened. 'Look, I'd love to meet Jenny and Tom – why don't I take them out on Friday too? While you're at the signing, I could pick up Tom – he must have a folding wheelchair that'll fit in the Bentley – then come to Molland's for you and Jenny.' He moved towards the door. 'Shall we call on them now and see what they say?'

She found it so easy to say yes, put the door on the snib and go downstairs to introduce him to Jenny and Tom. For a start, it got him out of her flat. And she felt much more relaxed about dinner for four than dinner for two. And finally, it would fill a void – because there was no chance of spending the rest of Friday evening with Rick; no chance at all.

Chapter Forty-One

When Rick turned up at Frenchay Hospital in Bristol on Thursday afternoon, he was surprised to find Roger waiting for him in Reception.

'Something you need to know,' Roger said gruffly, 'and Lou's not in a fit state to tell you herself.'

Rick swallowed. 'What's happened? Has she had a relapse?'

'Good God, no – sorry, I should have chosen my words more carefully.' Roger passed his hand wearily across his forehead. 'She may just be going through a phase, part of the recovery process, but ...'

'But what?'

The other man sighed. 'She doesn't want you to visit any more.'

Silence; then a guarded, 'Why?'

'It upsets her, reminds her of the accident, that sort of thing.'

'Is that all?'

Roger frowned. 'Isn't that enough?'

'What I mean is – is there another reason?' He paused. 'Like James Benwick?'

'Ah, so you know.' A relieved smile. 'That makes things easier.'

Even though it was what Rick had expected, even hoped, something flipped in his brain. Easier? Who for? He'd been through twelve days of hell – guilt, remorse, worry, frustration; sleepless nights, agonising waits, dreading each call on his mobile in case it was Roger or Barbara with bad news. Fending off people's comments at events – usually sympathetic, but not always; giving any media reports a wide berth, to avoid raising his blood pressure.

And now his services were no longer required. What if he'd actually been in love with Lou – did they have *any* idea how he'd be feeling now?

He took a long steadying breath. The main person to consider in all this was Lou. She'd been through more than any of them, and she was going to be all right.

'It does make things easier, doesn't it?' he said at last. 'Still, now that I'm here, can I see her for a minute?'

He followed Roger into the lift, up a couple of floors, along a corridor and, finally, into a little room where Lou was sitting in an armchair, looking through a sheaf of papers. He sat on the chair next to her, while Roger hovered in the doorway.

'Hi,' he said. 'How are you doing?'

'Good, thanks.' Her speech was still slow, but he noticed that her mouth was less lopsided than on Sunday. 'This is much nearer for Mum and Dad, and Henrietta comes every evening.' A pause. 'Yesterday she brought Anna and Mona with her – I'd forgotten how awful Mona is.' She smiled, and for a second or two she was the old Lou. 'James sent me some beautiful poems this morning. Do you want to read them?'

'No, but I'm glad you like them.'

She stared across at him and her eyes filled with tears. 'I wish you'd written me a poem or something.'

He shifted uneasily in his seat. 'I'm not a poetry sort of guy.'

'What sort of a guy are you, Rick?'

That was a very good question, and one he didn't know how to answer at this precise moment. So he merely said, with an apologetic grin, 'Not the right sort for you, but I hope James is. Goodbye, Lou.' And he raised her hand briefly to his lips.

A few minutes later he walked out of Frenchay Hospital, his step far lighter than when he'd walked in.

Chapter Forty-Two

Mona's text came late on Thursday evening, just as Anna was getting ready for bed: 'Know why you haven't heard from James B? Ring me.'

Anna almost didn't bother; she'd never expected James to call her, and she sensed that Mona was just looking to score points. But any news about James might also involve Lou, and Rick. So, with great reluctance, she phoned Mona.

'Thought you wouldn't be able to resist!' her sister said, triumphantly. 'But first things first. Henrietta and I are coming to Bath for the weekend – we're trying to get into The Royal Crescent, but it doesn't look too hopeful. You won't see much of us, I'm afraid – I've told Walter we can't make tea with Lady Dalrymple.'

'Lucky you.' The previous day, Anna had come home to a handwritten invitation – hand-delivered, she suspected, by the ever-attentive William. It requested the pleasure of her company in the Garden Villa Suite at The Royal Crescent on Saturday afternoon, followed by the theatre at night. Lady Dalrymple had apparently taken three boxes containing eight seats: herself, the four Elliots, Henrietta, William and Cleo. If it hadn't been Chekhov's *Three Sisters*, she would have given it a miss ...

'... at the theatre, though,' Mona was saying, 'because we'll be *very* visible – always a reason to buy a decent dress – and of course I want to meet William. The rest of the time Henrietta and I'll be either at the shops or in the spa – I can't wait!'

Anna made what she hoped were enthusiastic noises. She knew better than to ask about James directly – Mona would use delaying tactics to great effect – so she moved the conversation on to marginally safer ground. 'How did Ollie's concert go last night?'

'Oh, it was bearable, I suppose. *He* should have done the solo, of course – that teacher doesn't seem to realise who I am! Instead it was the son of one of the school governors, very average – and you should have *seen* what the mother was wearing!'

As Mona paused for breath, Anna said, 'I'm sure Ollie will have his chance, if he wants it.' Then, before Mona could retaliate, 'What's the latest on Lou?'

'Ah.' Anna could almost hear her sister settling herself more comfortably. 'That's partly why I'm bringing Henrietta to Bath. I've been telling Charles right from the start that Rick and Lou would never last – and today's just proved it.' She took a gulp of something – wine, no doubt – and continued, 'You know James Benwick's been visiting, and on Sunday Rick bumped into him? Well, that seems to have made Lou's mind up and she told him today that she didn't want him to visit any more.'

'Who – James?'

'No, you idiot, Rick. And now Barbara says Lou and James are madly in love and he's written more poetry in the past week than he did in the twelve years he was with Julie. Having read one or two of the latest efforts on his website, all I can say is – no wonder she left him.'

'How – how is Rick?'

A scornful laugh. 'Bloody relieved, I imagine. But you're at his book signing tomorrow night, aren't you? You can find out for yourself.'

Anna closed her eyes; she wouldn't be doing anything where Rick was concerned until she was sure ... 'But is it really over – or is Lou just playing hard to get?'

'That'd be a first, wouldn't it? No, it's over, Roger was

there when Rick said goodbye to her. He said himself that he wasn't the right man for her.' Mona added, in that bossy tone that Anna knew so well, 'So, you find out the lie of the land with him, then I can decide the best approach for Henrietta. Maybe a cosy little lunch on Sunday where they can help each other de-stress after the trauma of the last two weeks – I don't suppose you can recommend anywhere nice and romantic? No, probably not.'

Anna bit her lip; couldn't Mona see that her interfering would do more harm than good? 'But I don't think he'll stay in Bath after the signing, he's more likely to go straight to Uppercross and spend some time with his sister.'

'Oh, didn't you know? The Crofts are coming to Bath for the weekend – Rick's treat for their wedding anniversary or something – so they're meeting up with him there.'

Anna sat through the rest of the call in a daze. So much to think about: such as why on earth Lou would want James instead of Rick ... and whether she could believe Mona's assurances that Rick was OK ...

But, most important of all, how he'd react when she came face to face with him tomorrow night.

Chapter Forty-Three

Typical – at half-past six, just as Dave dropped Rick at the top of Milsom Street, it started to rain. But he brushed aside Dave's offer to pick him up later and insisted he had the night off. He wanted to give his plan every chance of succeeding.

An umbrella would come in handy, and it seemed that luck was on his side; because, as he walked down the street to Molland's, he passed a shoe shop. Like most shops these days, it had diversified into other things; five minutes later, he'd bought a telescopic black umbrella – which he immediately put to good use. Outside the bookshop, however, he wasted several minutes trying to fold it neatly enough to fit inside its silly little sleeve. In the end he gave up and stuffed the sleeve into his coat pocket.

Inside, a tall blonde girl – he didn't quite catch her name – ushered him up a narrow twisting staircase to the top floor. There were already twenty or so people there; no Anna yet. He gave the audience a vague smile, handed his damp coat to the blonde and propped his umbrella against a nearby table. The girl made him a cup of excellent black coffee and went through the format: introduction by the shop manager, talk from Rick for twenty minutes or so, then signing the books – she indicated the table piled high with copies of *Sex in the Sea*.

He nodded and responded with 'Yes' and 'Fine', watching every new arrival out of the corner of his eye. All women, but no Anna among them. Maybe she hadn't got a ticket at all; or maybe she'd torn it up after he'd stormed out of her flat. Shit, he'd been so confident she'd come tonight, in spite of everything.

Three minutes to seven, and there were only two seats spare at the back. The manager approached, cleared his throat, introduced himself as Tim – or was it Jim? Just then, two women hurried in; one a stranger with short red spiky hair, and the other – the other more familiar than his own heartbeat.

At last she was here and, even though she wouldn't meet his gaze, he felt his spirits soar. Now he could put his plan into action.

'If he keeps on staring in our direction,' Jenny murmured beside her, 'I think I might faint – in the hope that he'll rush over and give me the kiss of life.'

Anna risked glancing up; but now Rick's attention was on the manager as he introduced the event. She had to admit that he looked a lot better than when she'd last seen him, pacing the floor of her flat; if he was distraught at being dumped for the second time in almost as many weeks, it certainly didn't show ... And he must have got caught in the rain because his hair was curling at the ends, as it used to if he'd been swimming. When he started his talk, he took off his jacket and she worried that he was feeling feverish; although it *was* warm – there weren't usually so many people crammed into this room ... But no one else seemed to share her concern. When he eased open the top two buttons of his shirt, a little expectant sigh rippled through the audience – making him stop short, with an embarrassed smile. So if he wasn't feverish he was certainly nervous; and yet giving lectures and talks must be second nature to him, as it was to her.

She made an effort to rein in her thoughts and listen. He was talking about the French angel fish, something about it being fiercely territorial during the spawning cycle. Then he moved on to describe – in graphic detail, much to the audience's delight – the antics of the deep sea angler fish: how the male tracked his chosen mate and literally joined himself to her, their skin fusing and their bodies sharing a common blood supply. Not surprisingly, he talked at length about sea horses and sea dragons, their courtship and mating rituals, and the strange role reversal where the male looked after the fertilised eggs: the sea dragon carried them embedded on his tail, the sea horse in a special pouch on the front of his abdomen. An impromptu demonstration – involving his jacket and some plastic balls left over from a children's event – went down particularly well.

Finally he paused, glanced at his watch and adopted a summing-up tone. 'The species I've talked about tonight are all mentioned in my book. And they've got something else in common that's very unusual under the sea – they practise monogamy.' Another embarrassed smile. 'Monogamy's an interesting concept for people today, isn't it? In the past, it was synonymous with "a mate for life" – which is becoming increasingly rare in our society, with its liberated attitudes to sex and marriage and, of course, increased life expectancy. And yet ...' He hesitated, as though searching for the right words, then gazed into the distance and said, 'I don't know about you, but monogamy's something that I'm used to defining in purely physical terms, probably because I'm a biologist. One sexual partner at a time, that sort of thing.' Another pause, while he studied the floor. 'Recently, though, I've begun to realise that it can be much, much more. And so, for what it's worth, my personal message to you –' a fleeting look around the room, before he fixed his gaze on something in the distance again – 'is that, as humans, we must never give up hope. "A mate for life" needn't be a limiting biological fact, an impossible dream because of how we've behaved in the past. Why not redefine it as "a mate for the rest of your life" and keep the dream alive? That's what I'm telling myself tonight – it's never too late to have a second chance to live my dream.'

The blood drained from Anna's face. She stared at him and – along with every other woman in the room, it seemed – held her breath for his next words. When he spoke, however, it was just to mutter, 'Thank you, thank you for listening.' The audience breathed a collective 'aahh' – adoration, Anna wondered, or disappointment at the lack of any further confessions? Then the applause started. It didn't last long, because one or two women broke ranks and soon there was a disorderly queue clamouring for him to sign books.

Anna's heart was pounding as she took her place at the end of the line and responded automatically to Jenny's chatter. Never mind if half the audience were within hearing distance – she would ask Rick what his dream was, and hope for the answer she wanted.

When it came to the crunch, Rick couldn't bring himself to say what he'd planned – not in front of all these people. It was for her ears only, just as he needed to keep private the elation or despair that would follow.

And now the book signing was taking ages, because everyone wanted to chat. That was the trouble with revealing your personal thoughts – people felt they had to reciprocate. So he had potentially thirty life histories to contend with, when there was only one that interested him. But he would be patient and wait ...

Eventually it was the turn of her redheaded friend. She thrust a book at him, pushed a pair of glasses on to her nose and said eagerly, 'Wonderful talk, you had us eating out of the palm of your hand, especially at the end. Mind, you could have read extracts from the phone book and it would probably have had the same effect!' He found himself laughing with her. 'My name's Jenny Smith,' she went on. 'I'm here with Anna – you know Anna Elliot, don't you?'

He nodded, wondering how much Anna had told her.

Not a lot, judging by the way she got straight down to business. 'If you can sign it "To Jenny and Tom", that'll be great.' A deep sigh. 'I wish I could believe in second chances, you know. But Tom – that's my husband – was paralysed in a car accident five years ago and, well, it's hard to keep hoping that he'll walk again.' She blinked rapidly, took the book with a trembling smile and moved away.

Great. Here he was, trotting out platitudes about hope and second chances – and there was Jenny, coping day after day with a person whose life had been shattered. He felt such a fraud …

There was only one person left in the queue, and it was the one person he'd been waiting for. And the way she was looking into his eyes made him want to just grab her across the table and kiss away the need for any words at all. And the longer she stood there staring at him, the more certain he was that in five minutes or so, when they were out of here, he'd be doing exactly that …

As if she could read his thoughts, she blushed, looked down and fidgeted with the book she'd bought; his book, in those small, delicate hands. 'I wanted to ask you about your talk,' she said at last, and she sounded strangely, wonderfully breathless. 'It – it wasn't at all what I expected.'

He said in a low voice, so only she could hear, 'I remember you saying that about something quite different.'

She blushed more deeply and didn't reply; gently, he took the book out of her hands and placed it on the table. That had the desired result and she looked up at him again; but her eyes were watchful.

'Tell you what,' he said, boldly, 'how about you save the interrogation until I walk you home?' He reached under the table for the umbrella. 'Don't worry about the rain, I've come prepared. This should keep us both dry, provided we stay close.'

She seemed to be trying not to laugh. He glanced down at the umbrella; huh, so much for his attempt at being romantic – the thing looked like a deranged crow.

'Here.' She took it from him, gave it a brisk shake and secured the flapping wings with a little belt that he hadn't even noticed. As she handed it back, he caught her fingers in his and felt desire spiral through him.

He took a deep breath and blanked out everyone else. 'Anna, I–'

But then a man's voice cut in with 'Sorry I'm late, darling!' A self-satisfied voice, horribly familiar, just as intrusive as it had been at Lyme; and that same smug face, leaning in close. 'Had to show Cleo how to work the TV in her room *again*. Honestly, at times she's as thick as two short planks.'

Anna started, as if waking from a trance. The umbrella, suddenly redundant, clattered on to the table. And Rick knew that he had more chance of walking on the moon than walking her home.

The man tugged at her arm. 'We have to find Jenny. Tom's waiting in the car outside, and our table's booked for eight, remember?' He picked up the copy of *Sex in the Sea*. 'Signed and paid for? Right, let's go!'

'No, William, wait.' She wrenched the book from him and held it out to Rick. 'Please sign my book. Write whatever you were going to say. Please, Rick.'

The expression in her eyes was so soft and pleading that he almost believed her; but of course he was a fool – a naïve fool who talked about dreams and second chances as if they really existed! He opened the book at the title page, gripped the pen between index finger and thumb and signed two words with an aggressive flourish – 'Rick Wentworth'. Nothing more, nothing less.

He didn't wait for the ink to dry, just closed the book with a snap. Then he snatched up his umbrella and jacket and marched off to find his coat.

Chapter Forty-Four

'Here's your cup of tea, Jen.'

'Thanks.' Jenny sat up in bed and gave Tom a smile that rapidly became a grimace. 'Ouch, my head's thumping! How's yours?'

'Fine. But then I wasn't knocking back the champagne like you and Anna.'

'Well, we don't often get the chance, do we?' She took a sip of tea. 'God knows how much that meal cost last night – I hope our host thought we were worth it.'

This should have been the lead-in to a cosy little chat about William Elliot-Dunne, except that Tom was too preoccupied with his previous train of thought. 'Unusual for Anna to drink like that,' he said, anxiously. 'Perhaps you'd better go and see if she's OK.'

'At least it brought her out of her shell. To begin with, she was even quieter than usual, wasn't she?'

'Maybe she didn't really want us along–'

'She did, I asked her at work yesterday.' Jenny gave a little sigh. 'She said she wasn't in a hurry to encourage William. But, as he reminded her last night, they're having tea together this afternoon. I can't figure it out.'

'Neither can he, judging by the look on his face when she wouldn't invite him up to her flat.' Tom frowned. 'You're sure she made it up those stairs?'

'Absolutely. I counted the right number of steps, more or less, then I heard her open her door – must get round to oiling those hinges! – and shut it again.' Jenny paused, before steering the conversation firmly in the desired direction. 'So, be honest, what do you think of him?'

He shrugged. 'Seems like a nice guy. Must be loaded, judging by his car and the way he was throwing money around. And he seems very keen on Anna. She could do a lot worse.'

Jenny laughed, then winced as her head pounded. 'Spoken like a typical man. Yes, in financial terms Anna could do a lot worse. There's just something about him … I'm not convinced he's right for her. But don't worry – I'm not going to say a word. For the time being, at least, I'll give him the benefit of the doubt.' She took another sip of tea. 'Maybe I'd better go and see if she's OK, like you suggested. And I want to compare notes about last night.'

'I thought you weren't going to say anything to her about William?'

'I'm not, it's Rick Wentworth I want to talk about. I tried at dinner, remember, but she wouldn't rise to the bait. She probably thought it was a bit off to drool over another man in front of William.'

'On the other hand, *you* were quite happy to drool over another man in front of *me*.' Tom sounded amused rather than offended; but, just in case, Jenny reached across and kissed him.

'We both know only too well that I'm yours for eternity, whereas Anna and William don't know each other very well at all. Although if William has anything to do with it,' she added wryly, 'that won't be the case for much longer.'

The umbrella was a constant reminder of her. Last night Rick had needed it on the long wet walk to his hotel, and he'd left it by the radiator in his room to dry. This morning, when he woke up, his stomach knotted at the very sight of it.

He remembered the way she'd laughed at it; except now he knew she'd been laughing at *him*, at his arrogant assumption that he'd be walking her home. He remembered how deftly she'd folded it; huh, she must have been laughing about that, too, and thinking, Can't he even work an umbrella properly? And he remembered the thrill of her touch as she handed it back …

He pulled his laptop savagely towards him and checked his email. Nothing of interest, so he turned to his list of recently viewed websites. For whatever reason, the one that jumped out at him was James Benwick's. He clicked on the link; same dreary old site, except that he could find no trace of 'Move on You'. In its place was something equally grotesque, entitled 'Lady in White' and dedicated 'To my brave angel Louisa':

In the white room,
In the white bed,
She lies white-faced.
Only poetry brings
A blush to her cheek,
A gleam to her hazel eye.
Poems from my heart
For the lady in white.

'Give me strength!' Rick resisted the urge to hurl the laptop across the room – but only just. If Lou actually liked this trash, she must need her head examining. He gave a mirthless laugh as he realised she'd had plenty of *that* over the last two weeks.

His mind wandered back to Anna. James may have lost interest – and he suspected that she'd never been interested in him anyway – but what the hell was going on between her and that jerk last night? Dinner – and then what? Back to her flat, passionate kisses on the sofa – opposite the painting that he'd come to think of as theirs alone, not to be shared with anyone else? Or maybe they made straight for the bedroom, tore each other's clothes off and–

'Please God, *no*!' Had he simply whispered the words, or shouted them out loud?

Strange how it had taken until this moment for everything to fall into place. When he'd first met her again in Charles and Mona's kitchen, and he was free of Shelley, he should have realised it was a second chance. But he was feeling shocked and raw, and he'd always been in denial about the Anna Elliot part of his past. If only he'd had the sense to stop and think – to face his feelings about her openly and honestly – they might have had a future.

Then he'd made a major error of judgement and become embroiled far too quickly with Lou. But hardly had he extricated himself from that relationship when here was Anna with someone else in her life – a man who seemed to be part of her past, just as he was. Had he really expected her to wait patiently until he sorted himself out and decided she was the only one for him?

What a sodding mess …

And now he had to go through the motions of being alive and kicking: this morning he was meeting Sophie and Ed for coffee and this afternoon he had another signing in Bristol. Finally, there was the theatre tonight with Guy: an unexpected pleasure, thanks to Marie-Claude being held up in Paris. By a strange coincidence, the play was called *Three Sisters*.

No prizes for guessing who he'd be thinking about all evening.

The phone rang just as Anna was blow-drying her hair. She didn't recognise the mobile number; all she knew was – it wasn't Rick's. She deliberately hadn't stored it that time he'd rung her out of the blue, but she was sure his ended in 651.

Not that she was expecting him to contact her again, not after last night. If she really wanted to know how he felt, she'd have to make the next move ...

'Anna?' A woman's voice, vaguely familiar.

'Yes?'

'Sophie Croft here – and I mean here. Ed and I have just arrived in Bath for the weekend.' A rich chuckle, so like her brother's from long ago. 'And for once it's not raining!'

'You could be tempting fate.' Anna managed a little laugh. 'Where are you staying?'

'The Royal Crescent Hotel, the most gorgeous suite, all expenses paid – a present from Rick for our fifth wedding anniversary. I wish he was staying here too, but there weren't any rooms left.'

Thank God for that, Anna thought, imagining what might happen if Rick and Walter bumped into each other at breakfast. But all she said was, 'Very nice – and congratulations. How long are you here for?'

Sophie sighed down the phone. 'Three whole days – which sounds a lot, but there's so much we want to do! Including seeing you – you had to turn down that cup of tea with us in Uppercross, remember? When are you free?'

'I'm not sure – what are your plans?'

'Let me see ... We want to try the hotel spa, of course, probably later today. Then I'd like to visit the Abbey again, and the Roman Baths. But first we're having coffee with Rick, it's the only time he can fit us in – that's the trouble with having a famous brother! He couldn't manage lunch because he's off to Bristol for a signing, and he can't do dinner because his publicist is taking him to the Theatre Royal.' Another chuckle. 'I'll be surprised if Rick can sit still long enough to watch a play for three hours!'

The Theatre Royal, tonight? Anna shelved that thought until later; for the moment, she wanted to establish if she'd have any other opportunities to meet him.

'Can't he see you tomorrow, then?' She hoped it came across as an innocent question.

'No, he's going up north, leaving straight after breakfast. He's got twelve solid days of signings, then he's coming to us for a few days before he flies back to Australia.' Sophie added, 'He's opening our garden centre the weekend after next – I hope you can come.'

'I'd love to,' Anna said automatically; but all she could think was, 'Two weeks, then he'll be gone. And I might never see him again.'

'You've heard about him and Lou, haven't you?' Sophie's voice sharpened. 'I know everyone thinks *she* dumped *him*, but it wasn't really like that. He just felt he had to do the right thing and stand by her. Thank God she recovered and let him off the hook!'

'Mmmm.'

'It certainly seems to have taught him a lesson – d'you know, he actually told me that he should have taken my advice and worked out what went wrong with his previous relationship before starting a new one? Incredible.' She paused. 'Did you go to his talk last night?'

'Yes, I did.'

'I thought you might,' Sophie went on, breezily. 'He sounds fine on the phone, but what did you think when you saw him?'

Anna struggled with a hot wave of humiliation as she recalled how the signing had ended. She'd been stunned by Rick's reference to a far more intimate moment – *I remember you saying that about something quite different ...* And excited by his offer to walk her home ... She'd found his awkwardness with the umbrella endearing, the touch of his fingers disturbingly familiar ... Then William had turned up, and Rick had become as bleak and unapproachable as before. And, although he'd not said a single word, she'd felt his anger rise between them like a barricade …

The bizarre thing was, when she'd thought it over in the middle of the night, his behaviour had given her a flicker of hope. But the time to do anything about it was running out – fast.

She decided to give Sophie a version of the truth. 'He gave a very … *interesting* talk, but I couldn't really tell how he was feeling.' Then – deep breath – 'I didn't have a chance to ask him some questions. Would you mind if I joined you for coffee?' She steeled herself for a polite refusal.

'Of course not!' Sophie made it sound like the best idea in the world. 'We're meeting in that lovely little deli on George Street at eleven o'clock. Come as soon as you like.'

Chapter Forty-Five

In the middle of the bustling café-delicatessen, Rick greeted Sophie and Ed even more warmly than usual; it seemed like years – not days – since he'd last seen them. And, for a split second, he forgot he was a minor celebrity. Then people started to stare and he made for the most secluded corner.

'Hotel OK?' he said, after they'd settled themselves at one of the chunky wooden tables.

Sophie beamed at him. 'More than OK, as you know very well.'

'Or as you would know, if you'd managed to get a room there yourself,' Ed put in with a sly wink.

Rick laughed. 'Don't rub it in any more, thank you – although the place I've got is pretty good.'

'How did your talk go last night?' Sophie said, as she scanned the menu.

He decided to be truthful. 'Mixed. Some things went to plan, other things didn't.'

She looked up. 'Maybe you should – ah, here's Anna.'

He wondered if he'd heard her correctly. The next moment, however, a pink-cheeked Anna was pulling out the chair opposite his, and smiling at everyone, even him ... especially him.

It was a second chance. Wasn't it?

Sophie picked up the signs immediately.

Rick wasn't supposed to be getting involved with *anyone*, until he'd worked out what had gone wrong with Shelley. Yet here he was, asking Anna if she recommended anything on the menu, using his seductive smile and what she called his chocolate-fudge-cake eyes – dark, delicious and deadly – to their fullest effect.

What was that famous Robin Williams quote? Something like 'God gave man a brain and a penis, and only enough blood to run one at a time.'

When they'd ordered coffee and – surprise, surprise – chocolate fudge cake for Rick and Anna, Sophie returned to their earlier conversation. 'So was it your usual talk, Rick, or something different?'

'Both.' Another smouldering look at Anna. 'The usual stuff at first – a talking trailer for the book – but, for that particular audience, I added something new. You see, all the creatures I mentioned last night have one thing in common – monogamy, a mate for the rest of their lives.'

Ed gave a loud guffaw. 'I'd have paid good money to hear about that – from you!'

'So would I,' Sophie said dryly, glancing sideways at Anna. The poor girl had a dreamy expression on her face, no doubt deluding herself that his talk had been aimed at her. 'Not much monogamy around these days, is there? With or without marriage.'

Anna seemed to rouse herself from her trance. 'I think you two are great adverts for monogamy. And Rick obviously thought your wedding anniversary was worth celebrating, otherwise he wouldn't have arranged this weekend.'

Another guffaw from Ed. 'Good one, Anna. And another thing – I'm always suggesting weekends away to Sophie, and she's always got a reason to stay at home. But as soon as Rick arranges something, she's packed and in the car, nagging me to hurry up!'

'Complete rubbish,' Sophie retorted, then paused as the waitress brought four coffees and two huge slabs of death by chocolate. She went on, 'I don't always do whatever Rick wants. Some of his ideas are ridiculous, like wanting me to emigrate to Melbourne almost as soon as he arrived. As if I'd have given up my life here, when he might only have stayed out there three years! And I also had Mother to think about.'

Anna started, and her gaze flicked across to Rick. 'Your mother? In what way?'

Rick didn't answer, so Sophie explained. 'She'd just moved to Spain, mainly for health reasons. I was responsible for her legal and financial affairs – Rick was still a student, a post-grad by then, and out of the country a lot. There was always a chance that Mother wouldn't settle and she'd come back to England.'

'And did she?'

Rick cleared his throat. 'No. She loved Spain – which probably meant she put the fear of God into the community of Ancient Brits out there – but she died after a few months.'

Anna's big grey eyes filled with tears. 'Oh, I'm so sorry … What happened to your father?'

Sophie grimaced. 'The less said about him the better. He hasn't been part of our lives for years, and we've lost touch.' Then, in a brighter tone, 'But, you know, I'm really glad I didn't let my brother persuade me to emigrate, because otherwise I wouldn't have met Ed.'

Ed stirred what Sophie considered far too much sugar into his cappuccino, and gave an exaggerated sigh. 'Whereas I keep hoping Rick still wants Sophie to go and live in Australia. Without me!'

'Well, I'm always open to persuasion,' Rick put in.

And there was a sudden intensity in his voice that made Sophie think he wasn't talking to Ed at all.

Anna had thought it impossible, and now it was actually happening: she and Rick were relaxing with Sophie and Ed over a coffee.

Except that it wasn't very relaxing – because, every time she met Rick's gaze, she wanted to lean across the table and kiss him. Good job Sophie and Ed hadn't noticed.

Piecing together the precious personal fragments of the conversation, she realised that life must have been hard for him when he first went to Australia. Not only did he have the aftermath of their break-up to cope with; Sophie had refused to leave England, and then his mother had died – and his father had obviously been out of the picture.

And just how was she meant to interpret that last remark: 'I'm always open to persuasion'? Was he suggesting they might have a future together? Things were different now – they were older and wiser, they'd completed their education, built their careers – but not necessarily easier. They would still have to make sacrifices, and really *want* to take the risk – so where did persuasion come into it?

Unless it was all about persuading yourself to decide what mattered most ...

But she was moving too fast, ready to make life-changing decisions based on a few enigmatic looks and ambiguous words. She made a determined effort to tune in to what the others were discussing; it turned out to be Rick's last-minute invitation to the theatre that night.

'If it's the Chekhov play, I'll probably see you there,' she said recklessly.

His face lit up. 'Great, I'll look out for you.' A pause, then he continued with a wicked grin, 'Any of your favourite heroes in it?'

Her eyes danced. 'How can you even ask that? When I told you who they were, I never even mentioned Chekhov.' She turned to Sophie and Ed. 'We were having a few drinks at the time, so no wonder he can't remember.'

'I remember it perfectly,' Rick said, in mock indignation. 'One of your heroes was ... James Benwick?'

She pretended to give this nonsense serious consideration. 'James meets the main criteria, I suppose. He's an Action Man – when he needs to be ... And he's thoughtful and kind – at least, to a certain person recovering in hospital ... A man of honour? Probably ... But there's nothing heroic about his writing.'

Another grin from Rick. 'You've seen his website, then?'

'Yes, I looked at it yesterday.'

She was about to contrast it with *Sex in the Sea*'s narrative style – spare, yet vivid, and at times incredibly moving – when Sophie chipped in. 'Rick, it's quarter to. Aren't you meant to be leaving for Bristol?'

He stood up. 'See what she's like, Anna? Always on my case, has been for the past thirty-two years.' With a mischievous glint in his eye, he shook Ed's hand, bent to give Sophie a brotherly kiss and received a playful slap in return.

Then he came round to Anna's side of the table. 'Until tonight,' he murmured; and his lips brushed the curve of her cheek. Instantly, she felt the blood rush to her face. It might have looked as casual as the kiss he'd just given Sophie, but it certainly didn't get the same flippant response.

She watched him walk away, and wished she could go with him; but Sophie was talking to her, something about lunch the next day. 'That sounds great,' she said, vaguely.

'The Royal Crescent it is, then. The restaurant's first class, apparently.'

Anna's eyes widened in dismay. 'Actually, can we meet somewhere else? My father and older sister are staying there too, and I'd rather not–'

A peal of laughter from Sophie. 'Neither would I! Right, how about the Pump Room Restaurant, at twelve-thirty?'

'That would be wonderful, it's one of my favourite places in Bath.' Anna turned her attention to finishing her cake although, without Rick there to share the experience, it had lost most of its appeal. She could almost feel her waistline expanding; at this rate, she'd never get into her coral dress tonight. Except ... why not splash out on something new?

Minutes later, she said goodbye to Sophie and Ed and headed for Jolly's. Shopping for clothes with a man in mind was an unfamiliar sensation, but she found something that looked good enough to justify the price.

Back home, instead of going straight upstairs, she decided to knock on Jenny and Tom's door. After a little while, an ashen-faced Jenny answered, shuffled Anna through to the kitchen and switched on the kettle.

'Where've you been?' she said. 'I've just been all the way up to your flat to see if you're feeling as bad as me.' She raised one eyebrow, very gingerly. 'If you are, you don't look it.'

'That's because I stuck to champagne, whereas you had red wine with your main course, didn't you? And it was very good champagne, so no after-effects.'

'You certainly seemed to enjoy yourself.'

'I suppose I felt safe with you and Tom there.'

Jenny frowned. 'Don't you feel safe on your own with William?'

A pause. 'I find him disturbing.'

'And is that good, or bad?'

'I'm not sure.'

Silence, while Jenny made them both a coffee; then she said, 'I found Rick Wentworth's talk disturbing.'

Anna glanced sharply at her. 'Why was that?'

'Oh, it made me think about Tom and whether we should be trying some of the new treatments we've read about. Of course we'd never get them on the National Health, but we can't afford to go privately unless we sell the house.' She sighed. 'And, at the end of the day, life's not too bad as it is.'

'But that's just what he was getting at,' Anna said eagerly.

'We can all go on as we are, doing nothing different. Whereas "hope" is an action word – or should be. Something aspirational, like – how did he put it? – living our dream. But, to achieve it, we usually have to come out of our comfort zone and change in some way.'

And she'd made up her mind. Tonight *she* would change – be proactive, ask Rick if they could go somewhere and talk. She'd tidy the flat, too, in the unlikely event that they'd come back here …

Jenny was saying, '… very convincing, ever thought of becoming an after-dinner speaker? Maybe you and Rick could join forces and combine *Sex in the Sea* with nineteenth-century Russian literature.' She put on a hushed David Attenborough tone. 'Meet Anna Karenina, a typical female sea dragon, leaving her child for hubby to bring up.'

Anna giggled. 'You're ridiculous! Although it would be a way of freshening up my lectures, which I've been meaning to do this term. What could Prince Myshkin be – the deep sea angler fish, making the ultimate self-sacrifice and fusing himself to the female?'

But by now Jenny had spotted Anna's carrier bag. 'You've been shopping – is it something to wear at the theatre? You *are* a dark horse, telling me you're not in a hurry to encourage William.' Her eyes sparkled. 'Come on, let's see what you've bought.'

Anna opened her mouth to tell Jenny that it wasn't William she wanted to impress – then quickly shut it again. No point in making things more complicated than they already were.

Chapter Forty-Six

Taking afternoon tea in the conservatory of Dottie Dalrymple's Garden Villa suite ... nodding wisely at her complaints about the scandalous price of practically everything ... adorned – and adored – by Lisa on his right and Cleo on his left ... Walter felt that life could not get much better. Once William arrived and he could gaze at himself reincarnated, he would be truly content.

At last there was a knock at the door – and in came William, profusely apologetic, with Anna. The dear boy had insisted on fetching her in case she forgot about having tea with Lady Dalrymple. Unfortunately, there'd been quite a delay between him finishing lunch with them and setting off for Bennett Street. Something to do with helping Cleo find the remote control for her TV – Lisa had been obliged to remind him that that's what the hotel staff were paid for.

Walter noted that, once again, William was wearing an almost identical outfit to his own. Although this was extremely flattering, how he knew what Walter would choose was a mystery. Unless Lisa was behind it? He could quite understand her wanting the two men in her life dressed to the same high sartorial standard.

Dottie offered Anna the seat next to hers; but when William sat down beside Lisa, she edged her chair away from him. Walter sighed to himself. It was only a matter of time, he was sure, before these two carried on from where they'd left off. For the moment, Lisa was blowing hot and cold.

And now Cleo was asking what had taken them so

long, and William was explaining that they'd bumped into someone Anna knew in the hotel grounds. 'Someone Walter knows, too, apparently,' he added. 'Ed Croft?'

Walter smiled benignly. 'A tenant of mine – or very soon will be. No doubt hired to do some gardening – the name of Sir Walter Elliot throws open a multitude of doors.'

'Actually, Ed and Sophie are staying here,' Anna put in – rather spitefully, he thought. 'They've got the Sir Percy Blakeney suite over in the main house.'

Walter almost choked on his lapsang souchong. For God's sake, didn't people like the Crofts know their place? The Sir Percy Blakeney was one of the most prestigious suites in the hotel! But when Dottie – sounding genuinely impressed – said, 'Dear me, Walter, you must be a very astute businessman to find tenants who can afford The Royal Crescent,' he recovered instantly.

'Oh, Croft's quite the entrepreneur in his own little way,' he told her. 'He and his wife are opening a garden centre in a couple of weeks' time, just down the road from Kellynch. They haven't actually asked me yet, but they'll be expecting me to do the honours. Cut the ribbon, make a speech, and so on – *noblesse oblige*, you know.' A long-suffering sigh. 'And I've spent a small fortune getting The Lodge refurbished for them, let's hope they're suitably grateful.'

Lisa patted his hand. 'Don't worry, they won't be, tenants never are. Actually, I'm more worried about them using the relaxation pool in The Bath House while they're here.' She shuddered. 'The husband's fingernails are enough to give you nightmares, let alone the rest of him.'

Walter nodded. 'Quite right, darling, I'll have a little word with them.'

'I wouldn't advise it,' Anna said, with one of her deceptively sweet smiles. 'The Crofts are here as guests of Rick Wentworth. I'm sure he'd be very annoyed if he knew you'd had one of your little words. And, by the way, they've asked *him* to open their garden centre.'

He felt his jaw sag in astonishment – and hastily lifted it. How dare she suggest that he, Sir Walter Elliot, could possibly be upstaged by a man whose only claim to fame was a book that no respectable person would be seen dead with?

He was about to say as much, when Dottie gave a little crow of delight and reached behind her chair. 'Look what I'm reading at the moment!' To Walter's horror, she held up a book with 'Sex in the Sea by Dr Rick Wentworth' brazenly splashed across it. And no doubt the photograph on the cover was the upstart himself, flaunting his tan and his muscles for all he was worth.

'It's absolutely fascinating, I'll never think of a barnacle in quite the same way again,' Dottie went on, panting with incomprehensible excitement. 'Is Rick Wentworth staying at The Royal Crescent too?'

While Anna shook her head, Cleo purred, 'We 'ave met 'eem, Lisa and me. 'E eez a *vairee* sexy man.'

This was adding insult to injury. 'Where on earth did you meet him?' Walter spluttered.

'At Kelleench.'

'*Kellynch*?' Good God, had the enemy breached his ramparts without him even noticing?

As always, Lisa read his mind. 'I didn't let him in the house,' she said soothingly. 'He just came to see how The Lodge was progressing.' She gave him a meaningful look. 'If Lady Dalrymple wants to meet him, I'm sure you could arrange something with the Crofts.'

Once again he silently thanked the heavens above for this blessing of a daughter, while Dottie gushed, 'That would be wonderful, Walter. Let me know when he can call and I'll make sure I'm here, with my book ready for him to sign.'

Walter squeezed some enthusiasm into his voice. 'Delighted, just leave it to me.'

Luckily, William changed the subject. 'Didn't you want to hear about tonight's play, Dorothea? Anna says it's classic Chekhov, very subtle, all about the decay of the privileged class.'

'Decay?' Dottie said, in a puzzled tone. 'Good gracious, is it a comedy?'

Anna gave her an appraising look. 'More a tragic reality – and not just in pre-revolutionary Russia.'

Walter didn't quite understand her meaning, but he sensed it wasn't intended to be complimentary. Time for a distraction; he certainly didn't want to risk falling out with Dottie all over again.

He fixed an indulgent smile on his face, peered across at Anna and said, 'Well, my dear, aren't you going to let us into your little secret?'

She started, blushed and looked round to see who he was talking to. An awkward pause, then – 'Wh-what do you mean?'

'Your skin, it's almost radiant! What have you been using on it – Crème de la Mer?'

Next to him, Lisa said under her breath, 'Fat chance, on a university lecturer's salary.'

'I haven't used anything,' Anna said flatly.

Walter wagged a playful finger at her. 'Come along, there's definitely something different about you. It must be Crème de la Mer, I bought some for Cleo the other day and she's seen an improvement already.'

Cleo seized his hand and laid it against her face. 'Sir Voltaire eez always so generous.'

'Not at all, I'm simply a man who invests in beauty,' he said, with a modest little laugh. He peered again at Anna, stroking his own silk-smooth cheek thoughtfully. 'Or have you had a course of treatments somewhere? Not at the hotel spa, of course, that's for residents only, but perhaps the Thermae Bath Spa? I was quite tempted by their Luxury Caviar Facial myself.'

Anna gave a tight smile. 'I've just told you, I haven't used anything.' She got abruptly to her feet. 'I'd better go, I've got a few things to do before tonight.' She turned to Dottie. 'Thank you so much for inviting Mona to the theatre, she's really looking forward to it. You did know that Henrietta's not coming, didn't you? She's meeting up with some friends, so there'll be a spare place and I wondered–'

'Not any more, Minty's taken it,' Walter said triumphantly, positive that Anna had been about to ask if the Smith woman could join their party.

'I phoned her as soon as I knew we were one short,' William put in. He added anxiously, 'I thought you'd be pleased.'

'Of course,' Anna said, looking anything but. 'Anyway, thank you for tea and I'll see you all later.'

Walter exchanged glances with Lisa. Anna had obviously promised the Smith woman that she could join them; now she'd have to tell her she couldn't. No doubt the woman would be terribly disappointed, but did she *still* not realise that the Elliots – apart from Anna – were very particular about the people they mixed with?

Then he noticed Lisa's face darken. Looking round, he was just in time to see William hurrying out of the room after Anna. Why, Walter couldn't imagine – except that the dear boy was too helpful for his own good.

But wait a minute – hadn't Mona been complaining to Lisa that Anna was desperate to break up her marriage? No wonder she'd been rattled just now when he'd asked her about her little secret! Well, making one sister jealous could be seen as an unfortunate lapse of judgement; making both sisters jealous, however, was the act of a wanton relationship-wrecker.

From that moment, Walter resolved to do anything – *anything* – to keep William at Lisa's side.

'Anna, darling, whatever's wrong?'

She whirled round to find William standing unexpectedly close.

'Nothing,' she said automatically, slipping into her coat.

As she turned to open the front door and escape, his hand shot out and held the door firmly shut. 'Is it anything I've done – like inviting Araminta to the theatre?'

A grim smile. 'No, although I know someone who'd have jumped at the chance of going.' She hesitated, then decided to trust him with the truth. 'It's more the whole Lady Dalrymple thing – or rather Walter's behaviour when he's around people like her. I'd forgotten how nauseating he can be.'

And she couldn't help comparing this afternoon's pretentiousness with the easy camaraderie of Rick and the Crofts earlier; but she wasn't going to say that to William.

She went on, 'Look, I've come to tea, which is what you all wanted, so I'm off home now – if you'll let me go.' A pointed stare at his hand on the door.

'If it was up to me,' he said softly, 'I'd never let you go.'

Once again, these were the words that she wanted to hear from someone else. She bit her lip and looked straight at him. 'Go back to the others, sit and enjoy their inane conversation and narrow-minded opinions. That's not me, though. I prefer clever, well-informed people, like Jenny and Tom last night.'

'Don't underestimate the value of networking with the Dorotheas of this world – believe me, they have their uses.' A dazzling grin. 'But otherwise I agree, last night's company was the best – and not just because of Jenny and Tom.' He took her hands in his and dropped a light kiss on each palm.

She pulled her hands away, wrenched open the door and frowned at him. 'Please understand – I'm not like my father. Flattery will get you absolutely nowhere.'

'I'm not flattering you, I'm simply speaking the truth.' He paused. 'I was hoping you'd know the difference.'

Her only answer was to slam the door behind her.

Chapter Forty-Seven

Whatever the going rate, Rick thought, a box at the Theatre Royal was probably a bargain from a PR point of view. Overhanging the stage at one end of the Dress Circle, it thrust him and Guy almost literally into the spotlight. As the auditorium filled, they became the object of mainly female attention; faces turned their way – some with theatre glasses, others without – and a few women even pointed their fingers. Thank God his mother wasn't here to see them; 'don't point, Frederick' had been one of the many don'ts of his childhood.

'Did you have to take a box?' he said to Guy. 'It's like being in a bloody goldfish bowl.'

Guy shrugged. 'I thought it would impress Marie-Claude and, anyway, everything else had sold out. I only got this because the old bird who hired the other boxes didn't want it. She'd heard it was haunted by the Grey Lady, whoever she might be.'

'You certainly know how to arrange a relaxing night out at the theatre. While the lights are up, we've got people watching our every move. And when the lights go down, we'll be wondering if the resident ghost has joined us.'

But Guy was too busy checking his BlackBerry to retaliate. So Rick scanned the crowds below for what seemed like the tenth time, hoping to catch a glimpse of Anna. That was the only good thing about this box – she'd see him a mile off. But until she did, he'd have to be patient; bit of a tall order after this morning …

Guy interrupted his train of thought. 'Great news, the manager at Molland's is offering another signing for a week on Friday. There's been a cancellation at a much bigger venue and, based on the number of people who wanted tickets for your talk last night, he thinks he can fill it easily.' He looked across at Rick. 'It'll mean not going to your sister's until the next day, but it's only an hour or so from here, isn't it?'

Rick nodded slowly while his brain raced through the implications. If everything went well with Anna tonight, he'd have to wait nearly two weeks to see her again – unless she came to see him during his northern tour? And if it didn't go well tonight, he'd make one last attempt as soon as he returned. Which meant that the event Guy was arranging in Bath was a no-brainer.

'OK, I'll do it,' he said, with a pretend scowl. 'Consider it a thank you for putting up with me.'

The response was a broad grin and a sarcastic 'Deep down you're a real softie, aren't you?'

While Guy typed a reply on his BlackBerry, Rick returned to his search. This time, his gaze rested on the box directly opposite; the twin of this one, not yet occupied. Below it was a box for three, and entering it – flanked by her up-his-own-arse father and a little roly-poly woman in a fuss of green frills and gold feathers – was Anna, straight and slim and enchanting in an off-the-shoulder silver-grey dress, clinging to every curve.

At that very moment, the little woman trained her theatre glasses on him and nudged Anna excitedly. She glanced up ... and his whole body stilled in anticipation. He was too far away to read the expression in her eyes; but, when she turned and left the box, he knew exactly what she was trying to tell him.

He muttered his excuses to Guy and went to meet her.

Anna hovered between the two staircases leading up to the

Dress Circle, looking anxiously at the faces milling around her. She'd reckoned that this was the obvious place – but where was he?

She slumped back against the wall. They must have missed each other, or perhaps he hadn't understood what she wanted him to do. She glanced at her watch. Ten minutes or so until curtain up; the noisy crowds were starting to thin and, in a moment or two, she'd have to return to her seat. She closed her eyes and tried to compose herself for the evening ahead. What a prospect – Lady Dalrymple asking more stupid questions and her father listening obsessively to her answers, in case she gave offence. And all the time she'd be wondering how to meet up with Rick ...

'Anna.'

She opened her eyes to see him standing in front of her, smiling the little smile that used to make her melt into his arms. Smart, tight-fitting jeans; sky-blue V-necked sweater, hinting at the tanned, muscled chest beneath; hands in the pockets of a black jacket – the only concession to formality. He was wearing something that would fall between 'travesty' and 'tragedy' on her father's style barometer – and he looked amazing.

His gaze flicked over her bare shoulders and back to her face. 'Nice dress.'

She felt herself go red. 'You too.' Even redder now. 'What I mean is, you look nice.' How *tame* – think of something ... provocative. 'About coffee with Sophie and Ed earlier – I sort of invited myself along. And I'm really glad I did.'

'I've never enjoyed chocolate fudge cake as much as I did this morning,' he said, his voice warm with amusement. 'In fact, since I was last in Bath – walking out of your flat, being unforgivably rude – *everything*'s turned out far better than I expected.'

Deep breath. 'Do you mean with Lou – or me?'

The slow familiar bedroom laugh; eyes dancing an invitation, as they had that summer in France. 'I mean both, definitely both. We'll come to you later–' her heart missed a beat – 'but first I need to explain about Lou. On that walk at Uppercross, I made a right idiot of myself – no wonder she thought I wanted to jump into bed with her. From then on, I spent most of the time telling her to take it slow so that we could get to know each other. But the damage was already done, as the accident at Lyme Regis showed–'

'Remember what Henrietta said, you couldn't have prevented it.' She put out her hand to reassure him, then stopped. Too public here, people were already staring at them – they recognised Rick, no doubt – and the play would start soon. Later, when they went somewhere to talk properly, it would be different …

But to him, it seemed, other people didn't matter at all; before her hand could drop to her side, he caught it in his and said wryly, 'Let me take the credit for my own stupidity. But I have to give you some credit for James and Lou getting together, although I can't imagine you knew that when you turned him into a hero on the Cobb.'

She laughed. 'You're right – I never expected it! Anyway, it's probably more down to Lou's personality change.' Then, in case he'd not heard it from Ben, she added softly, 'Henrietta says James is already applying for teaching posts in Somerset. Apparently Roger and Barbara have invited him to move into the Great House until he and Lou can get a place of their own.'

The light faded from his eyes, and he let go of her hand. 'That's just like the Musgroves, isn't it? Makes a big difference if the parents are supportive.' He looked down at his feet. 'A big difference. But all the same …'

'All the same – what?' she prompted.

He cleared his throat. 'I think Lou's a great girl, and I

260

really hope she and James will be happy. It's just ...' He looked up at her, his face set. 'You'll know from talking to him that he's a really clever guy, always reading, and writing his poetry, however crap it might be. Trouble is – Lou's not at all intellectual, whereas Julie, his ex, most certainly was ... And I think he'll miss that, once the novelty's worn off.' A pause; then out rushed more words, spilling over each other like waves on a shore. 'Maybe he should have asked himself why Julie left him, and fought to win her back, because compared to Lou she was special, very special, and you don't get over someone like that, ever.' His voice was low and urgent now, and he held one clenched fist to the left side of his chest. 'I *know* you don't.'

She stared at him, sensing that he was talking about himself as much as James. She wanted so much to believe that she was his 'someone special'. But, equally, it could be any woman from the past ten years; she knew so little about his life in Australia ...

Later, when they had more time, she would ask him who he meant. Not yet. Not here. Instead she said shyly, 'What did you think of Lyme?'

'Lyme?' He frowned. 'Pretty, quaint, typically English. I can see its attractions – but, after what happened, I'm not in a hurry to go back.'

'Please don't say that.' She gave him an apologetic smile. 'You see, Lyme's one of my favourite places. I went there a lot as a child, with my mother, and once–'

'Anna!' A voice like the crack of a whip – Minty, just a few yards behind Rick, with William next to her.

Rick jerked his head round. Anna couldn't see his expression – but she could see Minty's, cold and condemning. And William's, a bland, impenetrable mask.

Then the bell rang, long and loud, for curtain up. Without

another word, or even a look, Rick stabbed his hands back in his pockets, turned his back on her and walked away.

He didn't take his hands out of his pockets again until he was in the box, safe from temptation. The temptation to reach out and trace the pale curves of her shoulders above the silver-grey dress – which, when he got close, turned out to be made of the finest wool, smooth as a second skin. The temptation to cup her face in his hands and kiss her hard, over and over and over again. And finally, just as overwhelming, the temptation to flatten that smug-looking man with a single smash of his fist. Oh, and to tell the Russell woman – or The Godmother, as he'd nicknamed her in one of his darker moments – that she was welcome to pick up the pieces.

'You OK?' Guy whispered, as the curtain went up.

He gave a curt nod and stared down at the stage: a sunlit sitting room, with three young women coming to life. The one in blue spoke first.

'It's exactly a year since Father died …'

He didn't hear the rest. A movement across the auditorium caught his attention and he looked over. The box for two was no longer empty; in the light from the stage, he could make out a blond man leaning in close to a dark-haired woman as they shared a programme. So close, in fact, that it was obvious he wanted to be sharing much, much more – if he wasn't already.

And the woman's dress was silver grey.

Anna wished she'd made a fuss and insisted on returning to her original seat. With her thoughts still full of Rick, she hadn't realised where William was leading her until they were almost upstairs in the Dress Circle. There was no sign of Minty, and she presumed that she'd taken her place between Lady Dalrymple and Walter. She couldn't face fighting a path through all the people behind her and asking Minty to swap; but she resolved to do exactly that as soon as the interval came round.

She was dimly aware of William placing a programme on her lap and the curtain lifting; but she couldn't concentrate on the opening scenes of the play. Her mind kept twisting Rick's words this way and that like a kaleidoscope. *Nice dress* ... Everything's *turned out far better than I expected* ... *We'll come to you later* ... *Compared to Lou she was special, very special, and you don't get over someone like that, ever. I* know *you don't* ... When she viewed it as him trying to tell her that he still loved her, she felt exquisitely happy; when she viewed it in any other light, she felt utterly miserable. And that was the trouble – it was all too open to interpretation.

At last she forced herself to tune in to the play; just as well *Three Sisters* was one where she could instantly pick up the thread. She'd almost grown up with it, intrigued by the title as well as her mother's passion for Chekhov. When she was young, she couldn't make much sense of it; but by her twenties she'd come to understand it only too well – and, instead of identifying with only one sister, she found traces of herself in each of them. Like Olga, she was practical and conscientious. Like Irina, she was idealistic about finding true love – but, ultimately, resigned to a life without it. And like Masha she'd fallen for someone at eighteen ...

Now William was murmuring in her ear – something about needing her to explain which sister was which, and why soldiers were garrisoned in the Russian provinces. She answered his questions as briefly as possible, then pretended to focus all her attention on the play. When she sensed him doing the same, she stole a sideways glance at the box opposite, wondering if Rick was finding it equally difficult to concentrate. But he was staring, stony-faced, at the stage.

And no wonder. Irina was talking about Masha's unhappiness – 'She married when she was eighteen, when he seemed to her the wisest of men. Now it's different.' After seven years of marriage, Masha was totally disillusioned and on the brink of a doomed affair with Vershinin, the soldiers' commanding officer.

Would it have been the same for Anna if she'd gone away with Rick at that age? One thing was certain, Rick wouldn't have been as forgiving as Masha's husband Kulygin ...

No change of scenery between Acts One and Two, just different lighting to suggest evening. And soon came the words that Anna knew by heart, spoken by Masha: 'Surely we must believe in something, or at least seek some sort of truth, otherwise our lives are empty, empty ... To live without understanding why cranes fly, why a child is born, why stars light up the sky ... You've got to know what you're living for, or there's no point to anything.'

Her mother had always interpreted this as a justification for religious faith. But now, for the first time, Anna saw it as a crystallisation of her personal philosophy. Her happiest times had been with her mother, and then those few weeks in France with Rick. Which wasn't to say that she depended on another person to make life worth living; it was rather that, for her, a soul mate gave everything a clearer, brighter purpose.

Soul mate. Memories of Rick last night, sharing his thoughts on monogamy and his dream of a mate for the rest of his life ...

These words of Masha's were a call to action. Time to believe in something, or at least seek some sort of truth.

Chapter Forty-Eight

As soon as the curtain went down after Act Two, Rick was on his feet.

'Need some fresh air,' he muttered to Guy.

The other man grinned at him, unperturbed. 'A drink, more like. You look as though you've just seen the Grey Lady!'

Rick twisted his mouth into a smile and left the box. He'd been haunted by the Grey Lady all right; but she was flesh and blood rather than a ghost.

At first, he hadn't been able to take his eyes off the couple in the box opposite, following every contact between them, almost or actual, with a sort of macabre compulsion. However, he could detect nothing more than the odd brush of hands – apparently accidental as they consulted the programme – and an occasional exchange of words, initiated by the man. Just as well; if there'd been anything else, he'd have been over there in a flash and lining himself up for a charge of grievous bodily harm. Not the sort of publicity Guy probably had in that plan of his …

Eventually, reassured that Anna seemed far more absorbed in the play than in the jerk next to her, he'd switched his gaze to the stage. Ironically, what was happening there only served to remind him of her: three bloody sisters – and the middle one feeling like she'd thrown her life away, at eighteen, on the wrong man.

But now his instinct was to find Anna again, and recapture that feeling of happiness tinged with misery. Or was it misery tinged with happiness? Not that it mattered. All he knew was that he had to be with her, and pain or pleasure was pretty irrelevant.

Forging his way down the stairs, pushing through the crush of people, he saw her before she saw him. She was standing where they'd met earlier, midway between the two staircases – hemmed in by both sisters, the father and The Godmother. The jerk wasn't with her, thank God.

It was the first time he'd seen the three sisters together and he couldn't help comparing them. Despite their different colouring, Mona and Lisa wore the same vibrant make-up and bored expressions. Both good-looking women but, in his opinion, overrated – like their namesake on display in the Louvre. Next to them, Anna was a unique and infinitely more subtle work of art, with a value beyond price. And how desperately he wanted a private viewing …

She still hadn't noticed him; in fact, she seemed to be having a heated discussion with The Godmother. For once, though, he was grateful to be recognised by complete strangers. Heads turned, women squealed and gasped, 'Rick Wentworth!' – and Anna looked up at last. He held her gaze, vaguely aware of The Godmother's Medusa-like stare.

'Rick darling, over here!' Mona shrilled in a far-too-loud voice, leaving no one in any doubt that they were on first-name terms.

He saw Anna press her fingers to her temples, as if trying to ward off a headache. Perfectly understandable – ten years ago, he'd threatened two of the people there with violence if their paths ever crossed again. Not explicitly, of course; 'I won't be responsible for my actions,' had been the gist, minus expletives.

The Russell woman certainly looked as though the feeling was still mutual. But, to his amazement, the father's ridiculously wrinkle-free face stiffened in a rictus grin. Bemused, Rick found himself going up to the man he'd once wanted to castrate – assuming that someone hadn't already beaten him to it – and, God forbid, shaking his hand. It wasn't a pleasant experience – rather like attempting to catch a jellyfish – and, thankfully, it was over in a split second. Then, taking her father's lead, Lisa leaned forward and brushed his cheek coldly with her lips; at which point Mona, not to be outdone, kissed him full on the mouth. No kisses forthcoming from anyone else, however. The Godmother turned pointedly away, while Anna–

Where was Anna?

Her father was speaking in that pompous voice of his, each vowel mutilated beyond recognition. '... a very dear friend of mine, Lady Dalrymple – a dowager viscountess, in case you didn't know.' He addressed the floor, as if he couldn't bear to look at Rick any longer than was absolutely necessary. 'She's here tonight, but don't embarrass her by introducing yourself. It's best if you make an appointment through me.'

'An appointment?' Rick repeated, blankly. Where had Anna gone? To meet the jerk? Bit of a coincidence that they were both missing ...

'To sign her book, that's all,' the father said, dismissively. 'Nothing you can't handle, I'm sure.'

This time, the words sank in, and the condescension behind them was unmistakable. 'I hope it's just a case of making my mark,' Rick said, through clenched teeth. 'Writing my name could be more of a problem – simple, uneducated peasant that I am.' And he spun on his heel and went, before he did something he wouldn't really regret at all.

The bell rang; five minutes until curtain up. Anna, waiting at the entrance to the box where Rick had been sitting, bit her lip; he must come soon, surely? Then she heard his footsteps approaching and tried to decipher his mood – man in a hurry, or man in a strop? One look at him confirmed it was both, and his face darkened even more when he saw her. She put her hand out, tentatively, but he stepped back out of reach.

'Where the hell did you get to?' His eyes flashed his resentment. 'I've been looking for you everywhere, and now the sodding play's about to start.'

'Rick, please can we talk–'

'We're talking now, aren't we?'

'I meant later.' She hesitated. 'I thought we could go for a drink somewhere–'

'Won't your boyfriend object?'

'*Who?*'

'The man who interrupted us in Lyme Regis. The man who interrupted us last night. The man who – with his sidekick, your delightful godmother – interrupted us downstairs. See some sort of pattern emerging?'

'Oh, you mean William.' She smiled, eager to set the record straight. 'He's just a friend – a family friend, actually. Ages ago, my mother and I spent a month with him and his mother in Lyme. And I hadn't seen him since – until that morning when I was having breakfast with you. Turns out Lyme is as much a special place for him as it is for me. So we–'

'Spare me the details.' His face shuttered. 'Have you got a painting of Lyme at home, too? Not relegated to the living room, of course, like that other one. Above your bed, perhaps? Oh yes, a special place for "a special place"!'

She stared up at him. 'You're *jealous*, aren't you? Jealous of William!'

He glared back. 'Have I got reason to be?'

It was almost funny; how could he *think* … 'No, you haven't, but that's not the point. You can't trust me, or anyone else, because – because you can't trust yourself!'

'What the hell does that mean?'

'Work it out for yourself. And when you've done that, then maybe we can talk about the future.'

He looked straight at her, but his eyes were empty. 'We had a future ten years ago, and you threw it away,' he said quietly. 'Let's just leave it at that.'

Without another word, he turned and walked off.

Chapter Forty-Nine

'Oh, Annie ...' Rick woke on a sharp, shuddering breath and sat bolt upright, his mind groping to piece everything together ...

Hadn't she followed him out of the theatre, stolen up behind him and slipped her arms round his waist? He'd looked down at those small pale hands, covered them possessively with his own, then turned and gathered her to him, whispering brokenly, 'I'm sorry, I'm sorry.' The silver-grey wool dress was so soft and warm he could have stayed there forever ... But then he noticed it was raining, and he'd forgotten to bring his umbrella. So he took off his jacket, wrapped it carefully round her, bent his head and kissed her. And it was like being on the boat with her all over again – kissing without needing to hold back ...

The next thing he knew, they were here – in this room – and he was peeling off her damp dress ... Except that it was more like his bedroom in Australia, and he was telling her that her dress would dry in no time if he spread it on the veranda. She laughed and asked what she could wear while it dried, and he said simply, 'Me.'

Now, in the grey morning light of an English autumn, he risked a glance at the stark white pillow beside him. Empty, as he'd feared it would be; and smooth, to show she'd never been here at all. Because this had just been a dream, an achingly vivid dream. And the worst thing was – yesterday he'd had the distinct feeling that he could have made it a beautiful reality. She'd sought him out, looked at him in that old familiar way, made him think – oh, lots of things, but mainly that she wasn't interested in anyone else.

Then, during the interval, he'd lost it. Big time.

He wanted to blame her father, or The Godmother. They hadn't changed in ten bloody years, despite the father's token attempt at civility. But he hadn't changed either, had he? Same old knee-jerk reaction, defiance before discretion, letting what other people thought of him get under his skin ...

You can't trust me, or anyone else, because you can't trust yourself.

Of course he trusted himself, and he trusted others. At work, he was always giving post-grads more responsibility if he thought they were up to it. With personal relationships it was different, he had to admit; he'd never let himself get close to a woman since Anna. So in that sense she was right: he couldn't trust himself.

And yet here he was, wanting a second chance with her, telling her that he was always open to persuasion; but that meant he had to be prepared to take a risk.

First, though, he had to communicate a slight change of plan to his sister. He reached for his mobile, selected her number and counted the rings – three, four, five. 'Sophie?'

'What's wrong?' Half-asleep, she still managed to sound anxious about him.

He sighed down the phone. 'Why do you think something's wrong?'

'It's very early, you must have something on your mind.'

'And you're on holiday – sorry, I forgot.'

She chuckled. 'Don't worry, I'll get my revenge. A few extras on the hotel bill, maybe. Anyway, you'd better tell me what's bothering you.'

'It's no big deal. Guy told me last night that Molland's are arranging another event in Bath. It's a week on Friday, in the evening, so I won't be coming to you until the Saturday morning. I'll make sure I'm in good time for the opening ceremony, of course.'

'You could still come to us on Friday night, couldn't you? The event won't finish that late.'

'No, I – I need to sort something out here.'

Her tone hardened. 'Something female, I take it?'

'What a nasty, suspicious mind you've got. But you're spot on.'

'I hope you're not hitting on some poor girl just before you go back to Australia.' In the background, he heard Ed telling her to leave her brother alone. 'That's Ed, siding with you as usual,' she went on, adding waspishly, 'Did you stay awake at the theatre?'

'I did – but I'd have been better off asleep,' he said heavily. 'And I pissed Guy off because I left at the interval.' His apologetic text claiming illness had apparently been less than convincing. 'Look, I need to go, Dave and I are leaving shortly. I'll phone you later, when I get to Leeds.'

And he had someone else to phone later, too; but there was no point in sharing that with Sophie. At least – not yet.

'You seem to be screwing *everything* up at the moment,' Mona announced later that morning, as she flounced into Anna's flat. Henrietta followed, slanting a sympathetic look at Anna.

Anna shut the door reluctantly behind them. She might have enjoyed this unexpected visit if Mona was in a better mood; or, more likely, if Henrietta had come on her own. 'I have no idea what you mean. Do you want a coffee?'

'We're not staying.' Mona flung herself on the sofa and narrowed her eyes at Anna, while Henrietta hovered between them. 'Let me get this straight. Sophie Croft told you yesterday morning that Rick was going away today, but you didn't think to mention it until last night, when it was too late?'

'Too late for what?' Henrietta put in.

Mona ignored her. 'It's not as if you've got a chance with him yourself, we've been through that already. So why spoil someone else's chances?' She jerked her head in Henrietta's direction.

'What – were you planning to set me and Rick up on a date?' Henrietta's eyes widened. 'Thank God you didn't. I've decided I'm very happy with Kyle for the moment – and, if I ever want anyone else, then *I'll* do the asking, all by myself. Anyway,' she added with a shrug, 'a girl would be mad to get involved with Rick when he's only here a couple more weeks. You'd just be getting to know him, then – whoosh! Off he goes to Australia and you never hear from him again. Broken-heart territory, pure and simple.'

Anna swallowed. Henrietta's down-to-earth take on the situation made it sound so hopeless. Just suppose she went to the opening of the Crofts' garden centre and the impossible happened – she got back with Rick. Wouldn't it simply be history repeating itself – a few days of complete and utter bliss, then big decision time? And now, despite her regrets, would she actually drop everything and follow him to the other side of the world? She felt sick at the thought that maybe, when it came to the crunch, she wouldn't …

Mona examined her nails. 'Actually, I'm not that impressed by Rick Wentworth any more. Seems to have a massive chip on his shoulder – he was quite rude to Walter during the interval last night.'

'Oh? I must have missed that.' Anna forced some indifference into her voice.

'Yes, you took ages in the Ladies, or wherever you went. Were you ill or something?' She pressed on without waiting for an answer. 'Anyway, Walter was just trying to fix up for Rick to go and see Lady Dalrymple, to sign her copy of *Sex in the Sea*. But Rick said he was treating him like a peasant and stormed off. Unfortunately, Lady Dalrymple's still desperate to meet him – which is the only reason why Walter was looking for him after the play. And then you conveniently remembered that he was going away first thing this morning, so it was all pretty pointless anyway.' Mona checked her watch. 'I'm wasting valuable time, let's hit the shops.' She swept towards the door, throwing a careless, 'Don't suppose you're coming?' over her shoulder.

Anna shook her head. 'Sorry, I've been invited out for lunch.'

'Ooh, anyone we know?' Henrietta said. 'Is it William what's-his-name?'

On her way out of the door, Mona turned and rolled her eyes. 'That's another example of you screwing up. I made more headway with William during the second half of that dreadful play than you've made in two weeks!'

Anna said nothing. Last night she'd felt only relief when Mona had taken her place beside William. She'd spent the rest of the evening sitting with Lisa and Cleo in the box beneath Rick's, wondering about all sorts of things. Such as – had he returned to his seat, and how could he possibly be jealous of William?

'Don't you want to know what I found out?' Mona prompted.

She shrugged. 'If you want to tell me.'

'He's absolutely mortified about the Brandi Berette episode – but he feels that, in a funny sort of way, it's given him an invaluable insight into Walter's infatuation with Cleo. He's come to Bath to get Lisa back – she's not making it easy for him, but he says he enjoys a challenge. And he also wants to get rid of Cleo – in fact, he told me he spent the whole of the interval last night interrogating her in the pub next door. I must admit, I did wonder where they'd got to.' Mona gave a little smirk of triumph. 'And he can't figure you out at all. He thinks you're weird.'

'Good.' Anna smiled across at Henrietta. 'Because I'm having lunch with the Crofts, not William.'

Henrietta's interest evaporated. 'Oh. Right.'

'Are you sure they didn't invite me as well?' Mona said sulkily. 'Very strange.'

'Not really – as you live so near, they could invite you out any time, couldn't they?' Anna couldn't resist adding, with a mischievous grin, 'If they really wanted to.'

Chapter Fifty

Walter toiled back up towards the Royal Crescent, pausing every few minutes as if to admire the view. In reality he was a little – only a little – out of breath from his walk round The Circus; and, he had to admit, rather bored with his own company. He missed Cleo strolling beside him, linking her arm through his, commenting on the fashion gaffes and physical deformities of passers-by. Of course, she invariably ended with a shrewd observation about his superiority on both counts, but that wasn't the point.

Apart from their visit to the theatre, he'd hardly seen her – and it wasn't as if she was off somewhere with Lisa. No, over the last week she seemed to have discovered some mysterious life away from them both, a life of early-morning outings and secretive shopping expeditions that they weren't invited to share. Take today – she'd told him last night that she'd be going to Holy Communion at the Abbey, to cleanse herself of 'eempure zoughts'. He'd instantly offered himself in the role of father confessor; but, eyes bright with tears, she'd explained that she daren't lay herself bare to him, of all people. That had been enough to trigger some impure thoughts of his own ... It seemed, however, that there was no risk of Cleo expecting him to turn thought into action; she'd become strangely reticent on the subject of them having a bath together in search of his sacral chakra.

And another thing – earlier, he'd checked with the hotel and found that Holy Communion at the Abbey was at eight o'clock, and could last no more than an hour because the next service was at nine fifteen. It was now after twelve. Surely Cleo hadn't spent the entire morning on her knees?

''Morning, Sir Walter.'

He started and peered at the woman who'd greeted him, as though she was merely one of countless acquaintances he had in Bath – when in fact he'd recognised her voice immediately. 'Mr and Mrs Croft! Where are you off to?'

'We're having lunch with Anna,' the husband replied, extending his paw-like hand.

Walter shook it gingerly. 'Anna?'

'Your daughter,' Sophie Croft put in. 'Such a lovely girl, she must take after her mother.'

He had a sneaking feeling that the woman was matching her brother for insolence, but he didn't want to alienate this couple until he'd got what he wanted. So he stared down his nose at them and said languidly, 'Anna does look like my wife – which I find very distressing, even now. Except that Irina was one of the St Petersburg Petrovs, a leading Russian émigré family, and always behaved like a true aristocrat.' He sidestepped memories of her more outspoken moments and continued, 'Which reminds me – a dear friend of mine, Lady Dalrymple, would like to meet your brother. She's staying at the hotel, so it's simply a question of him making an appointment to call on her before he leaves the country.'

Sophie Croft shook her head. 'Unfortunately he's a very busy man. But he's doing another talk here a week on Friday – she can meet him there, if there are any tickets left.'

Walter gave one of his most condescending smiles. 'I'm afraid Lady Dalrymple is extremely busy herself. I doubt she'll be able to fit it in, but I'll let her know.' He paused, then said brightly, 'I could always see if she's available to open your garden centre? Now that would be a real coup – she is a dowager viscountess, after all.'

'*Such* a tempting offer, isn't it, Ed?' There it was again – that thinly veiled insolence! She went on, 'But one we'll have to refuse. Who do you think people would rather meet – a young, handsome celebrity with something relevant to say about the world we live in, or an old dear whose only claim to fame is being part of an antiquated system of privileges that she hasn't had to lift a finger for?'

And off they marched, leaving Walter momentarily stunned. He soon recovered, however; and, as he resumed his slow, lonely journey back to the hotel, he was glad that he'd never allowed the Crofts anywhere near Dottie Dalrymple. It would have been catastrophic, positively catastrophic.

He had no doubt that Sophie Croft was already regretting her little outburst. She must realise, surely, that she'd just thrown away the chance of a lifetime? He'd give her until this evening to come begging for an introduction to Lady Dalrymple; and he'd make it quite clear that, if she was lucky enough to get an appointment, she was to leave all the talking to him.

Sophie didn't give Lady Dalrymple another thought, her mind far more happily occupied with the prospect of seeing Sir Walter's least favourite daughter. She and Ed arrived at the Pump Room Restaurant in good time; but it was nearer quarter to one when Anna arrived, out of breath and slightly dishevelled.

'Sorry I'm late,' she said, dropping one of her gloves and scrabbling under the table to rescue it. 'Just as I was going out, my godmother rang to invite me to lunch. When I said I couldn't make it, she gave me the third degree – who was I meeting, where, what time and so on. In the end, I had to be quite abrupt to get her off the phone.'

She looked so horrified at her own behaviour that Sophie laughed. 'Don't worry, just sit down and relax.'

'That was a nice surprise yesterday afternoon, seeing you at the hotel,' Ed put in. 'For me, anyway.'

Anna let out a heartfelt sigh as she flopped on to her chair.

'Me too. And it delayed tea with my father and his entourage for a little while longer.'

'Ed told me you seemed to have one of your own,' Sophie said, pretending to study her menu.

'One what?'

'An entourage. A very attentive one.'

'Oh, you mean William.' Anna sounded offhand but, out of the corner of her eye, Sophie saw her blush.

'Someone special?' she asked hopefully, mindful of the Rick effect yesterday morning. Far better for Anna to find someone more reliable.

But Anna shook her head and promptly changed the subject. 'How's the garden centre coming along?'

'We're on target for the opening, thank God. Now we just have to hope my brother is.'

'Your brother?' The blush deepened.

If blushes were anything to go by, Sophie thought, poor William was no competition for Rick. 'Yes,' she said, in mock exasperation, 'he's suddenly decided to stay in Bath the night before. Which means I'll spend most of Saturday morning wondering if he'll remember to turn up.'

The colour went from Anna's face as fast as it had come. 'Oh! Did he – did he say why he'll be in Bath?'

Sophie gave her an appraising look. 'It's another talk, arranged by the bookshop that hosted his event last Friday.'

She was going to leave it at that, but Ed added, 'That's the official version. Then there's the unofficial version – a bit of bedroom activity.'

Anna's eyes were huge and unblinking as she looked at each of them in turn. 'You mean he's spending the night with a woman?' Her small hands gripped the menu, knuckles as white as the tablecloth.

'Definitely,' Ed said, grinning wickedly. 'Knowing Rick, he'll be – ow!'

Sophie didn't particularly enjoy kicking her husband under the table, but it was the safest way to shut him up. Because he'd inadvertently provided her with an opportunity to warn Anna off Rick – and she didn't want him to spoil everything.

'Yes, I think he met someone at the book signing in Bristol.' She gave Ed another kick, just in case he contradicted her. 'Let's order, shall we? What are you having, Anna?'

'I-I don't know yet.' Anna stared down at her menu. Sophie had the uncomfortable feeling that she was close to tears and, for the first time in her life, she wished her brother far away. Still, with any luck, once he was back in Australia it would be 'out of sight, out of mind' for Anna; until then, Sophie resolved to keep the conversation a Rick-free zone.

Eventually, they were ready to order. They all opted for the roast lamb and, while they waited, Sophie started outlining their plans for the garden centre. Anna seemed to collect herself, managing a smile as she told them about her father calling there a few years ago and finding Mr Farley, the previous owner, peeing on his compost heap. According to Walter, the man didn't bat an eyelid and even had the effrontery to try and sell him a 'pee bale' for Kellynch! Needless to say, once he heard that Mr Farley had been selling them to stately homes the length and breadth of Somerset, Walter ordered several on the spot. When it became apparent that only male urine would do, being less acidic, the last remaining male member of the household staff – Clifford, the gardener-handyman – ended up performing this duty single-handed, so to speak, on Kellynch's own compost. Poor old Clifford had never spoken to Mr Farley since.

Sophie and Ed laughed and Ed said, eyes twinkling, that he was a firm believer in compost peeing too, and perhaps he'd put on a demonstration at the opening of the garden centre. But then, just when things seemed to be going well, a man and a woman stopped at their table – and Sophie came face to face with Rick's rival.

Trust Minty, Anna thought angrily. If she couldn't have William and Anna at the same table for lunch, then she'd settle for them being in the same restaurant at the same time. Or maybe, after seeing her talking to Rick last night, Minty just wanted to make sure they weren't enjoying a cosy little lunch together. Huh, as if that was likely, when Rick was making plans for a return visit to Bath that obviously didn't include her …

Meanwhile Minty was in full flow, informing the Crofts – and everyone else in the room, whether they liked it or not – that William was the future 9th Baronet of Kellynch. 'Already like a son to Sir Walter,' she added, 'and we're all expecting him to become a son-in-law one day. Isn't that right, Anna?'

Anna pretended to misunderstand her. 'That's if Lisa will have him,' she said tersely.

William gave her a quizzical look before shaking hands with Sophie. 'Araminta forgot to mention my other credentials.' He switched on a dazzling smile and a frank, wide-eyed gaze. 'I advise businesses and high net-worth individuals on their investments. So, once your garden centre's up and running, I'd be delighted to offer my services.' He placed a couple of his cards on the table.

Sophie laughed. 'Given the amount we've had to borrow, I can't see us having any money to invest for the next decade at least. But thanks anyway.'

'Araminta tells me the opening is a week on Saturday,' William went on, his smile even broader. 'I may well pop along and see how many punters show up.'

'Feel free – Anna, you're coming too, aren't you?'

Sophie sounded so enthusiastic that Anna couldn't bear to disappoint her. She mumbled a 'yes', then allowed her mind to wander to Rick, and the 'someone' he'd met in Bristol.

No wonder he'd been furious when she'd challenged him last night about trust ...

Minty's voice scolded her back to the present. 'Now, Mr and Mrs Croft, you haven't moved into The Lodge yet, have you? Because I'd like to show William round tomorrow. He's very anxious to buy a little house near Kellynch – and you couldn't get much nearer than The Lodge!'

Ed frowned. 'Hang on – are you suggesting that Sir Walter is going to cancel our tenancy agreement?'

'Good gracious, I'm not suggesting anything of the sort.' Minty raised her eyebrows, as if struck by a new thought. 'Of course, Sir Walter *did* enter into that agreement before William arrived on the scene.' A delicate pause. 'And I'd hope that, if William made him an offer he couldn't refuse, you'd allow him to benefit from it as soon as possible.'

Anna stared at William. She could think of a number of reasons why he'd want to be near Kellynch – winning Lisa over and extracting Walter from Cleo's clutches being the main ones. But, assuming he was successful with Lisa, she couldn't imagine her sister being content to live in The Lodge. For a start, where would all her clothes go?

Sophie was saying icily, '*If* that happens, we'll consider our options under the terms of our agreement. In the meantime, we'd like to try and enjoy our lunch.'

With a gracious nod, Minty bent and kissed Anna swiftly on the cheek, then summoned a waitress to show them to their table. William lingered, shaking hands yet again with Sophie and Ed and stooping to kiss Anna. She half-turned away, but his lips homed in as if branding her as his property. And she had no doubt that his, 'See you later, darling,' was calculated to convey a closeness between them that, in her mind, simply didn't exist.

But what did that matter, now that Rick was coming to Bath – to see someone else?

Chapter Fifty-One

Later that day, Rick phoned his sister for the second time. 'Hi there. Everything OK?'

'Wonderful, we're just having a rest in our suite before dinner – that has such a nice ring about it, doesn't it? Ed's even reading *The Scarlet Pimpernel* – fancies himself as Sir Percy Blakeney, obviously. How was your signing?'

He groaned. 'A queue three deep. There's an article about me in today's *Sunday Times* – apparently I'm just a sad git who needs the love of a good woman – so the good women of Leeds were out in force. I knew it was a mistake to give that tosser an interview.'

He could hear her trying not to laugh. 'Oh, I don't know – his article sounds pretty accurate to me.'

'Thanks a bunch. So, how was your day?'

'Fine – except, talking of tossers, guess what Sir Walter's up to? Cancelling our tenancy agreement for The Lodge!' He heard Ed's voice rumbling in the background, then Sophie's impatient, 'I know he hasn't told us as much, but I wouldn't be in the least surprised.' She spoke into the phone again. 'The heir to the title – William somebody – has turned up, looking for somewhere to live on Sir Walter's doorstep. If he likes The Lodge, I imagine that'll be it – which will be a total pain. It doesn't make as much sense to rent the greenhouses at Kellynch if we can't live there – and we can't stay on in the cottage at Uppercross, because our landlord has new tenants lined up. So we may end up living above the shop after all, which will mean redecorating – in the run-up to Christmas, just when we need to be working all the hours God sends!'

She paused for breath, and he said quickly, 'Did Anna tell you this – yesterday, after I'd gone?'

'No, it was Lady Russell – she and this William character were in the same restaurant as us today, obviously on a mission to ruin our lunch.' A loud sigh of irritation. 'I just can't stop thinking about it, *so* annoying.'

'But is Anna … part of the plan?' He silently cursed the catch in his voice.

'What do you mean?'

'Is she … oh, I don't know … are she and this – this man likely to live there together?' It could be her ideal scenario, he thought bitterly, despite her protestations last night about the jerk not being her boyfriend. Living back at Kellynch, surrounding herself with memories of her mother – without being under the same roof as her father. Women could make the most ridiculous decisions if they wanted something badly enough; just look at Shelley, running off with a complete stranger because he said he wanted marriage and children.

'What's it to you?' Sophie countered.

He wished he'd never asked the question. Sophie hadn't given him the emphatic denial he'd hoped for; and he had the distinct feeling that, for some reason, she was on her guard. Which would suggest that he'd stumbled on the truth …

'Nothing,' he said, bleakly. 'Nothing at all.'

Anna rarely bothered with a Sunday paper – there was enough reading matter in Saturday's *Times* to last her all weekend. In any case, she could usually rely on Jenny to bring any articles of interest into work the next day. This Sunday, however, it was different; she'd barely returned from lunch and a listless tour of the shops when Jenny knocked at her door.

'Couldn't wait until tomorrow.' She rushed in, thrust a flapping sheet of newsprint at Anna and veered off into the kitchen. 'Shall I make us a coffee while you read it? I'm dying to know what you think – to me, it sounds nothing like the man we met.'

'What are you on about?' Anna straightened out the page she'd been given, but saw only book reviews.

'It's an article about Rick Wentworth,' Jenny called above the hiss of the kettle. 'Not very complimentary – oh, you haven't got much milk left. We've got loads, I'll pop down and get you some.'

'Thanks,' Anna said miserably, turning the page over and staring at the large colour photo of Rick caught in an off moment – eyes dark slits of accusation, mouth a taut line. The words above it, 'Rick Wentworth Under the Microscope', suggested a no-holds-barred interview. She went over to the table and pulled out a chair. If this article was going to reveal all about his love life, she'd need to be sitting down.

A deep intake of breath – and she began to read.

"My perfect mate is a sea dragon," were Dr Rick Wentworth's parting words after our lunch together. And, unfortunately for any unattached female readers, I don't think he was joking.

On the face of it, this man has everything going for him – film star looks, a body to match and not one but three successful careers. For years he's been a leading expert on sea dragons, a highly specialised field of marine biology and one that conveniently requires him to be based near some of the best beaches in the world. Next, he added TV to his CV, which turned out to be an excuse to stride half-naked round the coast of Australia in pursuit of endangered species. Most recently, he's joined the ranks of celebrity authors with *Sex in the Sea*, a glossy door stopper about strange goings-on under water that has the women of Britain queuing up for him to sign their copies.

There may be plenty of sex in the sea, but I have a feeling there's been a distinct lack of it in Wentworth's life since he arrived on our shores last month. It's the most likely explanation for the man's sheer grumpiness. When I asked him what his book was about, he told me to read the blurb on the back. When I asked what he was writing next, he said, 'Nothing'. But if this is just part of his natural charm – well, no wonder his former girlfriend, Australian supermodel Shelley McCourt, looked round for better company as soon as he'd set off for the airport.

A mug of coffee appeared at Anna's elbow and she looked up, startled. 'Oh – thanks.' She hadn't even heard Jenny come back into the flat.

'Where are you up to?' Jenny adjusted her specs and leaned over to look, as Anna pointed silently at the third paragraph. 'Hmm, I thought that bit was totally unnecessary – sounded like sour grapes on the journalist's part. I know we've only met Rick briefly, but I can tell he's a far better man than this guy makes out.'

'But why give an interview if you haven't got anything to say?' Anna said slowly.

'I expect it's all planned way in advance. And if it was just after Lou's accident, no one could blame him for being grumpy.'

'Isn't that part of being a celebrity, though? Whatever you feel like inside, you're expected to put on a brave face in public.'

'True.' Jenny cocked her head on one side. 'Anyway, I bet it's all backfired.'

'What do you mean?'

'Well, if this journalist – what's his name?'

Anna glanced at the article, carefully avoiding the photo of Rick. 'Duncan Taylor.'

'Ah yes. If Duncan Taylor wants to turn people against

Rick, he doesn't seem to have realised that most women find a troubled, misunderstood man irresistible. They each think they're the answer to his prayers. Mark my words, there'll be bigger queues than ever at his next few signings.'

Anna folded the page in half, with Rick's grim face safely on the inside, and handed it back to Jenny. 'I won't read the rest, I've got a bit of a headache. By the way, is there any mention of Lou – or anyone else for that matter?'

Jenny squinted at her. 'You do look a bit washed out. Want to come and have something to eat with us tonight?'

'No, I've got some work to do. But thanks.' And just answer my question, she pleaded silently.

A gusty sigh. 'Pity, Tom would have liked your company. As soon as we've had our meal, I'm off out – Christina's invited me round to taste her sloe gin. Needless to say, I'm not taking the car.' Jenny grinned and went out of the flat.

A second later, she poked her head round the door. 'There's nothing in the article about Lou, and nothing to suggest he's got a woman in his life at all – hardly surprising, given the way that journalist's presenting him. But there's bound to be one, isn't there? And, if he's got any sense, he'll keep his private life exactly that – private.'

Anna managed a smile. Then, as soon as Jenny had gone, she curled up on the sofa and stared at the picture of Pornichet; re-living those few days on the boat and ignoring the persistent ring of the phone.

A freezing cold night, but what did it matter when you'd had several sloe gins for insulation? Jenny glanced up at the black void overhead, where stars glinted like pinheads. If only Tom was walking beside her. Oh, they often shared the same stunning view on a car journey, but nothing like this – the strolling-arm-in-arm, spur-of-the-moment romantic stuff that she used to love.

By now she'd reached Crescent Lane, which bordered the buildings at the rear of The Royal Crescent Hotel. Further along, she would pass the public entrance to The Dower House Restaurant. Before that, set into a high wall, were two doors leading to the hotel's self-contained garden suites. An added attraction for visiting film stars, according to a guy she'd once met who worked there; they could come and go from their rooms in relative privacy.

Odd, then, to see one of those doors ajar …

As she drew level, she went to pull it shut – then hesitated. No harm in having a little look, was there? So instead she pushed it further open, stepped noiselessly across the threshold and found a small, well-lit courtyard with–

'Oh!'

If she'd gasped out loud, it didn't seem to have disturbed the man and woman in the far doorway: a couple in a fevered embrace, a couple she couldn't help but recognise. She stood stock still, sucking in the cold night air, feeling it sear through her lungs as she took in the scene before her. The man was fully dressed and obviously the one who'd carelessly left the outer door open; he must have a key, even though she knew he wasn't a hotel guest. The woman was wearing only a loosened towelling robe, but presumably the man's constantly caressing hands kept her warm. Their ragged, urgent sighs carried towards her, silenced only when their blindly searching mouths met.

She staggered back out of the little courtyard, leaving the door wide open, feeling her stomach heave. Oh God, how she wished she'd never gone for that little look.

If only Tom was here … But she wasn't far from home now, the home that he filled with his solid, familiar, loving presence.

She broke into a run.

Chapter Fifty-Two

'And you're certain it was William?' Tom swung the pan of frothing chocolate-coloured milk off the hob and poured it expertly into two mugs. 'You know what your eyesight's like.'

Jenny gave a weary sigh. 'And *you* know it's my short sight that's the problem, I'm fine if things are further away. Thanks,' as he handed her one of the mugs, 'let's hope I don't throw this up, I still feel sort of sick ... Believe me, I didn't *want* it to be William – and I probably wouldn't even have seen his face if he hadn't been twisting about like – like a cobra preparing to strike.'

'But the woman – you've only ever seen her in that brochure Anna showed us. Was it definitely–'

'Cléopatra Clé and her Hands of Love? Yes.' Jenny blew gently on her hot chocolate and gazed unseeingly at the dispersing foam. 'Oh Tom, I so want Anna to be happy – like us!'

'That's up to Anna though, isn't it?' he said gruffly. 'There's only so much you can do.'

'I know, it's just – I've got to tell her about this, haven't I? She must like him a lot, splashing out on that dress for the theatre – completely out of character.' Another sigh, as she picked up her drink. 'When we went out with him on Friday evening, I thought there was something ... untrustworthy about him – remember? But I decided to give him the benefit of the doubt.'

'Well, you can't any longer.' He patted her hand. 'You'll have to tell her – and soon.'

This is a struggle, Anna thought, as she paused for a sip

of water in the middle of her eleven o'clock lecture. But then what did she expect after so little sleep? Last night, in bed, she'd stared into the darkness and gone through all the words and looks from the weekend, starting with Molland's on Friday evening and ending with lunch at the Pump Room Restaurant; shuffled them and turned them over in her mind, like a pack of cards. And only one scenario made sense, the one where Rick was trying to get some closure on the past before moving on. She supposed she was doing the same, in her own way. Except that he wanted to move on to someone new, whereas she'd merely discovered why the old love meant so much.

She switched her attention firmly back to her students. 'As I was saying, Turgenev writes particularly about missed opportunities. Take *First Love*, for example, a poignant tale of being in love with the wrong person ...' So much for work being an escape from her troubles.

Back home, she made a pretence of eating dinner – a few mouthfuls of tinned tomato soup and half a bread roll – while watching *Friends*. Sat at the table looking listlessly through her notes for tomorrow's lectures. Ignored the ringing phones – landline and mobile – because, for a change, she wasn't in the mood to humour someone else's needs.

A knock at the door – that sounded like Jenny. Anna had seen her briefly at lunchtime but, as she had a later start on Mondays, they'd travelled to and from the university separately. She let her in, hoping – for once – that she wouldn't stay long.

And – for once – Jenny hovered by the door, as if telepathic. 'You know I don't like to interfere,' she began, venturing a smile.

Anna rubbed her temples and waited.

'Um, can we sit down?' Jenny said.

'Of course – sorry, I must have been in some sort of trance.

Do you want a coffee?'

'Got anything stronger?'

'Yes, some red wine–' Anna broke off as she recalled William opening her last bottle. Needless to say, his promise to replace it had never materialised. 'Actually, no, I haven't.'

Jenny heaved a sigh as she crossed to the sofa. 'Don't worry, I'm probably better doing this stone cold sober.'

The first pang of alarm. 'What's wrong?'

'Look, why don't you sit down?' Jenny patted the sofa beside her.

But Anna's legs seemed concreted to the floor. She stayed near the door and stared over at Jenny. 'Just tell me.' It was about Rick and the new woman in his life, she was absolutely certain. She steeled herself, eyes darting to the painting of Pornichet as if for reassurance that she, too, had once been new and exciting.

Jenny was saying, 'Last night I saw something that I wasn't supposed to see – and it's going to upset you.'

'OK.' This is it, she added silently – but how did Jenny know it was going to upset her? With Jenny, she'd always been very tight-lipped about Rick; not like with Sophie and Ed, when she'd more or less given herself away …

She forced herself to listen as Jenny continued, 'It was about eleven o'clock, and I was walking back from Christina's along Crescent Lane. One of the back doors to The Royal Crescent Hotel was open and – you know me – I couldn't resist a quick peek.' A pause; then, almost apologetically, 'I saw far more than I bargained for – your father's masseuse and a man we both know, all over each other.'

Something drummed in Anna's ears, as though her heart was trying to burst from her body. She heard someone croak, 'Who was the man?' and realised it was *her* voice, a husk of its usual self.

Jenny eyed her carefully. 'William.'

Anna frowned back at her. No way – no way on this earth – could she have mistaken that for 'Rick'. As it sank in, she smiled – a big, beaming, idiotic smile.

Now it was Jenny's turn to frown. 'It's true, I saw his face!'

And Anna felt her voice recover its strength and bubble out of her in a laugh. 'Good! They deserve each other.'

An incredulous look. 'You mean you're not bothered?'

'Why should I be?' Anna flopped down on the sofa beside her friend; those concrete legs had suddenly turned to jelly.

'Because – well, I thought you cared for him.'

'I do, I suppose – but not in that way. Definitely not in that way.' There was only one man she cared for in *that* way … She blinked rapidly, forcing the tears back. Oh shit, she mustn't get upset like this; thank God Jenny wasn't wearing her specs.

'But why did you buy–' Jenny stopped. 'Never mind, I'm just glad you're OK with it. Although it does beg the question – why's William shagging Cléopatra Clé?'

Anna took a deep calming breath. 'I imagine he's desperate to keep her away from Walter, in case any little Walters come along and stop him becoming the 9th Baronet of Kellynch. He can't sell the baronetcy, but it still has considerable value to him. There'll always be people who trust a man with a title more than a man without, for whatever reason – pretty useful if you're flogging expensive investment advice.' She made a face. 'And who knows? If Cleo really is working miracles with Walter, she must be pretty good in bed.'

Jenny chuckled. 'From what I saw, they'd never have made it as far as her bed.' A pause, then she added, 'Wait a minute, if William's going to seduce every deluded female who has designs on your father – or, more likely, Kellynch – he could be a busy man.'

'I suppose so.' Anna thought for a moment. 'But then, so far, Lisa and Minty have been a pretty formidable barrier. Cleo only got under Lisa's radar because she performed a useful function – making Lisa feel beautiful. And I heard yesterday that William's looking to live near Kellynch, presumably to keep a closer eye on Walter. Between the three of them, they should see off any future Cleos.'

'Do you think Lisa and William will get back together?'

'If she doesn't find out about Cleo – yes, I do. But if she does – I'm not so sure.' Anna bit her lip. 'Which puts me in a bit of a quandary – should I tell Lisa about this, or not?'

'What would happen if you didn't? Wouldn't she find out herself, sooner or later?'

'Probably. But I'd feel guilty that, for a while at least, I knew – and she didn't.'

'Tell her, then. Just don't be surprised when she shoots the messenger.' Jenny got to her feet. 'Well, I'd better go and put Tom out of his misery. He was worried you'd be distraught about William.' She made for the door, then spun round. 'By the way, did you see the email from BRLSI?'

'No – what about?' They were both volunteers for the Bath Royal Literary and Scientific Institution in Queen Square, helping out at events and exhibitions. Along with many of her university colleagues, Anna had given talks there herself; there seemed to be an indefatigable interest among BRLSI members in the likes of Tolstoy and Dostoevsky and their impact on western culture.

'Bob's desperate,' Jenny was saying. 'Remember he emailed the other day to tell us that the science lecture a week on Friday was cancelled? Now Molland's want that date for another Rick Wentworth event. They reckon they can fill the place – starting with the people who missed out on tickets last Friday.' She sighed. 'Only trouble is, Bob can't be there – after the cancellation, he decided to book a weekend break. Any chance you can stand in for him? I can't, Tom and I are going out.'

She would go, even if it was just to say goodbye. No more Missed Opportunities.

'Thanks for letting me know.' She forced a smile. 'I'll check my diary, but I think I'm free. Can't let Bob down, can I?'

Chapter Fifty-Three

Away on his tour of northern England, in an attempt to keep his dark mood at bay, Rick had acquired a new routine. Before it was light, he got up and went for a run, enjoying the early-morning anonymity if not the autumn chill. Next – shower, breakfast and his first encounter of the day with Dave. He always went through the motions of checking the itinerary, but in fact Dave could have driven him to the same place each time and he'd have been practically none the wiser. Except when he went back to his old secondary school in County Durham – Stephenson country, as railway-buff Dave called it; there he did a different talk, all about making the best of yourself and finding work you could feel passionate about. In an area where the only job security was at the local unemployment office, and coming from a man who'd forgotten what passion felt like, it all sounded rather hollow.

He spent most of his days travelling with Dave, eating with Dave, giving talks and signing books for people he didn't know and never would. Back in his room – each night a different hotel, yet they were all uncannily similar – he made a rule never to open the mini bar. Mind you, he usually had a couple of pints with his evening meal; he realised how much he'd missed the rusty tang of English beer. Finally, to the drone of some late-night film on TV, he would drift off to sleep.

And then the dreams would start. Oh, Annie …

But gradually, he came to see what he'd shared with Anna more clearly – and to accept it as a unique and amazing part of his past, even if it would never be part of his future. What about the present? Well, he resolved to get through the rest of his visit to England and, along the way, show Anna the same generosity of spirit that she had shown him ever since he arrived.

That was why he wanted to phone her, or so he told himself; to apologise for storming out of the theatre and arrange to see her again. Except that he rang her mobile several evenings running and got no answer. Then, at last, she picked up.

'Anna?'

Silence.

'It's me.' A pause. 'Rick.'

'I know.'

'I just wanted to say I'm sorry. Again. And I'm back in Bath next Friday–'

'I know.'

'Can I see you?'

Another silence; then, 'If you want. I'll be at your talk.' And she hung up. Even worse, when he rang back she didn't answer.

Then Ben phoned to say that he was planning to come to Bath on the same day as Rick. 'I've got a meeting at the university in the afternoon, then I thought we could meet up for a few drinks.' He chuckled. 'I was even going to come to your talk, but I can't get a ticket – they've sold out.'

'You can come as my guest,' Rick said, 'as long as you don't heckle.'

'Now there's an idea – I could tell the audience about some of your exploits from our student days, I'm sure they'd be riveted.'

Rick forced a laugh. 'I'll look forward to it, haven't had any adverse publicity since last Sunday.' He cleared his throat. 'Just one problem – there's someone I need to see straight after my talk, and I don't know how long it'll take.

Are you planning to stay overnight?'

'If I'm out with you – definitely! And of course, when you've got three small kids, the thought of an uninterrupted night's sleep is always appealing.' Ben paused. 'Got anywhere in mind?'

'I'll text you the number of the hotel where I'll be staying. There's a decent pub just round the corner, so we won't have far to stagger back after a beer or two.'

It was a relief to think that, as soon as he'd seen Anna, he'd be able to go and drown his sorrows with Ben. There'd be no time to dwell on anything; no time at all.

Chapter Fifty-Four

For Anna, the days leading up to Rick's talk dragged so much that even a visit from William – or at least an attempt at one – was a welcome distraction. He rang her doorbell the evening after Rick's phone call, making her jump and wonder if it was Rick himself ... But it wasn't, of course.

He drawled over the intercom, 'Special delivery for Anna Elliot!'

She played dumb. 'Which company are you from?'

'Anna, darling, just let me in. It's bloody cold out here.'

'Shame, it's bloody warm up here,' she said, flippantly. Then, in a sterner tone, 'What exactly do you want?'

'Where do I start?' His voice turned to honey, sweet and slow and thick with complacency. 'I've got a crate of red wine, to replace the bottle I opened. Some exciting news about Kellynch. And Moët & Chandon, for a little celebration.'

'What are you celebrating?'

'I can't talk to you like this,' he wheedled. 'Why don't you just buzz me up and I'll reveal all over a glass of champagne?'

'I never let strange men into my flat.' There – she'd thrown down the gauntlet; although she didn't feel as calm and collected as she hoped she sounded.

'Anna, darling, what can you possibly mean?' But, for the first time, she detected a thread of unease running through the silky-smooth charm. 'I've already been in your flat, just the other week. You didn't think me strange then, did you?'

'But I do now.'

A nervous laugh. 'I think you'd better explain that cryptic

little comment face to face. Buzz me up, there's a good girl, before I freeze to death.'

'But I'm not a good girl.' She took a deep breath and went for it. 'And is it any colder than Sunday, when you were enjoying the night air outside the back door of The Pavilion?'

Silence. Then a guarded 'What did you see?'

'Enough. I haven't decided when or how to tell Lisa – yet. And I'll have to tell Walter, I suppose, although I'm sure you'll give him some bullshit about sacrificing your own happiness with Lisa to save him from social and financial ruin with Cleo.'

'But Anna, that's exactly what I'm doing – sacrificing my own happiness.' He paused, then rushed on, 'Don't judge me too harshly, I'll tell you everything if you'll just let me in.'

'But William – don't you understand? You don't need to tell me *anything*. What there was between us in the past – a brief, teenage friendship – no longer exists.' She added, with a sigh of irritation, 'And your sudden interest now just doesn't add up, you could have got in touch with me when you first met Lisa in London – but you didn't.'

'When I met her, I was in a mess – and I was afraid that you wouldn't like me any more.'

Anna gave a short, mirthless laugh. 'And did you honestly think I'd still like you after you'd dumped my sister for a millionaire's lifestyle and drug-fuelled sex – or whatever was on offer from Brandi Berette?'

'Believe me, I've changed. Can't you see I'm trying to redeem myself?'

'Oh yes, fawning over Lisa, keeping your options open, while–'

He cut in with, 'I wouldn't give her the time of day if I thought there was any chance with you!' His voice trembled, as if with emotion. But wasn't that just part of his act?

'You've as much chance as a snowball in hell,' she said, coolly. 'Unlike you, I'd rather have no one at all than make do with second best.' And she flicked the intercom switch firmly off.

Now, at last, it was the day of the BRLSI talk and she was trying to relax in the hottest, bubbliest bath she'd had for a long time. No more calls from Rick as far as she could tell, thank God. Maybe, like her, he'd realised that there was no point talking on the phone. She hadn't seen or heard from William since his attempted visit; and, unusually, Minty hadn't been in touch either – which suggested that she'd heard William's side of the story and wasn't in a hurry to listen to Anna's.

Anna's thoughts turned to Lisa, who she'd invited out for a coffee last Saturday morning. Lisa had reacted to the news about William and Cleo as negatively as Jenny had predicted, slamming her cup down on its saucer and accusing her sister of being insanely jealous and intent on sabotaging William's relationships. Apparently, during his visit to Kellynch with Minty the previous Monday, he'd fallen in love with the place and was full of plans for 'sweating the asset'. This would, of course, involve him moving into The Lodge – the ideal base for turning his plans into reality. As soon as Anna had wondered out loud whether, being at some distance from the main house, it would also be the ideal base for secret assignations with Cleo, Lisa had stormed out of the café.

With only a couple of hours to Rick's talk, however, it was time to forget family feuds and calm the butterflies in her stomach. Even if his new woman was with him at the talk, she thought as she slipped into her pale-grey wool dress, she'd behave with dignity and wish him well. She brushed her hair until it gleamed, sprayed Cool Water on her pulse points and pulled on her black suede boots. A glance in the mirror told her that she looked just as she had at the theatre.

Oh God, if she closed her eyes, she could still hear him saying, 'Nice dress' …

She wrapped herself in her heavy, dark-green coat, locked up the flat and set off on the short walk to Queen Square.

Friday evening promised to be free of rain, and Dave didn't need much persuading to have the night off. Rick took the umbrella with him, just in case – although, he reflected with a rueful smile, based on what had happened at his last talk in Bath it was hardly a lucky mascot.

There was a spring in his step as he walked with Ben from their hotel to Queen Square. In a matter of hours, the Anna situation would be resolved; he'd then have a few days with Sophie and Ed to look forward to, before returning to Australia. He was determined to tackle his work with fresh enthusiasm and renewed focus; finding ways to make the marine world a better place would offer enough challenge to fill his life for the foreseeable future.

In this positive frame of mind, he even welcomed Ben's news that Charles would be joining them. Since Lyme Regis, Charles had been bombarding Ben with emails about fishing management; when Ben had mentioned coming to Bath to meet Rick, Charles – already in Bath for a business seminar – had leapt at the chance of continuing their discussions face to face. OK, so Rick would have preferred a night out where the conversation didn't revolve around fish stock assessment methods and catch effort sampling strategies, but beggars couldn't be choosers. And, as far as Anna was concerned, weren't he and Charles in more or less the same boat? He imagined a ridiculous scenario where, as the beer flowed, they shed their inhibitions and compared notes.

Which reminded him, had he brought his notes with him for tonight? He slipped his hand inside his coat and felt in his jacket pocket. Yes, he had. By now, of course, they were a prop rather than a necessity; he'd got his talk – a longer version of the one he'd done at Molland's – word perfect over the last twelve days.

They reached the square and Rick glanced round appreciatively; it was a jewel of Georgian architecture, discreetly floodlit, with a slim stone obelisk in the centre. The BRLSI building was on the west side and, as they approached the main entrance, Ben asked about the timings for the rest of the evening so that he could text Charles.

'I'll be talking for exactly thirty-eight minutes,' Rick said. 'Say forty, by the time you top and tail it with a few words from the bookshop manager.' He walked swiftly through the outer and inner doors, into a large reception area intersected by free-standing display boards – some sort of art exhibition, by the look of it. 'Probably best if Charles meets you here at about quarter-past eight,' he went on. 'Then you two can go to the pub and I'll come along later.' He recognised the tall blonde girl from Molland's standing by the front desk, and flashed a smile. 'The book signing will take a good hour, depending on numbers, of course. Then, as I said before, there's someone I need to–'

His voice sheared off into silence. The blonde had moved away to reveal a woman sitting at the desk. A woman in a silver-grey dress that drew his eyes to the pale satin skin of her shoulders and throat. A woman who blushed and gave him one brief, conscious look that pierced his soul and sent wild, wonderful hopes soaring …

'Hey – it's Anna, isn't it?' Ben said cheerfully, walking up to her. 'I didn't realise you'd be here.'

Her colour deepened. 'I'm one of BRLSI's regular volunteers, they were desperate for help tonight.'

Was that the only reason she was here? Just as abruptly, Rick's wild, wonderful hopes plummeted to earth.

'So you're the same as me – giving up your Friday evening to see Rick's fan club in action?' Ben chuckled. 'I hope – for all our sakes – that the talk's worth listening to.'

'Anna's already heard it,' Rick put in. He stood right beside the desk – so close that he could have captured her small, slim hand in his – and heard himself say, with a ragged intake of breath, 'You told me it wasn't what you'd expected, remember?'

He willed her eyes to meet his; but she lowered her gaze to the neatly typed page of A4 in front of her and said gravely, 'At least I know what to expect tonight.' Then she jumped to her feet, all brisk and business-like. 'I need to show you where you're giving your talk. It's the Elwin room, on the first floor.' She called across to the blonde who was studying one of the display boards. 'Amanda, would you cover the desk for me, please?'

As they followed Anna out of the room, Ben said, 'Is there anywhere to leave our coats?'

She nodded. 'You can use the Lonsdale room, which is also upstairs. In fact, you might be better staying there until it's time for the talk to start.' She turned to Rick and added gently, 'It'll be more private, if you need to collect your thoughts.' He flushed; did she know that they'd scattered far and wide as soon as he'd seen her?

Climbing the stairs behind her, he couldn't help reflecting that her dress really was like a second skin ... And then he had to get his brain in gear as they entered a large, rectangular, high-ceilinged room, with row upon row of chairs facing a long table and a lectern at one end.

'Elwin seats a hundred, but we've also opened up Murch – through here.' She walked towards the speaker's table and gestured to her right, where folded-back partition doors gave access to a little ante-room. Rick did a quick count of the chairs set out in Murch, then went to stand at the lectern.

'So, there'll be about twenty people to my left,' he said, frowning in concentration. 'Which means I need to remember to make eye contact with them, as well as everyone else.'

'Exactly. Your books are here–' she indicated neat piles of *Sex in the Sea* on a smaller table in the corner – 'and I'll make sure you have a carafe of water. I'll take you to Lonsdale now, if you like.'

They followed her back through Elwin and into a smaller room, with chairs around a large table and the skeleton of a massive reptile-like creature sprawling across one of its cream-coloured walls.

Rick looked at the skeleton and gave a long, low whistle. 'A plesiosaur!'

Anna smiled. 'Probably the most famous item in the BRLSI's collection. A nineteenth-century plaster cast, rather than the original fossil – but impressive, all the same.'

'Some sort of marine super-predator, wasn't it?' Ben said, scanning the information panel just below the skull.

Rick nodded slowly, still stunned. 'Otherwise known as a 200-million-year-old sea dragon.' He glanced across at Anna and then wished he hadn't; her face was alive with the look of someone who'd just seen their thoughtfulness rewarded – a look of pure, unguarded delight. And it took him back to their time together on the boat, moment after moment of pure, unguarded delight ... He cleared his throat. 'No wonder you suggested this would be a good place to collect my thoughts – thank you. And now I'd better start reading through my notes.'

'That's what I do, too, before all my lectures.' She hesitated, then became brisk and business-like again. 'Can I get either of you a drink?'

'Not for me, thanks.' Rick went to the table and pulled out a chair, while Ben explained, 'We'll be having plenty of liquid refreshment later – what you might call a boys' night out.' He turned his attention back to the information panel.

She frowned, as though puzzled by his answer; but all she said was, 'I'd better go and see what's happening downstairs.'

She didn't go immediately, however; and, when Rick propped his umbrella on the chair next to him and took off his coat, she stared at his black jacket, blue jumper and jeans so intently that he wanted to ask, Do you like these as much as you said you did at the theatre? Because that's why I'm wearing them – at least you'll remember me at my best when we say goodbye.

And then, as he dropped his coat over the chair, she darted forward and retrieved the umbrella, clutching it to her as if it was the most precious thing in the world.

'You might forget this later.' Her voice was barely more than a whisper.

'How could I?' he said, just as quietly. 'Some things are unforgettable.'

A long pause, her big grey eyes soft and searching. 'But still unforgivable?'

He held her gaze, took a deep breath and was about to reply when Ben called over, 'Anna, I think I will have a drink after all. Coffee, white, one sugar – if that's OK?'

'Coffee. Yes. Of course.' Anna gave Rick one last, lingering look, laid the umbrella carefully on the table and left the room.

And, once again, those wild, wonderful hopes took wing.

'Some things are unforgettable.' Did she dare believe that he was talking about her rather than the umbrella? Could it be that, like her, he was deliberately wearing the clothes he'd had on when they last met? And had she heard Ben right when he said they were having a boys' night out?

The questions circled in her head, but the answers were back in the Lonsdale room; and, when she returned there with Ben's coffee, her heart was pounding at the prospect of discovering them. She needn't have worried, however; Rick was sitting reading at the table, and he kept his head down as she came in.

Ben was still studying the plesiosaur. 'Thanks,' he said, taking the coffee from her. As she turned to go, he added, 'By the way, I've spotted the deliberate mistake.'

She gave him a quizzical look. 'You mean with the plesiosaur?'

'That's right.' He lowered his voice. 'The forelimbs and the hindlimbs are the wrong way round. Let's ask the expert over there if he's noticed anything.'

'He seems absorbed in his notes, it would be a shame to disturb him.'

'True. Maybe his talk isn't as slick as he'd like.' He sipped his coffee. 'He said you'd heard it – what did you think?'

The question caught her by surprise. She heard herself say softly, 'I loved it. I'd been expecting just a rehash of his book, but he made it much more personal. He spoke about monogamy – how rare it is under the sea, but how relevant it still is to the human race, despite the barriers of sexual liberation and increased longevity. So what if, for many of us, "a mate for life" is no longer possible? It's believing in "a mate for the rest of your life" that matters.'

Ben chuckled. 'Sounds like a good chat-up line.'

She gave a faint smile. 'No, I think he really believes it.'

'Oh, I'm sure he does. So does James, with Lou – and he certainly did before, with Julie.' He pursed his lips. 'That's what I can't understand – how could James switch his loyalties that soon?'

And Anna, recalling Rick getting together with Lou on that awful walk just after his break-up with Shelley, said more loudly than she'd intended, 'Because men are realists. When the woman they love is no longer available, they move on.' Out of the corner of her eye she saw Rick's head lift, as though he was listening. She felt her face grow hot and turned away.

Ben was saying good-naturedly, 'And women aren't? What about the archetypal gold digger? You couldn't get more of a realist than that.'

Another faint smile. 'You're right, of course. But that's financial realism and, until comparatively recently, wasn't it driven by the fact that most women weren't financially independent?' She watched him drink his coffee, enjoying the unexpected debate – but fully aware that it was the other man in the room who was shaping her thoughts. 'I'm talking about a different sort of realism – emotional, for want of a better word. My theory is that a man needs the woman he loves to be part of his everyday life. If she can't be, he finds someone who can.'

'So women are more emotionally independent? Some men would take that one step further and call them heartless. Not me, of course, I'm far too happily married.' Ben gave a shout of laughter. 'In the natural world, though, the female of almost every species is deadlier than the male. And then there's the literary world – where good old James can give you all the examples of heartless women you could ever wish for!'

All this time, Rick hadn't made a sound. Now she heard him shuffle some papers, his seat creak slightly as he shifted about, coins clink as he felt in his jacket pocket. He must be locating a pen, she thought, to make a few changes to his talk.

She kept her voice low, anxious not to distract him. 'Hardly surprising – has James ever read anything written by a woman? Whereas I have, of course, and I can retaliate with plenty of examples of heartless men! Yes, biology and literature have a lot to answer for.' She hesitated, fumbling to give expression to something that she'd left unspoken for ten years. 'It's just that ... oh, I know this is a sweeping generalisation ... and, don't worry, it doesn't make us any happier, quite the reverse ... but I think women are different from men because – because we can keep on loving someone who's no longer part of our life.'

Ben nodded thoughtfully; before he could say anything in response, however, Amanda burst into the room.

'Anna, can you come and help?' she gasped, eyes wide with alarm. 'There's a horrible man downstairs, with a funny little woman, and he says they don't need tickets for Rick's talk because he's Baron Lynch and she's Lady Drimple. But I've never heard of them – have you?'

Chapter Fifty-Five

As Anna left the room, Rick put down his pen and stared after her. Was he doing the right thing? He shook his head impatiently; he was doing the only thing possible, and if this didn't work–

'Nearly done?' Ben eased himself on to the chair next to Rick's and finished his coffee in one gulp.

'Just a couple more minutes.' Rick placed his hand casually over the page; what he'd written was intended to be read by one person only – and it certainly wasn't Ben. He added the last few lines, signed his name, slipped the page in with his other notes and dropped his pen back in his pocket. Then – deep breath – 'Can you do me a favour?'

Ben grinned. 'Only if you tell me what's wrong with that plesiosaur.'

'The forelimbs and the hindlimbs are the wrong way round,' Rick said, without looking at the skeleton.

'Those were my words exactly! Were you listening in on my conversation with Anna?'

Rick ignored the question and went on, 'And there's something else – the two forelimbs are identical copies of each other.'

Ben looked across the room for confirmation, then laughed. 'OK, OK, you win! What's the favour?'

'Go and tell Anna that Baron Lynch and Lady Drimple can be my guests–'

'So you know them?' Ben put in. 'I thought they must be a couple of characters from the local pantomime.'

'You're not far wrong.' A grim smile. 'Sit them at the speaker's table – my publicist can't make it tonight, so no one else will be sitting there apart from you and the bookshop guy. Just make sure they're at the other end from me.'

'And here's me thinking you're choosy about your guests,' Ben grumbled. 'Ah well, I'd better go and tell Anna the good news.' With an exaggerated sigh, he got to his feet and went out of the room.

Once he was alone, Rick let his shoulders slump and his eyes close. 'At least it'll soon be over, one way or another,' he muttered.

And he wasn't referring to the talk.

For the third time, teeth clenched in exasperation, Anna said to her father, 'If you haven't got a ticket, there's nothing I can do.'

'Actually, we don't *need* to go to his talk at all,' Lady Dalrymple whined from the mangy embrace of an ancient fur coat. 'Just call him down to have a little chat and sign my book, there's a good gel.' She waved her hand dismissively, enveloping them all in a heady waft of moth repellent.

It was the second time in as many weeks that someone had used this line to try and persuade Anna to do something. She was on the verge of saying, as she had with William, 'But I'm not a good girl,' when Ben appeared, grinning broadly.

'Problem solved, I believe.' He winked at Anna and Amanda, then turned to Walter and Lady Dalrymple. 'Dr Wentworth would be delighted if you'd be his guests tonight. Would you like to follow me?'

Walter raised one of his perfectly arched – and no doubt painfully plucked – eyebrows in Anna's direction. 'As always, my name opens more doors than one could ever imagine,' he said modestly. He trapped Lady Dalrymple's furry arm in his and strutted off after Ben like a hunter parading his prize catch.

Amanda rolled her eyes. 'Isn't he ridiculous? Does Rick

realise what he's letting himself in for?'

'Oh yes,' Anna said quietly, 'I think he does.'

The other girl gave her a curious look. 'So they're friends?'

'Acquaintances. They met briefly when Rick was in Bath before – or so I heard.' Anna bit her lip – too much information. Why let on that she knew either of these men any better than Amanda did?

Thankfully, Amanda was too busy glancing at her watch and gasping in dismay. 'It's nearly time for the talk! I *so* want to hear it again, do you mind if–'

Anna interrupted her with, 'You go and get Rick out of Lonsdale and take him into Elwin. I'll man the desk until seven-thirty – and for another fifteen minutes or so, in case there are any latecomers.' An apologetic smile. 'Oh, and I meant to put a carafe of water on the speaker's table. Would you–?'

'No probs. Thanks, Anna!'

Amanda hurried off, leaving Anna to reflect on a nightmare scenario – her father and Rick in the same room for almost an hour. Of course, Walter would be on his best behaviour in front of Lady Dalrymple, but that might be provocation enough.

A further thirty or so people to greet and direct to the Elwin room – then there was nothing left for her to do except lock the front door and make her way up the stairs. At the top, she hesitated. Better to go into Murch – where there'd be only twenty people staring at her – rather than the main room. She opened the door a little way, edged round it – and Rick's presence hit her like a huge swamping wave. His voice, deep and dark as the November night, the words drowned out by the drumming in her ears ... His hands, confident and charismatic, speaking a vivid language all of their own ... His face–

She pressed her back against the wall and closed her eyes.

She could still see him; was this how it would be when he'd gone – his face haunting her, just like last time?

Desperate for a distraction, she opened her eyes again and sucked in her breath. From here the speaker's table was in full view. Lady Dalrymple sat at the far end, coat tethered safely to a nearby chair, gazing at Rick with rapt attention and hugging a copy of his book to her breast. Next to her, Walter seemed torn between admiring the backs of his hands and rather ostentatiously consulting his watch. Then came Ben – a man at ease with himself and the world, his face alight as if on the verge of laughter. Beside him, Tim from Molland's was surveying the audience, no doubt enjoying the prospect of a good evening's book sales.

Eyes back to Rick – and the realisation, ripping through her like an electric shock, that he was looking straight at her. She felt colour flood her cheeks; he hesitated, seemed to lose his train of thought for a moment, then switched his gaze away and continued with his talk. She listened, hearing only the rise and fall of his black-velvet voice, and the thought crashed into her mind like a stone through a window–

She would risk another ten years of regret to spend tonight with this man.

Time to wrap up and hand over to Jim – or was it Tim? – for a final few words, followed by prolonged applause from the audience. Rick gave a nod and a smile of acknowledgement, then turned and grabbed a copy of *Sex in the Sea* from the top of the pile behind him. Back at the lectern, as the applause started to die down, he rifled through his notes – found the page he wanted, slipped it in the front of the book and let out a long, controlled breath.

He cleared his throat and held up his hand for silence. 'Before we move on to the book signing, I just wanted to say thank you to all the BRLSI volunteers who've turned out

312

tonight at such short notice. And I'd like to give the person in charge, Anna Elliot, a small token of my appreciation. Is she here?' He made a show of looking round until he reached the door of the ante-room. She was still there, thank God, but pink-cheeked and reluctant, coming forward only when the audience began clapping again.

He met her half-way, shook her hand and presented her with the book. 'Just in case you haven't got one already.' He said it lightly but loudly; the audience laughed, and he made it an excuse to keep hold of her hand a little longer. His eyes burned into hers, willing her to see something much, much more in this apparently pointless gift of a second copy of his book.

She wouldn't meet his gaze, however; as she murmured her thanks, her face – and probably only he could detect it – dimmed with disappointment. Then she pulled her hand back, turned and walked away. The book looked as though it might fall unheeded from her grasp, which wasn't the plan at all ...

A tug at his sleeve – Lady Dalrymple, thrusting a book at him and babbling about barnacles. Rick forced a smile, took it from her and retreated to the speaker's table. This was reality – and for the moment he'd have to put his dream on hold. Except that he could do his best to get the signing over in record time, couldn't he? So, starting with Lady Dalrymple, he sat signing book after book as quickly as possible, keeping conversation to a minimum; just as well Guy wasn't here – he'd have had a fit.

After a while, however, he became aware of a little altercation at the other end of the table. Lady Dalrymple, now incarcerated in the most hideous and no doubt ridiculously expensive fur coat, was refusing to part with a paltry fifteen pounds for what his publishers described as 'a quality hardback with fifty-six colour photos'.

'It's my own copy, I brought it with me!' she shrilled at the blonde from Molland's, while beside her Anna's father spluttered, 'Disgraceful!' and, 'Don't you know who this is?' every three seconds.

Pen poised to sign yet another fly page, Rick hesitated. Should he bail the mean old bag out, or let her be arrested for shoplifting?

And then he heard Anna's voice, low and calm and soothing. 'It's all right, Amanda, I happen to know that Lady Dalrymple bought this some time ago.' He watched in horror as she left her copy of *Sex in the Sea* on the table and took Lady Dalrymple's, leafing quickly through it. She paused midway and pointed at something. 'Look at those tea stains, she can't have got those on it tonight, can she?'

Amanda gave a begrudging shake of her head, while Rick held his breath. One crisis averted – but what if Anna's book ended up in the wrong hands? He had a sudden vision of Lady Dalrymple avidly reading its contents before bearing down on him like a giant furball.

Talking of which – oh shit, the ghastly woman had picked the book up and was about to open it. He leapt to his feet, muttered an apology to the people waiting in line and reached the other end of the table in two strides.

'Lady Dalrymple,' he began, rescuing the book none too gently from her clutches, 'since you're so interested in barnacles, could I send you an academic paper I'm writing on their settlement behaviour in different flow environments? I'd really appreciate your views.'

The distraction worked. She fluttered her eyelashes and instructed him to mail it to her at The Royal Crescent Hotel where, she assured him, she would be staying at least until Christmas. Then she swept triumphantly off, the 8th Baronet of Kellynch clinging to her arm like one of her beloved barnacles.

So far, so good. But when Rick handed the book back to Anna, she took it with even less enthusiasm than before. He said in an urgent whisper, 'Read what's inside!' and she replied tersely, 'I already have.' A cold finger of fear snaked down his back until she added, 'I bought a copy after your talk at Molland's, remember?'

'I don't mean the book,' he said softly. 'I've written you a letter.'

Without another word, without even a glance, he returned to his seat and kept his eyes fixed firmly on the books he was signing. No way did he want to look up and second-guess her response from the expression on her face. He would know soon enough, and only then would he allow himself to think about the consequences.

'I've written you a letter.' That drumming in her ears again – and now a tight band round her chest, a dryness in her throat. A letter – for what? To profess his love, or assure her that he'd moved on?

She stumbled towards Lonsdale, driven by some masochistic impulse to collect her thoughts in the same place she'd suggested to him. As she entered the room, she instinctively glanced over at the plesiosaur – the 200-million-year-old sea dragon, as he'd called it. Life, preserved in plaster. Was it so different from her life – lived in all its fullness for such a short time, a starburst of feelings that she'd never experienced before or since, preserved in a handful of memories?

And now those feelings were about to be revived. Because, whatever the letter actually said, it would bring his voice into this room to talk about the past. And he knew only too well that she wouldn't ignore it; after all, she'd never been able to resist the written word.

Was this a second chance or a final goodbye? She hesitated,

then sat down exactly where he had been sitting. His coat still hung over the chair next to her, his umbrella lay where she'd left it. She put his book down on the table and opened it. A piece of paper stared up at her, the words dashing across the page in a bold, open scrawl that expressed the very essence of the man who'd written them.

Steeling herself, she let his voice into the room.

I once wrote you a letter and you never replied, which makes me wonder if you ever received it. This time it's a more personal delivery – and I need a reply, even if it's not the one I want.

I'm listening to you – I can hear every word, however softly you speak – and I'm half-agony, half-hope. You're saying that men are realists – that, when the woman they love is no longer available, they move on. Well, believe me, I tried – and I thought I had. But seeing you again, after so many years, just proved how little I knew ...

You told me to trust myself. So here I am back in Bath, putting everything on the line for a second chance with you. Is that what you want, too? Whatever your answer, remember this: I may not deserve you – when I think of how I've behaved, I know I've shown little self-control and even less forgiveness – but I've never stopped loving you.

You're talking about heartless men ... But I have a heart, and it's the same one you almost broke ten years ago, and it belongs to you, and only you, even more than it did then. And yes, I'm a realist: if you no longer love me, I will accept it. But don't say that only a woman can keep on loving someone who's no longer part of her life! Because I will keep on loving you until there are no stars in the sky.

Tell me tonight how you feel. If there's any chance of you loving me back, then I'll wait for you as I should have waited before. If not, say the word and I'll leave you in peace. But I'll never forget you, or what we had, or what might have been.

Rick

She read the letter over and over, afraid she might have mistaken his meaning. Gradually, however, she fought off her daze of disbelief. As she closed the book and took it downstairs, she felt amazingly calm.

It must look, she thought, like any other copy of *Sex in the Sea* – yet it had just changed the course of two people's lives.

Chapter Fifty-Six

The book signing was over at last. Rick managed to foil a few lingerers' attempts to engage him in conversation and went into the Lonsdale room to fetch his things.

To his surprise Ben was there, on his mobile. He waited until the other man had finished the call, then said anxiously, 'What's up? I thought you'd gone to the pub ages ago.'

'That was Charles – he's only just arrived. Apparently he bumped into an old university friend on his way here and went for a quick half.' A wry smile. 'All I can say is – it wasn't quick and, judging by the way he was slurring his words, it certainly wasn't a half.'

'Whereas you must be dying of thirst – good job you had that coffee earlier.'

'Yeah, and it kept me awake during your talk! No, seriously, I was riveted. Anna was right – you really believe that stuff about "a mate for the rest of your life", don't you?'

Rick pulled on his coat, then picked up the umbrella and cradled it in his hands. He kept his voice low, as if frightened of breaking a spell. 'Is she still here? Have you spoken to her since – since my talk?'

'Haven't even seen her, let alone spoken to her – but she must be around somewhere.' Ben chuckled. 'She and I had a very interesting conversation earlier about the differences between men and women – I'll tell you about it in the pub. If Charles can't walk in a straight line, we'll have to get a taxi – but you're seeing someone first, aren't you? Maybe we could get a taxi together, then Charles and I can wait while you–'

'Not really, it might take a while,' Rick said hurriedly. 'And anyway, she lives in the other direction from the pub.'

'Ah, *she*.' Ben rolled his eyes. 'In that case, there's a pretty good chance you won't be coming to the pub at all.' He grinned and headed for the door.

Rick felt his stomach knot as he followed Ben out of the room and down the stairs. In a matter of seconds, he would have his answer. One word from her – one look, even – would tell him all he needed to know. As Ben veered off to the Gents, he strolled into the reception area and tried to appear composed; but his heart was racing, and his eyes were restless as they scanned the thinning crowd ...

There she was, standing by the desk with her back to him. Not ready with her answer, as he'd hoped; in fact, her words and looks were directed at someone else – Charles sodding Musgrove, of all people.

'And I'm not coming to the pub,' she was saying. 'I've got other plans.'

Rick cleared his throat. 'Anna.'

She whirled round – and Charles looked over as well, with a beery smile and a drunken little wave. It was easy to ignore *him*; but far more difficult, even with a scientist's powers of observation, to read the expression in those startled grey eyes.

Ben appeared at his side, slapped him on the shoulder and said, 'See you later, at the pub?'

'Yes,' Rick said, automatically. But the grey eyes were sparkling now, like a sunlit sea. Did that mean ...? 'Maybe,' he said; then added recklessly, 'Maybe not.'

She smiled; and he smiled back, because now he knew everything was going to be just fine. Absolutely-bloody-wonderful, in fact.

'Come on, Charles,' Ben said, 'I don't think we're wanted.' But there was amusement in his voice rather than offence.

With an effort, Rick switched his gaze away from Anna. 'Sorry, Ben,' he said. 'I'll definitely see you in the morning, before I go to Sophie's.'

And that was the most he could commit to, he decided, as he saw the two men safely outside. Because he had a feeling that an awful lot was going to happen between now and tomorrow morning.

There were other people around, looking at the art exhibition on their way out – but he didn't care. And neither, it seemed, did she. As he strode towards her, she ran into his arms.

It was what he'd wanted, deep down, for ten long years: to hold her close and feel the beat of her heart.

Wrapped up in each other, they climbed the stairs to her flat with hurried steps. At the top, she reluctantly let him go, opened the front door and felt for the switch. Before she could flood the room with light, however, his lips brushed her neck just below one ear. Her hand stilled. Wordlessly, she spun round and–

The fierceness of his kiss made her gasp. It was like being back on the boat, when she'd realised that everything before had been a masterclass in restraint. This time, during the long tense weeks since their first meeting, the restraint had been far greater. And, she thought with a deep, drawn-out ache of anticipation, so would be the release.

They broke apart, struggled out of their coats, kicked off their boots. With clumsy, impatient movements, she at last flicked on the light, coaxed the front door shut and pushed the snib home. She smiled to herself as she saw his umbrella lying discarded – evidently forgotten, in the haste to revive older memories …

As she helped him shrug off his jacket and sweater, she noticed that her hands were shaking. It was, she decided, the thrill of knowing what would happen next. Savouring that knowledge, she allowed her fingers to slow and skim his taut, bronzed chest. At her touch, his eyes closed and the breath sighed out of him.

She unfastened his jeans, then paused. 'Rick?'

He dragged his eyes open and tilted her face up to his. 'Yes?'

'It's just …' Despite the assurances in his letter, she needed to hear him say the words. 'How long are you planning to be around?'

He didn't answer immediately. Instead, his mouth gently traced the line of her neck, right to the curve of her shoulder, while his hands pulled her dress down … and down. 'Oh, I reckon it'll be …' he kissed the soft swell of her breast, 'an eternity or two. Long enough to bring up a family and grow old together.'

'That,' she said, when she'd remembered how to breathe, 'sounds perfect.'

More kisses, while her dress and his jeans fell to the floor. As cool air met hot skin, she trembled – and, instantly, he cocooned her in his warmth. The seconds ticked by; but there were no kisses or caresses, only the sense that he'd somehow withdrawn.

'What is it?' she said quietly.

'I'm looking at that painting.' His voice was thick with emotion. 'A picture of our past. You had it as a daily reminder, whereas I …'

'Shhh.' She leaned back in the circle of his arms, put her finger to his lips. Later, she would tell him how she'd talked Katya into capturing her jumbled impressions on canvas, adjusting and re-adjusting the final result until it was real enough to send shivers down her spine. But not yet. She took his hand and led him into the bedroom, steering a sure path through the shadows to switch on the bedside lamp. And, as it cast its pale-gold glow on to the little table underneath, he glanced at the book that she'd left there.

'What are you reading?' He sounded oddly apprehensive – but no wonder, when the title was in Russian!

She smiled up at him. 'It's called *First Love* – what else?'

He smiled back – and it was that special little smile, the one she'd always thought of as reserved for her alone; only now she was absolutely certain about it. And the rightness of it all – of being with him, like this – stung her eyes with tears.

Later, when their bodies locked in an instinctive rhythm, when he whispered 'Annie' as a passionate, loving refrain – she knew that, this time, she would never let him go.

It was the same old magic, enriched by a new understanding – that the pain of loss only made the joy of rediscovery more intense.

Downstairs, back home after their evening out, Jenny emerged from the wintry depths of the larder clutching a bottle, which she promptly handed to Tom. 'You're nearer the corkscrew, I'll get the glasses.'

He raised his eyebrows. 'Wine – at this time of night? What are we celebrating?' Then, as he noticed the label, 'Bloody hell! I thought we were keeping this for Christmas Day?'

'Christmas has come early – for some people, anyway.'

She fetched the best glasses while he opened the wine. When he placed the bottle on the kitchen table to let it breathe, she shook her head impatiently. 'Pour it straight out.'

As soon as he'd done so, she raised her glass. 'To Anna.'

'To Anna,' he repeated automatically. Then, with a puzzled frown, 'Why on earth have we opened a bottle of very expensive Burgundy just to drink to Anna?'

'All right then – to Anna and the man she's brought back to her flat.'

'*What*? How do you know she's got a man up there?'

'You mean apart from hearing a distinctly masculine laugh outside a few minutes ago?' She allowed herself a smirk of satisfaction. 'Well, let's see, there were definitely two of them going up those stairs. Oh – and you know that noisy front door of hers? There was a very long pause between the creak when it opened and the creak when it shut, as if she'd been well and truly distracted. Good job I didn't oil those hinges after all.'

He sipped his wine – and frowned. She was about to ask if it was corked, when he said anxiously, 'You're sure it couldn't be William? That wouldn't exactly be something to celebrate.'

'No way could it be William. You didn't see her face when I told her what he'd been up to – she was almost relieved.' Now it was Jenny's turn to frown. 'Which means I was completely wrong about the theatre.'

'The theatre?'

'Whoever she wanted to impress there with her new dress, it certainly wasn't William.'

Tom raised his glass a second time. 'To Anna.'

'What for now?'

'For getting the better of you.' He chuckled. 'That doesn't happen very often, does it?'

And Jenny was determined it wouldn't happen again – at least, not for a while. The next morning, at exactly eight-thirty – she simply couldn't wait any longer, even though it was a Saturday – she knocked loudly on Anna's door.

No response. Undeterred, she raised her hand to knock again – and the door opened. She stopped herself just in time from hammering on the tanned, muscular chest in front of her, and looked up.

'Oh – it's *you*,' she whispered. In her confusion, she lowered her eyes. But the sight of only a pair of boxer shorts – obviously pulled on in a hurry, because they barely covered the necessary – made her gaze flick swiftly upwards again.

'Sorry, couldn't find my clothes,' Rick Wentworth said, not bothering to hide his amusement.

'Don't mind me,' she croaked. 'Is Anna around?'

'She's still asleep. Anything I can help with?'

Jenny recovered her voice at last. 'I just wondered if she wanted something from the shops?'

'Possibly – although we're at my sister's all day.' He grinned. 'I'm meant to be opening her garden centre.'

'Let's hope you can find your clothes, then.' She grinned back. 'Or maybe not. Get yourself a baseball cap and you'll look as though you've just walked off the cover of your book.'

He laughed. 'A bit chilly for that. And I'm not sure my sister would be too pleased – today's all about promoting her business, not my book. Anyway,' he went on, 'I'll tell Anna you called and I'm sure she'll be in touch.'

Very unlikely, Jenny told herself as she went downstairs. Given what else was on offer, Anna would hardly be thinking about her shopping list.

She found Tom in the kitchen, catching up with the *Bath Chronicle* over breakfast. 'Well, I met the mystery man,' she said, in a deceptively casual tone.

He looked up immediately. 'And–?'

'Anna Elliot is a very lucky woman.'

'So – who is he?'

'Rick Wentworth.' She watched his forehead crease in surprise. 'Just one teeny-weeny problem, of course,' she added, glumly. 'He lives on the other side of the world.'

Bliss, utter bliss. To wake up and know that love was only a touch away.

Anna shut her eyes to the dull morning light edging round the curtains, and stretched out her hand. Instantly, his fingers curled around hers; and she wondered if he'd been lying awake, waiting ...

She opened her eyes. He was sitting next to her, on top of the duvet; and he'd obviously been up and about, although he wasn't dressed. 'Come back to bed,' she whispered.

He let go of her hand, but only to trace her mouth with the tip of his finger. 'Wish I could,' he said, gently, 'but I've got a garden centre to open.'

The bed gave a soft groan as he got up, and she turned away. Love was no longer a touch away – and that was reality, wasn't it? Other things crowded in; and love, if it was a wise love, made room for them. But she couldn't help a little niggle of disappointment.

And then – his weight on the bed again, nearer now, right behind her; his body warming hers, and his voice in her ear, low and caressing. 'I love you.'

She rolled over to face him, blinking back the tears. 'I love you, too. And I don't want you to go.'

'To Uppercross? Aren't you coming with me?'

'I mean back to Australia, next week.'

He let out a long, ragged breath. 'I've already decided to cancel my flight – I'll make some phone calls first thing Monday.' A grave look, burdened with déjà vu. 'This time, I'll do whatever *you* want.'

'No.' She gave an emphatic shake of her head. 'This time, we'll work out what's best for both of us.'

Silence, as he gazed down at her; then his mouth relaxed into a grin. 'As long as it doesn't involve living with your father, or either of your sisters.' He glanced across at the desk. 'Or having a computer in our bedroom.'

She pulled him close, laughing. 'Getting picky, aren't we, Dr Wentworth?'

'Oh, I've always been picky – particularly about the love of my life.' A lingering kiss. 'But now I need to call Dave, or we'll be late. Although I know Sophie and Ed will let me off when they see *you*.'

'Mmmm.' Anna wished she shared his confidence. Judging by that embarrassing discussion with Sophie and Ed in the Pump Room, she'd be the last person they were expecting Rick to turn up with.

But then Rick saw things very much in black and white, she reflected, as she listened to his phone conversation with Dave. He was brief to the point of being abrupt, and totally focused on the matter in hand – getting Dave to pick them up in forty minutes. Whereas her phone call to Jenny a little while later, while Rick was in the shower, was the opposite of brief and focused. She was unusually nervous as she dialled the number; sharing this part of her past was uncharted territory.

She needn't have worried – Jenny's voice was warm with approval. 'Well, you're a dark horse! I got the shock of my life when I knocked on your door this morning and *he* appeared.'

Anna giggled. 'He's just told me you called. About the shopping, I haven't got a clue–'

'Don't worry, it was the best excuse I could think of to find out who you'd brought home.'

'Look, Rick and I–' Anna hesitated, then rushed on, 'It's not what you think.'

'Don't be so ridiculous!' Jenny said in mock despair. 'If it's not what I think, if you've had that man in your flat all night and done nothing with him, then you're a disgrace to womankind.'

Anna refused to be drawn on that particular subject, however. 'What I mean is – this isn't something sudden. Rick and I met a long time ago and, to cut a long story short, things didn't work out. But now–'

'But now everything's going to be wonderful?' Jenny put in, dryly. 'All I can say is – you like making life difficult, don't you? You couldn't have chosen a longer-distance relationship if you'd tried – apart from dating an astronaut. Still, I'm sure you'll either tell me to mind my own business or come out with something cheesy, like "Love will find a way".'

Anna bit her lip. 'No, I won't, because you're right – our biggest problem is how to be together. We need to talk through the options, so he's not going back to Australia next week after all.' As she said the words, she realised she was grinning from ear to ear.

'I'm glad to hear it. Why don't you come to lunch tomorrow, so that Tom can meet him?'

The grin widened, if that was possible. 'I can't think of anything nicer.'

'If that's true,' Jenny said, with an exasperated sigh, 'then you've got a *very* limited imagination.'

Chapter Fifty-Seven

Rick held Anna's hand at every opportunity – outside on the pavement while they waited for Dave, then in the back of the car, and even at the hotel when they called to collect his things. Holding hands had the advantage, he decided, of making explanations about their relationship unnecessary. And, just as important, it felt bloody great.

Dave made no comment when he saw them; but he broke his usual habit and turned on the car radio – more for their privacy, Rick guessed, than his own entertainment. On their many journeys together, he'd always preferred talking to listening.

Ben, on the other hand, ran down the front steps of the hotel and greeted them with a whoop of delight. 'So I *was* right! I told Charles last night there was something going on, but of course I couldn't prove it. And d'you know what? He bet me fifty quid that Anna wouldn't be interested in a shark wrestler! Pity he was drunk at the time – he'll probably deny all knowledge.'

A quick handshake and a rash promise to visit Ben and Megan the following week were all they had time for. When they'd picked up Rick's luggage and were in the car again, Anna said quietly, 'How long can you stay in England?'

He looked down at her small hand, safe and warm in his. 'A couple of months. I'm on sabbatical now, but I need to be back at university in early January for what we call the summer session.' He hesitated and looked up. 'What are your plans for Christmas?'

Her face clouded. 'I usually go to Mona and Charles, but I'm not sure that's a good idea.'

'No,' he said softly, 'it's not. Will you come away with me instead?'

'Yes.'

'Somewhere like the north of Scotland, or the depths of Wales, where we don't need to bother about anyone else?'

'Yes!'

He felt he corners of his mouth quirk in a tense little smile. 'On honeymoon?'

'Oh, Rick …' She leaned over and brushed her lips against his.

Still that tense smile; trusting himself didn't come naturally – yet. 'Will you marry me, Anna?'

'*Yes*. Did you doubt it?' She kissed him – properly this time – and he felt again that rush of exhilaration at being with her; then she drew back, waited for their breathing to steady, and said, 'But after Christmas?'

He said simply, 'I'll have to go back to Melbourne, even if it's just to hand in my resignation.'

Her eyes blazed. 'No – that would be like throwing away all your research!' She frowned in concentration, her mind pursuing a glimmer of coherent thought. 'Look, you have to be in southern Australia to do your work – but I don't have to be in Bath to do mine. At least, not next term. I'll have exam papers to mark, which I can do anywhere, and they've always said I could take time off from teaching to turn my PhD into a book. So, if I give them enough notice, I'm sure I'll be able to go to Melbourne with you in January.' She paused, and looked down at their joined hands. 'It's just – I don't know if I could bear to be so far away from Kellynch. The place,' she added hurriedly, 'not the people in it.'

'It needn't be for long, we could come back here towards the end of February – I've got a week's break. After that …' He sighed. 'As you said earlier, we'll work out what's best for both of us.'

She nodded. 'The main thing is that we're together – right?'

His hand tightened round hers. 'For now, that's more than enough.'

'Told you he'd be here on time,' Ed said, as they watched a black Jaguar swing through the gates of the garden centre.

Sophie turned away from the office window and allowed her shoulders to relax – but not her voice. 'By the skin of his teeth!' she ground out.

'Fifteen minutes to spare, actually,' Ed corrected her good-naturedly.

She pretended he hadn't spoken. 'I've been trying his mobile for the last hour, but he's got it switched off! It's just not good enough, he could easily have called to say he was on his way.'

'Don't think so – looks like he's had his hands – pretty full.'

Oh God, Sophie thought, suddenly contrite, what was up with Ed? He sounded short of breath, as if ... She whirled round, and discovered him struggling not to laugh. Before she could demand an explanation, however, a movement in the yard caught her eye. She glanced out of the window again – and her jaw dropped.

There was her brother, large as life, helping a woman out of the back of the car. Nothing odd about that; he could act the gentleman as well as anyone – when it suited him. But this was a man transformed – brimming over with a happy-to-be-alive energy, the Rick she'd last glimpsed when they were much younger. And the woman ... the woman was none other than Anna Elliot!

She saw them give their driver a friendly wave, then link hands and amble towards the shop as if they had all the time in the world. People overtook them, turning round for a second look and nudging each other, and in the distance a few press cameras clicked; but Rick and Anna seemed oblivious.

At the entrance to the shop, Rick paused beside Sophie's pride and joy – a large display of evergreen foliage and silk rosebuds in vibrant jewel colours. An appealing alternative, she hoped, to the potted poinsettias and holly wreaths that people usually bought to decorate their homes at Christmas. She'd spent many hours – and a vast amount of money – sourcing and arranging them to her satisfaction.

Now she watched her brother pluck a deep-red bloom from the very centre of the stand and present it to Anna.

'Right, that's done it!' Grim-faced again, she rushed out of the office – leaving Ed to follow at an extremely safe distance.

It was like being in a dream, a beautiful, never-ending dream, where everything Rick said and did showed her how much he loved her.

He tucked the silk rosebud in the top buttonhole of her coat. 'When we're back in Bath, I'll buy you real ones.'

She gazed up at him with heavy-lidded eyes. 'And scatter the petals across our bed?'

He laughed – and it was his bedroom laugh, deep and rich and unhurried. 'Keep on looking at me like that, and I'll get Dave to drive us home right now.'

'Over my dead body!' a voice snapped behind them; Sophie, as Anna had never heard her before – almost hoarse with anger.

Rick turned towards her, smiling serenely. 'Good morning to you, too, Soph.' Then, eyebrows raised in astonishment, 'What's the matter? You didn't honestly think I'd go off without opening your garden centre, did you?'

Anna risked a look at Sophie and immediately regretted it; she was the image of her brother at his most hostile.

'Frederick,' Sophie said coldly, 'put that back *at once*. You've ruined my display!'

Until now, Anna had barely registered the stand of flowers and foliage a few feet away, with its uniform swaths of colour. Oh God, Sophie was right; the small hole Rick had made in the middle drew the eye like a magnet and completely spoiled the overall effect. She gasped an apology, took the rosebud out of her buttonhole and put it carefully back in its place.

'Thank you.' Sophie sounded as if she was thawing to her usual friendly self; but a moment later she iced over again. 'And another thing, Frederick – how can you *do* this to Anna?'

'Do what?' Rick said, blankly.

And Anna, recalling that conversation in the Pump Room, finally understood Sophie's anger. *She* may have left Sophie in no doubt of her feelings for Rick – but had *he* ever given his sister any hint that those feelings were mutual?

She tugged at his sleeve. 'Sophie doesn't know about our ... history, does she? So she's worried that I'm just a time-filler until you go back to Australia.'

'History?' Sophie repeated, her stunned gaze flicking between Anna and Rick as if they'd each grown another head.

Ed arrived, grinning broadly. 'This garden centre'll be history if we don't open it soon. The shop's full to bursting and the press are here in force. Come on, let's get on with it.'

'In a minute.' Rick turned to Sophie. 'There's no need to worry,' he said quietly, and Anna felt his fingers close round hers. 'I don't believe in wasting second chances.'

Sophie's eyes were suspiciously bright. 'I'm very glad to hear it. You know, I've always thought–'

'Hell's teeth!' Ed put in, his grin fading as he stared across the yard towards the main entrance. 'Looks like Sir Walter's decided to honour us with his presence. Anyone have any idea why?'

Chapter Fifty-Eight

In the back of William's Bentley, Walter reflected that Cléopatra Clé had exited his life as unexpectedly as she'd entered it. According to Lisa, she'd checked out of The Royal Crescent Hotel that morning, without so much as a thank you. So – no more purrings addressed to 'Sir Voltaire', no more delicious massages, no more saucy threats to attend to his sacral chakra …

It was probably just as well, now that this new business venture of William's was gathering pace and taking up an increasing amount of everyone's time. They'd soon be checking out of The Royal Crescent themselves, and Walter – not William – would be moving into The Lodge while the main house was refurbished. Hardly fitting accommodation for a baronet; but William had assured him it was the best option in the short term.

And, of course, Walter would agree to anything if it kept William at Lisa's side.

Now the Bentley glided to a halt in front of Farley's Garden Centre and Walter had a blurred impression of freshly painted buildings, vivid splashes of colour and dim shapes milling about the yard. The opening ceremony wouldn't have started yet – he might still be asked to step in at the last minute. How he'd enjoy keeping Sophie Croft guessing as to whether he would accept!

He closed his eyes to run through the speech in his head. 'We were truly delighted, though not at all surprised, when Mr and Mrs Croft begged us some months ago to open their humble little–'

'Isn't that Anna?' William said, and the catch in his voice

was unmistakable.

Walter jerked his eyes open. Trust *her* to be here, lying in wait for the dear boy – just when he and Lisa were making the final arrangements for their ...

Fortunately, Lisa was on to it like a flash. 'It is – and she's wearing that dreadful coat, as usual. I told her it made her look like a hobbit when she bought it two years ago.'

Two years ago! His middle daughter was simply beyond comprehension. Why on earth would anyone keep anything longer than one season? Walter gazed fondly at his brand-new tweeds, then frowned as he noted William's cream wool suit. Lisa, it seemed, was no longer interested in dressing both the men in her life to the same high sartorial standard. There was an obvious explanation: cream was their main corporate colour and William wore it almost daily, whereas Lisa knew it made Walter look like a living corpse. When he'd mentioned their matching outfits, however, Lisa had pretended she didn't understand what he was talking about. But who else had been able to find out what Walter would wear, and give that information so promptly and discreetly to William?

A horn blared behind them. That would be Minty; William had offered to pick her up on the way, but she'd insisted on meeting them at the garden centre. Apparently she had a long-standing engagement earlier that morning to enlighten All Saints' Young Mothers Group on the virtues of thrift. Walter wondered how she could be taken seriously in that Rolls-Royce.

'I'll get out – I want a word with Minty,' he said, taking a handful of brochures with him.

It seemed that she was just as eager to have a word with him. When he reached her car, the window was already wound down and, before he could speak, she hissed, 'Have you *seen* who Anna's holding hands with?'

He could truthfully answer, 'No.'

'Rick Wentworth!' She allowed this bombshell its full impact, then launched her next missile. 'I read somewhere recently that his grandfather was a miner, and a communist! What *would* dear Irina think?'

Walter was too busy doing some thinking of his own to worry about Irina. 'Now, now, Minty – the man may lack breeding, but he's got money and he's generally thought to be extraordinarily good-looking. Physically, he rather reminds me of myself – a few years ago, of course.' He paused, in case Minty wanted to elaborate on his superiority even now; but she said nothing. Closing his mind to the memory of exquisite 'Sir Voltaire'-laced compliments, he continued smoothly, 'Last but by no means least, Dottie Dalrymple finds him an inspiration! We've left her in Bath reading every book on barnacles she can lay her hands on.'

'Barnacles!' Minty gave a grotesque snort. 'Look, I know it's not like last time, when Anna was so young and her place at Oxford was at stake–' She broke off, and her whole face began to twitch and tremble – most unattractive; and he had to bend lower to hear what she was saying between revolting, hiccupping sobs – most inconvenient. 'But, Walter – you do realise – if she still wants to be with him – we'll hardly ever see her? He lives on the other side of the world!'

Exactly, Walter thought. As far away as possible from William and Lisa.

Aloud he said, 'You may be jumping to conclusions, my dear. I'll go over and have a little chat with them, do some subtle probing to find out the lie of the land. No need for you to come – just leave it to me.'

Anna's heart sank like a stone at the sight of her father mincing towards them. She could see what was going to happen: at best an altercation between Walter and Rick, at worst a fight – all diligently recorded by journalists and photographers – and the opening of the garden centre ruined.

Not her life, though. This time, she would stand firm.

Everyone greeted each other civilly enough. But when Ed tried to hurry them all into the shop, Walter announced grandly, 'We're here to publicise our new business venture. It won't launch for another six months, but we're taking bookings now.' He brandished half-a-dozen expensive-looking brochures in their faces, as if distributing largesse to the poor.

'Sir Walter,' Sophie began angrily, 'we really haven't time–'

'It's in a different league from other local enterprises, of course,' he went on, with a dismissive nod at Sophie and Ed's shop, 'and destined to be a resounding success. Thankfully, there will always be those who value a noble lineage over fly-by-night celebrity, taste and refinement over tacky mediocrity. That is, after all, how we secured considerable investment to restore Kellynch to its former glory.'

And, instantly, Anna had to know – *what* was he up to? 'Let me see that!' She grabbed one of the brochures while Rick tightened his grip on her other hand; as he looked over her shoulder at the embossed gold script on the textured cream cover, she felt the reassuring warmth of his body at her back.

'Brides of Kellynch', she read out, in a strangled voice. 'The ultimate wedding venue – a touch of class for your special day.' She hesitated over the next two words, wondering if she could ever bring herself to utter them. '*Noblesse oblige*,' she managed at last, through gritted teeth.

Walter gave a pompous smile. 'And the best news of all – my eldest daughter, Elisabeth, will be the first "Bride of Kellynch" when she marries William Elliot-Dunne.'

'More like "Bride of Dracula" then,' Rick murmured.

But if Walter heard this taunt, he didn't rise to the bait.

'A late spring wedding, we hope,' he simpered, 'when our extensive facilities are complete – the Cherished Moments Chapel, the Royal Reception Hall, the Select Spa, the Bridal Bower for outside photographs, and so on.' He looked straight at Anna and Rick and said, without any preamble, 'If you two are getting married, we'll try and fit you in somewhere. We might even agree to a small discount – for family, as it were.'

'A very generous offer–' Rick sounded amazingly composed, Anna thought – 'and one that will get all the consideration it deserves.'

'*Noblesse oblige.*' Walter nodded benignly at him, then swivelled his cold blue eyes accusingly in Anna's direction. 'Haven't you anything to say?'

But Anna couldn't trust herself to speak. She was imagining her beloved home over the coming months, and its inevitable desecration. Living in Bath – even though she knew she would have Rick beside her – might prove too close to Kellynch for comfort.

Suddenly, Australia didn't seem too far away after all.

Epilogue

In The Lodge, Walter turns this way and that, admiring the cut of his new Ascot-grey morning coat in each of his reflections. This has become a daily ritual, even though it's only late February and Lisa's wedding is still some months off. The Lodge's second bedroom is barely adequate as a dressing room – so cramped with all these mirrors – but downsizing is his contribution to the greater cause, Brides of Kellynch. Best of all, it gives Minty no ammunition to complain about his extravagances.

Minty, however, has bigger fish to fry. As financial controller for Brides of Kellynch, she has a budget that exceeds her wildest dreams – and the meddling power that goes with it. Up at the main house, she sits in her new office – handily situated to ensure a good view of both the front door and the tradesmen's entrance – and prepares her weekly report for William and his idiot of an accountant. She occasionally stops mid-sentence to wonder aloud what dear Irina would think – but there is nobody around to listen.

Across the hall, Lisa harangues the architect about various plumbing problems at the spa complex in the west wing. She threatens to sue him if Select Spa isn't ready in two weeks, reminding him that it is opening well ahead of the rest of the wedding venue as a private members' club. Its manager, Mrs Clay, has worked day and night to deliver a very exclusive client list – all local dignitaries, eager to experience the beneficial effects of massage.

In the spa, behind locked doors, the conscientious Pat Clay is busy giving William a thorough ... debriefing.

Despite jet-black hair and a broad Somerset accent, she bears a startling resemblance to a certain Cléopatra Clé. Her future here is secure: as well as the private members' club, the Brides of Kellynch brochure promises 'a relaxing massage for the bride and groom, separately or as a couple', so she is sure her Hands of Love won't be idle.

Recovering from his one-to-one with Mrs Clay, William contemplates his good fortune. He has two women in his life who seem to have one purpose in theirs: making him happy, without forcing him to choose between them. Furthermore, his plans to sweat the Kellynch asset are on track. And, finally, his future father-in-law is extremely biddable, so William has no problem letting him out of The Lodge now and then. In a display of breathtaking audacity, he has even allowed him to meet Mrs Clay; but, as he explained to Lisa, given Walter's poor eyesight and aversion to her 'common' accent, they can safely assume that William will one day inherit the title he's already prone to using. Life couldn't be sweeter, except … But he is becoming more and more adept at blocking that pale, heart-shaped face from his thoughts.

Along the road at Farley's Garden Centre, Sophie and Ed Croft have been up for hours. Business is slow but, despite Walter's assurances to the contrary, they are building up a loyal following. And Sophie is relieved that they ended up living on the premises instead of moving into The Lodge – the rent on the greenhouses at Kellynch is prohibitive enough. Although she's heard a rumour that Brides of Kellynch is seeking planning permission to turn them into something known as the Glass Garden, an alternative to the Bridal Bower on rainy days …

A little further away, in their magazine-strewn bedroom at Uppercross Manor, Mona complains to Charles that their wedding was really crappy by today's standards. She thinks they should renew their vows, and she's already made enquiries at Brides of Kellynch. Of course, once the Musgroves see how things really should be done, they will want *all* their family events at Kellynch, not just weddings. And it shouldn't cost anything because, in return, Mona will offer her home-grown public relations services – Lisa doesn't have a clue how to handle the press – and vet the list of prospective brides. One can't be too careful when the family name is at stake.

But Mona ends up talking to an empty room. Charles storms downstairs, rounds up Ollie and Harry and makes for the sanctuary of the Great House. Here, his parents and sisters – with their partners – are having one of their frequent family get-togethers and Charles knows that, briefly, he will forget his troubles.

In Bath, Jenny and Tom are getting to know their new tenant, one of Rick's colleagues at the University of Melbourne who's over here on a two-year contract. Jenny has high hopes of pairing him off with Christina – only not just yet. She's already lost the company of one very good friend in recent months.

On the other side of the world, somewhere off Kangaroo Island, a man and a woman sit on the deck of a boat watching the stars. It's a time for reflecting on the past, dreaming of the future, and celebrating …

… the power of persuasion.

About the Author

Juliet describes herself as 'a nineteenth-century mind in a 21st-century body – actually, some days it's the other way round'. The youngest of four girls, she was born and bred in North-East England, where she met her future husband. Unlike Anne Elliot in Jane Austen's *Persuasion*, she got married despite pressure to wait until she'd finished her degree, and emerged from the University of Nottingham with a First in French and Russian. Thirty years later she is still married, has two teenage children and lives in Harpenden, Hertfordshire.

Her debut novel *The Importance of Being Emma* was shortlisted for the Melissa Nathan Award for Comedy Romance 2009.

Juliet's stories are modernisations of Jane Austen's novels.

www.julietarcher.com
www.twitter.com/julietarcher

More Choc Lit

From Juliet Archer

The Importance of Being Emma

A modern retelling of Jane Austen's *Emma*.

Mark Knightley – handsome, clever, rich – is used to women falling at his feet. Except Emma Woodhouse, who's like part of the family – and the furniture. When their relationship changes dramatically, is it an ending or a new beginning?

Emma's grown into a stunningly attractive young woman, full of ideas for modernising her family business. Then Mark gets involved and the sparks begin to fly. It's just like the old days, except that now he's seeing her through totally new eyes.

While Mark struggles to keep his feelings in check, Emma remains immune to the Knightley charm. She's never forgotten that embarrassing moment when he discovered her teenage crush on him. He's still pouring scorn on all her projects, especially her beautifully orchestrated campaign to find Mr Right for her ditzy PA. And finally, when the mysterious Flynn Churchill – the man of her dreams – turns up, how could she have eyes for anyone else?…

Visit www.choc-lit.com for more details including the first two chapters and reviews, or simply scan barcode using your mobile phone QR reader.

Why not try something else from the Choc Lit selection?

Starting Over
Sue Moorcroft

New home, new friends, new love. Can starting over be that simple?

Tess Riddell reckons her beloved Freelander is more reliable than any man – especially her ex-fiancé, Olly Gray. She's moving on from her old life and into the perfect cottage in the country.

Miles Rattenbury's passions? Old cars and new women! Romance? He's into fun rather than commitment. When Tess crashes the Freelander into his breakdown truck, they find that they're nearly neighbours – yet worlds apart. Despite her overprotective parents and a suddenly attentive Olly, she discovers the joys of village life and even forms an unlikely friendship with Miles. Then, just as their relationship develops into something deeper, an old flame comes looking for him ...

Is their love strong enough to overcome the past? Or will it take more than either of them is prepared to give?

Visit www.choc-lit.com for more details including the first two chapters and reviews, or simply scan barcode using your mobile phone QR reader.

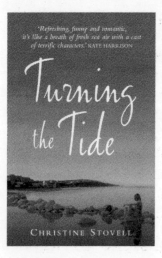

Turning the Tide
Christine Stovell

**All's fair in love and war?
Depends on who's making
the rules.**

Harry Watling has spent the
past five years keeping her
father's boat yard afloat,
despite its dying clientele.
Now all she wants to do is
enjoy the peace and quiet of
her sleepy backwater.

So when property developer
Matthew Corrigan wants to turn the boat yard into an
upmarket housing complex for his exotic new restaurant, it's
like declaring war.

And the odds seem to be stacked in Matthew's favour.
He's got the colourful locals on board, his hard-to-please
girlfriend is warming to the idea and he has the means to
force Harry's hand. Meanwhile, Harry has to fight not just
his plans but also her feelings for the man himself.

Then a family secret from the past creates heartbreak for
Harry, and neither of them is prepared for what happens
next …

Visit www.choc-lit.com for more details
including the first two chapters and
reviews, or simply scan barcode using
your mobile phone QR reader.

All That Mullarkey
Sue Moorcroft

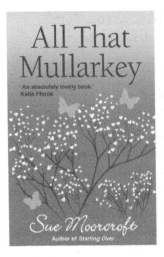

Revenge and love: it's a thin line ...

The writing's on the wall for Cleo and Gav. The bedroom wall, to be precise. And it says 'This marriage is over.'

Wounded and furious, Cleo embarks on a night out with the girls, which turns into a glorious one night stand with ...

Justin, centrefold material and irrepressibly irresponsible. He loves a little wildness in a woman – and he's in the right place at the right time to enjoy Cleo's.

But it's Cleo who has to pick up the pieces – of a marriage based on a lie and the lasting repercussions of that night. Torn between laid-back Justin and control-freak Gav, she's a free spirit that life is trying to tie down. But the rewards are worth it!

Visit www.choc-lit.com for more details including the first two chapters and reviews, or simply scan barcode using your mobile phone QR reader.

Trade Winds
Christina Courtenay

Short-listed for the Romantic Novelists' Association's Pure Passion Award for Best Historical Fiction 2011

Marriage of convenience – or a love for life?

It's 1732 in Gothenburg, Sweden, and strong-willed Jess van Sandt knows only too well that it's a man's world. She believes she's being swindled out of her inheritance by her stepfather – and she's determined to stop it.

When help appears in the unlikely form of handsome Scotsman Killian Kinross, himself disinherited by his grandfather, Jess finds herself both intrigued and infuriated by him. In an attempt to recover her fortune, she proposes a marriage of convenience. Then Killian is offered the chance of a lifetime with the Swedish East India Company's Expedition and he's determined that nothing will stand in his way, not even his new bride.

He sets sail on a daring voyage to the Far East, believing he's put his feelings and past behind him. But the journey doesn't quite work out as he expects …

Visit www.choc-lit.com for more details including the first two chapters and reviews, or simply scan barcode using your mobile phone QR reader.

Want to Know a Secret?
Sue Moorcroft

Money, love and family. Which matters most?

When Diane Jenner's husband is hurt in a helicopter crash, she discovers a secret that changes her life. And it's all about money, the kind of money the Jenners have never had.

James North has money, and he knows it doesn't buy happiness. He's been a rock for his wayward wife and troubled daughter – but that doesn't stop him wanting Diane.

James and Diane have something in common: they always put family first. Which means that what happens in the back of James's Mercedes is a really, really bad idea.

Or is it?

The Silver Locket
Margaret James

Winner of CataNetwork Reviewers' Choice Award for Single Titles 2010

If life is cheap, how much is love worth?

It's 1914 and young Rose Courtenay has a decision to make. Please her wealthy parents by marrying the man of their choice – or play her part in the war effort?

The chance to escape proves irresistible and Rose becomes a nurse. Working in France, she meets Lieutenant Alex Denham, a dark figure from her past. He's the last man in the world she'd get involved with – especially now he's married.

But in wartime nothing is as it seems. Alex's marriage is a sham and Rose is the only woman he's ever wanted. As he recovers from his wounds, he sets out to win her trust. His gift of a silver locket is a far cry from the luxuries she's left behind.

What value will she put on his love?

First novel in the trilogy

Visit www.choc-lit.com for more details including the first two chapters and reviews, or simply scan barcode using your mobile phone QR reader.

The Golden Chain

Margaret James

Can first love last forever?

1931 is the year that changes everything for Daisy Denham. Her family has not long swapped life in India for Dorset, England when she uncovers an old secret.

At the same time, she meets Ewan Fraser – a handsome dreamer who wants nothing more than to entertain the world and for Daisy to play his leading lady.

Ewan offers love and a chance to escape with a touring theatre company. As they grow closer, he gives her a golden chain and Daisy gives him a promise – that she will always keep him in her heart.

But life on tour is not as they'd hoped, Ewan is tempted away by his career and Daisy is dazzled by the older, charismatic figure of Jesse Trent. She breaks Ewan's heart and sets off for a life in London with Jesse.

Only time will tell whether some promises are easier to make than keep …

Second novel in the trilogy

Visit www.choc-lit.com for more details including the first two chapters and reviews, or simply scan barcode using your mobile phone QR reader.

Please don't stop the music

Jane Lovering

How much can you hide?

Jemima Hutton is determined to build a successful new life and keep her past a dark secret. Trouble is, her jewellery business looks set to fail – until enigmatic Ben Davies offers to stock her handmade belt buckles in his guitar shop and things start looking up, on all fronts.

But Ben has secrets too. When Jemima finds out he used to be the front man of hugely successful Indie rock band Willow Down, she wants to know more. Why did he desert the band on their US tour? Why is he now a semi-recluse?

And the curiosity is mutual – which means that her own secret is no longer safe …

Visit www.choc-lit.com for more details including the first two chapters and reviews, or simply scan barcode using your mobile phone QR reader.

The Scarlet Kimono
Christina Courtenay

Abducted by a Samurai warlord in 17th-century Japan – what happens when fear turns to love?

England, 1611, and young Hannah Marston envies her brother's adventurous life. But when she stows away on his merchant ship, her powers of endurance are stretched to their limit. Then they reach Japan and all her suffering seems worthwhile – until she is abducted by Taro Kumashiro's warriors.

In the far north of the country, warlord Kumashiro is waiting to see the girl who he has been warned about by a seer. When at last they meet, it's a clash of cultures and wills, but they're also fighting an instant attraction to each other.

With her brother desperate to find her and the jealous Lady Reiko equally desperate to kill her, Hannah faces the greatest adventure of her life. And Kumashiro has to choose between love and honour …

Visit www.choc-lit.com for more details including the first two chapters and reviews, or simply scan barcode using your mobile phone QR reader.

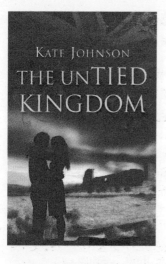

The UnTied Kingdom
Kate Johnson

The portal to an alternate world was the start of all her troubles – or was it?

When Eve Carpenter lands with a splash in the Thames, it's not the London or England she's used to. No one has a telephone or knows what a computer is. England's a third-world country and Princess Di is still alive. But worst of all, everyone thinks Eve's a spy.

Including Major Harker who has his own problems. His sworn enemy is looking for a promotion. The general wants him to undertake some ridiculous mission to capture a computer, which Harker vaguely envisions running wild somewhere in Yorkshire. Turns out the best person to help him is Eve.

She claims to be a popstar. Harker doesn't know what a popstar is, although he suspects it's a fancy foreign word for 'spy'. Eve knows all about computers, and electricity. Eve is dangerous. There's every possibility she's mad.

And Harker is falling in love with her.

Visit www.choc-lit.com for more details including the first two chapters and reviews, or simply scan barcode using your mobile phone QR reader.

Love & Freedom
Sue Moorcroft

New start, new love.

That's what Honor Sontag needs after her life falls apart, leaving her reputation in tatters and her head all over the place. So she flees her native America and heads for Brighton, England.

Honor's hoping for a much-deserved break and the chance to find the mother who abandoned her as a baby. What she gets is an entanglement with a mysterious male whose family seems to have a finger in every pot in town.

Martyn Mayfair has sworn off women with strings attached, but is irresistibly drawn to Honor, the American who keeps popping up in his life. All he wants is an uncomplicated relationship built on honesty, but Honor's past threatens to undermine everything. Then secrets about her mother start to spill out …

Honor has to make an agonising choice. Will she live up to her dutiful name and please others? Or will she choose freedom?

Visit www.choc-lit.com for more details including the first two chapters and reviews, or simply scan barcode using your mobile phone QR reader.

Star Struck
Jane Lovering

Our memories define us – don't they?

And Skye Threppel lost most of hers in a car crash that stole the lives of her best friend and fiancé. It's left scars, inside and out, which have destroyed her career and her confidence.

Skye hopes a trip to the wide dusty landscapes of Nevada – and a TV convention offering the chance to meet the actor she idolises – will help her heal. But she bumps into mysterious sci-fi writer Jack Whitaker first. He's a handsome contradiction – cool and intense, with a wild past.

Jack has enough problems already. He isn't looking for a woman with self-esteem issues and a crush on one of his leading actors. Yet he's drawn to Skye.

An instant rapport soon becomes intense attraction, but Jack fears they can't have a future if Skye ever finds out about his past …

Will their memories tear them apart, or can they build new ones together?

Visit www.choc-lit.com for more details including the first two chapters and reviews, or simply scan barcode using your mobile phone QR reader.

November 2011:

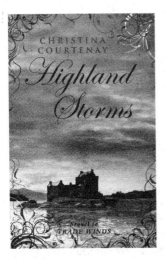

Highland Storms
Christina Courtenay

Who can you trust?

Betrayed by his brother and his childhood love, Brice Kinross needs a fresh start. So he welcomes the opportunity to leave Sweden for the Scottish Highlands to take over the family estate.

But there's trouble afoot at Rosyth in 1754 and Brice finds himself unwelcome. The estate's in ruin and money is disappearing. He discovers an ally in Marsaili Buchanan, the beautiful redheaded housekeeper, but can he trust her?

Marsaili is determined to build a good life. She works hard at being a housekeeper and harder still at avoiding men who want to take advantage of her. But she's irresistibly drawn to the new clan chief, even though he's made it plain he doesn't want to be shackled to anyone.

And the young laird has more than romance on his mind. His investigations are stirring up an enemy. Someone who will stop at nothing to get what he wants – including Marsaili – even if that means destroying Brice's life forever …

Sequel to Trade Winds

Visit www.choc-lit.com for more details including the first two chapters and reviews, or simply scan barcode using your mobile phone QR reader.

Introducing the Choc Lit Club

Join us at the Choc Lit Club where we're creating a
delicious selection of women's fiction.
Where heroes are like chocolate – irresistible!

Join our authors in Author's Corner, read author interviews
and see our featured books.

We'd also love to hear how you enjoyed *Persuade Me*.
Just visit www.choc-lit.com and give your feedback.
Describe Rick in terms of chocolate and you could win a
Choc Lit novel in our Flavour of the Month competition!

Follow us on twitter: www.twitter.com/
ChocLituk, or simply scan barcode using
your mobile phone QR reader.